# THE HUNT INITIATIVE

# THE HUNT INITIATIVE

A NOVEL BY

DILLON M. WALLACE

Sometimes Y Publishing

THE HUNT INITIATIVE


Published in the United States by Sometimes Y Publishing
Shawnee, KS 66217

ISBN (paperback): 979-8-9897815-0-8
ISBN (hardcover): 979-8-9897815-2-2

*Cover and book design by Dale Ley III*

First Edition Published May 2024

For *you*.
May you find what makes you tick
and always keep your time with it.

“Power is in tearing human minds to pieces and putting them together again in new shapes of your own choosing.”

— George Orwell, *1984*

*Ffpt! Ffpt! Ffpt! Ffpt . . .*

The panicked patter of heavy footsteps stomping across a back-alley pavement quickly doubles in tempo. In between the crescendo of hurried feet are bottomless breaths, each burning huff harsher than the last, gasping for every necessary bit of lung-calming air.

For a hold on the situation.

For life itself.

A dribble of dark maroon beads its way down the exhausted man's slick forehead from a fresh gash atop his sweaty crown. Slow and fine at first, then faster—thicker—until the crimson cascade starts to geyser from his scalp like a turbulent spigot. The flash flood south merges with the stockpiled salt and oil on his bogged brow and ladened lashes, distorting his already weary vision in a blinding burgundy haze.

He doesn't care.

He can't care.

Not right now.

He has no choice but to push forward even as the red rapids continue to surge past his flushed cheeks, pooling in the corners of his winded lips. The hint of wet rust teases his dehydrated senses.

Right now, it's simply life or death. To keep going at all costs.

For the first time in several blocks, he hears nothing but welcomed silence sandwiched between his weighted treads and sputtered wheezing.

Nobody shouting.

No choir of car engines purring in pursuit.

And, most importantly, no humming overhead from a targeted convoy of determined drones.

It's quiet. Too quiet.

The man lurches ahead, checking the blind spots behind and above him almost as often as the impulsive path set before him. The paranoia is more than warranted as the faintest sound of buzzing in the distant sky kickstarts a thrashing alarm on his eardrum. Before he can even see it round the corner, the drone is back on him in full-propelled pursuit. He flees in response, sprinting as fast as his numb legs can carry the tired load. He doesn't know it yet, but he's just entered a competition with himself to see which will break first, his body or his spirit.

As the muffled hum from the miniature propellers becomes audibly sharper upon approach, the flared red rings emanating from the drone's camera dot grow in circumference. But the robot bird's-eye view recording is the least of his worries overhead as multiple gunshots join the chaotic commotion below, ringing out several stories above from one of the apartment alley windows. All misses, but far too close for comfort.

Despite his fatigue, nowhere in the man's oxygen-deprived mind does he consider stopping to count his blessings. He's barely able to function as it is, relying solely on diminished reserves of adrenaline and fumes of sheer willpower to keep moving—keep surviving. In the past thirteen hours, he's been grazed across the shoulder, chest, and scalp by a hair-off-target buckshot, viciously stabbed multiple times in the side of the abdomen—somehow miraculously missing his vital organs—and relentlessly pursued by a multitude of bloodthirsty strangers and a fleet of facial-seeking drones.

A tireless gauntlet of threats from above and below that have led him to this exact moment. This exact place.

A crossroads, in more ways than one.

Slowing at the alleyway's sudden intersection of indecision, he halts momentarily to peek his head out from around the narrow four-way passage. Leading with careful eyes in one direction, he catches a delayed glimpse of the charcoal SUV he thought he'd successfully lost two blocks back zoom into his periphery. With no time or energy to react, he's forcefully introduced to the car's windshield, cracking the glass upon impact like fresh prey caught in a spider's web.

A second later, he crashes against the waning-summer-simmered blacktop while new wounds draining fresh life force begin to puddle around him on the stovetop pavement. The pain is unbearable. Several ribs are shattered. His left arm, uncooperative. And his jaw, inches unhinged from its natural socket by the violent drag across the jagged asphalt. The road rash is worn all the way through to the white mandible underneath his once-intact chin. A flap of exposed skin now bobs where his goatee once lay.

He rolls to his side in agony, gathering the last morsel of his depleted resolve to climb back to his badgered hands and knees. But there's nothing left inside him to keep going. He can't crawl. He can't even move.

A long strand of bloodstained drool streams down what's left of his chin, swirling like strawberry soft serve to the ground he was just so forcefully acquainted with.

The sheer affliction should be more than enough to consume his mind, but only thoughts of despair flood his concussed head.

How did he think he could run?

Was escape even possible?

Deep down, he knows he never actually believed he'd make it in the first place.

No one ever has.

All four doors of the dark SUV fling open as an equal number of passengers, each toting different instruments of destruction, step out. They close in, gradually surrounding the injured man on all fours. Taunting him, even.

The driver, a tall, short-haired beanpole of a man with thick-lensed glasses leads the pack. He's gripping a splintered Louisville Slugger nearly as thick around as he is.

"Well, well . . . looks like this is the end of the line, boys," he boasts, inciting jeers and snickers from the other three.

Bleeding and broken in every possible way, the victim struggles to utter a word between involuntary mouthfuls of red syrup.

"Pl-pl-, please . . . I'm s-s-sorry," he mutters, before a violent coughing fit overtakes him, producing a red Jackson Pollock effect on the asphalt. "I . . . I didn't mean to . . . have m-m-mercy, pl-ease. For god's sake—"

"You? Mercy? God?" A rosy-cheeked pudge of a boy, not a smidge older than a warm body in a high school classroom, bellows. "You hear that, guys?" he asks, raising the shotgun he's holding above his broad billowy shoulders. "He's apparently a man of the cloth now."

The third passenger, an elderly man, supporting a frail frame of wrinkled flesh and what's left of his wispy, white hairline, juts in.

"God can't help you now, son," the old sack of bones slurs, unsheathing a serrated hunting knife fitted with a black rubber handle from his belt. "He's on our side."

The remaining member of the foursome, a twenty-something, bearded man with an athletic build, wearing a black backwards ball cap and wielding a revolver, slithers his way to the head of the group. His approach is slow and calculated, stalking his downed prey. When he reaches the defeated man helplessly sprawled out before him, he lowers to a knee.

"So, you want mercy, Eddie? Is that what you want?" he asks, looming just above his grounded prize.

Eddie, wincing in agony from just the subtle act of breathing, struggles to reply through his dislocated jaw, "I di-didn't mean t-to . . . it wa-wa—" His teeth drowning in glossy crimson. "—was an accident."

"Tsk, tsk," the man in the baseball cap shrugs with a casual wave of his pistol. "You see, that's where I don't believe you, Eddie. First-degree murder with intent doesn't just happen. And I find it incredibly hard to believe that it was just an *accident*—as you so innocently plead—the night you decided to follow her home."

He places two calloused hands around Eddie's soiled shirt collar and lifts his fractured figure off the concrete. They meet eye-to-eye. Eddie's left sclera is so bloodshot from the trauma that his blue iris looks almost hazel from the encroaching red mixture.

"Tell me, was it just an *accident* that after she went to bed you broke into her ground-floor apartment, raped her, and then slit her throat?" He pauses a beat to gather himself. A single tear forms in the corner of his right duct. "Your own student. My . . . little sister."

The revelation is something unforgivable, but it's not the guilt that causes Eddie to break down into uncontrollable sobs for clemency. It's the fear of knowing what comes next—the inevitable. And in between the wild fits of choking on a river of his own blood and tears, the familiar combination of rust and salt once again overtakes his raised tastebuds.

"I'm sorry . . . Pl-eeeease, I'm sick. I can't h-help my . . . I'm so s-s-sorry."

"Yeah. Well, let me show you exactly where sorry gets you," counters the man in the black cap, who has yet to break eye contact. "You wanted mercy? Here it is. Burn in hell, you piece of shit. It's where you belong."

He rises back to his feet and wipes away the lone drop of concentrated sorrow as his parting words are consumed by the echoing crack of gunfire. Eddie returns to the pavement yet again, gracefully giving way to gravity. This time he lies there motionless. No attempt to get up. To keep running. The still-smoking bullet lodged deep inside the temple of his skull makes sure of that.

He's dead.
The way they all end up.
After all, no one has ever survived *The Hunt Initiative.*

. . .

# CHAPTER 2

Under a tired sigh, Clayton Sparks shakes his head and kills the live coverage of the latest Hunt on his living room TV. He tosses the remote onto a perfectly patinated, secondhand, leather loveseat and trudges his way into the kitchen to pour himself a generous—and much needed—second cup of "wake the hell up" for the morning. These new ass-crack-of-dawn-shifts have been anything but an easy adjustment so far, and he'd be the first to willingly admit that he's never been anywhere remotely close to sniffing the fresh pot of a morning go-getter. Maybe it's because any time after midnight always sounds like an appropriate bedtime. Or maybe it's the dreaded thought of having to actually make himself look presentable so goddamn early in the day. After all, his medium-length dirty blond shag and chin scruff may look disheveled, but the imperfect appearance is more than deliberate. And while he'd much rather be asleep, or at the very least, sneaking in a quick pump session if having to be up with the sun, he doesn't have much of a choice. It's not exactly like a thirty-two-year-old ex-con has the pick of the litter when it comes to viable job opportunities.

Interrupted in mid-yawn by a timid meow, he looks down to see

Scout staring up at him through a slow-waking pair of vertical slits. He weaves in and out of Clayton's legs in a figure-eight greeting, delivering his morning barrage of mews and purrs with a few extra headbutts thrown into the mix. The Halloween-themed tortie cat's body language seems to politely say, "Good morning, friend, please feed me. It's breakfast time." But Clayton knows the correct translation for those hungry morning meows is, "Food! Now, bitch." He's just happy to see the ol' furry ball of sass hasn't lost a step in this new rise-and-shine tango routine of his.

Clayton shuffles his way down the hall of the modest two-bedroom apartment to the hallway closet, still fighting the transition from morning zombie mode to land of the living. As a night owl, he's used to treading his steps carefully, having noted which planks of the old oak floor creak more than others under his 180 pounds of concentrated weight. It's like a minefield, only in this case, a wrong step won't trigger the blast from a life-ending bomb, just an angry explosion of verbal shrapnel from a tired girlfriend awoken far earlier than expected on her lone day off.

Glancing down the hall past the wooden blast zone, he sees a tiny sliver of light escaping from the bottom of the bathroom door. Trish is already awake. Surprising for her day off, especially since she was up late last night finishing the final piece for her latest exhibition. Scout seems to notice she's up, too, because he's now firmly planted himself right outside the door, pawing at it in a pathetic plea of despair in hopes that one of his incompetent human roommates will finally feed him.

Clayton chuckles at the ridiculous begging tactic and opens the closet door to grab the cat food. At the familiar crinkling sound of the plastic bag, Scout's trained ears perk up and he scurries back down the hall to the kitchen, purring loudly between giddy struts now that he's finally got his wish. Clayton digs a brimming scoop of kibbles from the bag and whispers, "Mom says only half a cup . . . but I won't tell her if you won't, buddy."

He studies Scout who is now aggressively slamming his furry cheek into Clayton's calf in between Richter scale-level purrs. "Although, I gotta admit. You are looking more like an overstuffed link of sausage with nubs for legs every day, pal."

Carefully, Clayton walks into the kitchen and empties the fat scoop of dried-up mystery meat into Scout's ceramic "Paw-Lease & Thank-Meow" bowl that Trish made him years ago when he was just a kitten. There's still some food leftover from yesterday, but the tubby tortie goes to town as if he hasn't eaten in days. For being the smallest of the three mammals in the home, he easily eats the loudest. And most often.

"Geez, buddy, take it easy," Clayton orders. "I don't have time to clean up one of your signature piles of pre-digested upchuck in the next five minutes."

While Scout gets his breakfast binge on, Clayton sets his coffee down on the counter bar and prepares to gingerly ease into one of the teak seats. Sure enough, as soon as his ass kisses wood, the stool wildly weeble-wobbles, but he catches himself just before enough inertia can build to buck him off. Realizing he just saved himself from yet another morning ride on the rogue rodeo stool, he heaves a sigh of relief before carefully adjusting to regain a perfectly balanced position atop. Once the coveted center of gravity has been achieved, he lets out a second chuckle. Twice his usual quota for this damn early in the morning.

He's only told Trish time and time again that they need new stools, but she's adamant about keeping these midcentury modern "bargain antique store treasures." Her words, not his. That's one of the things he's always loved about her, though. Despite coming from a family that has it all, she's always been one to carve her own path. Make her own life. When her father became the face of corporate America—branded as one of the world's most influential figures, and adorning the country's most coveted covers of *TIME* and *Forbes* more times than years Clayton's been alive—Trish went the opposite direction.

A life out of the public spotlight. No politics. No corporate business ventures. Just a love for art and the creative process behind it.

He continues laughing to himself as he looks aimlessly around the limited square footage confines of the apartment. Trish's serene still-life paintings from college and her more recent abstract projects and contemporary pieces breathe vibrancy and color into the plain beige walls that outline the humble two-bedroom abode. Affectionately infusing the small bland space with a warm sense of grandeur—of much-needed life and love—they work overtime to make the cramped surroundings feel like home.

Clayton goes back to sipping his cup of coffee while autopilot-thumbing through the latest Hunt news on his phone when he hears the bathroom door creak open.

"Hey, babe, what are you doing up so early? Thought this was your only day to sleep in," he yells down the hall, while carefully getting up from the merry-go-round stool and polishing off the remainder of his Joe. "There's a little coffee left in the pot, but you better hurry up before some asshole drinks it all."

Without noticing, Patricia "Trish" Klein enters the kitchen under timid steps. Even though she just woke up, her coal-black hair seems to crash delicately in all the right places, hugging her slender shoulders, accentuating her smooth, swan neck. A natural beauty with velvety eyelashes and rich cherry lips positioned atop a decanter-shaped figure just a smidge over five feet tall, she slouches underneath the low archway that separates the dining area from the apartment's sad excuse for a functional kitchen. She's still wearing her plaid night robe, and her usually fierce, ocean-deep blue eyes are wavering with uncertainty under bowed eyebrows and infiltrating rays of dim morning sunlight. It's a distant gaze that would normally indicate anxiousness, maybe even fear, but her cerise grin says otherwise.

Clayton, still totally unaware of her looming presence, pours himself a hearty bowl of cereal, dousing the processed sugar with a tsunami wave of milk.

"We're also fresh out of cereal," he shouts, rattling the empty box. "Someone, and I'm not pointing any fingers here, needs to quit with all the late-night munchies," he adds jokingly, through an even thicker pour of sarcasm. But as he finally looks up mid-bite, milk gracefully dribbling down his stubbly chin, he notices her uneasy aura. Clearly, she has something far more serious weighing on her mind than the apartment's lack of available breakfast options.

"Oh, hey, mornin', babe I didn't see you . . . Trish? What's wrong? Um, are you . . . okay?" he presses, his greeting growing more trepid with each fumbled question.

Rather than find the right string of pleasantries to answer him, she just shows him the test. One little white and blue stick with two solid pink lines etched into a small oval viewer. She starts laughing, but the smile quickly contorts itself 180 degrees into hysterical sobs.

The surprise news and its corresponding shock are almost too much for Clayton to process this early in the morning. They register, but in a delayed reaction, like his brain just stubbed its toe or had one too many aggressive licks of ice cream.

Finally, the mental duo sinks in.

"Wait! You mean—you? Me? We?" he spurts, eagerly pointing at Trish and then himself repeatedly, still fumbling for the right words. "We're gonna have a baby? Like, our baby? Like a you-and-me baby?"

Trish bobs her head in between a new tide of tears.

"What? This is crazy!" he shouts. "We're gonna have a baby!"

With his emotions revving in overdrive, he mindlessly casts his bowl of cereal onto the countertop. "Holy shit! Holy. Shit." He juggles in a back-to-back emotional combination of glee, then shock. "I'm gonna *be* a dad! I'm going to be a *dad*?"

Before he can further overthink the surprise situation, Trish runs over and drapes her arms around his neck. Together, they wipe away happy tears in between dumbfounded stares at the pregnancy test, making sure the blur from their marshy eyes isn't deceiving them with an imaginary second line.

"One. Two," he reiterates, physically counting them aloud. "Wow, this is real. Like, this is really happening. Right now. I just . . . this . . . *hmm*. It all makes perfect sense now," he continues.

Trish tilts her head and wriggles her nose. "Huh?"

"Oh, I mean, I heard you the other morning, calling up some dinosaurs in the bathroom. But I just figured it was from the rest of the bottle of mezcal we polished off the night before."

Trish gives a little snort, and they laugh even harder, giddy from the major morning news. Even now, as he gazes with glassy goo-goo eyes at the woman he loves, catching a glimpse of himself in her own waterlogged pair, he realizes just how far he's come. There was a time when everyone had given up on him. When he had given up on himself. He had plummeted on a downward spiral that finally landed him behind bars from a past life of regret, but Trish never judged him. Never held it against him. Despite the glaring disapproval from her father, Clayton finally realizes just how good he has it. A loving, loyal partner. And now, a beautiful, albeit unexpected, baby on the way. The makings of a new family. A second chance at life.

"So, what do we do next? Do we call the doctor? What do we name him? Or her? Do we even find out the sex? Are gender reveal parties still a thing? Ugh, I hope not. How much are diapers? Oh god, I've never actually changed a diaper—" he yacks, in a reflexive verbal vomit spewed from a runaway train of thought. "And when you wipe, is it front to back? Or back to front? Crap, I don't know shit. Like, literally."

Trish cuts him off, laughing in between diminishing sobs of joy.

"Whoaaa there, cowboy! Pump the brakes. We're going to figure it all out together as we go—one step at a time, okay?" she insists, and places her hand against his flushed cheek. Her touch is soft, calming. Just what he needs. "I've never done this before either, you know. But hey, we got this." Warmly adding her second hand to the other side of his face, she pinches his rosy pair together. "Besides, your parents did the bare minimum job on you, and you turned out okay, well, kind of," she teases with a playful smirk and spins around for the coffee pot.

"Woooww. Low blow, Mama," Clayton chuckles through a smirk of his own. "Try to keep the gloves up, will ya? That's what landed us in this situation in the first place."

"Hmm . . . Mama," she imagines aloud, reveling in the revered title while finishing off the pot. "I'm gonna have to get used to the sound of that."

"Oh *yeah*?" he flirts with a suave bouquet of pouty lips, determined eyes, and a solo-cocked brow. "How about we head to the bedroom, and I *help* you get a little more used to it?"

Clayton leans in for a kiss, gently tugging at her robe's loose sash. He reaches up to her shoulders, thinking to himself that her skin has never felt smoother, silkier—more delectable. The robe teasingly droops down her biceps, peek-a-booing the upper half of her teardrop breasts when the phone rings, successfully, yet unfortunately, cockblocking the forthcoming celebratory coitus.

"Ah, seriously? Who could possibly be calling this early?" he moans, as Trish side-steps his man sprawl for the phone. "Let's just pretend it's not ringing," he adds, inching back in for another chance to play hooky with take two at morning nooky.

"Now, where were we again?"

"Not so fast, baby daddy," she says, halting him in his tantalizing tracks. "Anyone calling this early probably has a good reason. We should answer it."

"Ugh," he groans and drops his head. "It fucking better be the best reason. I just had the perfect morning sex session stolen from me. I wouldn't have even had to pull out. So, whoever it is better be dead or dying, or so help me god, I'll see to it they end up one or the other."

Trish rolls her eyes at the drama from the empty threat and reaches for the phone. She instantly tosses it to Clayton, who hot potatoes it twice before securing it.

"Wha-hey! I don't want to answer it."

"Well, I can't answer it . . . it's a video call and I'm kind of . . . well, naked, thanks to your premature shot at morning delight."

"Eh, I'd say that baby is solid proof that there's nothing premature about me."

"Okaaay, big boy. I'm leaving now," Trish concedes and saunters out of the kitchen toward the bedroom. Halfway down the hall, she yells out, "Oh, and be nice!"

"Huh?" Clayton grumbles, as he finally looks at the incoming caller ID. "Ah, for fuck's sake, your *dad*? Really?" he shouts down the hall in return. "Et tu, Brute?" He pauses. "Goddamn Judas!"

Her faint voice carries from their bedroom at the opposite end of the hall. "Don't be a little bitch. Show no fear."

Clayton mumbles under his breath, "This should be fun" as he transfers the call to the TV.

A smug man with a silvery Selleck-meets-Reynolds-inspired mustache, who's actually sixty-five but looks closer to fifty, pops up on the seventy-five-inch flat-screen. His peppered hair is perfectly kempt, delicately manicured into its patented plastic combover. Not one gray, white, or black hair awry.

"Morning, Mr. Klein," Clayton answers. "Thought I was the only one in this family that woke up with the roosters?"

Simon Klein, a stern man of immense power and fame, doesn't miss his chance for a far-too-early berating.

"Well, Sparky, when you're as successful as I am, you're up before everyone else because that's how you make something of yourself. When the sheep are sleeping. Although, I guess that can't be said for everyone—"

Clayton grits his teeth before putting on the fakest smile that even a cheerleader would envy. He quickly chants in his head—*Give me an F. Give me a U. Give me a C-K and a Y-O-U. What's that spell?* He imagines a crowd of foam middle fingers waving in the air accompanying the cheer. After all, he's been chanting it long enough over the years that he's easily varsity by now.

First off, Klein knows damn well that Clayton hates it when he calls him Sparky. But that's only scratching the surface beneath the thick prick comment he just made. Chalk it up to another backhanded exchange in their long-standing string of petulant pleasantries. If Clayton's learned anything from their "talks," it's that a strong offense is the best defense.

He fires back without hesitation.

"Well, you know what they say, sir, 'All work and no play makes Jack a dull boy.' For your secretary and executives' sake, I sure hope there aren't any sharp objects nearby, like, say an axe."

"Ah. Always with the jokes, aren't you, Sparky? Maybe if you put half of that effort into improving yourself and providing for my daughter, instead of working on the latest smartass comment, you'd be more than just a lowly security guard. At *my company*, mind you. After all, it's not like I had to bend over backward and look past your lengthy history of misdeeds to even get you the job in the first place, am I right?"

On the outside, Clayton is calm, collected, and cool. He's taken a verbal punch—or a hundred—from Klein before. It's not like this childish game is anything new. But inside, Clayton is cussing out this asshole in every language he can think of, which is just English. So, needless to say, it's a lot of back-to-back four-letter words.

"And I appreciate you looking past . . . well, my *past* to offer me the job, sir," Clayton says, swallowing his pride, wanting more than anything for this conversation to end faster than it began. So, he quickly changes the subject and asks the pivotal question to hopefully bring that reality one step closer. "Anyway . . . what can I do for you this morning?"

Unfortunately, the olive branch is snapped in the attempted handoff as Klein continues to spare no peace or pleasantries.

"Well, for starters, you can get my daughter on the phone," he huffs, looking down at his watch. "And judging by the clock, it looks like you can also get your ass to work before you're even later than you are already."

Clayton glances at his own wrist.

"Oh, shit! Trish, babe? I gotta go. I'm late again," he shouts down the hall. "I'll see you later, Mama!"

Trish shuffles back into the living room in her favorite pair of paint-stained sweatpants that she's had since her high school art days and Clayton's vintage AC/DC "Monsters of Rock '91 Tour" concert tee. Clayton plants a drive-by kiss on her lips, snatches his work gear from the counter, and rushes toward the door before spinning back around at the deadbolt.

"BT Dubs, I just loooove your dad and I's little conversations," he whispers while making a noose gesture before opening the front door.

Following close behind in his footsteps, Trish shoots him the all-too-familiar "I'm sorry my dad is such a dick" face as he quickly vanishes out of frame. She leans out the apartment entry and yells down the hallway, slowing his hustling heels with her parting words.

"Don't forget about my dad's party tonight! Seven o'clock sharp, Mr. Always Late." She sugarcoats it with a kiss.

Clayton turns around while speed-walking backward and sarcastically replies, "Gee, if it's anything like our talk this morning, shoot me now . . ."

Smirking, Trish gently closes the door. She takes an extra beat to compose herself, then turns her attention to the television in the other room.

"Hey, Daddy, sorry about the wait, been kind of a crazy morning. Is everything okay? You never call this early."

"Of course, honey, everything is just fine. I didn't mean to worry you," he says calmly, reassuring his only child. "But did I just hear him call you Mama a minute ago?"

Trish panics. She loves Clayton. More than anything. And while she's overjoyed to be having his baby—unexpected as it may be—she's not in any way, shape, or form ready to break the news to her father. Especially with his history of known disdain for her choice of a current suitor. Not to mention, that whole not being married thing. So, she quickly squashes the ensuing conversation-to-surely-turn-heated-argument before it ever has a chance to gain traction.

"Huh? What? No, Dad, don't be ridiculous," she sputters, before finding the right footing on her best Clayton-inspired, conversation- veering tactic. "So . . . if everything's okay, why the early ring, Daddy?"

"Oh, no real reason. I just wanted to call and remind you that today is the twenty-five-year anniversary of The Hunt Initiative, and to confirm if you were still planning on attending the festivities tonight?"

"Of course, Dad. You know I wouldn't miss it. I've only told you that like fifty times. I just reminded Clayton on his way out this morning. We plan to be there at seven p.m. Is that okay?"

"Yes, seven p.m. is perfect." There's a dramatic pause before he continues. "I thought Clayton had to work a double shift tonight?"

She knows where this conversation is headed. But she cordially steers the dialogue back into a safer direction.

"He did have to work a double today, but he got Jayson to cover for him tonight. Funny thing about that," she says, scrutinizing him through a squinted gaze with one eyebrow cocked. "Clay never works a double on Fridays, but for some reason, he was scheduled to work one tonight . . . of all nights. You wouldn't happen to know anything about that though, would you, Dad?"

Her father pauses momentarily, but the silence seems like forever. He's caught and he knows it, but that won't stop the infamous Simon Klein from pulling out a compelling excuse from the *B* tab in his rolodex of bullshit.

"Hon, you know I don't have anything to do with managing security. I'm president and CEO of the company; I've got bigger fish to fry than worrying about Sparky's work schedule," he adlibs, finishing the lie with a flash of his patented pearly whites.

"Ugh. Dad, you know I've told you not to call him that. He hates that name."

"Sorry, honey, must have just slipped. My apologies. I'll see you and *Clayton* at seven p.m. tonight. Until then, dear."

He cuts off the call before she can get in another word. He always does. Like it's some kind of cop-out power move to win the argument without ever having to find a resolution. It's the same story every time she talks with her father. She loves him. And he loves her. He doesn't need to love Clayton. But he could at least accept him. If not for him, at least for her.

She wonders what her mom would think of all this if she were still alive. The thought plays in her mind briefly before the reflection is interrupted by an unscripted sprint to the bathroom. Another bout of morning sickness eager to prove that double-striped pee stick right.

"Damn. Rickers is gonna have my ass," Clayton mumbles, frantically scoping his watch again.

There's no feasible way he can make it around the corner and down four blocks in less than a minute. He'll just have to catch the next bus. And be even later, and more ass-had.

His scurry finally slows its stride as he helplessly watches his 6:55 ride vanish around the corner without him on it. *Guess the 7:10 one will have to do*, he thinks to himself. It's not like he has any other options. Besides, what's really another fifteen minutes when you're already late?

With fresh time on the expired shot clock, Clayton continues his tardy trek to the 18th and District Street bus stop at a more casual gait. Nestled in the heart of Bannerton's Arts District, the neighborhood is a melting pot of progressive college students, young middle-class families, and lots of old blue-collar households—White, Black, Latino, Asian—pick a color and you'll find it here. It's also home to some of the best mural work in the city. What was once just an overlooked stretch of condemned property, now serves as a communal gallery of blank canvases turned into vibrant works of art and blended culture. A little over twenty years ago, this was a rough neighborhood, a time when these same magnificent murals and their desolate buildings were nothing more than graffiti tags and gang hangouts. Territory markers from the rings that ruled the surrounding area. They were the kind of streets you didn't want to be caught walking alone down once the sun fell. Hell, you weren't even safe alone under the false security of broad daylight.

But now, it's a lively haven, gentrified as a product of The Hunt Initiative. Where startup families, artsy university kids, and the diverse working-class all socially and economically coexist under the scrutinized surveillance of drones buzzing four hundred feet above the ground and facial recognition cameras stationed on every corner. The gangs may have stopped patrolling, but that's only because they've been replaced by the watchful eyes of Big Brother, always looking to end any crime before it can even begin.

As Clayton rounds the corner of District Street, the animated billboard across the intersection plays a live breaking news clip from coverage of this morning's latest Hunt. The same rape and murder story he was just watching back home. Ever since The Hunt Initiative passed legislation twenty-five years ago—to the very day—massive billboards like this one and facial recognition cameras at nearly every major intersection were planted all across the country—in every state, every city, every small rural town in buttfuck America—to help aid the public in their pursuit of justice. The adopted ideology that fear is the best way to create peace. After all, you can't get away with a crime, especially murder, if everyone already knows who did it?

In large part, it's the sole reason why no one has ever escaped the Hunt. Clayton knows this, everyone does. You simply can't escape a system that has eyes on your every move. Your every decision. It's how the program was designed. For the accused to fail. For murderers and prospective killers to fear the result of their cruelest intentions. To uphold to the highest degree that absence of thought does not void consequence of action. To fulfill some semblance of what Clayton believes to be nothing more than a misplaced sense of self-righteous vengeance. A society playing judge, jury, and executioner with Klein leading its reckoning in a sadistic game of Simon Says. It's an unpopular opinion in a new nation whose founding principles of justice are grounded in the nationwide acceptance that the penalty for murder is murder. The immortal notion of *an eye for an eye*, adapted into an institution for the twenty-first century.

On his belated hike to the bus stop, Clayton passes by several people along the route, all nonchalantly living their lives while the graphic recap of this morning's Hunt replays on every screen as far as his eyes can see. A society once vehemently opposed to censorship now numb to the ironic violence it's created in its stead.

He looks on in silent observation as a determined woman on a morning stroll with her baby, looking anything but leisurely, zooms down the sidewalk while pushing a three-wheeled, aerodynamic spaceship of a carriage. Across the street, construction workers lay trivial orange cones about the road, irritatingly siphoning the flow of traffic to one lane for what Clayton feels like is the seventeenth time this month. While next door, a group of college kids are camped outside the Java Plaza, debating something artsy and likely brimming with an underlying preamble of pretentiousness that he can't quite make out in the distance. None of them have abandoned their ordinary tasks at hand or seem the least bit fazed by the current Hunt's happenings. It's as if they're not even aware of the news. Or they simply don't care. Like their individual fears have transformed into collective apathy. But just like politics, there are extremes. For every citizen that's indifferent, or for the select few, like Clayton, who stand against what The Hunt represents, there are two, three, even four times as many counterparts that feed off the Initiative. That live for the Hunt and its pursuit of redefining what true justice looks like.

Clayton finally arrives at the bus stop and glances at his watch again. It reads 7:08 as the bus pull up. Two minutes early, but he's already eight minutes late. He starts calculating in his head how long it will take if the bus makes minimal stops and the traffic isn't horrible. Under the most ideal circumstances, he's looking at a best-case 7:25 arrival. But he knows it's probably more like 7:30.

Fuck.

"Shit, shit, shitty shit," he mutters under his breath, while anxiously shuffling his feet, encouraging the automatic doors to stop taking their sweet ass time and just open already. "Rickers is really gonna have my ass for this."

He lunges inside at the first sliver of an opening and places his thumb on the ID scanner. Just another bit of personal tracking technology courtesy of The Hunt Initiative. No scan, no fare. As the touchpad examines all the intricacies that make his thumbprint uniquely his, Clayton's name, photo, and metro account balance appear on the accompanying digital toll screen, verifying approved entry.

He waddles his way to an open starboard window seat in the middle of the packed bus and plops. Peering out the cloudy pane of neglected public transport glass, he sees a small gathering of riders congregating around another stop down the street for a different metro route. With nothing to do but wait, this particular group is glued to the bus stop's news screen. Unlike the apathetic art students and overly eager jogger he passed on the way, this captive audience is transfixed by the Hunt coverage like moths to a flame, branding in their fluttering minds a sense of civic duty while being oblivious to its undertones of subconscious control. Just like the Initiative was scripted to do.

As the bus doors close, the engine revs, and the oversized shocks and brakes squeal to free the commercial vehicle from rest. Normally, Clayton would pop his earbuds in and zone out on the twenty-minute commute, but he left in such a hurry this morning that he forgot his trusted travel buddies on the kitchen counter. Instead, he rifles through the pocket of his black, finely pressed work pants to fish out his phone. Looks like aimless scrolling will have to suffice as his sole source of entertainment, but two seats down and across the aisle, he can't help but overhear two fervent passengers talking anything but quietly about the latest Hunt.

"Did you see how they caught him?" politely asks an innocent-looking, middle-aged lady with a good-girl, shoulder-length, brown bob and thin, clear-framed glasses.

"No, I missed it," responds the older gentlemen beside her with a faded brown bowler cap and thick Civil War-era sideburns. "I was watching the livestream last night but kept drifting off on the couch, so I just went to bed." He pivots himself toward her, adjusting his body language to elicit a reception of curiosity. "What all happened?"

The woman perks up at his ignorance, and the veil of her prior innocence is instantly stripped away, replaced with a slit pair of hungry eyes. The dark glint inside of them somewhat more devious, more savage than before. Almost maniacal.

She turns in her seat, a physical equivalent to her turn in demeanor. She's almost salivating, ready to divulge every detail with vivid color commentary.

"Well, it was the girl's brother and his friends. They'd been tracking him in their car all night."

"A dark SUV, right? That was the last thing I remember seeing on the broadcast."

"Yes, a coal-colored SUV!" she exclaims, the volume of her voice gaining decibels. Growing more passionate with every disclosed detail. "Except they lost him in the early hours. Apparently, he was hiding out in a dumpster in an alley downtown for quite some time. Fitting place for the garbage he was if you ask me."

"So how did they finally catch him?" the man asks, his increased inflection working to match her enthusiasm.

Clayton can hear it growing in the woman's tone. See it in her posture as the level of excitement continues to rise with each new development in her regaled narrative. As if she's reliving the Hunt and relishing in the prize of death.

"—and then *BOOM*! They slammed right into him full force as he tried to run out of the alley he was hiding in." She gestures, smashing her hands together. "He flew off the windshield like a deer in highway headlights."

"Wait, so they killed him with the car?" the man interjects for clarity. He too, becoming visibly invigorated from her retelling, like a child at storytime waiting for the climax.

"No. He was still alive, barely. Lying there with blood all over his face," the woman says, waving her hand over her own forehead. "Pooling around him all over the ground. From the live drone footage, his arm looked like spaghetti, bending in more places than there are joints. It was awesome."

The man scoots in closer for the grand finale as she continues recapping the account, practically yelling at this point with zeal.

"That's when they all got out of the car, and the brother walks up. He says some stuff to him as he's lying there begging for mercy. Then *BAM*!" she blurts out, accompanied by her thumb and index finger in the shape of a gun. "Shoots him dead, right in the head."

Pleased with her short, yet thorough, summary, she leans back in her seat, smiling as she eagerly anticipates her audience of one's reaction.

"Glad he finally got his. That disgusting rapist had it coming," the man adds, and also leans back, shaking his head. "As the father of a daughter myself, I just can't imagine. Would've loved to pull the trigger myself."

The two continue avidly covering details about the Hunt as Clayton's concentration is redirected by an equally passionate conversation taking place just a couple rows behind him.

He shifts his eavesdropping to the dialogue in the back. He can't see what the passengers look like without turning around, but based on the gravelly voice of the man who's dominating the discussion, he predicts it belongs to a heavy-set, blue-collar worker type. Jaded from years of hard manual labor and the little appreciation to show for it, the man is most likely a big fan of discovering the bottom of a bottle several times a day, every day of the week.

"I still remember my first Hunt. Been about eleven or twelve years now," the husky voice carries with pride. "Remember that woman who burned her husband and kids in that house fire across town? Trying to collect his life insurance policy and flee town with her new boy toy?"

The youthful voice that responds sounds like it belongs to a barely awake college kid on his way to morning class. Clayton can tell he's not invested in the conversation. He's just being polite despite his best effort to sound interested.

"Umm . . . not really. I think my parents watched it, but I don't know. I was pretty young."

Oblivious, Blue-Collar Bob takes his mannerly response as an open invitation.

"Well, a group of us had that crazy bitch cornered inside an old, abandoned house downtown. All exits covered. Nowhere to run." The gruff man pauses as if he's about to deliver the most exciting news this kid is going to hear all day. All year, even. "So, you know what we did?"

Again, the kid reluctantly indulges him. Shrugging his shoulders, "Hmm?"

"We burned that bitch just like she did her family." The man lets out a hearty, bowel-deep laugh. "Now, I ain't no writer, if you couldn't tell, but that sounds like poetic justice if I've ever heard it."

He continues chuckling to himself in a deep, raspy laugh that sounds like it's been fermenting for a while in his pony keg of a belly.

"Yup, now that was a good Hunt," he recalls, indulging in the memory like the bottle of opened whiskey he'll be reacquainting himself with in a matter of hours. "In fact, I've had the pleasure of being part of a few memorable Hunt parties," he continues, further outstaying his conversational welcome.

"Let's see. There was the hotshot country club accountant who clubbed his wife and her golf pro-lover to death after he found out she'd been cashing in on more than overpriced lessons. Kinda gives a whole new meaning to teeing off, huh?" He snickers, nudging the unamused student with his ashy stump of an elbow. "Then there was the school shooting kid that we bagged a couple years back. To this day, I've never seen so many Hunters contribute to one manhunt. Such a good turnout." He continues reminiscing, totally unaware that his audience of one is quickly becoming an audience of none. "Oh, yeah, and I can't forget that malpractice case where that doc killed her elderly patient with an overdose or something like that."

"Wait." The quiet student perks up. "But that was just an accident, right? I read somewhere that she didn't know her patient had been taking a new medication that was prescribed on the side by another physician."

"Ha! Doesn't matter, kid," the walking kegerator scoffs. "You know the law. Absence of thought doesn't constitute for consequence of action. A life for a life. If you let one get away, it taints the whole system. And the system is perfect. No bias. No prejudice. Just justice."

There's a ding heard overhead for the next stop as the bus slows to a halt under the sharp squeal of tired brakes nearing retirement. Clayton watches a handful of passengers get up to exit, including the Pilsner Doughboy. After a struggle against gravity from the pull of his own mass, the grizzly man finds his feet and waddles his way toward the doors, clinging dearly to the handrail above the small series of steps like a precious last bottle of suds. He only stops to look up when he sees three teenagers board.

The kid in front has the sides of his pale head shaved and quarter-sized gauges doing their best to fight the elasticity of his stretched earlobes. He's wearing a politically charged black t-shirt protesting The Hunt Initiative. It enthusiastically reads *Open Season for No Reason*. The kid in the middle is toting a canvas satchel covered in a Tetris display of patches advertising several rock bands, skateboard brands, and pithy political quips. One of them reads *Fuck Hunting. Go Skating.* The teenager bringing up the rear is far more subtle in his overall anti-Hunt wardrobe choice, simply opting for a ballcap that reads *I've Got No Initiative.*

Like every major movement in American history, the younger generations, although somewhat naïve and easily impressionable to their peers, seem to have a third eye capable of looking beyond the black and white of modern society. The innate ability to think and live somewhere in the gray area while caught in a tug-of-war between two fallible sides recklessly competing for their allegiance. They can pinpoint the flaws in publicly adopted systems and the perpetual errors of their parents' and grandparents' legacies, but any room for correction is often wasted on fruitless rebellion, misplaced apathy, or one too many drugs. Born into this new world, they know nothing about what was except through the tainted lens of their elders, lawmakers, and history books. They only see what is. But so often *what is* doesn't translate well to their aspiring view of *what should be.* So, by the time they reach their parents' age—jaded from years of greedy nine-to-five careers, life-draining fiscal responsibilities, peers more interested in pinpointing failures than celebrating successes, and a media that can't define the word impartiality—they've become the spitting image of everything they once hated. Everything that's wrong.

Grizzly Adams notices the first kid's shirt as he exits, and mumbles to himself under his stale, hungover breath, "Fucking snowflakes."

As the bus continues toward its next stop, Clayton diverts his attention to the row of monitors that line the upper side of the bus like digital crown molding. The rectangular spots where printed advertisements used to clutter the walls have been replaced with a sleek bank of flush flatscreens. They're spaced every two seats apart, streaming all the same post-Hunt footage that's been playing everywhere all morning. The reporter on the scene adds her closing remarks before turning it over to Simon Klein, President and CEO at The Hunt for Justice and creator of The Hunt Initiative, for a special statement. The broadcast cuts to a live recording of Klein.

> "*Citizens of Bannerton and my fellow Americans, thanks to The Hunt Initiative we've been blessed today with yet another rewarding example of true justice being served in our beloved nation. And it's one for the history books. Today's Hunt in Cedar Springs, Arkansas marks nearly four months since the nation's last Hunt. The longest time between Hunts since the inception of the program twenty-five years ago, to this very day. I find it incredibly fitting, and I couldn't be prouder that today, of all days, we can all honor the anniversary of our nation's salvation with a fruitful Hunt . . .*"

Clayton turns away from the screen as Klein continues his ramble. He doesn't know if it's from his personal disdain for the man, freshly fueled by this morning's skirmish, or if he's just growing tired of all this holier-than-thou Hunt bullshit. Maybe, it's because he's got a baby on the way to think about now. To care for. To raise in a world he's not so sure he believes in. Whatever it is, he doesn't have time to think about it now because the bus is slowing down for its next stop.

His stop.

The metro doors part, and Clayton hops off the bus with an extra pep in his step. Partly because he's beyond late at this point, but more so, it's from replaying the news that he's going to be a father, and he can't wipe the shit-eating grin off his face.

When he makes it to the end of the block and around the corner, he's greeted by the most magnificent piece of architectural excellence he's ever seen. And even though he's been working here for a while now, the definitive skyscraper never fails to amaze him. As headquarters for The Hunt Initiative, The Hunt for Justice Tower is a one-of-a-kind technological triumph in both size and scale. It was built from the ground up and fitted with the latest and greatest everything that money can buy, just like the new justice system it so zealously enforces. It also happens to easily be the tallest building in Bannerton's already staggering skyline. In any city's skyline. A deliberate feat created to touch the heavens—something not achieved by mere coincidence. After all, Clayton did always feel Klein fancied himself as someone sent from above.

At the rear gate entrance, he leans in to align his eye to the corresponding retinal scanner. A faint red line skims across his pupil and the lock light, accompanied by a crisp clank, turns green. He pushes the horizontal bar inward and enters the metallic, triple-reinforced steel door. Inside, the long, sprawling concrete hall gives the illusion of fading infiniteness under the buzzing haze of stale overhead fluorescence. Not more than three steps down the hallway's illuminated blackhole, he spots Sean Javorsky, a baby-faced rookie who just started security detail with the unit less than six months ago. He's posted outside the floor's main entrance.

Sean looks up at the clock on the wall with gritted teeth.

"So, you want the bad news or the worse news?" He grimaces.

"Hmm, real tempting options. What about the *good* news?" Clayton counters, optimistically.

"Hate to say it, man, but I'm fresh out of that."

"Damn," Clayton responds, intent to keep walking and talking in his already hurried state. "Dare I say bad news first then?"

"Well, other than the Bulls's pathetic streak of losing it in overtime again last night, Rickers is on a witch hunt for you. Also, again."

"Yeah, I caught that OT. How the hell are you going to pass up the final shot like that?"

"Right? That's exactly what I said!"

"Looks like it could be another rough season for our boys in red and black."

"Same old Chicago."

"Unfortunately. So, what's worse news than Rickers trying to burn me at the stake?"

"Well, maybe it's nothing, but he is looking exceptionally pissed this morning."

"Of course, he is. I'd hate my life and everyone in it, too, if I cashed in my whole existence squabbling for the scraps from Klein and this hellhole. The dude really needs to get laid in a bad way, like yesterday."

"Maybe, but unless you can help him find a dance partner for the horizontal tango, I think you're better off laying low this morning.

Jayson's already tried his best to cover for you, but even Mr. Smooth himself only has so much charm."

"Speak of the devil," Clayton interjects, as he catches Jayson barreling around the corner down the far hall, his slim silhouette illuminated by the harsh glow from the succession of hanging LEDs.

"I'll catch you later, Sean," Clayton says with an accompanying wave.

"Good luck, man," the rookie responds. "You're going to need it."

Jayson's distant profile and steps grow in size and volume the closer he gets until he meets Clayton face-to-face.

"Dude, you're late. Again," he heeds, and rolls his eyes. Their looping gaze falls to his wristwatch. "Nearly half an hour. Rickers is going to go ballistic."

"I know man, I just got . . . caught up in something this morning."

Jayson steps in front of Clayton to study his face. His demeanor seems far too cheery for a soon-to-be ass-chewing.

"Wait a second. Those sparkling eyes. That hidden grin. I know that look. I invented that look. Someone had themselves a little taste of morning glory, didn't they?" Jayson pries with a beaming smile. "Go ahead, just tell me I'm wrong. I'll wait."

As Clayton's best friend, Jayson Moore is stuck in a life of perpetual bachelorism. The tall, thin Black man is dedicated to his ability to charm anything with shaved legs and a peach for an ass while keeping a pristine box fade 365 days a year. As an unattached man with style to spare, Jayson changes women as often as he changes bed sheets. And since the two are cataclysmically linked, it's created a vicious cycle of lingering commitment issues and sleepless nights, literally. But despite his inability to pledge himself to any one of his many one-night stands, Jayson's loyalty as a friend is unquestionable. Clayton and him were hired on at The Hunt for Justice at the same time. And having spent orientation together and countless graveyard shifts, as well as acquiring a mutual hatred for Rickers, their dipshit security superintendent, they quickly formed an instant bond that grew into a friendship built on a breaking each other's balls, petty competition, and a shitload of empty twelve-packs of the finest Mexican lagers.

"Let's just say it was something like that," Clayton responds, hiding the tinge of a grin.

"You know, one of these days, I'm not gonna be here to cover for your ass."

"I know. You're probably right, but until then I'll just have to keep cashing in on those IOUs."

"Yeah, well those IOUs are piling up, and this ain't *Dumb and Dumber*," Jayson scolds, grabbing Clayton by the shoulders. "I mean, do I look like fucking Lloyd Christmas to you?"

"You're right. I'm sorry, man," Clayton confesses.

"It's fine. Just—"

"You could never pull off a bowl cut. Are you kiddin' me? You're way too Black. And besides, you're definitely more of a Harry anyway. Only your shaggin' wagon is the wiener dog in your pants."

"You know, if you weren't my best friend, I'm pretty sure I'd hate you. Like, a lot."

They share a quick laugh as they continue walking and jabbing each other down the next series of long, winding hallways. Corridors that feel more like constricted passageways of an underground bunker system than the distinguished bowels of corporate America. Eventually, they reach the security breakroom, and Clayton badges in.

"Which one was dumb, and which one was dumber, anyway?" Jayson asks, sincerely. "I've always wondered."

But before Clayton can answer the million-dollar pop culture question, Rickers bursts through the door behind them, storming into the room with his frantic scuttle that makes it look like he's got a broomstick stuck halfway up his ass. And judging by the look on his beet-red face today, the handle must be wedged even deeper up his poop chute than usual.

Sensing the expletive explosion that's about to take place, Jayson pats Clayton on the back and dips out.

"Uh, good luck, man," he adds before slinking off to safety somewhere outside of the ensuing blast zone.

But he doesn't even make it out of the room before Rickers unloads the verbal clip he's had cocked and loaded from the moment he caught whiff of Clayton's arrival.

"Well, look who decided to finally grace us with his presence. About goddamn time, Sparks," he barks, turning erection-red like the prick he is.

Rickers brushes the sleeves back over his pudgy, sausage-link arms and aggressively crosses them. His already round baby face, complete with a hearty helping of double chins, appears even more bloated from the influx of blood currently rushing to it, and his high crew cut with the bangs flipped up isn't doing him any favors in the slimming department. "I guess I didn't realize we all worked on your schedule. Tell me, what's the excuse today, Sparks? I've been waiting all morning to hear it, so it better be fucking good."

Sensing that a second argument before lunch probably isn't ideal, Clayton concedes defeat and goes with a simple apologetic response he thinks, or at least he hopes, will dilute the fire in Rickers's eyes.

"I'm sorry, sir, it won't happen again. I promise."

"*Ohh*. You promise, huh? Well, I feel so relieved now."

He thought wrong.

Rickers takes a step closer invading Clayton's personal space. He bends over even further as if that metaphorical broomstick just nudged itself north another inch or two.

"Thing is, Sparks, . . . your promises don't mean *shit* to me, and my name ain't *Jack*. If I had a dollar for every time you've made me a promise, I'd have enough money to retire from this place and not have to deal with the likes of your sorry ass ever again."

Maybe it's because he's already warmed up from his earlier spar with Klien. Or, maybe it's this morning's surprise news that he's going to be a father that makes everything else seem somewhat trivial now, but Clayton just can't resist the urge to poke the bear for once.

Higher road be damned.

He has zero fucks to give.

"Well, I don't know, sir, I'm beginning to think that you ride my ass so often because you secretly want it."

Caught completely off guard by the ballsy comeback, Rickers doubles down on his "World's Biggest Asshole Boss" routine.

"What the hell did you just say? You want to say that again, smart ass?"

Clayton knows he just dumped a giant pile of flammable trash on top of the dumpster fire he's already fighting to get out of, but he just doesn't care anymore.

Not now.

Not today.

Negative fucks to give.

"Now, see, there you go again, sir, talking about my ass," he says without attempting to hide his smirk.

Rickers, who is now just as red in the head as the two-sizes-too-small security shirt that his belly is raging its own side war with, gets all up in Clayton's face.

Eye-to-eye.

Nose to Rudolph.

"You talk a real tough game, Sparks. Even have your little petty rap sheet to show for it. But you want to know what I really think?"

"More than anything, sir."

"I think you're just a scared shitless little boy. All bark, no bite. And if you weren't fucking the daughter of the president, who personally hand-fed you this gig, I'd take pleasure in not only firing your pathetic ass but teaching you a lesson in respect in the process," Rickers says, tucking his shirttail back into his Winnie the Pooh waistline. But like a broken roll-down blind, it keeps raising back up, begging to continue its game of belly button peek-a-boo.

Clayton knows deep down that he'd love nothing more than to beat this pudgy, pompous prick to a pulp. Even now, he can feel the urge in his fingertips, a tinge of rage attempting to curl his hands into fists. But that's a life he gave up when he got out of prison and met Trish.

And he'd never jeopardize that.

He's sworn to it.

"Well, you know better than anybody, sir. I've never been a very good learner, so it might take a couple lessons."

Rickers's attempt to bait him into reenacting a violent flashback from his former life falls flat. He debates whether to push the envelope even further, but before he can think of his next goading comeback, a voice rings out on the intercom.

"*Clayton Sparks, Mr. Klein would like to see you in his office right away. Clayton Sparks to Mr. Klein's office. Thank you.*"

Rickers takes the opportunity for one last verbal jab before the bell sounds. "Looks like Daddy Warbucks to the rescue again," he swings.

As Clayton heads for the exit, he stops right before the door and spins his head back around toward Rickers. He looks down at his butt and back up to his boss, then back down again, accentuating his glutes. Rickers's eyes follow the flirtatious movement.

"Hey, Ricky! My eyes are up here," Clayton says accusingly, as a string of obscenities immediately chases him out of the breakroom. Their tone is distinct, but the big words aren't so clear as they're stifled by the heavy thump of the closing door. He knows he'll pay for that one later, but he can't help the smirk that spreads between his ears on his strut to the elevator. He's on his way to the lion's den, probably for another fight.

But it's okay.

Today is still a good day.

At the chime, Clayton steps into the nearby elevator. The lift, like the rest of the building, is heavily inspired by Klein's love for midcentury modern minimalism, but with all the bells and whistles of the latest and greatest tech that corporate America can afford. He reaches to badge for the penthouse suite while simultaneously bending over for the required retinal scan. The thin red line reads the caverns of his light blue iris while passing over the bridge of his broad nose and scruffy cleft chin. Meanwhile, the badge pad verifies his secondary authorization. A green indicator light blinks, granting him access, but as the elevator doors close, a hand reaches in to halt them.

"So? How'd it go with Rickers?" Jayson pries through a gritted grin tugging on his lips.

Clayton gives a subtle sigh.

"Oh, you know, the usual. Just Lil' Prick Rick being a big dick. Child's play compared to what I'm about to face," he says, signaling to the number for the penthouse punched into the elevator panel.

"Yeahhh . . . I heard the page," Jayson says, nervously rubbing the back of his neck. "You ready for round two?"

Clayton hits the penthouse button again for the 165th floor.

"Trust me, if this morning has taught me anything, it's that I can handle whatever today throws at me."

"Well, I feel like a broken record, but good luck, man." Jayson shrugs as he removes his hand from the stuttering doors.

"Luck? Nah. Luck would be a quick death, not this," Clayton adds, and tosses in a wink for good measure as the elevator doors shut, sealing his fate.

One would think that traversing 165 stories might take some time, but this is The Hunt for Justice, and its sophisticated system of souped-up pulleys, winches, and cables functions like a vertical bullet train shooting the lift up a seemingly endless barrage of floors in an instant.

When the elevator reaches the penthouse, its doors slide open and Clayton is greeted by Alexa Holbeck, Klein's personal assistant. Alexa has all the makings of your stereotypical rich businessman's secretary. Young, pretty, driven, but still naïve enough to all the corporate corruption. The type of innocent person who should have no business working for an asshole like Simon Klein.

Always the charmer, Clayton greets her with pleasantries that border on flirtation. He figures the least he can do to prepare for the tongue-lashing he's about to get is to have a pleasant buffer beforehand.

"Alexa! You look nice today," he says, stepping off the elevator. "New hairdo?"

Even with her olive skin, her tanned cheeks can't hide the sudden rush of red.

"Mr. Sparks, hi-hey," she responds, fumbling the welcome as her hand immediately goes to combing her hair. "Thanks, it is. I figured it's nearly summer and getting hot, so why not chop some off the top," she stammers, still anxiously running her hands through it. "Y-you like it?"

"I do. It suits you well. Really rounds out your cheekbones."

A fresh rush of blush again floods the current focal point of conversation as she tucks a tuft of freshly cut black hair behind her ear.

"Mr. Sparks, you always know the right thing to say." She looks down shyly at the floor. "Trish is a lucky girl."

"Ah, see that's where you're wrong. I'm the lucky guy," Clayton retorts. "And please, I've told you before. Just call me Clayton. Or Clay. Or, hey you. Literally anything but Mr. Sparks. Seriously, I'm far from a mister."

"Oh, I don't know about that," she says in a cute attempt to defend his honor for him. "But sure thing . . . Clayton."

She smiles, filling the silent gap in their exchange, before remembering why he's up here in the first place—to see Mr. Klein, not give her butterflies.

"Oh, uh, I'll let Mr. Klein know you're here," she says, reaching down to page him. "Mr. Klein, sir? Clayt . . . I mean, um, Mr. Sparks is here. To see you," she fumbles, again stumbling over her words. Her cheeks light back up in Pikachu mode.

"*Send him in*," a gruff and unwelcoming voice trebles back through the speaker.

Although still relatively new to working for Klein, Alexa is more than aware of the two men's history of "tension," for lack of a better word.

"Yikes," she grits. "He sounds extra in the mood this morning, so good luck."

Clayton pauses and shakes his head, letting out a chuckle. "That definitely seems to be the popular phrase for me today."

As he walks over to Klein's office door, he takes a deep breath in before reaching for the handle.

"By the way, there's no such thing as luck," he says with a nod toward Alexa.

Then, he exhales and enters.

It's showtime.

Every time he's been up here, which is far more times than he cares to admit, it's like a new game of find-the-latest-kill. As an avid hunter, the walls of the room are lined with *prize* animals claimed from Klein's numerous big game hunting expeditions across the world, including various other pelts and furs scattered among the clutter of stuffed and fluffed prey. On the bookshelf to Clayton's left, lie several lavishly framed pictures of Klein boisterously posing with the corpses of his kills, along with a small open box filled with several tiny vials that read "Acepromazine."

Whatever it is, Clayton's never heard of it.

All of the taxidermized head mounts that pepper the walls range from big game to the more obscure, everything from moose and giraffes to rhinos and lions, even a silverback gorilla. But just taking these majestic creatures' heads isn't enough. Not for Klein. He's managed to turn other prized parts of his kills into random office supply keepsakes and florid, one-of-a-kind decor. A huddle of walrus tusks have been fashioned into a set of ivory pens, giant squid tentacles made into legs for the dual lamps that flank his desk, and endangered crocodile hides used to wrap everything from his planner and mouse pad, all the way down to a set of coasters, in their embossed leather scales.

After a brief study of the room, Clayton spots the newest addition on the wall—a massive, eight-toothed hippo brandishing two gnarly incisors. The impressive, open-mouthed beast appears frozen in time, displayed as if emerging from the warm waters in the sub-Saharan. The thought of killing such a magnificent creature makes him sick to his stomach. But he thinks about his past and realizes—who is he to judge someone on their guilty pleasures? Their sins? When his own ledger is far from unscathed.

On the opposite side of the office-turned-trophy-room is a full museum-like exhibit displaying a complete history of barbaric weaponry. The ancient arsenal covers an evolutionary gamut of timeframes throughout the age of civilization. In the corner lies a rack of antique swords and blades. Everything from claymores and falcatas to broadswords and a Spanish rapier. On the adjoining rack of armaments hang a series of maces and double-bladed axes, while prehistoric bows, crossbows, and at least twenty rifles litter the neighboring wall.

It may technically be an office, but it sure as hell feels more like a barracks.

"Sparky . . ." Klein groans, as he peers up from staring down the sights of an old Winchester Magnum hunting rifle. The crosshairs pointed center mass right at Clayton's chest. *It's probably the exact same gun he used to kill that poor fucking hippo*, Clayton thinks to himself, reluctantly playing along by raising his arms in a gesture of surrender.

"Don't move," Klein directs, as he adjusts the sights ever so slightly. "Riiiight there. Perfect. *Bang*. You're dead."

His signature sinister grin flaunts itself underneath his targeted eyes. A villainous facial expression that aptly displays his narcissistic arrogance, like an evil picture worth a thousand scares. Knowing that he's set the stage for the impending conversation, Klein places the rifle back onto its empty rack behind him so that he can finish unloading the rest of his incoming unpleasantries.

"Sit down," he orders.

Clayton ambles up to the plain office chair that sits dwarfed before Klein's massive antique desk. An overelaborate piece of historic pre-Revolutionary War furniture made of some priceless 250-year-old wood from America's Founding Fathers. It even has an ornate lion head in mid-roar emblazoned in gold embedded upon its front. Behind the desk sits a throne. At least that's what it looks like—a chair fashioned for a king. It's lined in the finest Peruvian jaguar fur, and its ears are decorated with elephant tusks so enormous they could pass as priceless, prehistoric ivories from an excavated woolly mammoth. Hell, Clayton wouldn't be surprised if they actually were.

Clayton takes a seat, but before he can ask why he's been called up here, Klein cues his own question.

"Beautiful day, isn't it?" he asks, in a tone that suggests he's not at all interested in whether or not Clayton agrees.

Clayton leans back in his chair and coolly replies, "It was."

"Hmph," Klein sighs under his breath and through the slightest smirk.

He pours himself a healthy dose of Irish coffee—what looks to be at least number two for the day based on the residual amber ring inside the mug and the open bottle of Macallan on the desk—and takes a steadied sip. Upon swallowing, he wastes no more effort on small talk, diving right into one of his "Master of the Universe" monologues that Clayton has become all too familiar with.

"When I was twenty-five years old and fresh out of law school, do you know what happened to me, Sparky?"

"No sir, I—" but he's quickly cut off by Klein who clearly isn't looking for another sarcastic response.

"I had a dream. More of an epiphany, really. A calling that I couldn't ignore. That I couldn't turn off. I didn't just want to be someone that helped change the world. I wanted to be the *one* that changed the world. A man of stature. Of power. An unstoppable force. So, you know what I did?"

Again, Clayton tries to respond, but his open mouth is left silently hanging from just another rhetorical question with no intent besides dramatic effect.

"I worked. And I worked. And then I worked more. First one in. Last one to leave. Day in, day out. Nights, weekends . . . holidays. I traded sacrifices for something greater than you could ever conceive. I mean, do you think this, —" he preaches, gesturing to the luxurious penthouse around him "—all of this, was just magically handed to me? That I just woke up one morning and suddenly became who I am today?"

With his contribution to the dialogue well noted, Clayton doesn't even fake an attempt at a retort this time.

Klein slowly makes his way to his throne, still sipping on his generous three-finger pour. But he doesn't sit down. Instead, he rests his arm across the top of the chair's adorned tusks and just stares out one of the grandiose stained-glass windows behind him. The sight beholds an impressive, sprawling metropolis accompanied by an ocean of lush valleys and hills that surround it. It's a vast view that's unrivaled. He looks down at the people below. From this height, they look like nothing more than worker ants at the mercy of his thumb.

"With The Hunt Initiative, I've created something bigger than any one person, Sparky. A world where people are held accountable for not only their own actions but also for the consequences that follow. For all their transgressions. A justice system, born on impartiality and raised without prejudice or corruption. A twenty-first-century synthesis that fuses the golden rule with the proven teachings of *an eye for an eye*. Refining the Wild West's unspoken law of frontier justice with a voice to support a modern nation and a futureproof world. And it all centers around one, simple premise: *The penalty for murder is murder*."

He takes a large gulp from his heavily lubed java and swirls the remainder of Rare Cask whiskey with just a dash of coffee in his mouth, savoring the sting before swallowing. His graying mustache twitches as he turns his broad torso from the window.

"It's a system of equality that turns predators into prey," he continues, deviously wiping the cocktail of caffeinated depressant from the silver flavor saver above his upper lip. "Kill and be hunted. A life for a life."

Clayton repositions himself in his seat. Crossing his left leg over his right and then vice versa in a failed attempt to gain an ounce of comfort. To prepare for what he knows is coming next. The real reason for this lavish, holier-than-thou speech. He's been in this literal position enough times to know. It's like clockwork by now.

Still posing with his arm draped around his throne, like it too is some kind of trophy he just hunted rather than an actual seat, Klein continues.

"The Hunt Initiative isn't just an evolution of our judicial system. It was, and it still is, a revitalization. A reimagining of sorts. And since I implemented phase one twenty-five years ago to this very day, murder rates and cases of manslaughter have decreased ninety-three percent nationwide. In fact, they're nearly nonexistent right here in Bannerton. We haven't had a murder in almost a decade. And with The Hunt Initiative that I put into place, we've experienced a remarkable trickle-down effect across the entire criminal blackboard. A monumental drop in other subsidiary crimes from the top, down: theft and larceny, vandalism, trespassing, rape, arson, reckless endangerment—and a couple I know you're familiar with—burglary, and my personal favorite, assault and battery."

He reaches down to deliberately nudge the askew pad of paper on his desk parallel again with his keyboard, coaster, and other perfectly assorted geometric office supplies. "I'm one of the most influential people alive, Sparky. But do you think I'm content? That what I've done is enough to be satisfied with myself? With my family? With our future as the greatest nation to ever exist?"

Klein raises his mug once more. His beady eyes not so much lifeless as they are soulless. As if there used to be a person somewhere buried deep in there at one time, an actual, real human being capable of emotion and compassion, replaced long ago by an obsessed figure greedy for power and fame.

Clayton's never asked Klein why he felt so compelled to create The Hunt Initiative; he doesn't know if he wants to now, or ever. He can speculate that something happened in Klein's past to trigger the idea. As a big-shot lawyer with a bright future in progressive legislation, something had to have planted the seed to spur such a radical judicial evolution. But what? He thinks maybe it aligns somehow, some way, with the ambiguity surrounding the death of his wife, Rebecca Klein, who died when Trish was just a toddler. Clayton doesn't know all the circumstances around her death. Come to think of it, he doesn't really know about any of them. Just that it was some automobile accident that left Klein devastatingly motivated. Trish herself has little to no recollection of her mother as is, and he knows asking Klein now is beyond a fruitless endeavor.

Klein presses forward, starting in on the second act of his one-man homily.

"Up until now, this has all been just the beginning, Sparky. Because tonight at the anniversary celebration, I will finally reveal the next phase of The Hunt Initiative. The rollout of a Global Hunt," he says, pausing for an added layer of dramatic effect. "Soon, the entire world can eat, sleep, and live without fear, protected by justice in its purest form," he concludes, spreading his arms wide open.

The divine action reminds Clayton of how Jesus is depicted addressing his apostles at the Last Supper, as lord and savior of the free world. Preaching as if there's a full room of devoted followers hanging onto his every didactic word.

"I'm a visionary, Sparky. And what I see. What I dream—I do."

He finally makes a move to sit down in his seat of sovereignty, slowly lowering himself like there's a surrounding council anxiously awaiting His Highness to be at ease.

Although in good physical standing, especially for a man his age, Father Time and the cumbersome weight of the power Klein carries has expedited the wear on his most prominent facial features. Not enough to notice at a distance, or even at a first glance, but as Clayton stares across the table at the figure before him now, he sees a tired man desperately trying to mask his aging mortality. His smile is bright, polished, and aligned, but so much to the point that it's obvious his real teeth are shamelessly hidden behind a pair of pearly white veneers. Meanwhile, the crow's feet around his eyes have deepened and spread their footprints so far down his cheeks that they're more reminiscent of a vulture's claw. And no matter how many secret nip and tuck sessions he's undergone to stave it off, the loose skin on the underbelly of his chin continues to lose its hopeless war against gravity.

"Now, do you want to know what I see when I look at you, Sparky?" Klein asks at long last, doing his own personal evaluation of Clayton.

Bingo.

*Here we go*, Clayton thinks to himself. The moment he's been waiting for. Dreading. The real reason for being called up to Klein's office of death is finally taking shape.

It's not so much that he's afraid to answer.

It's that he knows he doesn't have to.

"Nothingness," Klein responds for him, and casually reclines back into his seat, reaching pinnacle king mode. Only there's an unsettling shift in his laxed demeanor. Clayton feels for the first time since he's known Klein that he's truly at the mercy of a ruthless tyrant, and not just a man. To bring a sense of ease back into the tense situation, he scouts the surrounding floor around him for any hint of a trap door.

Just in case.

Klein reaches for his mug, but he must have forgotten that somewhere in between his personal history lesson and proclaiming himself second savior of the New World, he drank it all. He subtly places the cup back onto the table and scoots it to the side, flashing another hint of his OCD.

"You're a blemish in my otherwise perfect existence, Sparky. You're not even a waste of potential because there's nothing prospective about you. Where you came from, who you are, what you've done. They amount to nothing more than a life of past regrets and a future bound for disappointment. I have absolutely no idea what my daughter sees in you, but your very existence insults me."

Clayton walked in anticipating a verbal scuffle, but even this is more than he was prepared for. Still reeling from the oral onslaught of character-crippling defamation, he finally finds the right muscles and reflexes to open his mouth and form some semblance of a reply.

"Um, I'm . . . sorry you feel that way, Simon."

"That's Mr. Klein to you. And save me the apologies. You're not here to be forgiven." Klein leans in, the grave scowl on his face more dire than ever. His eyes pure black. "You're here to be forgotten."

He's not sure if it's because he's still trying to process everything that's just been said, or if it was just the vague and suspiciously threatening nature of that last statement, but Clayton cautiously probes on for clarification.

"Forgotten? What are you talking about?" he questions. His voice is firm, but his demeanor is a tangled ball of nerves firing on all cylinders.

"Always the quick one, aren't you, Sparky?" Klein responds with precise cynicism, as he leans back into a less menacing position. "Allow me to spell it out for you simply. I'm a wealthy man. I could make your wildest dreams come true. All I ask in return is for you to just . . . disappear. Up and go without a trace. As if you were never in my or Patricia's life in the first place."

With his mind officially caught up to speed on the fucked-up situation he's found himself waist-deep in, Clayton has no other way out but to fire back.

"Are you seriously trying to buy me out right now?"

"Is it such an unreasonable proposition?"

"This is fucking crazy."

"Is it? Just give me a number, and we can both move on with our lives. Away from each other, where you're free to go pollute some other family. To brainwash another father's daughter. Tarnish someone else's reputation."

Klein reaches for one of the walrus tusk fountain pens and a croc-skinned notepad from his desk. He pushes the pair across the immaculately preserved eighteenth-century walnut toward Clayton, who freezes at the absurd validity behind the whole devious concept.

"Go ahead, Sparky. Just write it on the paper and we can both have what we want." He snickers as Clayton remains paralyzed by the shocking reality of the situation. Meanwhile, a maniacal sneer slithers under the perfectly sculpted confines of Klein's kempt mustache.

The smug, serpent-like smile is enough to snap Clayton out of his defeated daze. As his motor skills shift back into gear, he reaches down for the pen, bobbing it in his hand a couple of times. The heft alone and the gold-fashioned stylings attached to the smooth ivory easily indicate it's probably worth more than what he makes in a month, maybe two.

Slowly, he gestures toward the paper and begins to write.

Klein reclines back in his chair, reveling in yet another win in his illustrious history of getting whatever he wants. Perhaps one of his finest victories yet.

Clayton finishes writing and rips the top page from the leather notepad. Belligerently, he tosses the pen and pad atop what could be Thomas Jefferson's Grandover desk for all he cares. Folding the loose ply of paper, he slides it back over to Klein.

"See, Sparky, that wasn't so hard now, was it?"

Klein snatches the creased note and unfolds it to read the number. The arrogance on his conceited face flees as fast as the ensuing rush of red takes to fill it, leaving a wake of bubbling disbelief behind. Only, it's not shock at all. It's anger. More specifically, rage—like a hissing kettle that's reached its boiling point.

Scribbled on the piece of paper are four simple words:

"*Go fuck yourself, asshole.*"

Klein crumples up the humiliating note in his tight fist. The intensity behind the anger causes his knuckles to whiten. He deliberately places it into the trash bin under his desk and leans forward. As a man of precision, he slowly and meticulously removes his thinly framed glasses with both hands, folds them, and places them neatly onto the desk.

"Hrmm. You disappoint me, yet again, Sparky."

He looks directly into Clayton's blazing eyes. There's so much heat in the room it feels like the thermostat just got jacked up twenty degrees. The stare-down continues for an uncomfortable matter of time, in which nothing is said but everything is communicated.

Klein finally breaks the silent tug-of-war.

"Fine," he mutters, twitching his mustache in an almost nervous tick that Clayton's never seen before. "If it's not money, then what will it take?"

For the first time in their dueling dialogue, Clayton feels like he has the floor. It's not just another one of Klein's rhetorical questions of grandeur. Dozens of thoughts race through his mind, but he doesn't know where to begin. So, he just starts talking, hoping his mouth will catch up to the spewing speed of his enraged thoughts.

"You just don't get it, do you . . . *Simon*? Hell, you never have," he says, pressing the issue more than he ever has. "And apparently you never will. I don't want your fucking money. Jesus, I never have! I fell in love with your daughter, not your bottomless checkbook or your gaudy reputation. I want absolutely nothing from you. Not a goddamn thing. How hard is that for you to understand?"

Clayton rises from his seat. It's a small act, but a power move, nonetheless, giving him the higher ground and a more dominant position.

"Look, I know I fucked up when I was younger. But I've paid my dues for those mistakes. I'm a different person now. I'm not that scared, angry kid anymore constantly looking to end conversations with my fists instead of my words. And if you're more worried about what my past means for your future—for your own daughter's happiness, then you're more pathetic than I ever thought."

Clayton steps back from the chair and adjusts his security shirt.

"Now, if you'll excuse me, I've got to get back to work, *sir*."

He starts to walk away, but his eyes wander one last time to the new hippo trophy. He stops and turns back around to Klein who hasn't moved an inch or stopped glaring.

"Oh, and this—" Clayton gestures to the trophy, then everything around it. To the countless dead animals that wreathe the room, to the stacked racks of weaponry—to the building itself. "All of this. Everything you've *created*. It's all bullshit. You might be able to con millions into believing your perfect system of law and order is based on some altruistic form of justice. But when you scrape through the heaping pile of lies and deceit, you're really just in the business of profiting off people's misery by disguising it as vengeance. Exploiting their fear and sorrow through needless acts of violence. And I gave all that up a long time ago. So, you tell me, who's really the criminal here?"

Clayton continues his path toward the door. As he reaches for the handle, he catches an uncontrollable shaking in his hand as it rattles the knob. Not out of fear or anxiousness, at least, not anymore. But from a sense of liberation. Everything he's ever wanted to say to that smug son of a bitch was just laid out on the line. And although it's not exactly the way he ever pictured the metaphorical shit hitting the fan, he can't help but notice the upward curve in his lips that reflects just how good it all felt.

Back home at their urban crossroads apartment, Trish Klein faces a desperate dilemma of her own.

"Ughh . . . what the hell am I going to wear tonight?"

She throws her arms up in defeat as she storms out of the bedroom, away from the clothing massacre that looks as if her closet and her dresser just had a knife fight. Scout cocks one sullied eye open from his loafed position on the bed, less than amused to have been disturbed during his first of many quality slumber sessions for the day. He trots off down the hall for another room filled with less drama and fewer raging hormones.

Fully aware that the battle against her wardrobe has reached a stalemate, Trish follows the perturbed tortie down the hall into the kitchen. She looks over to find he's put resuming his nap on a temporary hiatus while he helps himself to a third breakfast.

"Stress eating, huh?" she asks, watching him choke down a mouthful of kibbles. Following his lead, she opens the freezer and digs for the fresh tub of Chubby Bunny chocolate chip cookie dough ice cream. She hunts out a spoon from the silverware drawer and scoops a heaping bite straight from the pristine surface.

"Me, too," she mumbles through the mouthful of creamy custard. Scout pays no attention as half of the kibbles make the short, expected journey into his mouth while the other half scatter onto the hardwood every which way.

After a couple soothing spoonfuls, Trish decides to shift her mood into what she hopes to be a happier light. She grabs her phone from the kitchen counter and types a text to Clayton.

*How long does it take for a baby bump to show? I've tried on my entire closet so far and I look like a cow in every dress I own!*

She hits Send and shovels in another bite as she anxiously awaits the three little dots in the other column to stop moving.

Finally, Clayton replies.

*LOL. Just relax. I'm sure all your dresses look amazing, and they'll continue to look even more amazing once that baby starts growing!*

She smiles as she reads the comforting message, her stress starting to balance itself back out as another one comes through.

*And if not, then you can always get some of those dresses that are like an oversized shirt meets a robe. What are those called again? They start with an M.*

She says to herself timidly out loud, "Muumuus?"

Another text comes through.

*I really hope you just said it out loud.*

And that's when the setup hits her.

She walked right into it like the front-row sucker at a stand-up comedy show. Her mouth grows big. Her eyes even bigger, then slit. She casts the Chubby Bunny aside as she plots her revenge text.

A kiss-blowing winky face emoji soon follows Clayton's jab. But it's too late. War has been waged.

*Excuse me?! Not even a day pregnant and you're already calling me fat? You better watch yourself or I might just MOOOO-ve all your shit out the apartment window.*

Trying to play nice, he replies.

*Touché, mama. But c'mon let's be honest, you laughed a little, right?*

Trish wastes no time as she goes in for the kill.

*Oh, sure I did. It was so funny that I can't wait to see who's laughing the next time you're looking to get some. Because thanks to you, this apartment is now a no-cow tipping zone.*

Trish tosses the phone onto the counter in exchange for the now half-eaten tub of savory sweetness. She lands another spoonful onto the runway of her tongue. Maybe it's the coolness of the ice cream or the belated humor of the situation, but she starts to chill out, giggling to herself.

A simple, harmless joke, but it was just the thing she needed to come to terms with her emotions. To realize how exciting their future will be. She isn't surprised; Clayton's always been able to talk her off the ledge one way or another. It's one of the things she loves most about him. For a man with a history that proves otherwise, Clayton has never been anything but a calming force for her since the day they met nearly three years ago. A moment she still remembers with vivid recollection. The first time she laid eyes on him at her favorite little coffee shop just down the block.

Trish had grabbed coffee from Java Plaza dozens of times before. It was her sanctuary during the craze of her Master of Fine Arts years, quickly becoming her go-to stop for a pick-me-up perk long after graduation.

One rainy Sunday in April, she was cuddled up in her usual cozy spot in the back corner of the café. Sitting on her favorite 70s-era velvet blue couch with Bob Marley not only playing on the record player in the background but hanging on the wall directly overhead, his portrait nestled next to other long-gone greats like Janis Joplin, Buddy Holly, and Kurt Cobain. She was nose-deep in *Dreamcatcher*—for the second time—soaking up the soft reading light of the nearby lamp's halogen glow and the warmth emanating from the hot mug of her steaming chai latte. Trish, who could never be found too far removed from the spine of a hardcover, was a fan of all genres, but nothing could fully possess her quite like the addiction for a nail-biting sci-fi mystery. In this case, even one she'd already read before.

More than two dozen customers probably walked into the shop within the hour Trish had been there stuck with her eyes firmly glued to King's Oxy-induced thrill ride about reunited friendships and a surprise alien invasion. But for some reason, the welcome bell on the door just sounded different when Clayton Sparks wandered into the shop that day. It wasn't his physical features that drew her in, although, they didn't hurt. At just under six feet tall with a semi-athletic build, Clayton was slightly better looking than your average cup of Joe. He sported a convincing five o'clock shadow over a defined jawline that bordered closer to ten p.m., and his dishwater blond hair, topped off by two wild cowlicks, fell delicately, yet imperfectly, in all the right places. Even his clothes were nothing special. She remembers he wore a plain maroon t-shirt, gray tapered sweatpants, and a smudged-up pair of black Chuck Taylors—a uniform that simply said Sunday errands.

For Trish, though, what caught her eye that drizzly day wasn't his traditional looks or nonchalant style. It was his aura. Something about the way he seemed to carry the weight of the world on his shoulders but did so without complaint or burden. As if he was *Tuck Everlasting*, a man who had lived centuries and had all the experiences—good and bad—to show for it.

To this day, she still has no idea why she did it. Although an extrovert at heart, it wasn't like her to be the one to make the first move. To be the pursuer, not the pursued. At least, she'd never done it before. She was traditional in that regard. But on that specific saturated Sunday, she couldn't help but put down her book and go talk to the real-life mystery that had just walked into her sanctuary—into her life.

Of course, falling in love with someone is always easier when it's only you and them. That young love period where the whole world just seems to stop, and it's just the two of you. Before the outside world of friends, family, and coworkers can cast judgment and jump to their own ill-conceived conclusions about who you are and what you deserve. She knew bringing suitors home to her father would never be an easy task. Not as the daughter of the infamous Simon Klein. But when Clayton finally came clean about his rap sheet early on in their relationship, she knew that gaining her father's approval changed from problematic to mission impossible. It wasn't that she couldn't take her father's snide remarks about her choice in men. She'd dealt with that on and off growing up. But in Clayton's case, it was the backhanded comments her father constantly hurled at him that boiled her blood. She thought she'd worked out an accord, but how do you reach a compromise with a man who has everything to lose and nothing to gain? Especially when that man is your own father.

After a few minutes of aimless self-reflection, Trish wipes away the salty trail of joy from her eyes and caked-on cookie dough from the corners of her lips. With a newfound spark, she heads back to the bedroom on a mission to end this wardrobe war once and for all. To leave no dress behind.

Halfway down the hallway, her phone rumbles again. Thinking it's Clayton ready to make an apologetically desperate plea for promiscuity, her eyes flicker in surprise when they read the word DAD on the incoming caller ID screen.

She answers the phone.

"Hi, honey," says the trebly voice on the other line.

"Hi, Daddy, to what do I owe the pleasure of two calls from you in one morning?"

"Oh, umm, nothing major, hon . . ." her father responds, but there's a noticeable pause on the line before he finishes his thought. "Say, you haven't talked to Clayton recently, have you?"

Under normal circumstances, flare guns would be going off in her head heeding all sorts of warning. In their entire relationship, her father has never once phrased such a vague question regarding her disapproved boyfriend. But since she just spoke with Clayton not more than five minutes ago, and he mentioned nothing unsettling, she doesn't overthink it. She's already done that enough this morning and there's a bedroom battlefield to prove it.

"Nooope. Why? Is there something he was supposed to tell me?"

That familiar pause returns as she awaits his response. The silence is so loud she can almost feel his thinking on the other line. If he's fishing for something, she has no idea what it is, nor does she really care right now. Her mind's already been overloaded with all kinds of emotions and uncontrollable hormones since her series of early up-chuck sessions this morning.

"No, no, nothing to worry about, hon. I just told him that you two were planning on arriving at the anniversary party at seven p.m. tonight, but he thought it was seven-thirty p.m. I just wanted to make sure you had the right time. That's all."

"Yep. We should be all good. We'll see you at seven p.m., Daddy. Oh, and do me a favor? Please behave yourself tonight," she adds, setting a best-behavior precedent for the evening. Just to make sure everyone is prepped to play nice. "I know you don't think much of Clay, but if you love me at all, you can at least accept him. Because he's not going anywhere anytime soon, okay?"

Another delayed response finally cuts through the static line. "Of course not, hon. I'll be good, for you. That's a promise."

"Thanks, Daddy. It would mean a lot. I love you."

"Love you, too, honey. Bye-bye."

Trish puts the phone down on the bed and after a quick game of eeny, meeny, miny, moe with her two top dress choices, she lands on the white backless look over the olive strapless number. She hears the muffled vibration of an incoming text against the queen bed's duvet.

She reads the new message.

*You know I just want what's best for you, hon. I'll see you tonight. Love, Dad.*

She smiles and tosses the phone back onto the mattress as she skips off toward the bathroom with the winning dress in hand. She thinks today couldn't get any better.

If she only knew the half of it.

By lunchtime, Clayton has had a couple hours to process everything that went down in Klein's office. But it's too much for him to comb through alone. After he finishes warming up the leftover Pad Thai that Trish made last night, he sits down next to Jayson at a table in the corner of the small, bleak security breakroom. Posted on the wall next to the occupied two-top are posters for workplace harassment, anti-discrimination protocol, and contact info for filing HR complaints.

He can't help but scoff at the irony.

"Wait, wait, wait—" Jayson repeats over a mouthful of his own bachelor noodle staple, a steaming cup of set-it-and-forget-it Easy Mac. "You're telling me he literally tried to buy you out? Like, for real? With actual money?"

"For real. He told me to write my price down on a piece of paper and slide it across the desk."

"Damn, man, that's some straight-out-of-the-movies mafia-type shit. He really went all *Godfather* on you," Jayson adds, choking down his sad, nuked excuse for actual pasta. "'I'm gonna make youse an offer you can't refuse,'" he jokes, jutting out his jaw in a sad attempt at his best Vito Corleone impersonation.

It's been a while since Clayton has seen Jayson this animated. But he's relieved to know that he's not the only one that thinks his whole rumble in the penthouse was anything short of totally, way-over-the-line fucked up.

"So, what'd you do?" Jayson asks, now so invested that he's totally ignored his "heat & eat" lunch.

"Oh, I wrote on the paper," Clayton responds, slurping up a bite of broccoli and loose tail of spooled flat noodles.

"No way? What you'd write?" Jayson doubles down in disbelief.

Clayton swallows and takes a drink from his water bottle. "Well, he told me to name a price, right?"

"Yeah, but you didn't. Riiight?"

"No! Of course not. I called him an asshole and told him to go fuck himself."

Jayson laughs so hard that he involuntarily bangs his fists onto the table, accidentally flinging his fork to the ground. Somehow, watching his friend lighten the heaviness from the situation causes Clayton to reluctantly join in the screwed-up hilarity of his own misery.

"Trust me, I wish I was joking, but it gets even more fucked up. Klein said, and I quote, 'I could make your wildest dreams come true. All I ask in return is for you to just . . . *disappear*.'" Clayton embellishes disappear for dramatic flair while Jayson regains his composure long enough to blankly stare straight ahead paralyzed, mouth agape as if Clayton just hit him with a stupefy spell.

"I mean, I know that old bastard never liked me. I've known that ever since we first met. But this? I gotta say, I never saw this coming."

Jayson snaps out of his hex and casts the first thought that comes to mind. "Well, you're gonna tell Trish, right? Like, duh."

It's a fair question. In all honesty, it's the only question that Clayton's been contemplating since he left Klein's office. Turning it over and over, back and forth in his mind like a washing machine set on heavy load. He knows he wants to tell her, of course, he wants to tell her, but what will it do to his already toxic relationship with her father? Worse yet, what if Trish doesn't believe him? He could lose everything. And the thought of that is just too much to handle right now.

Clayton looks up despairingly from his bowl of now-cooled leftovers. He's suddenly not hungry. Like his stomach just sensed everything that's weighing on his mind, and made the executive decision that not having an appetite is one less thing for him to have to worry about at the moment.

Sensing the looming hesitation in his friend's demeanor, Jayson echoes his previous statement.

"Man, you have to tell her."

He knows it's probably a feeble attempt to try to sell Clayton on doing the right thing, but that's what friends are for. And as his best friend, he feels like it's his duty to push the envelope here.

Clayton, still clearly battling his own inner turmoil replies, "I don't know, man. It's not that easy."

"The hell it isn't! Daddy 'Douchebag' Warbucks just tried to bribe you. You think he's just going to stop there? As if he's going to be all like 'Well, Clayton didn't accept my bribe, but I guess we can still try to be friends.' Fuck no, man. That dude has it out for you. You gotta tell her now before Skid Mark Avenue straight up turns into Shit Street."

But before Clayton has a chance to respond, he spots Rickers down the hall through the breakroom windows. Power-waddling with that metaphorical stick still firmly wedged up his balloon knot. Heading right for the breakroom.

"Speaking of shit, Rickers ten o'clock," Clayton sighs. "I gotta jet, man. I've taken enough ass-chewings today to hit my quota for the next six months. I'll catch up with you later, all right?"

He springs to his feet, tosses his nearly untouched lunch into the trash, and bolts for the side breakroom exit before Rickers finishes rounding the corner.

On his way out the door, he hears Jayson call out, "You gotta tell her, man!"

Seconds later, Rickers storms into the break room, aggressively surveying the confined space. He finds Jayson suspiciously finishing up his lunch alone.

"Okay. Where'd he go?" Rickers demands.

Playing coy, Jayson responds with as much false conviction as his voice can intonate. Looking around the room for added effect, he answers Rickers's question with his own question while taking a hefty swig from his soda can.

"Where'd who go, sir?" he mumbles in between fizzy gulps.

"Don't play dumb with me, Moore. You know damn well who I'm talking about. Thick as cow shit you two are. So where is he?"

Jayson leans back in his chair, picks up the napkin from his lap, and carefully wipes his mouth. The compiled seconds of added action give him just enough time to polish up a more believable excuse.

"I don't know where Clay is at, sir. Last I heard, he was called up to Mr. Klein's office earlier this morning. Haven't seen him since."

Rickers scans the lunch table like a detective. Investigating for any evidence that could suggest someone else was eating here. But there's nothing substantial to prove any foul lunch play has transpired.

"Well, when you do see your boyfriend again, tell him I'm looking for him," Rickers snarls, as he scopes his knockoff Rolex. "Now get back to work, Moore, your break is over."

He clomps his way out of the break room, back to his search and lynch party for Clayton.

Jayson picks his dirty fork up off the floor and tosses it, along with his empty cup of macaroni, into the trash. As he walks out the door, he shakes his head, chuckling to himself.

"Man, that dude really needs to get laid, like yesterday."

Barely escaping yet another tongue-lashing for the day, Clayton makes his way down the west basement corridor. Security used to be stationed on the twenty-second floor. But over a year and a half ago, the unit was relocated to B1, the building's basement. A relocation Clayton likes to refer to as the *bowel movement* because all the corporate big wig shit seems to flush down here.

Down here, the drab concrete walls provide no flourish like the rest of the modern marvel's public-facing areas. The toilet situation, or lack thereof, gives Clayton prison PTSD flashbacks. The security personnel's "offices" are just recycled broom closets cramped with little space and no windows to the outside world; even the building's storage—bins of outdated tech, old office supplies, holiday decorations, and the like—is slowly overtaking the underground facility's space one year at a time.

Clayton doesn't really think Klein would purposefully move the whole department to the basement of the nation's tallest, most luxurious skyscraper on the lone account of his disdain for him, but the transition did take place shortly after he was hired. And after today's clash in his office, he wouldn't be surprised in the least if Klein had displaced them in some petty and pathetic attempt at a pissing contest.

Typically, after lunch, Clayton makes his rounds of the premises. No frills, just standard clockwork stuff. The usual perimeter patrol routine includes checking that both north and south gate entrances to the building are secure, signing for deliveries, watching for any suspicious activity on the *Matrix*-inspired bank of security monitors, and patrolling key floors that house the records room, cafeteria, executive offices, and main building entrance. He's been working here just under two years, and there's only been one real red alert.

It stemmed from an out-of-state, sixth-grade science teacher who had lost his daughter to a kidnapping turned homicide. Turns out he was outraged that her killer was murdered on the Hunt by someone other than him. Just some random civilian that had no tie to the victim's family. He took the slight personally, something about not getting enough closure. As if her vengeance wasn't enough because he wasn't the one to physically seize it. To end up with the blood on his own hands. He was outraged that The Hunt Initiative had personally failed him. His loss and anger caused him to call in a bomb threat, but when authorities locked down the premises and scanned the building, they didn't find anything. The inconvenience sure did piss off Klein, though, so it wasn't all for nothing.

But most of the time, the biggest threat to the building is just a hit-or-miss scattering of pacifist protesters rallying out front against The Hunt. Waving home-crafted cardboard signs of love and peace that say token bumper sticker phrases like "Violence Doesn't Solve Violence" and "Compassion Is Not a Crime." They're nothing more than harmless modern-day hippies, but Klein hates them and their defiance to his Initiative with a passion, so they're all right in Clayton's book.

As Clayton turns another winding corner, he's met by a long and narrow window that stretches across the basement's vendor garage entrance. A delivery is taking place as a slender man in a gray uniform unloads several vending machine boxes from his truck. Clayton can see the entirety of the exchange taking place through the window, but for the delivery driver and everyone on the other side, it's just a sprawling reflection of themselves.

Finally, after what feels like a mile-long corridor, he reaches the entrance to the surveillance room. He badges in and immediately spots Hector "Hex" Marquez reclined in the control seat, feet on the counter, and phone in hand scrolling through what could almost pass as a photo gallery of softcore porn. Clayton shakes his head and grins. He could wait and see how long it would take before Hector notices him over the peek-a-boob slideshow of selfies—hell, if it were any other day besides today—he probably would. But he doesn't have the mood or the time for it right now, so he deliberately shuts the door with extra emphasis to make his unannounced presence known.

Hector's crisp Air Jordan 1s fly off the counter in a white and red blur as he swivels the control chair around to see who's there. His well-groomed mullet spins with him as the remaining black locks that were partying in the back catch up to the business taking place up front. His eyes give off the impression that he just got caught with his pants down. Which, from what Clayton just saw, might not be far off.

"*Mierda*, Clay! You scared the shit out of me, homes."

Containing his laughter to just a grin, Clayton takes the three steps down into the control pit, grabs the co-pilot surveillance chair, and plops down into its ergonomic memory foam cushion. He turns to Hector who still looks like he's just been depantsed in gym class.

"Oh, I'm sorry. Did you two—" pointing to Hector, then his phone "—need a moment alone to finish?" He jabs his thumb toward the door behind them. "Because I can *cum* back later."

"Man, it ain't like that," Hector defends, as he leans back in his chair, chin up, nervously adjusting his tucked-in gold chain. "Just . . . I haven't been home much, ya know? Been workin' doubles the past two weeks. So, the missus just sent me . . . a sneak peek at what I been missin'. Know what I'm sayin'?"

"Well, from what I saw, it looked like the only thing peekin' was what her top wasn't keepin'. You know what *I'm* sayin'?" Clayton jests with a playful laugh he can no longer contain.

"Yo! You can't tell Camila you saw that. Was hard 'nuf for me to convince her to send those pics in the first place."

"Heyyy, my lips are sealed, Hex," Clayton jokes, as he gestures zipping up his lips. "But my eyes can't lie."

"*Ha-ha*, Clay . . . go ahead and bust my huevos. But that's my mamacita right there. You'd be hard-pressed to find a *hermosa* like Camila interested in a lowly hombre like me. Those curves, that long black hair . . . her lips. Muy bien, homes. Muy. Bien."

At twenty-four years old, Hector reminds Clayton of himself when he was younger. Playful, yet unabashed. Stuck in a perpetual state of getting older but not wanting to grow up. He also just happens to share a rap sheet of his own for a history of petty crimes when he was a teenager—digital fraud, identity theft—small-time stuff. Nothing as serious as some of the marks on Clayton's ledger. They even know some of the same names from the overlapping circles of people they used to run around with. And while he's never outright admitted it to anyone, or himself, Clayton feels the urge to protect Hector from potentially slipping back into his old ways, especially with the recent birth of his daughter, Sophia, last spring. Like a good big brother, he hates the idea of Camila losing him and Sophia growing up fatherless from a stupid lapse in judgment. It's probably why they've become good friends since he started working here about five months ago. Clayton knows deep down it's why he's always subconsciously checking in on him. To make sure he stays out of trouble.

Clayton shifts his attention to the twenty-seven-by-fourteen-foot grid of thirty-two-inch surveillance monitors that line the room's massive wall. Each screen on the sprawling digital embankment displays its own personal story—a unique scene unfolding right this second, in and around this very building. It's always a lot to take in the first time he looks at it.

"How's today looking?" he asks, keeping his eyes glued to the wall of constant commotion, aimlessly scanning the mass of flickering screens.

Hector takes a swig from his big gulp-sized cup of some overly caffeinated neon green drink and relocates his eyes to the bank of moving pictures.

"Pshh, uneventful. As usual," he replies, and takes another nip from his eye-peeling energy drink. It never ceases to amaze Clayton at Hector's innate ability to continuously drink that sleep-override carbonated shit at any time of the day, every day.

Chewing on the side of his straw, Hector turns his gaze back to

Clayton as a sly smirk grows above his dark, wiry beard. "Although I hear your day has been anything but," he adds. His smirk now evolved into its full, shit-eating grin stage.

"Okay. What'd Jayson tell you?"

"Shit, homes, Jay didn't tell me nothing."

"Huh? Then how—?"

"I heard you get paged up to Klein's office this morning," he says, motioning to the monitor board in front of him. "I don't have a security alarm here for that, but I know that call means trouble."

"You can say that again," Clayton replies, looking back up at the sea of screens. His eyes appear glazed over, meaninglessly staring forward as they mirror the flickering movement of the feed before him.

The deadpan demeanor makes Hector think that maybe it's more serious than he initially thought. Replacing his joviality for sincerity, he probes deeper, "You wanna talk about it, amigo?"

Clayton takes a deep breath before responding.

"Just more Klein crap, man, but honestly I'm not really in the mood right—"

All of a sudden, Clayton's dazed gaze is diverted to commotion on one of the screens in the lower right quadrant of the rig's grid.

He mutters under his breath, "Speak of the devil."

Hector follows Clayton's trance to find Klein, accompanied by a mystery man, conversing in front of the elevator on the executive floor.

Hector chimes in, "Well, well, look who it is. *El Diablo* himself. Hey, who's that big, shady-looking hombre he's talking to?"

Clayton walks around Hector's control chair to get a closer look at the screen.

"I don't know, Hex. Never seen the guy before. He definitely doesn't work here," he answers, while studying the scene. "But you're right. He makes some of the baddest dudes I met in the joint look like buttercups."

Clayton and Hector focus in on the lone screen like it's the climax of a movie. The elevator opens and Klein and his mystery guest board the lift, but not before Clayton catches a quick glimpse of a shiny metal object with a black pleated handle tucked underneath the man's leather jacket.

"Did you see that?" he inflects, adding a grave undertone to his question.

"Si, looks like homes is packing," Hector confirms, inching forward to the edge of his seat.

Clayton sits back down and scoots the chair closer to the monitor. "Can you pull up footage in the elevator?"

"Sorry, *ese*, no can do. That's the executive elevator for the penthouse. It's basically Klein's personal lift, so he doesn't have to rub elbows with the rest of us little folk. Ain't no cameras in there."

"Damn." Clayton's mind jumps to the next logical step. "Can you at least locate what floor they get off on?"

"*Claro*, that I can do," Hector confirms. "Just a sec."

Methodically, he inputs a couple of command shortcuts from his central control panel.

"Looks like they got off on floor . . ." He points at a separate, side computer screen not associated with the security footage monitors. "Sixty-six."

The same light bulb flickers on in both their heads as they look at each other and simultaneously reply.

"RECORDS."

"What are they doing up there?" Hector asks, not hesitating for an answer. "No one ever goes up there unless it's for maintenance or there's a flux in the climate-control setting. The whole floor is basically just one giant server room."

Listening but not looking, Clayton's eyes dart from screen to screen until he locates the small quadrant of monitors on the wall broadcasting their current position.

"I don't know, Hex, but I've got to imagine it's not for a lack of meeting rooms," he responds, finally shifting his eyes from the monitor bank over to Hector's direction. "Is it just me or does something not feel right?"

"Si," Hector replies. "It's kinda, how do you say in English . . . smelly?"

Clayton's eyebrows cock with confusion.

"Smelly?" he asks.

"You know, like when something's . . . uh, suspect. Or shady."

"You mean, fishy?"

"Si! Fishy! That's it," Hector exclaims at his moment of English eureka. "This shit feels *muy* fishy, amigo."

Clayton nods in agreement as they both continue to watch Klein and his surprise guest make their way down the hall of the sixty-sixth floor.

Then, something deep down—an almost uncontrollable urge at the back of his mind—impulsively flips. Like an involuntary switch in his brain, immediately taking control over his body.

He goes into instant autopilot.

"Fuck it. I'm going up there," he says, flinging his chair aside and making a beeline for the exit.

Hector yells out right as he reaches for the door.

"Whoa, you all right, homes?" he asks, confused at the sudden spurt. "You want me to call this in or something?"

"No, no I got this," Clayton replies, trying his best to conceal any deeper concern. "Just turn your walkie to channel twelve and keep an eye on them. Let me know if they go on the move."

"You got it, amigo." But Clayton's already out the door, bolting for the elevator before the words land.

When he reaches the lift, he slams the UP arrow repeatedly, as if impulsively hitting it multiple times will make it arrive any faster. After more seconds than he cares to count, the double doors start to part, and he dashes in as soon as the gap is big enough to squeeze through. He pounds floor sixty-six and takes an anxious step back trying to plot his next impromptu move.

From B1, the elevator only takes a matter of seconds to travel sixty-seven floors, but the ride feels like it's in slow motion compared to the thoughts racing in his mind. Thoughts now interspersed by more questions without answers.

Like, *who was that guy?*

*Why did he have a gun?*

*How did he ever get it past security?*

*What are they doing on the records floor?*

*And what's his connection with Klein?*

The ride comes to a halt and the giant metal doors part. Clayton cautiously pokes his head out, peeking both ways like a trained kid trying to cross a busy road. The coast looks clear, but he doesn't want to risk it.

He unclips the walkie from his belt and brings it to his lips.

"Hex, you copy? Over," he whispers.

There's a slight pause. A moment of panic when he fears Hector might have forgotten to flip his walkie to the right channel during his hasty exit. After all, he did say it as he booked it out the door.

Then, a voice breaks through the static.

"Roger that. I'm here, amigo. Over."

"Whew. Okay, good," Clayton replies under a sigh of relief. "So where are they now?"

"Looks like they're headed down the northeast server hallway. Right outside the main records room."

"10–4. Keep your walkie ready in case I lose them. Okay?"

"Claro. I still don't really know what's going on, but be careful, amigo."

"Copy that, buddy."

Unlike The Hunt for Justice's other lavish levels chock-full of stylized office furnishings, the building's records floor resembles something closer to a sterile spaceship than a luxurious corporation. Comprised of four gridded server rooms—northwest, northeast, southwest, and southeast—the wing is divided by thick concrete walls and a metallic-trimmed hallway with a thin, runway strip of geometric-patterned carpet that intersects the building's floor plan to form a symmetrical cross smack dab in the center. The rooms themselves are littered with an array of unsynchronized blinking lights in a variety of colors and patterns, and bundles of chords that go who knows where, plugging into god knows what. The actual files housed in the large space craft-inspired storage units comprise the entire catalog of The Hunt Initiative, dating all the way back to its inception, and beyond. It's like a digital mausoleum of obituaries for all those murdered in the Hunts as well as the death records of the original victims, reaching back more than twenty-five years and counting. But that's not all. When Klein was mapping out the blueprint to create the foundation for The Hunt Initiative, he needed to gather as much research as he possibly could. That meant murder rates per capita, homicide statistics, autopsy reports for freak deaths, unsolved cases, and everything in between, even personal health information. As a result, all the existing murder, manslaughter, and missing persons cases, plus any other documented deaths prior to the Hunt's implementation—dating back at least another ten years—all live on the servers as well.

With so much data being housed in one central location, the entire space is built with soundproof walls to dampen the loud, orchestrated hum of hundreds of hard-at-work hard drives rumbling in unison. It's also kept at a substantially cooler temperature than the rest of the building thanks to its air-conditioned floors that help counteract the immense heat radiating from all the storage towers. No one actually works on the records floor, and you have to have certain access to even get in.

Coincidently, it's the exact kind of high-level clearance that the president of the biggest company in the world and that same company's lowly security guard both possess.

Clayton sleuths his way down the hall toward the northeast server room hugging the wall for every centimeter of added cover. As he rounds the southeast corner, he spots Klein and his guest at the far end of the hallway, talking just outside one of the room's doors. Only he's too far, and it's too loud, to distinguish what they're actually saying. It does, however, give him a better look at the mystery man of the hour.

He's quick to note that the guy looks even rougher around the edges in person.

Tiptoeing into full-on Pink Panther mode, Clayton's eyes transform into magnifying glasses, meticulously scanning their subject up and down from head to sole. Upon completing their drive-by inspection, they confirm the newcomer is a bald, burly brute of a man—almost as tall as he is thick—with what looks like a gnarly scar or birthmark carved along the contour of his right cheek. He also has some serious hand tattoos stenciled across his streetfighter knuckles. The kind of finger ink that typically says something introspectively unoriginal like, "FREE SOUL" or "STAY TRUE" topped off by a pretty rose on the back of the hand. But judging by this guy's ex-con disposition and mob-like starter kit fashion, Clayton's guessing those familiar prison hand tats say something more along the lines of "DEAD HATE" or "NEXT KILL," topped off with a skull for added don't-fuck-with-me emphasis.

He thinks to himself, *What could Klein, one of, if not the most, prestigious and well-known figures in the nation, possibly be doing with this thug on a floor that's highly restricted but not heavily monitored?*

Looking for an opportunity to inch closer to the action, Clayton waits patiently to make his move. When both men finally flash their backs to him, he dashes for the northeast corner and dives behind the wall. He slouches for safety, hiding for a few extra beats before concluding that he successfully made it undetected. He can hear the conversation better, but it's still not entirely clear. Only audible enough to pick up every few words or so.

He hears Klein first. "... and that's it? What about his record?"

Clayton peers out from behind the wall ever so carefully, cupping his ear for any extra decibels of amplification. Honestly, he's surprised he can hear anything at all. Not just because of the airplane-induced droning from the army of server fans, but because at the moment, his heart is beating so hard in his chest it's coming out of his ears.

"Yessir, untra ... *(garble)*. Just like ... *(garble)* ... your wife," the mystery man stutters.

"I told ... *(garble)*... goddammit ... *(garble)* ... never speak ... *(garble)* ... her ... *(garble)* ... not here," Klein barks in punctuated return. "Just give ... *(garble)* ... to me."

The man reaches into his leather bomber's pocket and pulls out what looks like a small, nondescript thumb drive. The action causes the shiny revolver in his chest holster to catch a glint from the overhead fluorescence. Clayton gets a good look at the piece.

The man hands the device to Klein, who quickly slides it into his suit's inner chest pocket before entering the server room.

"Damn," Clayton mutters under his breath. "Lost 'em."

He looks up at the security camera and gives the lens a *what next?* shoulder shrug.

Seconds later. "*Lo siento*, amigo," Hector chimes in from the speaker on Clayton's hip. "There aren't cameras in the actual record rooms. At least none that I have control over."

Clayton's frustrations escape him. He has no idea what's going on, but he knows he was close to finding out something.

"Shit!" he blurts out, before quickly muzzling himself at the realization they could return any second.

Muffled, he asks himself aloud, "What's Klein up to? And what does his *wife* have to do with anything?"

None of it makes any sense and this day continues to get more interesting by the hour. If "interesting" is the word you'd used to describe finding out you're a father-to-be, getting blindsidingly blackmailed by your baby mama's power-hungry father, and then stalking said father and his *Goodfellas* cohort, who clearly has an unchecked gun and a nefarious past, into a heavily secured sector of the nation's most notable enterprise—all in one morning.

"Clay, come in, amigo," a tin-sounding voice cuts in, breaking the silence and his focus.

He jumps at the startling sound of Hector reawakening his walkie while his hand dives for the volume knob before his mind can even process the action.

"Clay? You all right? Come in?" Hector asks again. "I think it's time you bolt, amigo."

"I'm okay," Clayton responds. One hand on the volume dial, the other across his pounding heart, trying to contain the drumroll. "I just . . . I gotta do one more thing."

"You've done enough, ese. Now get out of—" But before Hector can finish, Clayton kills his walkie. He wants to know what the hell is going on, and despite Hector's best interest, he's not ready to stop his investigation. Not yet anyway.

After staking out around the corner for a few minutes, Clayton's curiosity begins to win the battle over his patience. The thought that they could have left through the rear entrance also enters his mind, making that thin, sheer layer that separates the two human traits finally snap. Refusing to wait any longer, he starts the motion to get up from behind his post just as Klein and his lackey spill back out into the hallway from the northeast server door. Only this time they're not loitering around outside the door shooting the shit like before.

They're headed right toward him, and fast.

With the same involuntary reflex used to hush his radio, Clayton unconsciously sprints down the gridded hallway toward the northwest server room. But as he makes his impulsive first step, the walkie slips out of his hand and tumbles across the walkway.

He freezes and his stomach sinks—the bile acting like an aggregate mixture firmly cementing his feet to the floor. He has to make a costly call, and fast. Risk going back for the radio, potentially exposing himself to Klein and Tony Soprano Jr., or ditch the walkie, which they're sure to find, and just take cover. Either way, he's done the quick math and concluded that he doesn't need a number to tell him his odds are totally fucked.

Ultimately, his legs make the decision for him in real-time, but in his head, it feels like slow motion as he sprints over to the walkie and scoops it off the floor. He can hear their voices and the pace behind their steps growing louder, closer by the millisecond. Booking it faster than his worn work boots can gain traction, he peels out on the tile part of the flooring as his half-life soles fight against the glossy, nonexistent grit. Goodbye, plan A. There's no way he can turn back and outrun them now, so he dives for safety behind the northeast corridor's corner wall like a wide receiver leaping for the endzone.

Only this isn't a touchdown. But he wishes it was just a game.

# CHAPTER 8

Clayton lays sprawled on the ground as he hears the distant ding of the elevator down the hall. His heart is racing so fast that every one of the twenty-four bones in his rib cage is working overtime to contain it.

At the sound of the elevator closing, he finally gathers himself, slowly rising to his feet. He wicks away the beads of sweat that have splattered his forehead as he slinks his way back around the corner to the northwest server room. Reaching for his badge, he scans the card but there's no response.

He tries again.

No click.

No green light.

Nothing.

It's odd because he should have access to this floor. He's been up here once, maybe twice before, to check the server integrity from an overheating alert, and although it's been a while, his badge definitely had authorization. Running out of ideas and fresh out of nerves, he grabs the runaway walkie from the clip on his belt.

"Hex?" he whispers, greeted only by white noise.

He tries again.

"Hex?" he repeats. "You there?"

But only a long, deaf silence joins the monotonous hum of the surrounding servers.

Again, his lack of patience gets the best of him.

"HEX!" he shouts.

Still no response. Just a constant, static *Crrckkk* purring over the speaker. Nothing but his lone voice in a lost radio wave abyss.

Then, finally.

"Clay! You okay, amigo?"

Clayton deflates an elongated sigh of relief that practically sinks him right back down to the ground. Not just because it's good to hear Hector's voice after his far-too-close call, but because he thinks Hex just might be his key to getting into the locked records room. Literally.

"Hex, shit, man. It's never been better to hear your sloppy Spanglish."

"*Que te folle . . . ! Cabrón.* I thought you were fucked back there."

"That makes two of us."

"*Estas bien*, man?"

"Yeah, I'm good. But I could use a little help. Is there any way you can open this door for me from the control room? There's something I gotta check out."

"Si, homes," he replies, yet there's hesitation in his tone. "But are you sure about this?"

"Just do it, Hex," Clayton demands. "I have a feeling there's something weird going on, but I need in there to find out."

"That's exactly my point, amigo," Hector retorts. Trying to give advice to the one person he usually gets it from. "Why go poking the bear, eh?"

Clayton replays this morning's conversation with Klein in his head. His offer to buy him out.

Out of a job.

Out of love.

Out of his future child's life.

He always knew Klein was a self-serving, maniacally egotistical, power-hungry piece of shit, but seeing him conspiring with a mystery mafia man, that's a first. It just doesn't make sense.

"Hex," he pleads, fully aware that his friend doesn't know the whole story. And that he's not about to go into the ugly truth of telling it all. "I gotta know what they were doing in there."

Desperation sets in. "Please? I need this."

With his hands folded in prayer aimed up at the hall's security camera, Clayton waits. A matter of seconds pass before the automatic lock clicks and the light on the handle turns green. He blows a kiss to the security camera in the corner and flings open the door.

Upon entering the room, the dull buzz of servers swells to a cyclonic roar. Amid the deafening drone of the copter-sounding "chuff," Clayton assesses the room as blinking lights twinkle and flash around him like lightning bugs on a Midwest summer evening. He replays the exchange between Klein and the Tommy DeVito look-alike on steroids in his head. He heard the mystery mobster say something about Klein's wife. But why? What does she have to do with anything? She's been dead for more than two and a half decades.

Inside the server room, there's not much to the space other than a perimeter of towers on a temperature-regulated concrete floor. The room's high ceiling is comprised of a labyrinth of exposed pipes, vents, and a few large industrial fans, ensuring that the air maintains circulation to help further regulate the chamber's climate. On the wall, there are extra environmental controls, including a dashboard for the room's air purification system, in case additional action needs to be taken. And dead ahead, in the middle of the twinkling server room, lies a computer system stationed on a sleek, metallic desk with a matching ergonomic chair tucked neatly underneath. Just a lone monitor plugged directly into the mainframe along with a backup hard drive system, in the event that the surrounding embankment were to ever crash or malfunction.

Clayton works his way over to the desk and shakes the mouse, waking it from its stupor.

"Damn," he says to himself. "Of course, it's password protected. Why wouldn't it be?" As if he was going to just waltz in here and all the answers would miraculously be there waiting for him on the home screen.

Clayton doesn't want to do it. For more than one reason, he considers against it. He doesn't want to bring in an accomplice if things get iffy, and he certainly doesn't want the other guilty party to be Hector. Not after all he has on the line. But the more he tries to talk himself out of it, the deeper his feet sink into the plan.

"Fuck . . ." he mutters before punching the talk button on his radio. "Hex? I could use another assist?"

He explains the current situation to Hector the best he can, as fast as he can get the words out, before asking for help with the computer access.

"So, can you get me in?"

There's an elongated pause in the one-sided conversation before Hector responds.

"Sorry, amigo, I don't have that kind of access, but . . ." Hector trails off. "That doesn't mean I can't break it."

It's exactly what Clayton hoped it wouldn't come to but feared it might. And right now, despite the slight guilt, he's more than thankful it's an option.

As it turns out, Hector's own mini misdemeanor rap sheet is chalked full of many petty talents of thievery, and none more important right now than his uncanny ability as a hacker. In fact, it's largely because of his skills behind a keyboard that landed him this surveillance gig in the first place. Guess the authorities thought he had a brighter future playing security for the "good guys" on a plea deal than doing any real hard time as a bad guy. Convenient how the government is more than willing to turn a blind eye to things so long as it means their sight improves.

While Hector attacks the keys with newfound conviction, his true talent shines as he effortlessly breaks into the server mainframe and calls up the entire digital blueprint for the HQ, including floor schematics and the building's door lock inventory system within seconds. He punches into the sixty-sixth-floor RECORDS ROOM layout, manipulating the 3D-lined schematic to home in specifically on the northeast server room. After a few additional keystrokes, he locks in on the server room's computer IP address as Clayton watches the mouse on the monitor's screen begin to dance around with a mind of its own.

Hector finishes inputting his last command, a ballistic hacking algorithm that uses automated brute force processing to feed vast quantities of passwords into the system until one of them successfully registers. After a couple minutes of failed login attempts, it finally acknowledges one.

Clayton watches as the login window transitions to an open desktop view. Alphabetical folders of last names *G* through *M* methodically line the background among similar grayed-out folders containing the other nineteen letters of the alphabet.

He's in, just like that. And he did it all while making it look effortless.

Even Clayton is shocked. Hex had told him he was good, many times. Probably too many times. Apparently, humility isn't a strong suit for hackers. But seeing him in action—in his element—was nothing short of genius. It makes the whole plea deal with authorities make a little more sense. After all, it's better to keep your enemies closest, right?

"Hell yes," Clayton exclaims in a hushed shout over his radio. "I owe you one, man."

"De nada," echoes back from the walkie. "Just be careful, amigo. You're standing on the edge of a slippery slope."

Clayton couldn't agree more. It's why the less Hector knows, the safer he'll be.

"I appreciate the hand, man, but I don't want to risk getting you in any more trouble for this. I've already asked too much. I'll take it from here."

Resisting every urge to join the already illegal cause at hand, Hector thinks about what's at stake. Only a year removed from probation, another strike could cost him everything.

Camila? Most likely.

Sophia? Definitely.

"Si . . . all right, Clay. But I ain't going nowhere. I'll be on lookout. Just holler if you need me."

Clayton clips the walkie back onto his belt, next to his flashlight and retractable badge. Being responsible for protecting the headquarters of something as biblically violent as The Hunt Initiative, one would think the security personnel should be more equipped to handle physical altercations if any were to ever arise. Hell, other members of the security team carry defense weapons—taser guns, stun rods, and the like. Rickers even walks around with a firearm, a modified Colt Python revolver with an elongated barrel. The jests of him overcompensating for something have yet to get old.

Meanwhile, Clayton is left with a stern voice and a pair of fists if anything ever gets ugly. Maybe Klein never felt keen on the idea of giving him the opportunity to defend himself. At least, that's what he's always suspected in the back of his mind, and after today, he's about 99.9 percent sure that he's 100 percent right.

Getting back to work, he jogs the cursor that he's resequestered across the litter of alphabetized files. He hovers past the folders *I* and *J* before landing on *K*. He double clicks and a laundry list compiling the last names of all the *K* victims, murderers, and associated parties populates the screen. It's overwhelming to think this is just one list in the alphabetical sea of the last twenty-five-plus years of The Hunt Initiative's data. There are twenty-five other lettered folders just like this one comprising life that was.

He zips down the list, passing large chunks of names at a time only to slow his roll when he hits "Khan." A few more page flicks, and even slower yet, "Kinner" . . . "Klapson" . . . until he arrives at "Klein." His scrolling comes to a crawl.

*Klein, David M.*

. . .

. . .

*Klein, Leighann J.*

. . .

*Klein, Mitchell D.*

*Klein, Rachel A.*

. . .

. . .

Slow and steady until he finally comes to a complete stop. The mouse hovers over a single name. The one he's been so adamant to find.

*Klein, Rebecca N.*

Not looking to waste any more time, he quickly double-taps her name. A loading wheel starts to spin, matching the chaotic cadence of thoughts currently swirling in his head.

He can feel the sudden secretion of water, salt, and fat from his clammy hands start to adhere to the curve of the mouse and grooves of the keys with its every anxious rotation. He has no idea exactly what he's looking for. Or what he expects to find—if anything. He just knows that the whole situation feels fishy.

Or as Hex would say, smelly.

Either way, this shit reeks.

But when the file finally finishes loading, he's only left again with more questions than answers. In a surprising twist of fate, Rebecca Klein's file doesn't have anything of interest. In fact, it's practically empty. There's no statement from the first responders on the scene. There's no time or cause of death. No autopsy report. Nothing at all that gives any indication as to what actually happened to her. All the corresponding fields are blank, giving no insight into how she died. If it weren't for the tiny bit of personal info documented, it would be as if her death never happened—as if she never existed.

**Full Name:** Klein, Rebecca Nicole
**Home address:** 343 Carriage House Lane, Bannerton, IL 60203
**Marital Status:** Married
**Immediate Family:** Simon Caldwell Klein (husband), Patricia Lindsay Klein (daughter)
**Occupation:** N/A

At the bottom of her file, there's a button that reads [Full Report]. Clayton clicks on it, but the only thing to appear is yet another dead end. Just an access denied message along with an address to a place and street he's never heard of.

ACCESS NOT AUTHORIZED
15276 Westport Sq., Suite C
Bannerton, IL 60411

He squints, straining his eyes in one last hope-filled attempt to find anything else he might have missed on the page. He scans every pixel of the twenty-inch screen, praying for anything useful to magically stand out, but nothing does. There may not be any answers here, but that's validation enough to question the suspiciousness of this entire situation. Because none of this adds up. The Hunt's database shouldn't have any errors, not like this. Every person's file on these servers has been carefully collected by the authorities and automatically pooled, organized, and registered by the most modern, state-of-the-art software money can buy.

He drags his forearm across his beady chin, wiping the pooling perspiration away as he thinks out loud.

"What the hell? This doesn't make any sense. These are direct federal copies. There shouldn't be any incomplete files in The Hunt database . . . unless—" He raises his head in a moment of obvious eureka. "Someone intended it to be that way."

Clayton feels his left pants pocket vibrate. The jarring pulse is enough to snap him back into the moment.

He digs out his phone and sees the preview text from Trish awaiting his reply.

*Hey babe, it's almost 4:00. You on your way home soon?*

"Shit, I totally lost track of time," he mutters aloud, frantically eyeing his watch to double-check the time.

He opens the camera on his phone and quickly snaps a photo of Rebecca Klein's file—or lack of one, making a mental note of the mystery address. He closes the file and logs out of the server database, returning everything just the way he found it. Something weird is going on here all right, but right now he's more worried about what, if anything, he's going to tell Trish about today's rabbit hole of fucked up events. And if he does, will she actually believe him?

Hell, he's not so sure he even believes it all himself.

Clayton studies himself in the full-length closet mirror. He cinches the half-Windsor on his skinny navy-blue tie peppered with white polka dots and gives a couple extra tugs on his suit collar for good measure. The appearance of being well put together on the outside is being fiercely contradicted by the feeling of unraveling from within. There's so much consuming his thoughts right now that he just gawks, blankly staring at the image reflected before him. In less than ten hours, he's been on a roller coaster thrill ride of highs and lows. The happy, life-altering news of Trish being pregnant has taken a distant backseat to the thought of being bribed by her father, troubled by the mystery mob boss with the gun, and more than anything, baffled by the peculiar info—or lack thereof—on Trish's mom's death file. He keeps hearing those haunting words echoing off the dense walls of his skull.

"*Just like your wife.*"

What did they do for Klein's wife? According to her file, there's no record of any circumstances surrounding her death. Just an inaccessible file and a random address in some part of the city that Clayton's never been to, let alone heard of.

All at once, he feels the tension in his thoughts release as a delicate touch gently grazes his lower back. A slender hand appears in the mirror, adorned with a vintage pearl ring. It works its way up past his shoulders to brush his freshly shaved chin.

"Well, well, Mister Sparks . . . someone cleans up nice," Trish teases, breaking his stern silence. "I can't remember the last time I got you in a suit. But now that I have, I kind of want to rip it off."

Clayton softly reaches for her hand, lacing his fingers with hers.

He turns to meet her gaze.

She's breathtaking as always, but even more so right now. The perfect combination of elegance meets sensuality. The little, backless white dress that she rampaged her closet for earlier surrenders itself perfectly to her figure, hugging all her curves in all the right places, while skillfully exposing just enough of her silky-smooth legs so as to not leave much to be desired. Her hair is done up beautifully. Wild and wavy, yet somehow gracious. A way he's never really seen it before, like something straight off the cover of a bridal magazine. Dangling from her ears are a series of gorgeous golden hoops that bring a soft, warm glow to her cheeks while affectionately framing her diamond face.

He steps back and spins her around.

She twirls, smiling along for the playful ride.

"I'm sorry, ma'am, but there's a woman named Trish that lives here. She's kinda my girlfriend. Actually, my pregnant girlfriend. And I don't think she'd appreciate me having a mistress in our apartment. Especially our bedroom."

Trish moves in closer, her mouth hovers just below his grin. Their eyes lock in raging passion, in what one could only describe as true love.

Her lip curls up slightly to match his.

"Well, I guess we better leave quick then," she says, adjusting his tie and then stroking her fingers temptingly back down it. "Before she sees us."

Despite the serious four-inch suede stilettos Trish is wearing, she still has to rise onto her toes and lunge forward for the kiss.

The embrace is pure desire. Electric.

She lowers herself back down and wipes the ruby-red, satin lipstick from his mouth with the side of her thumb. The smudge perfectly matches the crimson color of her nail polish. She gives him a loving pat on the cheek before snatching her clutch from the dresser and walking down the hall toward the front door. Making sure to give her hips a little extra sway along the way.

Clayton closes the closet door and follows her lead. Halfway down the hall he just can't resist the urge.

"Those legs are gonna put me in a tomb," he quips thirstily.

She shoots him a playful look over her shoulder. "Oh yeah? Well, you're looking pretty drop-dead yourself, cowboy."

"If a cowboy is what you want, then I'm down for a little late-night wranglin'."

She gestures to her stomach, "Oh, because one little calf on the way isn't enough, huh?"

He shakes his head. "I'm still paying for that mumu joke this morning, aren't I?"

"Yep," she replies, slinging her jacket on through the first of her outstretched arms.

"And for how long will I be groveling exactly? Just asking for a friend."

"Well, that depends?"

"On?"

She finishes wiggling into the coat. "On how well you behave yourself tonight."

Clayton throws his head back. No verbal dispute but his physical protest says more than enough.

"Look, I've already talked to my dad, and he's promised me that he'll be on his best behavior, too," Trish says, stepping toward him. She drapes her arms around his shoulders, pulling him in closer. He falls even further into her eyes, which now carry a newfound sincerity in place of her previous playfulness. "Promise me, please?"

Against every bone in his body and his better judgment, against everything he's uncovered today, Clayton can't say no to those big, pleading baby blues. He's never been able to, and besides, what would he even say? "*Oh, by the way, Trish, your dick of a dad tried to literally bribe me today to never see you again. I think he might also be working with the mob. Oh, and if that's not enough of a conversation starter, I think he's into some shady shit regarding your dead mom. But yeah, I'm super psyched for this anniversary party. Let's do it!*"

The truth is, Clayton hasn't the slightest clue how to bridge the subject, especially on a night like tonight of all nights. That argumentative bomb can wait at least until the morning. And besides, he could definitely use the extra time to decipher what exactly in the actual fuck happened today.

He takes a deep breath in, bringing himself back to the moment.

"All right. I promise," he says.

But he doesn't mean it.

Trish smiles and pinches his cheek. It's followed up by another ruby-red copy of her lips on his clean-shaven canvas.

As she swings open the front door, Clayton follows behind, grabbing her keys from the ceramic dish on their vintage credenza-turned-liquor cabinet.

"Now, can we go back to that whole wranglin' talk again?" he teases. "I liked the way that locomotive was steaming."

"How about we save talking *3:10 to You-and-Me-ma* role-playing if you can actually make it through tonight, cowboy?" she replies with a soft grin and an even softer touch, this time upon his chest.

"I'm just saying—I'd be down for learning how to hogtie," he replies, gesturing a lasso motion in the air as he turns to lock the door. "That's a rodeo I could get behind, literally."

But Trish stops him in his train tracks. "Did you just insinuate that I'm a pig, now?" she heckles with accusing eyes. They're the loud, peering kind that say, "When are you going to learn to stop shoving your foot all the way down your stupid piehole, Clayton?" but without actually speaking at all.

Chugga Chugga, Choo *Oops*.

"What? No! Wait, I just—" he continues babbling like a flush-faced schoolboy caught creepily gawking at his crush. "I just thought a little bondage could . . . I wasn't insinuating . . ."

But she cuts him off before he has a chance to officially remove his own hoof from his snout.

"Relax, cowboy. I'm just fucking with you," she says through a teasing laugh. "Damn, you're really off your game tonight, Mr. Wayne. You've got a lot of cowboying to learn if you're gonna be as calm and cool as The Duke."

Clayton shakes his head, forcing a grin as he fiddles anxiously with the keys. The truth is, Trish is right. He is off tonight. Way off. And it's killing him keeping the reason for it all to himself.

They may be headed to a party, but he's in absolutely no mood to celebrate.

Trish's red hatchback is parked close, just across the street about a block down. The spot was a lucky find on a Friday night, especially since these midtown streets fill up early on the weekends thanks to their doormat proximity to the best twelve-block strip of local shops, restaurants, and of course, bars in the city.

Tonight's parking jaunt should be an easy walk through the grass, that is unless you're wearing four-inch dress heels. But Trish doesn't complain. Not a peep. She just owns the quick trip across several lawns as Clayton fumbles with the keys to cover up his drifting thoughts.

When they arrive at her car, he's alert enough to play gentleman, and so he swings around to open her door. With a somewhat restored air about him, he chivalrously offers his hand.

"Your chariot, mi lady," he says with a less-than-stellar British accent.

Playing along, Trish drapes her right hand dramatically across her heart, while surrendering her left to the grasp of his outstretched palm.

"Why, my prince," she swoons in her own terrible British accent while sliding into the passenger seat. "Thank ye."

Clayton shuts the car door and loops around back toward the driver's side. He squats in carefully, adjusting his tie as part of the settling-in process.

Scattered across the pleather backseat are chaotic piles of art supplies and random sketch pads. An assortment of blank canvases rest in tidy stacks on the otherwise messy floor, while paint tubes, various brushes, and a spilled folder of protruding drawings occupy the gray bench seat. Trish really wears that stereotypical "organized chaos is part of my creative process" badge well. At least at home, she does a better job of keeping the creative chaos confined to just her studio.

Clayton turns the key to start the ignition and for a few minutes, there's an unfamiliar silence in the car before they reach the highway. She looks over at him, measuring the weight of his thoughts through his heavy gaze. His eyes are on the road, but his focus is anywhere but between the dotted lines. He can't quite see her studying stare, but he can feel her examining him from his periphery. Still, he doesn't engage. He knows if he looks at her, there may be no escaping the truth.

Trish turns on the radio to kill the quiet, and another news report from this morning's Hunt fills the car's surround sound.

"*Earlier today, Gary Anderson, age thirty-four, a resident of Wichita, Kansas, and teacher at Mount East High School, became the latest victim in the name of justice. His legal execution adds one more tally to The Hunt Initiative's perfect twenty-five-year–to the day–record of righteous offerings. Mr. Anderson was found guilty of the rape and murder in the first degree of nineteen-year-old philosophy student Josephine Huxley, also a native of Wichita and former student of Anderson. Justice was carried out via shot to the head by Josephine's older brother, Shane Huxley, and a group of cohorts who had been tracking Mr. Anderson since the previous evening. Mr. Anderson is survived by his wife, Elaine Anderson, thirty-two, and two daughters, Paige Anderson, six, and Beth Anderson, three.*

"Ugh. They really love to drag these out, don't they?" Trish scoffs while tucking a loose strand of fly-away hair from her updo back behind her ear. "We get it already. He was a terrible person that did an unforgivable thing. He paid for it. There's no need to idolize it."

Despite her own father being the creator of The Hunt Initiative, Trish Klein has never fully agreed with the concept. Maybe it's the added violence that comes with it, but a life for a life just seems gratuitous to her. Like forcing two wrongs to make a right. She prefers to believe in people. Not the system. Although she would never tell her father that to his face. She's always been drawn to the idea that people are capable of change, that their futures can be brighter than their pasts. It's one of the reasons she continues to believe in Clayton.

Wanting something a little less downer for an already stressful evening, she punches the first pre-programmed button on the radio to her favorite local station. A folk-rock tune resonates from the speakers.

She checks the time, it's indie hour on 96.9.

"Hey! This is that new release from Midnight Theatre I was telling you about the other day." She listens, bobbing her head to the edgy banjo-inspired beat. "I like it. It's kinda trippy."

Clayton nods and gives a subtle grunt of approval.

She reaches over and slowly turns the volume knob down a few clicks—staring at him again, poised to crack the case as to what's weighing on his mind. She starts with something subtle. What she thinks should be harmless.

"So . . . how was work?"

Clayton shudders at the mention, doing his best to shift his attention from the confines of his thoughts to the pretty lady sitting next to him. He's played this moment over in his head a dozen times already. Now's the perfect setup to lay it all out, but he's not ready. To tell her everything right now, on the way to the party, would be catastrophic.

He digresses, keeping his response short and vague, trying not to overplay his bluffing hand with too much emotion.

"Um, work? It was fine. Got yelled at by Rickers for being late again. Made my rounds. Shot the shit with Jay and Hex." His eyes never leave the road. "You know, the usual."

She nods. Still wary but not wanting to push the envelope. Maybe if she can get him talking, sidetracked. Just a little more comfortable. He'll open up.

"Well, I've got some good news for you tonight. With our new addition—," she says massaging her stomach, "you've got yourself a designated driver." But a slight frown tugs down on the corners of her lips at the first realization she'll be attending tonight and the next eight-plus months of her life completely sober. "Ugh. Lucky you. Guys have it so easy."

Clayton glances over at her, forcing a smile.

"Must be fate," he adds. "Because I'm going to need all the drinks I can stomach to get through tonight."

"Oh, c'mon! It won't be that bad," she replies, rattling off tonight's incentives on her fingers. "First, there'll be all the overly priced brands of top-shelf booze you can drink, for *free*. Second, countless rounds of delectable appetizers that neither one of us can probably pronounce the name of. And third, there's sure to be the best live entertainment that federal funds and generous donors with pockets as deep as the Mariana Trench can buy—"

Clayton cuts in, finishing her statement. "And fourth, a pretentious, self-serving speech from your egomaniacal father."

Only he doesn't realize he's said it aloud until he hears the words himself.

Trish wastes no time in firing back an angry look. He can almost feel the heat radiating from her glare.

"That's not fair," she counters. "We had a deal, remember? You promised."

But Clayton can't help himself.

"I know, I'm sorry," he responds. Only he doesn't quite leave it at just that. It's like his mouth is running a rogue, one-orifice show, and he can't keep up. As if it's trying to self-sabotage the restraint his mind has been struggling to contain all day. "But am I wrong?"

This isn't where she hoped her prying would go, but now that he's finally talking, she might as well see it through. After all, her plan is working. For better or worse, she's getting somewhere. Figuring out what's really bothering him. One peeled-back layer at a time.

She only wishes she wasn't surprised that it's yet again centered around her father.

"Well, no, but what do you expect? It's the twenty-five-year anniversary of The Hunt Initiative today. It's everything he's worked for. Dreamed of. He's going to eat tonight up. And yes, before you say it, I know he's a self-absorbed workaholic and can be a bit of an asshole sometimes, but—"

"Sometimes? *Just* sometimes? Trish, the man totally hates me. No, no, he straight up despises me," Clayton exclaims, throwing any regard for his previous balance of caution to the wind. The admission of today teetering on the tip of his tongue. "He literally loathes everything about me—about us—and you know it."

Trish hates these arguments. She despises them as much as Clayton thinks her father despises him. They've been near non-stop since they first got together. But if there's going to be another knockdown drag-out, it's better now than at the party. So, she tries to squash it before it can blow up any more than it already has.

"He doesn't hate you. He just . . . he just doesn't understand you. Doesn't get us. He wants me to be with someone just like him. Think the way he thinks. Live the way he lives."

"You mean someone who's driven? Successful? Has money? Someone—"

Turns out her squashing tactic isn't working so hot. It seems the harder she tries to stomp out the fire, the more air she feeds the flame.

"—Someone to be a total asshole, just like him?" Clayton continues ranting.

"You're putting words in my mouth. I didn't say any of that."

"No. But you implied it."

Trish turns in her seat. She doesn't want this fight. She never wants this fight, especially not now. But it seems to always be there lurking in the shadows. Ready for a jump scare at the worst possible moments.

"Clay, you know I don't want all that. I never have. And I don't give a shit about what my father thinks is best for me. I'm a grown woman capable of my own thoughts and actions. I fell in love with you, for you. Nothing else. I don't need anything else. Just this," she finishes, grabbing his right hand.

Clayton eases his strangle on the steering wheel. The liberation is felt throughout his body as the blood returns to relieve the tension in his fingers. His mind's still an absolute clusterfuck, but there's no reason for him to take it out on her. She's done nothing wrong, and she doesn't deserve it. She never has.

"I know. I'm sorry." He sighs again. "It's just all really been nagging me lately, especially now with a baby on the way." He turns to look at Trish, who reciprocates with those big, beautiful blues of hers. He places his hand on her stomach. "I just want us all to be happy."

Her left arm extends over the center console like an olive branch, gracefully resting her leafy hand on the top of his thigh.

"We're in this together—just you, me, and this unexpected little tater tot that's aggressively staked claim to my uterus," she says through a giggle, as she places her hand against his on her tummy. Her touch is warm and soothing. Just what he needs right now. Everything he needs right now. "It's just the three of us, together. Well, technically four, if you include the demanding and soon-to-be super jealous fat ball of fur back home."

"Oh-hoh, he's gonna be so pissed," Clayton confirms, and they share a laugh.

After several seconds of letting the make-up session sink in and take root, the conversation takes an enthusiastic upturn.

"Oh, I almost forgot to tell you!" Trish shrieks, as she shoots up from her seat. "You know the vendor I've been talking to for like two months about my latest impressionist collection?"

"You mean the good-looking guy with all the hair?" Clayton shoots sarcastically.

"Well, well, is someone jealous?" Trish teases back.

Coolly, he responds, "Who? Me? Jealous? No way."

But his series of growing inflections prove one hundred percent otherwise.

"Why, Clayton Sparks! There's nothing to be jealous about. I've only got eyes for you, cowboy," she reassures. "Besides, the guy is totally insufferable. And beyond pompous, OMG."

"Oh, so he's like your dad," Clayton jabs light-heartedly.

It's an ill-timed quip he knows full well he could end up paying for all over again. But like a typical dumbass boy who didn't just learn his lesson not to touch the hot stove top, he can't resist the burn.

Trish impishly slugs him in the arm, letting out a laugh that teeters on insulted but totters back on playful.

"Oooowww, foul on the play," he wails, while rubbing his shoulder. "The ref takes a point away for unsportsmanlike conduct."

They meet eyes, trying to camouflage smiles that fail to hide their beaming faces. In this moment, everything feels good again. Like it's all almost back to normal.

Five blissful minutes later, they pull into the parking lot of the convention center. Trish motions for Clayton to hold up as he pulls into an empty stall, slides the car in park, and kills the engine. She flips the visor mirror down so she can apply a second layer of lipstick and give herself a final once-over for good measure. As she reaches into her purse to put the ruby-red tube away, Clayton notices the pearl ring on her left index finger.

"I've never seen you wear that one before," he says. "It's pretty. New antique store find?"

Trish spreads her fingers like a bride-to-be trying on a full display of overpriced wedding rings.

"No, not quite. It was my mother's, actually," she replies, wiggling it with her thumb on the same hand. "I don't typically have a fancy reason to wear it, so I kinda forgot I had it. But I found it when I literally put the *war* into the word *wardrobe* this afternoon. Guess I figured tonight would be the perfect night to revive it."

Thoughts of the records room, the incomplete file, the shady character Klein was talking to—it all comes surging back like a killer tsunami flooding his thoughts. If there were ever a perfect moment, he knows this is it. His chance to play Alice and get a glimpse of clarity into Wonderland through one of the above rabbit holes.

"It's beautiful," he remarks, knowing that the phrasing to his next question is everything. Probe enough to get something, but don't go too deep or he could lose everything. "Trish, how much do you remember about your mom?"

She lets out a soft sigh, reaching for an old box of dusty childhood memories stashed away in her mind's warehouse.

"Not much, really. I was just about three when she died. Sometimes I have these random flashbacks, almost like snapshot memories of her, you know like when I smell a certain scent or hear a certain song? God, she loved Fleetwood Mac. I remember her reading to me every night before bed. And the soft nature of her voice. How she used to lovingly brush my wild hair back behind my ears when it was covering my face from playing too hard. And some other random bits here and there from my dad, I guess, but not a lot."

Clayton probes a little deeper.

Just enough.

"What actually happened to her? You've never really told me much."

"Uh, I don't really know all the details. Just from what Dad tells me, and he doesn't like to talk about it. It's probably too painful," she says, taking a deep calming breath before continuing. "She was in a car accident. A hit-and-run or something like that. They never found the car or the person who hit her, though. I honestly think it's what really drove my father to start all this stuff in the first place," she adds, pointing through the windshield. Clayton's eyes follow her finger to the giant THE HUNT INITIATIVE 25TH ANNIVERSARY GALA banner hanging over the convention center's main entrance. "To create The Hunt as a way to cope."

But Trish's mind jumps ship before she's capsized by the ensuing swell of cresting emotions.

"Anyway, that's enough of that. We can save that sad story for another time," she remarks, pulling the visor mirror back down while she blots her glassy eyes with a crisp, clean pocket square from Clayton's jacket. After a couple of closing sniffles, she flips the visor back up, forcing a disposition suitable for celebration.

"Right now, we've got a party to attend. And you've got an open bar to see to. Speaking of which, I'll take the keys."

Clayton starts to ask a follow-up, but he stifles himself. Reluctant, yet smart enough to drop the topic before he triggers something to further damper the reclaimed mood.

He pulls the dangling set of keys from the ignition and drops them inside Trish's unzipped clutch.

She opens the door and hops out, but Clayton isn't so eager. He takes an extra moment to compose himself. If Trish's mother died in a hit-and-run, why wouldn't that be in her file? Why wasn't anything in her file? It doesn't add up. Nothing today has. But fuck it, maybe he just needs a drink, or ten.

Upon first glance, the convention center looks like Christmas on merry steroids. Thousands of ornate lights drape and line the front entrance to the building—every beautiful bulb twinkling soft, golden halogen in perfectly linked harmony. The accompanying glass anniversary signage and baroque outdoor décor seem to be etched in actual quartz or some kind of opaque crystal. There are even contemporary art ice sculptures carved in a variety of elaborate geometric shapes and cut from the clearest hunks of ice Clayton has ever seen.

Ushers dressed in getups of matching penguin-tailed, satin robes with corresponding top hats—more glamorous than anything in his own closet—await guests at the door with warm greetings and a complimentary glass of rosé champagne. It's as close to a wealthy winter wonderland for the One Percent as it can get. One thing is for certain, Klein made sure to spare no expense on making this night one for the history books—The twenty-fifth anniversary of The Hunt Initiative.

As Clayton and Trish ascend the concrete steps to the main entrance, he looks over at his date in awe. She looks even more radiant now under the soft yellow haze of the strategically strewn lights. He wants nothing more than to spend the rest of his life with her. To get down on one knee right now and make it official. But relationships are built on trust. On the promise of honesty. And Clayton's secrets from today are piling up, bending, and slowly breaking his intent to stay true to that vow.

At the entrance, Trish spots Jayson working the front door. She calls out to him from atop the last step.

"Jay?" she asks, quietly shouting.

At the sound of his name, Jayson spins around from his security post.

"Trish!" he yells in return, flashing that charming, thousand-dollar smile. "Wow, you look absolutely stunning, girl."

A step behind, Clayton chimes in, eager to not fill the third-wheel role with his own date. "What? No love for me, man?"

Jayson takes a moment, sizing Clayton's best duds up and down.

"Yes, I'm sorry, you're right, sir. The James Bond reject convention is actually across the street at the Applebee's. Now, if you'd kindly leave, I have a pretty date to escort inside with my *Goldfinger*," he jests, motioning for Trish to place her hand in his.

"Wow. Really, Jay? That cheesy line may do wonders on your wait-list of one-night stands, but it's not getting you anywhere near this *Octopussy*?" she claps back, dissing his gesture of douchey debonair without missing a beat.

"Ohhh, ouch. Well played, T. Well played," Clayton laughs, as he adjusts the silver cufflinks on his shirt sleeves before cinching up his tie for good measure.

"Besides, Jay, you *Dr. No* I make this look good."

Bested and knowing it, Jayson squeaks in one final weak rebuttal, "Pshh, whatever you say, Double-O-Negative."

"Okaaay, boys, that's enough now." Trish butts in, shaking her head. "You two can shoot off your big secret agent guns some other time, but let's try to behave ourselves tonight, yeah? Because you're really starting to fit the roles of *Dumb and Dumber* right now."

Clayton jumps in, "We were *just* talking about that movie earlier today."

"That's because you two are that movie. Even dumber than the sequels."

Clayton's cheery disposition drops like an admonished child at the fitting accusation.

"Sorry, you're right, babe," he admits, and then looks at Jay, extending a peace offering. "Truce?"

"Yeah, sure. Truce," he replies, accepting Clayton's hand. He leans in mid-shake. "But there's no way in hell I'm Lloyd. You're waaay dumber."

Trish can do nothing but shake her head amid the testosterone-induced hopelessness. She might be able to dress a man-child in adult clothes, but it doesn't mean he can act the part.

"Sooo, anyway, back to adult talk," she interrupts, looking to alter the declining trajectory of the conversation's slapstick trip down pop culture lane. "Jay, I thought you were covering for Clay tonight at the office? To what do we owe the privilege?"

"Ah, I was. Well, I still am, technically. But Rickers wanted a handful more of us here tonight to assist with the festivities. So, here I am. Fresh Prince of Charming, in the flesh. And I must say—" He pauses to check out a tall, timely woman in a slinky red thigh-high, side-slit dress, his eyes doing their best *Howlin' Wolf* cartoon impersonation. "It's a helluva lot better view than the basement at HQ. That's for sure."

Trish watches his prowling eyes as they migrate slowly back to their conversation.

"Oh, Jay, ever the perpetual bachelor," she jokes. "I *should* feel sorry you're terrified of commitment, but I'd probably pity the woman who has to be with you more."

"What can I say, T? I'll take a box of chocolates over a candy bar any day."

Ignoring the perfect opportunity for a well-timed bachelor jab of his own, Clayton chooses to revisit a previous point of conversation.

"Wait. So, Rickers is here? Tonight?"

Jayson shrugs his shoulders and gives him an "I'm sorry, it's true" look.

"Afraid so, man. I think he's working backstage somewhere though. Probably pissed off about something or someone new. Or remembering that he has a teenie weenie."

"In his string bikini," Clayton adds, as they both crack up like prepubescent boys trading fart jokes.

Trish just shakes her head again in embarrassing defeat.

"But seriously, that's a relief," Clayton mutters between bellows. "Let's just hope the ass-hunter stays backstage. I could use a hash in the win column today."

Only the laugh detour doesn't last long before it takes a hard turn back onto Shit Street thanks to Jayson and his inability to shut up or mind his own business.

"Speaking of today—" Jayson preps, as Clayton looks on helplessly, perfectly playing the role of innocent bystander in his own personal demise. "Trish, did Clay tell you what happened?"

It's a simple question. But the words knock the wind from him harder than a blow to the chest.

Trish tilts her gaze over to Clayton, who immediately stops gesturing the "shut the fuck up" hand across the throat motion at Jayson while mouthing every silent obscenity he can think of.

"Umm, no?" she says, her inflection reflecting the hint of rising confusion. "He didn't say anything eventful happened today. Just the usual."

"Huh, really?" Jason adds, coy as can be, unfazed at Clayton's silent threats and current death stare.

Trish looks back at Clayton who is attempting his darndest at a fake smile, biding his time for anything but the truth.

Not here.

Not now.

Not like this.

Fucking Jayson.

"Oh, yeah, today. Umm, it was nothing really," he dismisses. "Actually, I did kind of mention it on the way over here. Just an exceptional day of Rickers riding my ass for being late. You know, I really am beginning to think that man does, in fact, want my ass."

He forces a halfhearted laugh at the end for good measure.

"Aww, I'm sorry, love. He's probably just compensating for something," she jokes, holding up her pinky finger.

"See!" Jayson points at Trish. "Even you can't help it. The guy has PRICK written in Sharpie all over his forehead. He's just too dumb to read it backwards in the mirror."

"Well, babe, I think it's time we head inside and make our grand entrance," Clayton commands, placing his hand on the small of her exposed back in a near-herding motion. Eager to avoid any other potentially charged questions from Jayson "Blabber Mouth" Moore. "What do you say?"

Jayson shrugs and opens the event hall door to bid them adieu. He shoots Clayton an optic blast of guilt as they step into the lobby.

"You're right, Clay. Trish's *father* is probably waiting for you two."

As the couple enters, Jayson probes Clayton's eyes in a last-ditch attempt to plant the seed for him to tell Trish about the confrontation with Klein. To come clean about the bribe. Deep down Clayton knows he's right. That he needs to tell her everything. Just not right now. Not tonight. Besides, Jayson doesn't even know half of the whole truth about today—about the records room, the *Scarface* wanna-be with the gun, or Rebecca Klein's mysteriously empty file. Clayton hasn't had the chance to fill him in on everything. Hell, he hasn't even had enough time to process it fully himself yet.

Trish looks back. "Thanks, Jay, have a good evening," she imparts. "Oh, and try not to go digging too far into that box of chocolates tonight, mkay?"

"Hey, I can't help my sweet tooth, Trish, but I'll try my best," he quips back and closes the door, flashing two fingers and his pearly grin while Trish and Clayton proceed into the party, arm in arm.

The main lobby of the convention center is filled with guests dressed to the nines. Thousands, maybe even tens of thousands of partygoers are all gathered together looking to celebrate twenty-five years of The Hunt Initiative—a quarter of a century spent under the watchful eye of Klein's revolutionary vison. His dream of the so-called revitalization of the American justice system come true. As Clayton looks around the ritzy room, he wonders just how many of these present, first-class elite have participated in a Hunt, or Hunts. How many of these cultured attendees have had another's raw blood on their hands. Rich, poor, Black, White, male, female, gay, straight, trans, handicapped—the Hunt doesn't discriminate. It's not designed to. It's simply the worst traditions from the Old Testament retrofitted with the best innovations of modern times.

A person may be polite, poised, and proper on the surface, and you'd never know the unabashed vengeance raging inside. No preview into their history of violence. There's nothing to mark anyone who's ever killed in a Hunt. Or will kill in one. And that's both the beauty and the horror of appointing your peers as judges, jury, and executioners.

After a couple monotonous rounds of pleasantries between Trish and a few of her father's deep-pocketed investors, donors, and other big dick-swinging, old, white male executives that Clayton's met multiple times before—yet they never care to remember his name—the pair enter the grand archway to the celebration hall. Upon first glimpse, it's exactly like a page come to life from *The Great Gatsby*. Not just in its matching nouveau meets deco style and flair, but in the symbolic blurring of the American Dream. Where the hopeful pursuit of building a freedom-forward future has been corrupted by the insatiable hunger for fame and fortune, and in the Hunt's case, decades of fearmongering through a fascist father figure obsessed with societal submission. Clayton can't help but see through the masquerade of it all, but even he has to admit, it's simply a sight to behold. Only there's nothing simple about it.

In the center of the grand room stands a sprawling, extravagantly lit, and well-constructed stage with perfectly draped crushed blue velvet curtains. A glitzy lineup of barely dressed, pre-show burlesque dancers theatrically parades around its entirety in an appetizer-like effort to infuse excitement into the crowd and tee up anticipation for the remainder of the night's festivities. The most elegant and exquisite chandelier that Clayton has ever laid eyes on hangs marvelously from the ceiling's top canopy. Its thousands of pendeloque prisms seem to almost float in pure isolation as its diamond inlays somehow defy the laws of gravity and the limited knowledge of physics he possesses. It's been decorated all the way down to the finest symmetrical lines with flawless curved precision and geometric shading.

The tables where guests are slowly beginning to take their seats have been systematically scattered about the giant space. Each one fitted with its own lavishly unique floral and gemstone centerpiece—everything from emeralds and ambers to sapphires and amethysts. Apparently, the color scheme for tonight is from the gaudy rich palette.

On a second smaller stage, slightly separated from the main one, is a full orchestra composing classical tunes from the age of the big band. A sweeping archway of gold and black balloons twists and spans from wall to wall like inflated ivy, bobbing subtly across the entire room as waiters dressed in authentic 1930s concierge attire pass out obscure hors d'oeuvres and glasses of the most effervescent champagne ever poured, only rivaled by the iridescent shimmer of the gravity-defying chandelier floating overhead.

And above all the glamorous commotion happening below resides a large, lavish balcony with its hundred-year-old ornately sculpted railing leading way to a bustling casino space. Tables of all betting fashion, from poker and roulette to blackjack and you name it, line the upper tier. It's where Clayton spots the man of the hour himself, Simon Klein. Shooting craps and no doubt schmoozing his guests with his best Jay Gatsby impersonation on full display.

The whole ostentatious scene is almost too much for Clayton to take in, so he snatches a couple of extra bubbly flutes from a server's complimentary tray as one strolls by. He throws the first one back with little resistance.

"Good god, is this what the fifteen-year anniversary was like?" he asks, wiping his chin. "Look! They even have a giant saltwater fish pool behind the bar. And are those actual sharks? Jesus, this is un-fucking-believable."

Trish turns, looking at the impressive 5,000-plus gallon aquarium.

"This? Oh, no," she says waving away his incredulousness. "Ten years ago, it was a juggling lion balancing on a unicycle in a cage behind the bar. And they were giving away puppies at the front door instead of booze," she teases, shooting him a grin. "Guess it's been kind of a down decade."

"Yeah, who needs standards when you have a shit ton of money, right?" Clayton adds, piggybacking on her addictive sense of sarcasm.

They share a brief laugh before Trish, too, notices her father up on the balcony. He returns the sight from above, raising his drink as they lock eyes.

She turns to Clayton.

"Let's go say hello to my dad," she pleas, grabbing his non-champagne-holding hand. "I'm sure he's about to take the stage in a bit."

Underwhelmed with enthusiasm, he throws back the remaining champagne in his second glass, quickly stealing a third one from another server's tray as they corkscrew up the winding staircase. For Clayton, it's an extra dose of liquid courage as he heads back to the lion's den.

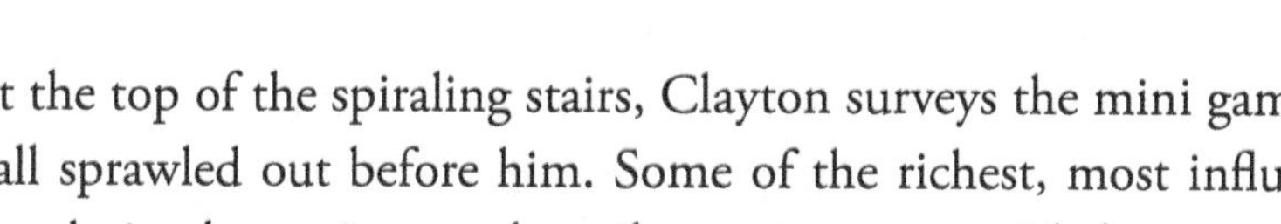

At the top of the spiraling stairs, Clayton surveys the mini gambling hall sprawled out before him. Some of the richest, most influential people in the nation are happily parting ways with large stacks of chips worth so much money he can't even tally the amount in his head. And even if he could, he wouldn't want to because he'd probably vomit at the absurdity of their lax high stakes.

The craps table seems to be the balcony casino's key attraction, which is exactly where Klein is still stationed as they approach. Dead center at the head of a packed table.

The grand, oval counter is brimming with hands reaching in and out of the ziricote-trimmed Cleopatra bowl. Colorful stacks of chips denouncing all denominations of money line the sides as players place their bets and hope for the best. When Clayton and Trish reach the table, Klein is in the midst of rolling the dice. He greets his daughter with open arms and a loving embrace, completely ignoring Clayton's existence.

"Patricia, honey, I'm so glad you're here. You made it just in time. I was just about ready to shoot. I'm on the pass line bet ready to toss the come-out roll."

Never having gambled a day in her life, outside of pulling the handle of a penny slot machine in a Nevada airport, Trish looks at the table totally overwhelmed. She has no clue what all the various numbers and words written on the table mean, or what the significance is of the little pucks labeled ON and OFF that litter the pristine red felt. It might as well all be a foreign language to her.

Slightly embarrassed, but doing her best to hide it, she smiles.

"I have no idea what any of that means, Daddy."

Klein chuckles and pulls her in for an innocent kiss on the top of her head like she's a naïve child.

"Everyone! Excuse me, *everyone*," he shouts over the hustle and bustle of the bowl. It falls silent instantly. "My good luck charm has finally arrived. This is my lovely daughter, Patricia." There's a sudden uptick in the roar at the table as a luxurious legion of complete strangers and a few of her father's acquaintances, who literally form the nation's upper crust, all welcome her. The slight embarrassment from before is now starting to show its true color, literally, as Trish's cheeks flush to match the pressed red felt of the game table.

Klein leans in toward his daughter. The bouquet of whiskey and Cuban cigars has left a hint of what smells like spiced band-aids on his breath.

"To put it simply, it just means I need a seven or eleven to win, darling." Klein holds out the dice in front of her face, gesturing for her to make the next move. "Just a little, for good luck?" Her cheeks are now firing on all crimson cylinders as she abashedly leans forward, giving the dice a lucky little blow.

"That's my girl," he says with a wink, before swirling the two six-sided dice in his hand one last time prior to letting them fly.

The dice bounce every which way, clanging together and then apart as they continue their wild route to the far side of the oval. The constant cheering from those gathered around the table grows quiet as the dice kerrang off the lip of the bowl before wobbling into their final resting places.

The dealer shouts out "Shooter rolls a two. That's snake eyes for Mr. Klein" as he whips his craps stick across the table to collect the set of dice that read double ones.

A collective and deflating sigh overtakes the table's bystanders, muting the short-lived crescendo of optimism.

"Well, I guess you can't win them all," Klein speaks out, as he finishes the last swig of thirty-year-old, barrel-aged, thousand-dollar amber in his rocks glass. "Now, if you'll all excuse me, I've got to get ready to give my anniversary speech and *wow* you all."

Cheerful sentiments from the congregation that has pooled around the action echo in the background as he steps away from the table.

"Sorry, Daddy, I hope you didn't lose too much money on account of my bad luck," Trish apologizes.

Her former embarrassment is now replaced by a new sense of guilt.

"Nonsense, honey, it was just a friendly game," he ripostes, placing his empty glass on a small bar table next to a series of finished flutes and backwashed bottles of beer. He looks fondly at his daughter, giving her a proper introductory hug. He may be a power-mongering, down-talking piece of shit to Clayton and those not entranced by his inner ring of world domination, but even Clayton must admit as he watches their loving interaction, he's always seemed to be a good father.

"It's good to see you, darling. I feel like it gets longer and longer between each time we see one another."

"I know, Daddy," she replies with her head buried in the shoulder of his suit jacket. "But you're a busy man."

"Be that as it may, I've always got time for my daughter. Who I might add looks absolutely gorgeous tonight," he says, as they part momentarily, giving her a twirl. He studies her formal, all-grown-up appearance, brushing that elusive strand of hair back behind her ear just as her mother used to. "You look just like her, you know? Like your mother." His eyes lock with hers. "She'd be proud of you, honey."

Up to this point, Clayton has been content letting them share their sentimental moment as he sits idly by watching the gambling unfold around him, downing the remainder of his third glass of champagne to ease his bubbling nerves. But at the sound of Klein bringing up Trish's mother, his ears perk up in a "welcome back to reality" moment. He steers his wandered attention from the poker tables back to eavesdropping on the side pocket, daddy-daughter convo at hand.

"Really proud," Klein adds.

Trish blushes yet again at her father's comparison.

"Aww. Thanks, Daddy." She wipes underneath her eyes at the hint of congregating moisture. "I feel like I miss her more every single day."

"Me too, honey," Klein says, placing a gentle hand on her shoulder. "Me too."

And then, just like a responsive faucet flipping from warm to cold, Klein turns his attention to Clayton. He makes no attempt to shake his hand or embrace him in any way. He doesn't even make direct eye contact. Just a bare minimum acknowledgment with the name he knows he hates.

"Sparky."

"*Oh, hi there, you absolute piece of human garbage. Made any other good bribes today, asshole? Or maybe you'd like to tell us about your burly bald buddy, Jimmy-Two-Toes, that I saw you conspiring with this afternoon?*" Clayton recites to himself in his ideal greeting. But the only two words to actually leave his lips are "Mr. Klein."

Always looking to deal the upper hand in their exchanges, Klein looks around at the boisterous gambling scene playing out behind him.

"No intention to partake in any of the high stakes, Sparky?"

Trish nudges her father in the ribs with an elbow, clearing her throat with the subtle blow. She's told her father a thousand times that Clayton hates that nickname. He knows it. And he knows Clayton knows he knows it.

"I mean—" mustering through clenched teeth at Trish's cue, "—Clayton."

But that's not even the real sear in Klein's backhanded attempt to once again cut him down. Clayton isn't fazed by the name bullshit anymore. Sure, it's petty, and he knows exactly why Klein continues to do it. Anything to dangle his power over him, like a carrot before the horse. No, he's more pissed off by the gambling remark because he knows it's just a poor, lowly attempt to point out his lack of wealth. Or more specifically, lack of class, yet again.

But not one to fold his cards so easily, Clayton responds with his own confident bluff.

"Too rich for my taste, sir," he remarks, grabbing his fourth drink, a bottle of pilsner from one of the craps table's servers. "Besides, I left my high roller money wad in my security pants back home. They're cargo pants. More pockets for all the Benjamins, you wouldn't know."

Sensing that the conversation is quickly sliding further downhill, Trish interjects, changing the subject.

"So, Daddy—" she practically shouts, wrapping her hands around Clayton in a loose, loving clinch. "When do you go on stage?"

Klein looks at his gold and silver-linked Cosmograph Daytona timepiece. The platinum dial from the nearly $30,000 Rolex indicates it's almost showtime.

"Right about now," he informs, adjusting the wings on his bow-tie and gold tuxedo cuffs. He leans in to kiss Trish on the forehead. "Sorry, hon, I hate to say hi and run, but duty calls."

"You know duty would have to actually stop now and then to ever call, Daddy," she jokes, slightly ushering him along. "Good luck. I'm sure you'll be great."

She smiles at him as he turns to make his way back downstairs toward the stage. He briefly stops to greet and bump elbows with a few additional high roller donors along the way, like a professional athlete being hailed by adoring fans.

Trish turns her gaze back to Clayton.

He returns the stare, losing himself again in her cool blues while all the chaotic thoughts from today flood his consciousness. Everything he'd like to tell her—has to tell her—right there on the tip of his tongue.

Before he knows it, he's talking.

"Trish . . . I . . . I . . . th-there's something I—"

She waits and listens. Her wide, welcoming eyes petitioning for him to just spit it out already. But their attention deflects direction to a soft voice stemming from their peripheral.

"Hi, Clayton."

They turn in unison to find Alexa Holbeck approaching from one of the balcony's poker tables. Dressed in a slinky, double thigh-slit green velvet number that could bend any man's will, she struts forward, flashing a delectable grill of starch whites sandwiched between billowing lips that are probably even softer than they look. Her hair is pulled up tight in an intricately weaved bun that looks like it belongs on the runway for Paris Fashion Week. The whole scene of her approach is like something out of a romantic comedy with the heads of all the old, rich gambling men turning together in slow motion—as if on timed swivels—to greet her every saunter, and doing nothing to hide it.

"Oh, hey, Alexa, I didn't see you up here," Clayton says, returning pleasantries. "You look nice tonight."

"Thanks," she responds, shyly, her voice as smooth and tender as her outfit. It's difficult to tell if her cheeks have flushed red with bashfulness or if the blush she's wearing is just working overtime. "You clean up pretty good yourself," she adds, averting her eyes to the floor.

Clayton reaches his arm around Trish, placing it on the dimpled small of her back. He maneuvers her forward a tad.

"Alexa, this is my girlfriend, Trish." He beams as they extend hands toward one another. "Trish, this is Alexa Holbeck, your father's—"

Clayton draws in a deep breath before shutting his mouth, cutting his own thought short. "Actually, what *is* your official title? Secretary? Personal Assistant? Babysitter?" he jests.

Alexa lets loose a giggle, "Executive Administrator, actually," she responds, taking a small step forward. "Hi," she says, releasing Trish's hand. "It's nice to finally meet you."

Trish returns the greeting, upping the pleasantries. "You, too. My father has spoken very highly of you since you started a few months ago. Which is good, because I can't say that for him about a lot of people," she jokes. "Or anybody, really."

The deprecating delivery is followed by a short, ice-breaking laugh.

"Well, he's quite an accomplished man," Alexa replies, gesturing to the entirety of the spectacle surrounding them. "It really is nice to finally meet you in person. Both your father and Clayton talk about you all the time. Is it weird to say I feel like I already kind of know you?" she concludes with her own friendly titter, while her eyes scan Trish's figure up and down, then back again. "You look amazing by the way. I love that white dress."

Trish's cheeks flash that familiar bit of red as she looks down and models her dress with a humble curtsey. "Aww, thank you. That's sweet of you to say," she responds, nuzzling back into the nook in Clayton's arm. "You'd probably laugh if I told you how long it took for me to decide on what to wear. It was like picking out a damn prom dress all over again, well, minus the early-2000s spaghetti straps, crunchy barrel curls, and glitter everything."

Clayton squeezes her tighter into the crook of his elbow.

"You could wear anything or nothing and still look breathtaking," he says, moving in for a peck on her cheek.

"Oh god," Trish heckles and rolls her eyes. "You're such a cheeseball sometimes. And your pickup lines need some serious CPR, cowboy."

"Well, I don't know CPR, but I can show you some TLC," he adds, now pressing his lips against hers.

As he pulls back, Trish looks up at him, smiling.

"Eh, better, but only because I set it up for you." She uses her thumb to wipe the red lipstick residue from his lower lip. "You really gotta stop kissing me or your face is going to look like you lost a fight with a red magic marker by the end of the night."

"You guys are adorable," Alexa cuts in. "What you have is special. Never let that go." She pauses briefly. Then, there's an awkward moment of silence among the trio that Alexa takes as her cue to leave the couple to their own romantic devices.

"Well, I hope you enjoy tonight." She breaks the hush. "I know your father has been excited for months about today. In fact, I should probably go check on him, in case he needs anything before he goes on. He might not show it, but he always gets really nervous beforehand."

Alexa turns and twirls her dress like a model at the end of a catwalk.

"It was really lovely meeting you, Trish. Goodnight, Clayton," she adds, and disappears back through the rowdy gamut of casino tables. All the gamblers are cashing out their winnings in preparation to take their seats for Klein's speech, but like a magnet, her physical presence again attracts nearly every set of betting eyes to look up from their cash-out piles for one last chance to ogle her exit.

Trish turns to face Clayton, who is now working on his fifth drink, a reimagined Vesper Martini. She grabs the skewer with its accompanying three olives, stirring it in an oddly seductive manner. After a few sensual stirs that James Bond would most definitely not approve of, she brings the skewer up to her lips and takes a suggestive mouthful of the first olive. The garnish's red and green undressing looks—and feels—like Christmas come early.

Clayton watches the amorous nibble, hoping to make the naughty list.

"Wow," he mutters, while his eyes make no attempt to blink. "Would you do that again . . ." he gulps. "Like, please?"

Ignoring his plea for provocative seconds, Trish swallows, then says, "Well, she was—"

"Nice, right?" he piggybacks, finishing her sentence and regaining some control over his enticed "Mommy kissing Santa Claus" desire.

"Nice?" she plops the skewer back into his cocktail. "All you've got to say is nice? Nice is how I would describe the adorable old ladies you see at the grocery store on weekday mornings. Nice is a smile from a happy baby. My Nani is nice. No, that woman was not nice. She was drop-dead gorgeous. Sexy as hell. A fucking fox. But sure, let's go with *nice*."

She starts stirring the drink again, anxiously rattling the remaining olives around the glass cylinder. "You know she likes you, don't you?" she asks, taking down a second olive, sans teeth.

Caught completely off guard by the question, Clayton responds after a forced snicker.

"W-wait, wh-hat?" he fumbles, placing his free hand behind the back of his head, nervously scratching his neck. "No. No, she doesn't. Why would you—"

"Duh," Trish says out loud, but even louder with her eyes. "Did you see her cheeks light up like sirens when you complimented her? Shifting her eyes toward me, the floor—on everything else in the room but yours."

"What that?" he innocently solicits. Totally oblivious, doing his accidental best to keep the ignorant male stereotype alive. "I thought I was just being nice. She's always like that."

"Always like that, huh?" Trish persists, cocking one eyebrow above the other. "Because she's totally crushing on you."

Clayton opens his mouth, but nothing comes out. Then slowly a grin starts to take shape.

"Wait a second," he says, now smiling from ear-to-ear. Beaming even. "Are you? You *are*. You're totally jealous."

Trish scoffs.

"I mean, how can I not be?" she asks, slitting her eyes and crossing her arms. "Hell, even I couldn't take my eyes off her. I mean, damn, you saw her. Everyone up here did. Most of them twice. I know because I was one of them."

Thoroughly enjoying this rare moment of vulnerability, Clayton is half-tempted to let it continue for his own amusement. But in a smart turn of events, he's willing to take the win while he still has the upper hand. He's not betting any of his money or his relationship on black tonight.

"Eh, I mean she's pretty and nice and all, but these eyes aren't looking," he says, brushing the situation off like it's nothing. He puts his hand around Trish's upper butt, drawing her closer. "Besides, I've already got myself a drop-dead gorgeous, sexy as hell, fucking fox of a baby-mama-to-be, right here. And I can't take my eyes off her."

Trish looks down and a tender smile now conceals her envious shame. She grabs the skewer from his drink for a third time, plunging it deep into her mouth as her sultry red lips work their way down the shaft from tip to tip until the last olive vanishes. She tugs it gently with puckered lips, freeing it back down the pole. Clayton can't help but feel it get a little extra steamy in his suit and jacket.

He loosens his tie to let out the sudden rush of warmth flooding his body.

"Pretty good answer, cowboy," she responds, as she grabs him by the tie and pulls him in closer. "Maybe you're not so bad at the pickup lines after all." Leaning in for another kiss, she hovers her lips over his like an airlock ready to dock. "So long as I'm the only one you're laying them on."

The kiss is slow and passionate, more explosive than any celebratory firework. More magical than any fairytale ending. Worth more than all the lavishness of this party and the large stacks of chips circulating through its pop-up casino combined. The overwhelming allure of its aftertaste makes Clayton forget about everything. Where he is. What happened earlier. How and when he's going to eventually break the news to Trish.

In this moment, none of it matters.

It's just him and her, together.

Nothing else.

# CHAPTER 12

Klein makes his way backstage where he's mic'd up and given his cue to take the stage as soon as the dancers finish their final number. You'd think being in the constant gaze of the public eye would help prep his nerves for moments of grandeur like this, but despite Klein's stoic demeanor, he can't avoid what so blatantly and unfortunately makes him human—emotion. He may think and act like a supreme being, but deny it all he wants, he's still only a man. Just flesh and bones. And the jitters in his hand only serve as evidence, a reminder of his resentful mortality.

There's a loud eruption from the crowd as the burlesque dancers finish their grand finale. As they pour in backstage from behind the closed curtain, they're moving in a synchronized, single-file exit. Klein takes one more generous gulp from the Glenfiddich in his rocks glass, gritting his teeth from the slow burn down. His attempt to numb the emotion raging deep within.

Nerves be damned, it's showtime.

One deliberate step at a time, he makes his way up the side staircase to center stage. Before he can even finish walking to his mark, he's met by resounding cheers and applause from the captivated crowd of thousands. Camera lights flash across the venue's mountainous silhouette of attendees, illuminating jillions of scattered bursts that flicker like tiny stars. Klein pauses in admiration from the sheer magnitude of this anniversary and what it took to get here. The will, the vision—the sacrifices.

The ovations gradually die out after he's had ample time to bathe in the gratuitous adoration. He takes a small step toward stage left, procrastinating because the praise is pure fuel.

Once the needle on his ego nears full, he begins.

"*The late Martin Luther King, Jr. once said, 'True peace is not merely the absence of tension; it is the presence of justice.' And while I respect the romanticism of his sentiment, I wholeheartedly disagree with the execution of the message. The idea that peace brings peace is foolish. It's juvenile in nature and naïve in concept. You see, true peace is not merely the absence of tension. It is the fear of it. The accountability and ownership that you are held responsible to the full extent of the law for the consequences of your own actions, regardless of thought. We're not just talking about the presence of justice; but the reimagination of it.*"

Klein works his way across the platform to stage right. He methodically adjusts the position of his glasses, and continues.

"*You all know me as a man of faith, a strong believer in the Good Word. After all, religion is the fundamental pillar for the foundation of everything The Hunt Initiative has been built upon. But I must admit, right here and now to you all, that I am at fault for doubting scripture. For committing sin.*"

A collective gasp sprawls across the crowd like a suffocating wildfire.

"*I tell you that in complete confidence, in the notion that The New Testament is but a glamorized contradiction of the books that came before it. Of the Old Testament that vehemently built and shaped the moral backbone of our disciplined and righteous society many millennia ago. Thus, I beseech you all to not uphold Deuteronomy: Chapter nineteen, verse twenty-one's practice of purging evil through an 'Eye for an eye. A tooth for a tooth' in any equal standing to the physical turning of the other cheek in Matthew: Chapter Five, verses thirty-eight through forty, for that latter lesson is nothing but a farce—a white lie proven to be far more harmful than ever intended. For there is no justice in handing your coat to a man who demands your shirt. That is a false creed of collective mercy we faithfully, blindly, and regrettably followed for centuries. And just look where it got us: the highest crime and murder rate per capita our nation has ever seen. Incarceration numbers that exceeded physical prison capacities by tens of thousands. Not to mention the increase in hefty government taxes on you, the people, as a direct result. But above all else, it failed those personally affected by the system itself. A total collapse in bringing closure and evenhandedness to the suffering and mourning of our lost loved ones. Those that had been taken from us before their time. Stripped from our safe and adoring embrace.*"

The previous gasp that swept the congregation's breath has transformed into communal praise. The acclaim upticks momentarily before residing in a unified hush-like Sunday mass.

"*Mohandas Gandhi, like his successor Mr. King Jr., believed in that same adolescent world—the idea of peace through pacifism. Like Matthew ignorantly proclaimed in The New Testament, Gandhi too preached turning the other cheek, because of the belief that 'An eye for an eye will leave the world blind.' But I have seen the truth. And what I saw—what we all can see with our own eyes—is that an 'eye for an eye' will only help us truly see, eye-to-eye. For the one-eyed man will do anything to keep from losing his sight entirely. Because no other person except for the one-eyed man sees as clearly the consequences of his actions. Or lives with as much farsightedness. For he knows firsthand the penalty of his transgressions, including the price for committing the vilest of them all—murder. Because there is so much more at stake when it's a life for a life and not simply an eye for an eye. For 'the rest will hear and be afraid, and will never again do such an evil thing.' Amen.*"

Hanging onto his every word, as if carabined to the edge of their seats, the audience lets out a roaring ovation.

"*This, ladies and gentlemen, is our new normal. An evolved sense of righteousness for a changed nation. The new foundation on which the American justice system operates. Where business is good, and justice is served. At any cost.*"

Klein walks to the side podium for a sip of water. The act of reprieve affords the crowd a moment to applaud themselves for the system they've faithfully adopted, but more importantly, to applaud him as its creator.

"*When I founded The Hunt Initiative twenty-five years ago, on this very day, I wanted to create something bigger than any one person. I had recently lost my wife, the first love of my life, to a reckless 'accident.' At least that's what the authorities called it. I was at my wit's end left searching for answers. For a reason why my beloved Rebecca had been taken, so suddenly stripped from my and my beautiful baby daughter's lives. But I found no solace in my pleas and prayers for a solution.*"

Trish reaches a hand over Clayton's armrest, but her gaze doesn't leave the stage. Her palm is clammy and warm as she squeezes his hand. He looks over and can see her eyes start to well up. He's not sure how much more hiding what he knows he can take. It's already eating at him from the inside out, and Klein's speech is only hastening the cannibalistic process.

"*It was the stepping stone I needed—that we all needed—to forge a nation where people would truly be held accountable for their actions. For their lack of thought. The birth of a justice system born on impartiality, raised without prejudice or corruption. A reincarnation of the golden rule for the twenty-first century. 'To do unto others as they have done to you.' Because to simply do unto others as you would have them do unto you, is nothing but a starry-eyed sentiment disguised in a fool-hearted execution. Just like Mr. King. Just like Gandhi. Even our brother Matthew.*"

He continues his pacing across the stage, pinging back and forth to ensure he hits all the marks equally that have been laid out for him during rehearsals. To treat this speech as a show.

If ever pressed, Klein would likely brand his theatrics as captivating; Clayton would skip the bullshit and call them what they really are—indoctrination.

"*I repeat, 'Do unto others as they HAVE DONE to you,'*" Klein reiterates. "*It's a simple premise centered around an enforced federal decree: The penalty for murder is murder. That comprises first- and second-degree murder, and all degrees of manslaughter. Of course, there are a few additional mandates behind the due process of The Hunt Initiative, but they too have been simplified to streamline the desired outcome of absolute justice. For starters, everyone here knows that:*

- *All suspects will have the right to trial unless their crime has been witnessed by a majority party, in which case, conviction will be expedited;*
- *Safe harboring an Initiative's prey will result in the same death penalty above for said guilty party;*
- *And, if successfully charged, tried, and convicted, the guilty has the freedom and right to attempt escape from the judge, jury, and execution of their peers.*"

Klein stops his pacing to face the audience head-on.

"*But no one has ever escaped The Hunt. And no one ever will. I can promise you that.*" With added emphasis, he hits each of the following words with dramatic flair. "*Because. That. Is. Justice.*"

The ovation echoes once again, as cheers and applause resonate through the packed convention center, skyrocketing the decibel level to new fidelities.

Slouched in his seat, Clayton thinks to himself, *Wow, this sounds familiar. The son of a bitch used part of his own "I am God" speech on me this morning. Right before he bribed me with his pick-a-number game.*

Klein continues his address, visibly enjoying the spectacle, feeding off the crowd's funneled energy.

"*We finally live in a justifiable nation where friends and families can seek retribution for their lost loved ones. Where any American can avenge the horrors of murder for their fellow citizens. Where trials aren't performed and drawn out in favor of a corrupt defense thanks to the fine print of a mendacious court system. Where it doesn't matter the color of your skin, your creed, or your sex. A life where we don't have to be afraid anymore. Because when you take away the father of all crime, the rest will fall into order. Like cutting off the head of Adam's snake. Because God promised us a paradise, and I am here to ensure its delivery.*"

With confidence now coursing through his entire being, Klein's early nerves are just as much a figment of the past as the former judicial system he's so infamously replaced. He now struts with a sense of unmatched arrogance to the front of the stage, his head aimed toward the heavens.

"*Good people of Bannerton—of America—and to our brothers and sisters around the world, tonight, we celebrate twenty-five years of The Hunt Initiative. Twenty-five glorious years of justice for our beloved nation—for our gone but not forgotten loved ones,*" he preaches, giving himself a round of applause that's reciprocated tenfold.

"*But I must admit, I stand here today still left unsatisfied—wanting more. For there is still so much work left to do. So many wrongs to right. Justice yet to be served.*"

He looks out across the dark abyss. The bright stage lights shroud the audience from any recognition beyond countless rows of black silhouettes. But he doesn't need to see them. He already knows they're groveling for him to continue his sermon.

He smiles, relishing the thought of reverence.

"*That is why I'm proud to say publicly, for the very first time, that The Hunt Initiative is just the beginning. The first step toward our new goal of global peace. Because soon the entire world can eat, sleep, and live without fear, protected by justice in its purest form.*"

The velvet curtains behind Klein slowly part to reveal an imposing rig of stylized LED screens. In the center, a massive central monitor, nearly fifteen feet wide, comprised of three smaller panels displays the ominous phrase "A New Hunt Is about to Begin" across it. Meanwhile, two large vertical panels more than twenty feet tall flank the stage's sides. At first glance, they support The Hunt Initiative seal, but upon closer inspection, Clayton notices it's a slightly modified version of the current emblem—an evolution of sorts. An emblazoned gold eagle with outstretched, razor-like wings overtakes prominence in the foreground as a gridded globe now nestles the space above its head. The eagle's breast bears a shield with a single star above seven stripes, a reimagining of the United States under the lone decree of The Hunt Initiative's foundational pillars: Persistence, Sacrifice, Ambition, Courage, Integrity, Faith, and Responsibility. Around the outer edge of the globe are the words "The Hunt Initiative" scrawled across the top. They're accompanied by the phrase "Justice for All" written along the bottom. Finally, just beneath the pose of the mobbing eagle, rests a banner with a line of Latin. It reads "*Vita ad Vitam*,"—A Life for a Life.

"*Ladies and gentlemen, it is my utmost pleasure to bring you the next iteration in our continued Hunt for justice. I present you with The Hunt Initiative: Global Pass.*"

The grand reveal is met with a growing undertone of collective "oohs" and "ahhs" that ripple throughout the hungry crowd. Thousands of audience members salivating at the palatable chance for a literal world bathed in bloodshed, all in the name of justice.

As Clayton looks around at the bloodthirsty crowd, practically drooling in their big donor seats, he feels a burning sensation throbbing in his head, and it's not from the sixth alcoholic beverage he just polished off. He's simply heard enough. His mind can't take any more bullshit for today or it might explode. Without explanation, he gets up from his seat and makes a deliberate push to the closest exit, fumbling over the motionless feet of entranced guests on his rush out of the aisle.

Alarmed by his abrupt departure, Trish quickly follows suit.

Once inside the empty lobby, Clayton wastes no time loosening his tie under a deep gasp for fresh air. He rushes over to a neglected tray of drinks and slams another glass of half-drunk champagne—lucky number seven for the night.

Trish witnesses the whole concerning ordeal from the exit.

"Clay? Babe? Are you okay? What's wrong?"

Completely unaware she followed him, Clayton whips around to face her with his mouth still ballooning from unswallowed carbonation. He forces a gulp and exhales harshly. His thoughts dribble out of his mouth at the same time.

"I can't do this," he huffs, catching up to his breath and his words. "I had to get . . . I just needed some air."

Doing her best to sympathize with his sudden burst of sincerity, she tries to commiserate.

"It's okay. I know, I feel it, too," she airs, placing a delicate hand on his back. "My dad can get a little . . . holier-than-thou. But—"

"No! You don't get it," he urges, slamming the now empty flute back down onto the table. The tall, thin glassware's stem shatters at the force, slicing the webbed flesh between his thumb and first finger. He's so worked up he doesn't even notice the slight red trickle. "It's not just that. Not entirely."

"Okaay," Trish replies timidly, afraid of anymore self-inflicted bloodshed. "What is it then?"

Clayton looks deep into those vast, seafaring eyes of hers, and instantly, he can feel himself drowning. He doesn't know where to begin. How to tell her about the bribe, her mother—any of it. So, he does what every scared, insecure man does and second-guesses himself instead—his past, their relationship, the baby—everything good about his life, everything he holds dear—ready to throw it all away in fear that he'll lose her either way.

"Why me, Trish?"

"Huh?" she asks, still trying to play catch-up with whatever personal demon is trying to free itself from his possession. "What are you talking about? What do you mean?"

"I mean, are you sure you want to risk a life of luxury on a guy that can't give you what you want? That can't give you all of this?" he poses, gesturing to the embellishments all around them. "I'm not a good person, Trish. My past is ugly. Messy."

Visibly confused and growing more teary-eyed at every slight to their relationship, she treads forward carefully.

"Clay, you're kinda freaking me out right now," she says through wavering words, a byproduct of the tremble in her lips. "Where is all this coming from?"

But he just ignores her question and fires another shot from left field.

"I'll never be able to give you and our baby what you deserve. You know that, right?"

Her buoyant eyes finally overflow from the incoming tide. The salty waves rush over her cheeks as she searches his castaway gaze for the true Clayton. The man she loves, not this cruel antagonist he's suddenly become.

"Look, I know you're scared. I'm scared, too. But I've never wanted any of this." She mimics his gesture of the swank space. "I've told you that so many times. Wh-why can't you believe me?" she asks, sniffling her way through the question. "I don't care about who you were, what you've done, or where you've been. I love you for who you are right now. For the man I fell in love with. I just want you." Delicately, she brings her hands over her belly. "*We* just want you."

Her words flood him with emotion, pulling him under with the current from her torrential ocean blues. The baptism is enough to cause an instant change of heart.

He steps forward and wraps his arms around her—around them.

"I'm sorry. I'm so, so sorry. I freaked out and lost control," he confesses, dabbing her glassy eyes with his shirt sleeve. "You know I love you more than anything. And I'd never do anything to hurt you, right?" He brings his hands to her hips and takes a step back. With every bit of sincerity reflected in his stare, "Ever."

"Y-you promise?" She sniffles.

This is the love of his life. The mother of his unborn child. His everything. No more secrets. He knows it's time to come clean or risk losing her for real.

He smiles and adds, "Always."

They hug in a silent embrace that says nothing, but everything. Muffled in the background of the Kodak moment, Clayton can faintly hear Klein wrapping up his speech.

"*By this time next year, The Hunt Initiative won't just be confined to the physical borders of our free nation. Soon, we—along with our brothers and sisters around the globe—will be able to partake in one, unified Hunt for world justice. No victim unavenged. No murderer safe from the grasp of righteous consequence . . .*"

They let go of one another and slowly regain their composure. Clayton seizes the moment of reprieve to figure out where to start. How to tell her the real reason behind his breakdown. Why he's been so on edge all night. Failing to imagine there's any kind of a good segue, he does exactly what he swore to himself he wouldn't do.

Just say it.

"Trish, there's some—"

"Ugh, I need to go freshen up," she interrupts, in between subsiding sniffs and aggressive mascara dabs. "I probably look like a drunk sorority girl who just broke down because Taco Bell was closed or something," she jokes, wiping away the diluted black lines streaking down her cheeks.

"Look Trish, I really need to—"

"Sorry, babe. Give me just a sec," she responds, holding up her hand already on a beeline mission for the restroom.

"But Trish, I—" Clayton mutters to himself, sighing out the rest of his planned sentiment in the wake of her trailing steps. "—really need to tell you something."

"I'll be right back," she shouts from the distance.

And just like that, he's left to wait again with nothing but the anticipation to tell her eating away at his every thought.

". . . *Ladies and gentlemen, together we are justice. This is the future. Happy Hunting.*"

Well, almost his every thought.

# CHAPTER 13

Inside the main hall, Klein delivers a triumphant coup de grâce to close his address. Before he can even finish his last word, the attendees rise to their feet like thousands of droids in programmed waves of jubilation. Their roar, deafening. It's a standing ovation fit for a king.

Never one to shy away from the limelight of gratuitous adoration, Klein basks in their worship like a miracle had just been performed. When his ego has sufficiently runneth over, he walks off the stage as if it were water. Like he was God.

Meanwhile, Clayton paces the dolled-up convention center corridor as he waits outside the restroom for Trish. In between anxious strides, he eyes another unattended tray of champagne flutes and decides *what the hell, one more can't hurt.*

He tosses the sparkling bubbly to the back of his throat for his eighth drink in two hours, and the not-so-subtle effects of inebriation begin to possess his senses. It's why he's hesitant to believe whether the mystery man Klein was talking to earlier today is, in fact, standing in the lobby or if he's just imagining it. After all, he's been obsessing about it all day, so a drunken fabrication is more than a possible culprit.

Clayton clinches his eyes and gives his head a vigorous shake—a scientifically supported tactic to decipher one's level of sobriety. Right up there with black coffee and cold showers, clinically proven to expedite the sobering-up process. When he reopens them, he's more than sure it's not just his intoxicated imagination. It's Tony Soprano all right, wearing the same black leather jacket and toting that familiar, up-to-no-good mobster mentality. He might as well just add the tattoo SUSPECT across his forehead to join his other works of prison art.

Clayton watches him from afar until he vanishes backstage through the lobby's side door.

He glances over to the restrooms, still no sign of Trish. Then, back across the lobby to the exit where Mr. Mafia suspiciously slipped away. He plays how the possible scenario in his head will most likely shake out, and against better, *sober* judgment, he decides to give chase. To take the initiative and go on his own hunt of sorts.

He slinks his way across the sporadic assortment of empty cocktail tables over to the side door, peering around like a buzzed thief in the night. Luckily, everyone is still in the main hall soaking up the lingering high from Klein's speech. He nudges the door open just enough and catches a glimpse of his target turning the corner down the hall. Leaving the exit door ajar, he follows. Careful to maintain a sufficient tail, he rounds the corner just in time to see the backstage door shut. He looks behind to see if anyone is watching.

Again, not a single person in sight.

Clayton gets right up on the door but pauses at the first sound of commotion. He cups his ear against the slab of wood, hoping to hear something, anything really. But all he can make out is the faint sound of muffled, indiscernible voices on the other side.

"Damn," he whispers.

Exercising patience in a situation that calls for action, he waits for a heavier exchange in the barely audible conversation to slowly inch the door handle free. He's hoping that between their exchange and the festivities wrapping up in the main hall, the duo of preoccupied voices won't take notice.

After enough concentrated leverage, the latch is ever so silently removed from its resting place and the door creaks open. The fresh two-centimeter gap reveals just a sliver of the scene taking place in the next room. Clayton quietly moves in, hunching over to align his eye just right with the vertical slit.

Finally, he can both hear and see what's going on. Sort of.

"Helluva speech, sir," says the mystery guest in a tough baritone rasp.

"Forget about that," Klein deflects, pouring himself another hefty glass of his favorite vice. "What's the status, Marco?"

Of course.

*The mystery mobster would be named Marco*, Clayton thinks to himself. *He's already a walking stereotype. Why not add to it?*

"Just like we talked about, sir, my guys are stationed at the apartment right now. I'm about to leave here and join them."

"Good. Very good. Just remember, only him. DO NOT touch the girl," Klein emphasizes. He takes a heaping shot from his stiff three-finger pour, emptying the glass. "That's my daughter. And the last thing any of your men want to do is cross me. Is that understood?"

Clayton shakes his head in disbelief, making sure it's not the alcohol again muddling his senses—because, well, science.

"No offense, Mr. Klein, sir, but you stick to what you do best. And let me and my men do what we do best," Marco replies, revealing the same silver gun with the black handle underneath his jacket. "Just like we planned, no one will be able to trace it back to you. It'll look like a routine robbery gone wrong."

Klein pours himself another generous single malt scotch. He takes the second one down in a gulp even bigger and faster than the first.

"And his file?" he seethes.

Marco acknowledges, "Like I told you at your office earlier, untraceable. Just like—well, you know."

Clayton's officially heard enough.

There's no other thought crossing his mind right now than to find Trish and run. To tell her everything and flee for anywhere, everywhere but here. But before he can slip away, a familiar touch graces his shoulder.

"Clay?" Trish asks, softly, her voice high with confusion. "I saw you come back here as I was leaving the bathroom. What are you—"

He tries to shush her. But it's too late. Even her subtle voice is enough to spur attention from the other room.

Klein's the first to bark at the uninvited noise.

"Who's out there?" he demands.

At the sound of his familiar voice, Trish pushes the door open.

"Daddy?" she queries, her confusion skyrocketing by the second. "What—" she continues, pausing momentarily at the sight of Marco. "What's going on?"

Without hesitation, Clayton lunges in front and ushers her safely behind him with a deliberate outstretched arm. It's the first time in his life that he's ever seen Klein look caught off guard.

Vulnerable.

Almost helpless.

"Yeah, Klein, why don't you tell her *exactly* what's going on?" he condemns.

Klein looks at his daughter—her eyes wide and unassuming—but he can't form the right words. Or any words, really. Only a symphony of Speech 101 don'ts spills out from beneath the tense shudder of his mustache.

"Hon . . . Ahem, honey . . . I, umm . . . Well, I uhh. I don't know what . . . We were just—"

"Let me help you out," Clayton interrupts, halting the stammer fest. "How about we take it from the top? Starting with the part about you bribing me this morning with your checkbook to leave her. To buy me out. Or, maybe we back burner all that bullshit and go right to you spilling the truth about her mother," he orders, each demand growing louder and more damaging than the last. "But most importantly, tell her about this fucking guy and your plan to off me tonight at our apartment." Now screaming, "Tell her about all of it!"

The mascara Trish just reapplied for the second time tonight streaks down her cheeks yet again. She's not sure what emotion to feel right now because there's more than one pouring in while her tears stream out.

Total disarray from what's happening.

Fear from the mounting tension.

Disbelief about the accusations.

Any and all of it.

Trying to process everything she just heard all at once, she side-steps Clayton's protective pose to address her father head-on.

"Da-daddy?" she sputters, as she chokes down the looming lump in her throat. "What's Clay talking about? What's he saying? I-I don't understand."

She looks back at the man she loves, and she hardly recognizes who she sees behind his newly donned mask of rage. A rage she's heard about in his past stories of regret, but one she's never seen in person.

Until now.

Klein's soulless eyes gaze tenderly upon his weeping daughter. For once, there appears to be a semblance of sincerity behind them, but the authenticity is gone the instant he opens his mouth and the same old lies spew out.

"Hon . . . honey . . . Clayton isn't well," he accuses, finally finding his angle of defamation. "He doesn't know what he's talking about. He . . . he's drunk. Completely delusional. Don't listen to him. He's crazy, dangerous. Listen to me, I'm your fath—"

"Cut the shit, Klein," Clayton jumps in, taking a step closer. "Tell her the fucking truth or so help me—"

Just then Marco, who's been a silent observer up until now, reaches into his jacket and unholsters the silver revolver. With one seamless action, he lines up the blunt barrel chest-high with Clayton, who backs up, skirting Trish behind him once again.

"Don't fucking move," Marco grunts.

"Or what? You gonna shoot me? Risk killing us both? Please," Clayton scoffs and turns to Klein. "Just tell me this, Simon. If I'm really the crazy one here—the *dangerous* one—then why is your hired muscle the one with a gun pointed at me right now?"

"Because he's protecting us from you, Sparks. You're unhinged," Klein continues, milking his innocent bystander approach. Each new lie coming more naturally than the last. "Trish honey, come over here. *Please.* Clayton is dangerous. He needs help. We can help him, together."

"You son of bitch," Clayton retorts, keeping Trish pinned behind. "Have you ever told the truth? Or is your whole life just one big fucking lie? Trish, babe, I'm not—"

He glances over his shoulder at her—the love of his life. The mother of his unborn child. She's trying her best to keep it together, but she's teeter-tottering between a total breakdown and absolute disbelief. She's scared, desperate—her whole world turned upside down.

"Trish, your father is lying. You know me. You know I'd never do anything to hurt you. You know that!"

At the seemingly harmless choice of words, Klein does what he does best and seizes the opportunity.

"Wouldn't hurt her, would you? Just like you never meant to hurt . . . Antoni Rivera?"

"Wh-what? How?" Clayton mutters, his rage instantly overshadowed by the total shockwave from the mention of that name.

A name he hasn't heard in a very long time.

A name he'd hoped to forget.

"That's right, Sparky. What? Didn't think I'd dig up *all* the info on your record? Even you couldn't be that naïve," Klein speaks up, re-adjusting his timid posture to a familiar footing of confidence. "I've read up on all your run-ins. Juvie. Your stint in prison. I know everything there is to know about you." He directs his attention toward his daughter. "But does Trish know the full story? Every last bloody detail?"

"Trish, babe, don't listen to him! He's trying to change the conversation," Clayton pleads. "He wants to turn you against me. To make me out to be the bad guy."

"Ahh, you see, Sparky, that's where you're wrong. I don't have to make you out to be the bad guy. You've already done that yourself. Your own history of violence proves it," Klein preaches, as if back on stage conditioning the masses. His brief lapse of power now fully re-instated. "Tell me, Sparky, did Antoni beg for mercy before you beat him to the brink of death?"

Clayton's heart plummets, cannonballing into the bile of his stomach. Splash from the reflux sends a blaze throughout every inch of his body.

"No. No, that's . . . you don't understand. That was a long time ago," he denies, as the internal fire rages, threatening to call up the eight drinks he put down earlier tonight. "You're wrong. It wasn't like that. I've changed. I'm not that guy anymore."

"Of course, you are, Sparky. People like you don't change," Klein pushes. A smile slithers out from beneath his mustache. "In fact, it's because of people just like you that I created The Hunt Initiative in the first place. To keep the rest of us safe."

"Shut the hell up, Klein! Enough of the self-righteous bullshit," Clayton screams.

Again, he turns over his shoulder to implore Trish.

"Babe, that's not me anymore. You know me. I'm not that man."

"We know exactly the kind of man you are, Sparky," Klein

interjects, his tone growing more assertive despite his voice getting any louder. "A man with a plagued past and dried blood on his hands."

Sensing that Klein has fully regained the upper hand, Marco takes a step closer. Undeterred that his pistol is still locked on Clayton, Trish mirrors his movement and maneuvers herself free from behind her boyfriend's guard. She paces toward her father. Clayton tries to usher her back, but she discards the halfhearted attempt, deliberately casting his arm aside.

Klein smiles at the failed gesture and extends his own genial hand toward her.

"That's my girl," he adds. "Come to me."

But she stops abruptly, mid-route. And so do her tears.

"Tell me what *really* happened to Mom," she says, her tone ensuring that the command is not mistaken for a question. "And don't you dare lie to me."

Klein's recovered arrogance is yet again replaced with the unnerving feeling of diffidence. His smug expression and balance of power quickly lose buoyancy as he feels his emotions and dominance start to skid. His daughter can see the answer already written in the blank flutter of his eyes. A horrible truth concealed in one giant, life-long lie.

His olive-branched hand falls to his side. He takes a couple of calculated steps back, readjusts the lapel of his tuxedo, and lets out a deep sigh.

He turns to Marco.

"Shoot him."

Marco cranks the hammer back on the gun and steadies his aim. Before he can feel the tension from the trigger, Clayton lunges forward, swiftly closing the short gap between them. Both men struggle in the sudden entanglement, fighting for position, trying their best to gain leverage over the firearm. Together, they hoist it overhead and then violently back down below their knees. Hunched over with both hands planted on the gun's grip, Marco forcefully throws a sucker punch with his elbow right into Clayton's cheek. He stumbles back from the surprise blow but wastes no time in re-engaging before Marco can reclaim aim.

Lowering his shifted stance to a near squat, Clayton drives through his heels in an explosive, off-balance thrust. He generates enough power and force from the move to heave Marco back into the near wall. The heavy impact causes the butt of his bowling ball head to leave a red scuff against the white brick.

Marco may have the size advantage, but Clayton has Father Time on his side.

He yells for Trish to run. But she's frozen in the corner of the room. Completely paralyzed by what's taking place, she doesn't know whether to cry, help, or scream. Even Klein looks lost on what to do other than just stand and watch.

The two men continue their tussle as Clayton acquaints his right knee with an opening on Marco's exposed torso. He hits him with it again and again, doling out successive punishment to his liver. Marco finally gathers enough strength to free himself from the wall and overpower Clayton, driving him back, but Clayton counters with a well-placed fist to Marco's temple. The equilibrium punch is enough to daze the bigger man, sending him stumbling back on rubber legs.

Clayton seizes the small window of opportunity to go for the gun. But in a last-ditch attempt, Marco finds the trigger and squeezes. The pistol jolts from his hand, firing one lone shot.

*BANG!*

Clayton finishes wrestling the gun free from his dazed opponent. With the advantage, he whips Marco across the bridge of his nose with the base of its hard rubber handle. Again, the brute staggers backward from the bone-breaking blow, giving Clayton enough time and space to gain control of the room.

Immediately, he forces both men into the corner, bobbing the hot barrel back and forth between them as they step back slowly in lockstep.

He touches his cheekbone, assessing the damage. It's swollen but not bleeding.

"Trish, go get help!" he shouts, without taking his eyes or the gun off Klein and Marco.

She doesn't respond, so he commands again.

"Trish! I need you to run and get—"

The horror consumes him the moment he turns to face her.

She's still standing motionless by the door, but she's cupping her belly. Her hands, scarlet and trembling. Her white dress, no longer immaculate. She peers up and meets his quivering eyes with a similar look of terror reflected in her own.

He dives toward her as she drops to her knees, catching her before the rest of her limp body can make contact with the floor.

"Oh my god, Trish! Babe? Love?" Clayton cries out, teetering on hysteria. "You're all right. Don't move. I've got you. It's going to be okay. Everything is going to be okay," he reassures over and over, more for himself than for her.

Attempting to stop the river of blood, he applies pressure to her belly with his equally trembling hands, but there's too much and it's flowing too quickly. He tries to press harder but only more escapes. Within seconds, all the color in her body has fled from the fresh wound. Like a boat sinking, all he can do is sit by helplessly and wait as the love of his life descends deeper into oblivion with every shallowing breath. Inconsolable, he feels the last bit of warmth in Trish's body delicately touch his cheek as she extends her stained hand to his face.

He cradles it in his grasp, bringing it to his lips.

"There I go again, getting red on you," she says quietly. Somehow able to crack a soft smile while her body tiptoes along the edge of shock and unconsciousness. "My cowboy."

Overcome with what seems like every human emotion competing all at once, Clayton picks the one he and Trish so often fell back on.

Lived on.

Loved on.

It's laughter.

"Yeehaw, baby," he jokes, while holding back his own river of tears.

Trish tries to laugh, but the action triggers a violent coughing fit. Blood fills her entire mouth and begins to seep from the corners of her lips.

Drowning in her own life-sustaining fluids, she composes herself just enough.

"Clay . . . y-you know I b-believed you, right?" Her body subtly shakes as the red streams slowly pool around her. "I-I've always b-believed in you."

"Shh, that's not important right now," he trembles, just rocking her in his cradled arms. "I love you, Trish. More than anything."

"Promise?" she gasps.

"Always," he whispers.

And with one final smile, the spark in her eyes is eternally doused. He continues to stare into her lifeless ocean blues, wishing he could drown in them to join her.

Slowly, he lowers her hand to the floor and lays it delicately by her side.

Then, he weeps.

Klein slumps in the corner, void of any reaction. His face is nearly as pale as that of his deceased daughter's. For a man who never loses, he just lost the only thing besides power that he's ever truly loved. Meanwhile, Marco just stands there and stares blankly through the purple and black forming around his eyes, unsure of what to do next.

Clayton's sobs are anything but quiet. Yet the ringing silence from the aftermath is what's most deafening.

After the moment of the initial shock subsides, Klein comes to, realizing time is of the essence. He looks at Marco who's still searching for a plan.

"Get out of here, now," he orders. "Take the back door and don't stop for anything or anyone. Understood?"

Marco does as he's told and bolts for the exit while Clayton continues to grieve, holding the loss of his entire world in his arms.

Within half a minute, event security bursts into the room. Rickers is the first one through the door. Jayson and Sean follow suit. A quick scan of the scene gives Rickers enough pieces to start putting a vague puzzle of the events together. Clayton, who's holding his boss's dead daughter with the murder weapon next to him, presents an overwhelmingly easy case.

"Mr. Klein, sir, what happened here?" Rickers inquires, reaching for his overcompensating firearm. "We heard a gunshot."

Without wasting a moment more to mourn, Klein takes aim of the situation and delivers his next perfectly placed, premeditated lie.

"It was him. It was *all* him—Sparks! He came in here furious. Something about being in financial trouble and owing the wrong people money. Lots of money. He threatened me and my daughter if we didn't pay up. Patricia tried to calm him down, but she got in the way," he spiels, giving an award-worthy performance with his uncharacteristically erratic delivery, acting more vulnerable than he's ever allowed himself to be seen. "The crazy son of a bitch shot her. He killed my sweet Patricia. Detain him, now. Right now, goddammit!"

Without hesitation Rickers moves to restrain Clayton, who is still crippled over, lost in utter shock. He does nothing to resist the feeling of cold metal against his wrists, just as Jayson can do nothing but watch in total disbelief as his best friend is forcefully handcuffed and read his rights as the newest "Prey to The Hunt."

"*Clayton Sparks, you are hereby, at this moment Prey to The Hunt Initiative until proven innocent. Your rights as a citizen have been waived, and you will await your chosen fate by the judge, jury, and execution of your peers. It is encouraged that you accept these terms with poise and steadfastness and make yourself a prime example of a good Hunt, should you be convicted and found guilty. Do you understand your rights and comply with your fate?*"

"B-But Rickers, sir, wait. We don't know what really happened here," Jayson pleads, finally finding an action while trying his best to bring needed gravity to the spiraling situation. "Clay wouldn't do this. He loved Trish, more than anything. There's no way he—"

"Quiet, Moore. Do as you're told," Rickers snarls. The riposte is further emphasized by Klein, who clearly shows offense to the challenge of his integrity.

"I saw the whole thing. I was right here. He threatened me. And her. He shot my little girl. My baby girl," he bellows. "Who are you to question me, boy? Now hurry up and take Sparks away so he can await his own fate."

Fighting out of his weight class and far from his jurisdiction, Jayson tries once more, hopelessly.

"With all due respect, Mr. Klein, sir," easing his delivery. "It's Hunt protocol to get both sides of the story first."

"Respect?" Klein scoffs, now yelling directly into Jayson's face. "You'll show me some goddamn respect by arresting this man, this instant, Officer, or I'll have you detained too for non-compliance. Do you understand me?" he threatens.

Jayson pulls back a deep breath, ready to Hail Mary another counter, but his sensibility wisely wins out.

"That's what I thought," Klein mocks.

Rickers and two other security personnel on the scene hoist Clayton up and drag him toward the exit. But before the crew can make it out the door, Klein halts the ensuing seizure. With pure malevolence fuming from his eyes, he jabs Clayton in the sternum.

Bullyingly, he leans forward and whispers in his ear.

"You're going to pay for this, Sparky. Welcome to The Hunt."

Led by Rickers, security ushers Clayton out from backstage to the main lobby. The throng of hypnotized attendees, captivated by Klein's keynote and now this sudden, mysterious mayhem have poured into the lobby, bumping elbows to witness all the commotion.

A majority of the crowd's initial speculation centered around fireworks, a possible jubilee to emphasize the grand reveal of The Hunt Initiative: Global Pass. But that celebratory thought quickly dissipated at the discovery of a lone, isolated bang and the escorted arrest of a bloodied man in handcuffs.

Whispers rustle throughout the crowded space, carrying speculation like gusts of wind across a dense forest, rustling every leaf with conjecture of a pending thunderstorm. A crime has struck their party. And this is the wrong type of ravenous gathering to tease with such a spark.

As security pushes their way through the parting sea of black tuxedoes and flashy ball gowns, an old woman wearing a gold, sequin-inspired flapper dress screams out from somewhere deep within the swarm.

"Murderer! Murderer!" she incites, urging her cohorts for agreement like a rally cry for the pack. "He's a murderer!"

Chants begin to ring out from the jungly congregation as the tension throughout the room tightens. Their groans grow louder as assumption turns to accusation.

A short, bald man with a ruffled cummerbund as wrinkled as his forehead yells out.

"He's a killer! Get him! Get the murderer! HUNT! HUNT! HUNT!"

Within seconds, the restless landscape of partygoers is no longer rustling peacefully. They're fighting to free themselves like a bitter autumn come early. Chaos quickly breaks out among the crowd in unison with the shattering of a champagne flute heaved at—but just missing—Clayton's head. More discarded cocktail glasses, along with empty beer bottles, and even silverware, soon follow a similar trajectory.

"Moore! Javorsky! Get Sparks the hell out of here, now," Rickers shouts at his nearest personnel. "I'll take care of this."

The active guards, with a shambling Clayton in tow, hasten their exit, taking cover to avoid the party shrapnel showering from every direction, yet Clayton himself makes little to no effort in deflecting any damage from the relentless downpour.

Once they make it out through the main entrance, Rickers barricades himself between the glass door and the swarming crowd turned starved sharks. They're just a whiff of chum away from becoming a shiver of apex predators in a full-fledged Hunting party.

Rickers shouts from the top of his stout lungs.

"People, please! Everyone! Justice will be served, I assure you," he roars, pushing an eager young woman in a lavish floral frock back into the stirring herd.

She snarls back like a hyped hyena.

"You all know the rules," Rickers continues. "He must be tried and prepped with due process just like everyone else." But his feeble attempt to be heard over the growling hush from the carnivorous crowd fails.

A frail man with a delicate silver combover in a burgundy tailcoat barks out from the front line, "If he's guilty, why wait? We want justice now!"

The thirsty question is met by a resounding roar as the peaceful partygoers turned hungry horde continue to salivate with a renewed lust for justice. For their right to feast.

Then, suddenly.

*BOOM*!

A deafening gunshot rings out from the back of the lobby, blanketing the hostile rally with a tranquilizing shush. They all turn in a single wave to examine the origin of the shot and are met with the image of Simon Klein, brandishing one of the many bolt-action hunting rifles from his collection. Peering over the crowd from atop the casino staircase above, he has yet again captured everyone's undivided attention for the evening.

"Ladies and gentlemen," he says over the silent awe. "My fellow patrons of The Hunt . . . my astute colleague is absolutely right. There is a process. And we should follow order."

He pivots, taking a small step forward as he begins to gently descend the winding staircase like a combative screw—one deliberate step down at a time. He slings the still-smoldering rifle over his shoulder, maintaining his gentle descent; yet, his fixed scowl conveys anything but docility.

"However—"

He takes another dramatic step down, scanning the ravenous faces of Bannerton's most sophisticated slayers.

"—Given the vile nature of the atrocity that has just occurred here tonight . . . witnessing firsthand the brutal murder of my *own* beautiful, beloved daughter, Patricia Klein, by the very man who swore to protect her. To love her." He purses his lips together air-tight, concealing the hint of a quiver from his lie. "I say to hell with order. Due process be damned. For true justice knows no bounds."

Roars erupt throughout the crowd signifying their unwavering approval and renewed commitment to the initiative Klein built exactly twenty-five years ago. Their appetite swells to right a wrong, by any means necessary.

Void of concrete evidence.

Without truth.

Simply fueled by their leader's word and a power above the law.

Klein looks out over his people—his disciples. At the world he has created—his dominion. And with his eyes on the prize for Clayton Sparks's head, he drags out a long, methodical breath before he gives the official order.

"Let The Hunt begin."

Society's most elite tear through the convention hall doors like a starved wolfpack on the prowl.

Hungry for justice.

Thirsting for blood.

And ready to stop at nothing until they taste both.

At the sudden cacophony of primal clamor stemming from the convention center's entryway, Clayton and company whip around to see the carnivorous collective that makes up Bannerton's upper crust rapidly approaching, nipping at their heels in an endless stream of determined droves.

There's a delay in their initial reaction.

And then.

"RUN!" Jayson shouts, kicking his feet into gear against the pavement. "Fucking run, now!"

The three take off in a dead sprint.

Somewhere in between the encroaching howls of the homicidal

mob defogging his brain and the crisp, outside air replenishing his lungs, Clayton finally snaps out of his postmortem trance. To say it's a rude awakening to the dire reality of their current situation is beyond an understatement. Impending doom tends to have that effect.

He turns to Jayson. "I didn't do it, Jay. I would never . . . I *could* never—"

"I know you didn't do it, man," Jayson echoes without skipping a beat. "But now's not the best time to get into it." Frantic, his eyes scan the packed parking lot, hoping to somehow manifest their unknown destination into existence. "Where the hell you parked, anyway?"

Clayton points over to the southeast lot while reaching down to grab his keys. Only he doesn't find them in his usual pants pocket. Desperately, he starts patting and digging all around his suit like a master magician failing at an amateur trick.

As if today's series of bad luck couldn't get any worse, it just did.

"Shit! Trish had the keys."

"Wait, what?" Jayson fires back mid-stride. "Okay then, new plan. Sean, we'll take your security car."

Only Sean's no longer neck-and-neck with them. His pace has dropped from a sprint to a jog to now barely a walk. Clayton and Jayson turn in unison to see him standing in the middle of the parking lot, completely idle.

Jayson mimics, screeching to a halt.

"Sean what the hell are you doing, man?" he demands in between winded breaths. We've got to go, NOW! C'mon."

Clayton stops, too, and adds, "Yeah, Sean, c'mon. We gotta move!"

But the rookie security guard just shoots Clayton a blank stare in return. The empty look says it all before he even opens his mouth.

"Clay, man, I like you. You've been nothing but nice to me since I started. But I can't help you. I can't interfere with The Hunt. I've got a family. I—"

"Oh, fuck this," Jayson mutters under his breath, but still loud enough for both to hear. "Are you kidding me right now, Javorsky?"

His irritation growing more visible with every precious millisecond wasted.

He takes a few side-shuffling steps back toward Sean.

"Enough of this shit. Let's go," he urges, while nervously watching the onslaught of hunters dressed to the nines make up valuable parking lot ground. "Clay didn't do it, man. He's innocent."

Sean takes a reflexive step back as Jayson encroaches into his personal space.

"That's not up to me or you to decide," he responds through a timid voice and apologetic eyes aimed at Clayton. "Look, maybe you are innocent, maybe you're not. I don't know. But I'm not ready to risk my own life or my family's lives to find out. I'm sorry, Clay. Truly."

At this point, Jayson's had it. They're running out of time, and the Hunters can sense it—their lynch-ready approach hastening exponentially as their distance dwindles.

"For fuck's sake, Sean! We don't have time for this bullshit," he belts, storming toward the rookie with his fists balled. But Clayton intervenes, side-stepping in front of him. The two friends stare at one another, face-to-face for the briefest of moments. Fully aware that time for an adequate pissing contest isn't on their side.

Clayton speaks up before Jayson can get a word out.

"He's right, Jay. He's not part of this. It's not safe for him." He places a heavy hand on Jayson's shoulder. "Or you."

Clayton turns to face Sean, who is noticeably twitchy from self-confliction.

"Sean, I'm not asking you to come with me, or to save me, but if you don't give me those keys, you might as well just kill me right here and now," he pleads, extending his hand. "Because I won't make it out of this parking lot alive."

Meanwhile, with every extra word in their untimely exchange, the horde continues its berserk advance as fast as their stilettos and polished Oxfords can take them.

They're no more than fifty yards away and closing.

Sean ping-pongs his glance between Clayton and the looming flock of highbrow Hunters. Their growls grow more audible with every infringing step, even distinct facial features are now discernable—everything from hairstyles and nose shapes, right down to their flared fangs. He clenches his whole body tight in a useless attempt to dispel his rookie jitters and digs a shaky hand into his front pants pocket. Looking down at the excavated keys, he debates his next move as if the right answer were miraculously etched somewhere on the metal ring itself.

The horde, now forty yards away, is closing in even faster.

All three men are jumpy, but nobody moves.

Clayton pleads with Sean one last time.

"It's now or never, Sean. What's it gonna be?"

Thirty yards away now, and again empty cocktail glasses and other miscellaneous utensils begin to rain down from the outside darkness like a thicket of arrows. Glassware shatters and fine china clangs all over the concrete, right before their feet.

Amid the silhouetted party favors cascading from above, Clayton watches as a set of car keys gracefully dance through the night sky.

He reaches out and snatches them mid-flight.

"Two rows down. To the right," Sean divulges, his voice sincere, yet his tone defeated.

The horde is under twenty yards out.

Clayton shoots him a grateful nod and then sprints in the instructed direction. Weaving in and out of the full lot, he quickly locates the security car and slides across the white hood from the passenger side while pounding the fob's unlock button.

As he flings open the driver-side door and hops behind the wheel, he turns to see Jayson immediately plop into the passenger seat next to him.

"What the hell do you think you're doing?" he asks, surprised.

"What's it look like?" Jayson wisecracks, despite the grave

circumstances. He clicks his seatbelt. "I'm coming with you. You're gonna need my help."

Clayton rebuts, "Look, Jay, I appreciate the thought but—"

He's cut short as Jayson snatches the keys from his hand and jabs them into the ignition. His usual cool and calm quickly swap for the appropriate level of fear and panic as another champagne flute collides with the car's windshield, cracking it upon impact.

"Just shut the hell up and drive already, will ya?" he shouts.

Clayton jerks his head forward and peers through the spider-webbed glass. The Hunting party is closing in now less than ten yards away. There's no more time to waste arguing. He thrusts the transmission into Drive and punches the gas pedal to the floorboard, squashing it like a bug with the full force of his toes. As he throws every bit of his weight behind it, the car's tires burn and squeal while it momentarily Flintstones in place—fighting every which way against the pavement to gain traction.

Finally, the four slabs of rubber find their collective grip on the coarse blacktop, and the car peels out of the parking spot, leaving a pair of fresh skid marks and a cloud of charcoal behind. Fishtailing briefly in a haze of burnt rubber, Clayton regains control of the wheel and weaves out of the way just in time past the first few eager Hunters on the scene. He brushes so close to two middle-aged men armed with dinner knives that he can hear the scratching of their fine dining utensils scrape along the side of the car as he zooms by.

He continues his pursuit for an exit to the street, but a panicked scan of the lot shows every main route to be blocked by legions of lavish partygoers turned bloodthirsty savages. All of them are keen on making this a fast Hunt. From across the lot, Clayton can see that the south exit is blocked too by a few guests who have tactfully moved their cars to form a pop-up blockade.

"Fuck, no south exit," Clayton deflates.

Jayson squints over his shoulder.

Past the blitzkrieg of anniversary attendees, he spots the west exit.

But a shifty blockade of the best SUVs money can buy is strategically placed alongside that way out as well.

He whips back around in his seat.

"No go on the west exit, either."

"Dammit! They got us boxed in," Clayton shouts. "We're screwed."

Scrambling to scan the entire parking lot for a solution at any logical escape, all hope seems lost. Jayson's stomach begins to churn. Maybe Clayton's right. Maybe they are screwed, and this is it.

Or maybe not.

He double-takes over his shoulder once more. Directly behind them at the far end of the lot, he spots a row of towering, perfectly manicured hedges organically fencing off the parking lot from the main drag.

He looks across the car at Clayton, his eyes wide, eyebrows cocked.

"Anything?" Clayton pleads.

"Well, I may have an answer, but I don't think you're gonna like it."

"It's not like this is multiple choice, Jay. Even true-false has more options. Just tell me!"

"All right then. You know the hedges behind us?" Jayson asks, motioning with his thumb toward the back window at the dense row of nearly twenty-foot shrubbery planted behind them. "That's our ticket out."

Clayton snaps his line of sight to the rear hatch window.

"Through those?" he yells. "No fucking way. They're huge!"

"Hey, if you're gonna oppose, you gotta propose, man," Jayson counters. "And I haven't heard either jack or shit from your side of the car. So what's it gonna be?"

There's a pause in Clayton's response. Scheming over the physics of the maneuver in his mind, he quickly concludes there's not enough time in the formula to flip the car around and attack the landscaping head-on.

The guests are closing in again, fast. Too fast.

A baseball-sized rock sails into view from the hazy glow of the stooped streetlamp above. The impact further fractures the windshield like a flaking plexus on a freshly frozen pond. The shattering sound is followed by the shriek of a crazed woman, clutching a black and silver stiletto in her dominant clubbing hand. She leaps atop the hood as Jayson yelps, jumping in his seat from the sheer shock value.

Less than an hour ago, this woman was a sophisticated, well-mannered societal member of Bannerton's upper crust. The city's elite. Probably a PTA member on her children's school board, maybe treasurer of a philanthropic foundation or charity, undoubtedly a never-miss-a-Sunday churchgoer, and more than likely, an all-around, well-respected business executive for some prestigious corporate marketing firm or other cushy, six-figure desk job. Now, she's stripped down to nothing more than animalistic instinct, infected with a rabies-like rage and the desire for blood—all in the name of claiming justice that isn't even hers.

Clayton throws the car in reverse and again reacquaints his full weight with the gas pedal. The familiar scent of torched rubber once more fills the air in a lingering black fog. The sudden inertia floors the car backward as the tenacious woman clings onto the gap in its hood with a white-knuckled grip. She begins smashing the fissured windshield with the reinforced point of her six-inch heel.

The spiderweb spreads, instantly weaving even more shattered strands throughout the remainder of the compromised glass.

Jayson shouts in horror, "Jesus Christ, this bitch is crazy!"

But Clayton doesn't risk breaking his concentration from the rear windshield. Because he knows that in a matter of seconds that crazy bitch is going to need both hands if she hopes to maintain her hold atop the car.

Without looking forward, he calls out to Jayson.

"Hang on! It's about to get bumpy."

Jayson locks one hand on the leather dashboard before him and braces the other against the ceiling. The car jolts over the curb dramatically as the complex physics affecting the woman's grip—a perfect combination of acceleration, mass, and gravity—quickly becomes too much for her to handle. She flies from the hood, tumbling onto the grassy knoll of the landscaped curb they just vaulted.

Clayton slams his foot against the pedal again, releasing all its horses to rejoin the gallop.

"Clay, buddy," Jayson inflects, watching the hedges grow larger, closer with each incremental tick on the speedometer. "I'm having second thoughts about this." Larger yet, closer still. "Maybe we should just—"

*KA-BAM!*

The car launches off the curb with convincing speed, using the bump as a makeshift ramp. It barely clears the three-foot-high brick planter before crashing through a deep-rooted row of massive, perfectly kempt, and healthy arborvitae hedges. The shrieks of outside snapping and drumming reverberate even louder on the inside of the car as twigs and branches rake across its exterior.

Once free of the terranean beating, they're hurled onto the street ass-end first. A splash of sparks soars from underneath the car's carriage as the trunk scrapes along the pitch-black backdrop of asphalt.

Clayton catapults the wheel hard left, while simultaneously throwing the car in drive. The chaotic combination somehow ends in a seamless transition, saving the small SUV from a disastrous barrel roll upon impact.

The two friends take off, gaining as much distance and speed between themselves and the convention center turned hunting grounds as the red meter will allow.

They're safe.

For now.

Clayton doesn't think, he just drives, weaving in and out of traffic with reckless abandon. No destination, just a race against time and any possible trackers hot-tailing in pursuit. Jayson manages to free the anxiety in his arms from shit-straining tension, but he's anything but relaxed.

"What the actual fuck? That was insane," he squeals, puckering his eyes as tight as his asshole.

Still clenched at ten-and-two with conviction on the roof of the wheel, Clayton speeds right through a stale red light without flinching. And then the next. The deadly game of chicken between their car and red traffic lights causes Jayson to put "Shit!" on loop, repeating the word like a life-saving penance as the car comes mere inches away from being double T-boned in the middle of the third ran-light's intersection. A few seconds later, at the revived realization of not being dead, he peels open his eyes to glare at Clayton who hasn't taken his own pair off the road, let alone blinked.

"Clay, what the hell?" Jayson screams, curling up in his seat like a fetus in the womb. "Slow down! You keep driving this crazy, and it won't matter that we got away because we'll end up dead anyway."

Clayton hears his friend's petition, but he doesn't waver. He's hardwired to put as many miles as fast as he can between themselves and the convention center.

At this point, it's simple math—the greater the distance the safer they are.

Their wild ride continues as the car acrobatically slingshots into oncoming traffic, flinging around a silver sedan, not going at a speed to Clayton's liking. Determined to be the back-to-back chicken champion, he reenters another high-stakes, first-to-flinch game, this time with a small, white Toyota. The advancing compact lays on the horn from twenty or so feet out, but Clayton doesn't act like he even hears it. In the last stretch of safety, the oncoming car finally surrenders, swerving across the wrong side of the yellow lines to barely avoid a paralyzing head-on collision with their bulldozing security vehicle.

Jayson yells out again. A desperate hope to finally break through to his transfixed friend.

"CLAY! Slow down, man, you're going to get us killed!"

At the sound of the word "killed," snapshots of the night's grisly events flash through Clayton's spellbound thoughts. The mental slideshow is enough to trigger a comeback to his senses.

"Sh-shit, I'm sorry, Jay," he admits, still shaking his head right. "I lost control back there for a bit, huh?"

Jayson eases himself back down from the edge of his seat with a deep huff in, then out. Just enough of a reprieve to catch his breath and muster up the right set of words to ask what Clayton knows he's been wondering from the get-go.

"Clay, what the hell went down back there?" he asks, still panting between hummingbird heartbeats. "What happened to Trish?"

The hesitation to answer his best friend's question mixes poorly with the fresh wound of his girlfriend's death. Where would he even start? Does he tell his friend about the mystery man at The Hunt for Justice? About Trish's mom's incomplete file? Does he give him the kitchen sink or the CliffsNotes?

He knows the answer before he's even finished asking himself all the questions.

"Jay, Klein's bribe this morning is only the tip of today's fucked up iceberg. He killed her, his own daughter. He didn't actually pull the trigger, but he did everything else to carry the bullet."

"Huh? What do you mean?" Jayson probes, confused. "Why would he do that to his own daughter? It doesn't make any sense. Did I miss something?"

Reluctant to rehash the recent past, Clayton knows he owes it to him. Not only because Jayson's his best friend but because he just risked his own life to save his ass.

"You remember when I slipped out of the lunchroom this afternoon, before Rickers could rip me a new one?"

"Yeah."

"Well, I paid Hex a visit in the control room."

"Uh-huh. So?"

"We were just shooting the shit like we normally do on my rounds, and that's when I spotted Klein talking to this mystery mafia man—just a real mean mobster-muggin' prick. You know, the kind of cartoon tough guy that looks like he considers good dental hygiene flossing with razor wire."

"You mean like Tony Soprano?"

"On steroids."

"Damn, okay. So, then what?"

"Well, I followed them up to the records floor. I just had this feeling in my gut that something wasn't right, you know? Especially coming fresh off Klein's bribe," Clayton recalls, gripping the steering wheel a tad tighter. "When I got up there, I spied on them talking and caught something about Rebecca Klein's file being untraceable, I think. I don't know. It was hard to hear everything over all the servers."

"Wait," Jayson chimes in. "Rebecca Klein as in Klein's former wife, Rebecca Klein?"

"Yeah."

"As in Trish's mom?"

"Yep."

"But she's been dead for like, ever, right?"

"Right."

"Like twenty-some-odd years or something, right?"

"Uh-huh."

"So, then what's she got to do with—"

"Jay, no offense but just shut the fuck up for a second, I'm trying to tell you," Clayton blurts out.

Hands in the air, Jayson defers. "Right. My bad. Go on."

"Anyway, something was said in their exchange that sounded like 'just like your wife,'" Clayton continues, repeating what he heard Marco blab. "So, after they left the room, I had Hex override the door's security lock and break into the database to pull her file."

"You did what? Clay, you know Hector just got off probation for hacking less than a year ago," Jayson scolds. "It's how he got the job in the first place—part of his make-good plea."

"I know, I know," Clayton admits, the guilt shaking his words. "I asked him for just the one—" There's a slight pause. "Okay, maybe it was two favors. But that's it. I didn't want to risk putting him in any more danger. But Jay, I had to find out what was going on. I mean, hell, the guy even had a gun. How'd he get it past security? Nothing, yet everything, was adding up to something. It was all way too smelly."

"Huh?" Jayson utters for clarification.

"Shit. I meant fishy."

"Oh." Jayson nods. "So, what did her file say?"

"Nothing." Clayton shrugs.

"What do you mean nothing?"

"Like, nothing."

"Like a *not what you were looking for* kind of nothing or—?"

"I mean like, fucking nonexistent file kind of nothing. It was almost completely blank other than some trivial personal information," Clayton clarifies.

Then, using the fingers on his free hand as a frustrated visual aid, he adds . . .

Thumb. "There was no record from the first responders on the scene."

Index. "No cause of death."

Middle. "No time of death or witnesses."

Ring. "No autopsy report."

Pinky. "Not a *goddamn* thing!"

He finishes counting and balls his trembling hand into a fist, striking the dashboard with an emotional exclamation.

"But Clay, that's not possible, man." Jayson eases in his rebuttal. "All records are direct copies pulled from central. The only way that could be feasible is if—" Ding. The reality of the thought clicks on like a lightbulb. "If someone who knew what they were doing altered her file from the inside."

"That's exactly what I thought."

"Okay, but how?"

"How what?"

"How do you find a file that doesn't exist?" Jayson asks, almost more of a rhetorical question to himself. "No file means no information. And no information means no case. And no case means good fucking luck."

"I know. It doesn't make sense. But I did find one thing that was kind of odd." Clayton digs for his phone. Striking digital gold in his jacket pocket. He pulls it out, taps the camera roll app, and hands it to Jayson. "When I clicked on her full report, no information surfaced, but it did prompt this weird message. I don't know, maybe it's nothing . . ."

Jayson cradles the phone, studying the photo.

ACCESS NOT AUTHORIZED
15276 Westport Sq., Suite C
Bannerton, IL 60411

Reading the random address triggers an old fuse in an area of his brain he thought had gone completely dormant. He dusts off the inactive canals and maps out the entire city like a 3D-rendered GPS in his visual cortex. Born and raised in the heart of Bannerton and employed as a delivery truck driver for nearly seven years before landing the security gig at The Hunt for Justice, Jayson knows this city in and out better than almost any man or machine.

Every major development.

Every urban sprawl.

Every obscure street and backroad like the back of his hand.

But this address. This specific street. He's never heard of it. It doesn't exist.

"Clay, this is a bogus address," he says, handing the phone back over.

"Wh-What do you mean bogus?"

"I mean bogus," he reiterates. "As in fake, not real, Santa Claus—pick one."

"What? But how?" Clayton deflates, the wind stripped from his sails. "That doesn't make any sense. Why would it be in her file then?"

"I don't know. For the same reason nothing else was? Because someone probably planted this."

"So, I'm screwed. Is that what you're saying?"

"Sorry man, I hate to break it to—"

But, before he finishes the sentence that will inevitably rip his buddy's sail clean off the mast, Jayson snatches back the phone. He analyzes the fake address again. Then, something unexpected clicks as the fuse in his brain regains even more power. Something vaguely familiar about the name, but not as a whole.

"Westport.

West-port.

West. Port." He repeats it again and again, breaking the name apart like a child learning syllables. All at once, flashbacks of his grade school social studies days deluge his memory. As the nostalgia kidnaps his thoughts, he recalls sitting in the back of Mrs. Snaudberry's classroom, catching wafts of her nose-turning cinnamon perfume as she would sashay between desks, the clickety-clack of her distinct walk in short-heeled, oversized clogs, and how she would annoyingly overcorrect anyone ad nauseum who would say "Can I" instead of "May I" when asking to go the restroom.

"I don't know, *can* you go to the restroom? Sounds like a personal problem to me," she would annoyingly tease every single time, for a joke that was never funny in the first place.

He also remembers the giant pull-out maps over the blackboard and having to painstakingly memorize useless state counties and every one of their cities. All these repressed memories come roaring back, including a reading on a chapter of the history of Bannerton's *West* Bottoms, which if his memory holds, served as the old stockyard and meatpacking *Port* for the expanding transcontinental railroad back in the late 1800s.

That's when it all starts to fit together, like the last few puzzle pieces of his childhood mind finding their rightful place. What if West-Port was a moniker for the long-forgotten West Bottoms and its old railroad port?

West *Bottoms*. Railroad *Port*.

West. Port.

Westport.

It may be a huge stretch but right now it's the best they've got. It's the only thing they've got.

"Holy shit," Jayson declares, nodding his head. "I think I might be onto something. Westport Square might be referring to the West Bottoms, which used to be the hub of the old stockyard railroad port. If this is real, and I'm still not totally sold that it is, it's got to be located somewhere in the old stockyard railroad district."

"Umm, Jay. I don't mean to burst your bubble of revelation, but there's nothing in the West Bottoms. Hasn't been for decades. It's a forgotten era, a goddamn ghost town. Like, literally," Clayton presses. "I'm pretty sure they do paranormal investigations down there."

"Hey, take it or leave it, man, but that's my educated guess," Jayson counters, sitting back in his seat, arms crossed. "Which last I checked is one more lead than what you've got."

He fishes out his phone from his pocket and takes a picture of the address on Clayton's phone with a snap from his own camera.

"And they do, by the way," he adds.

"Huh?" Clayton groans in response. "Who does what?"

"Paranormal investigations. They do ghost hunts and other spooky shit down there," Jayson continues, reconjuring the topic. "I took a date down there once because I thought a little night of fright might help get the libido right. You know, like a little apparition aphrodisiac. But instead, she got super freaked out and never returned any of my calls. Not even a text. She just returned my ghost tour favor by literally ghosting me back." A small grin finds its place across his lips. "Hmm. Makes a lot more sense now that I think about it."

He hates to admit it, but maybe Jayson's got a point—not about the ghosting but his lack of leads. Clayton has nothing to go on. Just a dead woman's empty file and the fact that Klein is a crazy, egomaniacal tyrant who will stop at nothing to save face and destroy him. Not to mention an entire city—a country even—that's about to be sold on the belief that he's a guilty, cold-blooded killer. Oh, and lest he forget, a horde of reinvigorated Justice Hunters, who he's sure are gaining precious ground on their escape party this very instant. The shudder of which makes him glance in the rearview to check if their tail is still clear.

"Look, Jay. I appreciate everything you've done to help me so far, but I can't drag you any further into this shit storm," he appeals to his friend. "I'm already in part responsible for losing Trish. I couldn't live with myself if you got arrested or hurt, too—or even worse, killed—just trying to help me."

Deep down, Jayson knows he's right. But what kind of friend would he be if he just stepped aside now and let the wolves have him?

"Clay, I'm only saying this because I love you, but fuck off," he states plainly, without hesitation. "I'm in this with you. So just accept it. Now, get off on the next exit. We need to swing by my place to get some things. Way I see it, you've got about thirty minutes—maybe an hour tops—before Klein and The Hunt for Justice have your Open Hunt photo planted across every nook and cranny in the city, and a fresh flock of drones out scanning every face in the streets looking for yours."

Clayton doesn't know what to say. He doesn't really need to say anything. It's all said in the silent exchange between their eyes and a subtle nod.

But, just for good measure, "Thanks, man," he adds.

"You'd do the same for me," Jayson states, rolling down the passenger-side window. "Now, first thing's first," he orders, and casually tosses Clayton's phone out the opening. It catches an 80-mile-per-hour gust of self-propelled highway wind and shatters upon impact with the blurred lines of the trailing interstate behind them.

Clayton's initial reflex is to lunge toward the passenger window in a far-too-late attempt at a rescue mission. "What the hell, man? My phone!" he shouts.

Jayson returns his whining with a blank stare.

"You know, Clay, for an ex-con, you're kind of a terrible criminal," he accuses, matter of factly. "Your phone is the first thing they're going to track."

Clayton sighs. Jayson's right and he knows it. But there's far more to it.

"It's not that, it's just—I had pictures on that phone. Texts from Trish. All our memories together." The realization that the love of his life is truly gone sinks in deeper than the shock. "I can't believe she's dead, Jay. What am I going to do without her? She was my whole world."

And that's when the question of all tempting questions snakes across his frail state of mind, hissing a whisper of hopelessness into his ear.

"Is all this even worth it?" he laments.

Jayson rears his head at the words of despair.

"Hey! Don't talk like that, you hear me? I know this is crushing, man. And I'm so, so sorry. I can't even fathom what you're feeling right now, and I won't pretend to," he sympathizes, sliding his hand atop Clayton's shrugged shoulders. "But her death will be for nothing if you end up dead, too. You've got to keep going. You gotta fight this . . . however you can. You feel me?"

Clayton hesitates at the question and ekes out a less-than-convincing nod.

It's hardly much but it's a good enough response for right now.

"All right, good. That's all I need," Jayson reassures. "But first, we've got to get you under the radar. Totally off-grid. Only I'm way out of my league here—a far cry from any criminal mastermind. Do you know anyone we can call? Anyone at all that could help?"

Despite his massive hesitation, Clayton knows the answer to Jayson's question immediately. He knows exactly who can help him lay low. Someone from his past life that he's all but forgotten. A life he swore he'd never go back to. He knows the answer. In fact, he's known for a while. He just doesn't like it. And he sure as hell doesn't want to accept it.

"Yeah," he sighs. "I do."

"Really? That's great. Who is it?"

"His name . . ." Clayton takes a reluctant deep breath. He pauses, then exhales with fledgling resolve like someone afraid to face their innermost demons.

"His name is Antoni Rivera. The man I almost killed."

# CHAPTER 16

Not only is Antoni Rivera probably the last person on earth who wants to see Clayton alive, but he just might be tied for first place with Klein on wanting to see him dead. Like Trish, Clayton has never told Jayson all the details surrounding his past life marred by youthful delinquency, a laundry list of bad decisions, and the regretful propensity of being in the wrong place at the wrong time—most of the time. It's not for a lack of Jayson trying, though. After the liquid liberation of a few beers, Jayson's favorite drunken pastime has always been to go fishing in Clayton's lake of lawlessness for any loose-lipped stories he could reel out. But some things are better left unsaid. Kept unknown, even among best friends.

That was then.

This is now.

Jayson sits silently in the passenger seat as they roll up to his house. As a precaution, Clayton flipped the headlights off a few blocks ago just in case any unwanted parties may be waiting for their arrival. He parks along the curb across the street and kills the ignition. The awkward silence lingers, amplifying the already quiet void that fills the car.

Jayson, who for once has used his ears tonight more than his mouth, breaks it.

"Just so I've got this straight . . . Rivera is the guy who sent you to prison?"

"Yeah," Clayton slips, reluctantly.

"A guy who you almost killed?"

"Yeah." Again, hesitant.

"The same guy that you now think is going to welcome the idea of helping you with open arms?"

"Yeeaahh?"

"Did you really just answer my question with a question?"

"Maaybeee?"

"You just did it again."

"Well, why are you asking so many damn questions?"

"Because someone has to! Because you're clearly not asking yourself the right ones," Jayson accuses, twirling his finger next to his temple. "Because you're talking batshit right now, man."

Clayton knows it, of course, he does. The whole thing sounds monumentally stupid, beyond a long shot. But it's the best idea he's got because it's the only idea he's got.

Jayson continues. "Man, Rivera's going to try to kill you the moment he sees you. Especially now, knowing that his long-awaited vengeance will be an act of justice under decree of The Hunt," he balks, emphatically making a strangling gesture with his hands to drive the point home. "You'd be nothing more than a stuffed pig with an apple in its mouth posing on a silver platter. Are you fucking crazy, Clay?"

"Look! There's more to the story than what I told you, all right," Clayton rebuts. "I know it sounds like a ridiculous suicide mission, but Rivera—he owes me."

"Owes you? For what, sending him a get-well card and a bouquet of roses while he was recovering in the ICU?"

Losing more and more patience from the ticking time they already can't afford, Clayton tries to squash the dispute with a different motive, the clock.

"Jay, we don't have time for all the details right now. We gotta keep moving. Just trust me on this one. Please?"

He flings open the car door and stomps out, a clear signal he's done arguing.

Jayson follows his lead.

The street is still. Almost too quiet. But they're not sure if it seems that way due to the added anxiety of their situation, or if it's just an unnaturally calm evening in the tucked-away neighborhood. Regardless, they pay extra heed, creeping across the street to Jayson's two-bedroom bachelor bungalow. After casing the place with a quick walk of the perimeter and a peek inside the exposed living room windows—thanks to Jayson who's never seen the return on investment for a set of curtains or blinds—they finally make for the front door.

The quiet quarters are even more eerie once they're inside. It's practically pitch dark in the house other than the soft, yellow hue from the streetlights out front, spilling in from the exposed windows.

Jayson reaches to turn on the end table lamp, but Clayton calls out in a raised whisper.

"No lights," he hushes, waving his hands for added measure. "Just in case."

Jayson nods and removes his hand from inside the canvas shade. He motions to Clay, pointing upstairs.

"Wait here. I'll grab us a change of clothes and some essentials."

Clayton gives him a thumbs up from across the room as Jayson tiptoes up the staircase. He's been over to Jayson's house at least a dozen or more times, but it's never felt more foreign than right now. The old house is already bachelor-barren, save for a few framed pictures hanging on the wall, an obnoxiously large flat-screen TV on a stand, brimming with the latest video games and their hardware, and a hand-me-down wool couch that laughingly fails to fill the void of the surprisingly spacious front room. But here, now in the dark, it feels desolate, lifeless—strangely unfamiliar.

Clayton makes his way around the haphazard excuse of a sofa to the solitary wall speckled with unlevel photo frames. He scans the stretch of eggshell-brushed drywall where portraits of Jayson's family break up the monotonous eight-foot section of off-white paint. Captured on film are photos of Jayson coaching his nephew's little league team, attending his younger brother's college graduation, and celebrating with his parents on their forty-fifth wedding anniversary cruise trip to the Caribbean.

Clayton's eyes stop when he gets to the last picture on the wall. A photo of Jayson, himself, and Trish toasting champagne flutes at last year's New Year's Eve party. He raises his hand to touch the captured memory of the woman he loved—and the child he lost—delicately caressing the outline of her figure with the pad of his index finger. A warm, salty teardrop catches his bottom lip. It's quickly accompanied by lemmings of others as his heart catches their ensuing undertow. It's drowned by a crushing wave of grief when he notices she's wearing the same backless white dress from tonight.

He can't help but hang his head and weep.

So much for being quiet.

It's the concentrated creak of bodyweight slinking back down the aged, wooden staircase that alerts him. At the first sound of Jayson's footsteps, he does his best to wipe the evidence from his eyes while turning around to face his descending friend. But it's too late. Jayson can see he's been crying from the way his sodden eyes twinkle in the moonlit darkness.

Not to mention he could hear his sobs from upstairs.

An overwhelming sorrow hangs in the reclaimed silence amid Jayson's helplessness. The thought that there's nothing he can do to mend his friend's suffering or make things right is—in itself—agonizing. This isn't like their past advice situations, easily hashed out over a twelve-pack of pilsners and a few strategically timed jokes. This is the ultimate grief. The worst kind of loss. All Jayson can do now is just hope and try to help preserve his future.

Jayson neatly places a pair of sneakers, jeans, and a t-shirt on the arm of the couch.

"Here, man, try these on," his voice almost muted. "Pants might be a little long, but they should fit your waist all right."

Clayton loosens his tie until he can slide it off without resistance from the tight double Windsor. He moves onto the buttons of his dress shirt, just now realizing that his hands are still caked in red splotches of clotted blood—Trish's blood. His emotions make another aggressive and abrupt push for the surface as he dashes for the kitchen sink, snapping the hot water handle back as far as the valve will go.

For longer than he should, he just stands there slouched with his hands on the counter and his head in the sink, letting the warm water stream down the drain like the tears from his eyes. He feels a soft hand rest on his shoulder while another one hands him a towel.

"Clay, I'm so sorry about Trish," Jayson confides, his voice faltering. "I know she was your world. She was my friend, too. I can only imagine what—"

"She was pregnant, Jay," Clayton interrupts between sighs, his face still overhanging the running farmhouse sink.

Jayson's face turns from needed support to utter despair. He fights for the words to make the situation right—or at least better in any way—anything he can do to console his friend. But they don't come. Nothing does. He just stands there with his hand on Clayton's shoulder as his best friend loses the battle against grief once again.

After another minute of mourning, Clayton regains his composure and accepts the towel from Jayson. He gently pats his face and dries his hands, tossing the soiled rag on the countertop next to a pile of days-old, dirty bowls and polished-off beer cans. Jayson directs him over to the kitchen table and they look at what's inside the backpack he hastily threw together upstairs in the dark. Clayton glimpses an LED flashlight, an old, sweat-stained ballcap, a small wad of cash tightly rolled in a rubber band, Jayson's phone and work radio, a rusty pocketknife, and a 9mm handgun.

He takes the gun out of the bag.

"I didn't know you had this," he says between fading sniffs.

"It was a Happy Birthday gift to myself a few years back," Jayson responds, adding a few protein bars and some bottled water from the pantry to the bag's cache. He snatches the gun from Clayton and checks the magazine and safety. "Turns out, a session at the range is a damn good stress reliever."

He plunges the pistol back into the bag as Clayton picks up the roll of cash. Reluctance paints his gaze, but Jayson cuts in before he can say anything about not feeling right by taking it.

"Don't. Just take it. I know it's not much, but it's all I've got on me." He tosses the money back inside the bag and zips it up. "What else do you think we need?" he asks.

Clayton thinks for a moment. He knows that every minute spent here is another minute closer to putting himself and his friend in danger.

"I think we're good, I just need to hit the head before we leave."

"Good thinking," Jayson agrees, handing Clayton the bag. "You can use the one by the front door, I'll go upstairs. But let's hurry. Only time for one shake, all right," he teases, in a feeble yet well-intentioned effort to lighten the mood.

Clayton nods and slings the backpack over his shoulder while Jayson tiptoes his way back upstairs again. Once he disappears around the wall of the second flight up, Clayton hurries over to the junk drawer, where thanks to many nights of heavy pre-drinking he knows Jayson keeps his assortment of keepsake bottle openers along with twist tied bundles of outdated charging cords, neglected pocket lighters in a rainbow of colors, and a random assortment of one-off Allen wrenches and their corresponding screws. The kind that comes with cheap pre-assembled furniture that people aren't sure whether to keep or throw away after assembly, so they just uselessly toss them in their junk drawers.

After rummaging through the crammed pull-out box, he finds what brought him there in the first place—Jayson's stash of office pens. He blindly grabs one of The Hunt for Justice gels, ignoring the current irony behind it, and rips off a paper towel from the countertop spool.

Jayson makes his way back down the stairs in a silent hurry, this time his scuffling feet sounding more like a muffled tap dance routine off the wooden planks.

"Clay, you ready, man? Let's hit the—"

Before he even gets to the bottom landing, he can feel it. That unconscious sixth sense that lingers when a room is completely empty, void of any life. He heads toward the kitchen with an odd leisure behind his stroll because he already knows. Even among the organized chaos of clutter that adorns his cup-ringed dinner table, he immediately sees the note.

*Jay,*
*I love you like a brother. That's why I can't risk you getting any more involved in this. Don't worry about me. I've got a plan. Thanks for everything.*
*-Clay*

*P.S. It's called cleaning. You should try it. No wonder you can't keep a girl.*

Jayson shakes his head as a tiny smirk twists his upper lip.

Quick to connect the dots, he looks to the front door that's been strategically left just ajar. He knows the car is already gone. There's no point in checking. Or chasing after.

He walks over and casually shuts the door. As he turns around, he softly bangs the back of his head against the old mahogany, tilting his chin into a position reminiscent of prayer—of hope.

"That son of a bitch," he murmurs aloud. "Be careful out there, buddy."

# CHAPTER 17

Clayton zips down the surrounding, moon-washed neighborhood streets, running through four-way stops like they're mere yield signs. About two miles from Jayson's house, he catches a pair of high beams in his rearview making a left turn onto the road behind him.

His first inkling—he's screwed. But he quickly curbs the panic with his second thought—a sharp right at the next intersection.

As he cuts the corner, he looks back to see if the trailing car imitates. Its lights temporarily sway out of his reflective center rectangle but land back into frame a moment later. If they're not following him, they're coincidently taking the same route while maintaining the perfect distance. Enough to make it feel suspect.

An escape plan evades his thoughts just when he needs it most.

How could they have found him so fast? His getaway wasn't flawless by any means, but he thought he'd bought himself at least a little more cushion. Then, it clicks. Totally obvious, really. He's driving Sean's security car, of course, it's being tracked.

"Shit. How could I be so stupid?" he berates himself, and slams his hands on the steering column.

Truth is, it's simple. His mind's not right, far from it. In fact, it's completely fucked. He just lost everything he holds dear, and now he's on a frantic run for his life for something he didn't do. There's nothing but a dense, dark haze engulfing every inch of logic in his scattered brain.

"Think, think, think," he repeats. His voice aggressive, tone panicked.

It hits him like a lightning bolt in the brainstorm that's raging upstairs.

There's a cemetery just a couple blocks south. If he can make it there without drawing any more attention, he's pretty sure he can lose just one car. But if this nightmare of a day has taught him anything, it's that nothing is going to be that easy.

Right on cue, after rehearsing his Día de Muertos-inspired game plan, two more cars join the pursuit, cruising closely behind his original trailer. What was just a game of cat and mouse is now officially a Hunt party.

All four vehicles methodically continue toward the cemetery in a single-file line, inadvertently forming their own funeral procession. Clayton may be scared shitless—fear, front and center, feasting on his psyche—but the sadistic symbolism doesn't go unnoticed.

As he pulls into the main entrance, the weathered and rusted-out cast-iron arch above him reads Vigor Gardens Cemetery—eternal residence to one of Bannerton's biggest boneyards. The front half of the memorial park is lined with a freckled array of modest single, double, and family plots with granite monuments ranging from simple date-of-birth to date-of-death headstones and conservative floral bouquets to far more extravagant statues and decorated marble tombstones fitted with bronze planters and full arrangements. Many bear the usual clichéd scripture passages inscribed upon their recently tended plaques. Toward the back of the cemetery, Clayton notices a labyrinth of imposing mausoleums surrounded by spectacular sculptures and flowing fountains that are all gated off from the rest of the foremost plots.

He checks the rearview again to see the convoy uniformly turn into the same gated entrance, itching for him to make the first move.

"Well . . ." he sighs. "Guess it's now or never."

He guns the gas, hurling the car on a collision course with the gated section of private mausoleums. The peeling wheels spit up chunks of earth and rock before ripping the old, rusted entryway from its haggard hinges upon impact. Once through, he slams on the brakes and kills the engine. Using it as a makeshift blockade, the car serves no further purpose. The only way in now is over the hatchback or scaling the ten-foot-tall, speared iron fence. He snatches the backpack from the passenger seat and takes off down the stretching labyrinth of the dead, trying his best not to join them.

It doesn't take long before he hears the slamming of car doors and shouting of men in the distance as he scurries through the maze of graves in a dead sprint, depleting his lungs with every thrilling stride. Beams of light from their flashlights bounce around the marbled indigo and onyx horizon behind him like haunted spirits in the night. He checks the mausoleum doors as he runs by each isolated crypt, but none budge. The old locks are still doing their due diligence decades, even centuries, after construction.

Which gives him an idea—distraction.

He stops dead in his tracks and quickly unzips Jayson's bag to dig for the gun. Even after all these years, the weight and cool touch of the steel feels all too familiar. Back on the run, he flips his grip and uses the butt of the firearm as a miniature battering ram to smash the lock of the nearest catacomb.

Then, the next one.

And the next one, as he continues to zigzag his way down the network of monuments, adding in a busted window here and there to further throw off their trace. He can hear his pursuers barking conflicting directions at one another, inaccurately instructing the rest of the group where they think he is based on the disconnected cacophony. It may be a cemetery, but there'll be no resting in peace tonight.

One man shouts out, "I heard him go into one of the big tombs over there!"

To which another man replies, "I think he's in that one."

And another. "No, he went in this one."

His plan seems to be working, but for how long? He needs an escape route, and fast. He picks up a palm-sized rock and chucks it thirty yards ahead as it ricochets off a large stone slab. He watches as the flashlights all turn in unison to examine the clack. Under the blanket of night and the pitter-patter beat of the park's water fountains, Clayton doubles back as his Hunters aimlessly push ahead to investigate the faux source.

Void of breath and heart racing, he makes it back to the mausoleum's entrance gate before spotting two men unenthusiastically standing lookout. Their half-hearted gaze lazily surveys the surrounding scene.

Upon closer inspection, they're nothing more than a couple of boys—barely teenagers—and based on their topic of conversation and the anxiety surrounding it, they've most likely been dragged here by their parents' misplaced desire for justice.

"You see anything?" asks the boy in a backward ballcap, his delivery as timid as his nervous demeanor.

His friend, who's wrapped in a hoodie and slouched against the grill of a pickup, responds, "Josh, for the last time, I haven't seen shit. I can't see anything. It's too fucking dark." There's no hint of timidness in his voice, just pure indifference. Like he'd rather be doing anything else, anywhere else than here.

"Dude, this sucks," Josh continues, finding some of his misplaced nerves. "How did we get stuck standing lookout anyway? I didn't even want to come. I was playin' video games, just about to beat the final boss in *Altered War* when—"

"Wait. Didn't you already beat that game?" asks Mr. Nonchalant in the hoodie.

"Yeah, but I'm replaying it in Insanity Mode."

With no subtlety obscuring his mockery, "Wow, man, that's like totally *insane* . . ."

"Pshh, shut up, Kale," he fires back, adding in a middle finger for good measure. "You couldn't even make it halfway through on regular difficulty."

"You're right. Because that game sucks, Josh."

"More like you suck at it." They both snicker, breaking one another's balls like grade schoolboys on the playground. And, in all honesty, not too far removed from one.

There's a slight pause before Josh, the ballcap kid's, next exchange.

"So, what'd this guy do anyway?"

"Murdered his wife, apparently," Kale, the boy in the hoodie responds. "At least that's what my dad said on the way here."

"Damn, man, that's pretty messed up."

Kale straightens up from leaning against the truck's hood. "You want to know the really messed-up part?"

"What's that?"

"They didn't even try him."

"Wait, what?!" Josh interrobangs, a newfound interest transitioning his tone. "But that's not, like, legal. Is it?"

"Hell no, it's not," Kale replies, adding fresh fervor where there was none just seconds ago. "But when has any of this Hunt stuff ever felt legal?" He goes back to lackadaisically leaning against the hood of the truck. "Or right?"

Clayton's heard about all he needs to make his next move. He realizes the extreme level of potential idiocy in the ensuing decision, but he's got a good feeling about it despite his exceedingly dreary shitstorm of a night.

He walks out slowly with his hands up from behind the monument where he was eavesdropping. The kids snap to attention, raising their guns to take aim, but the crosshairs are anything but steady in their shy hands.

The boy in the ballcap speaks out, his words more trepid than before, "S-s-top right there, m-man."

Clayton continues his advancement forward, just slower.

"Look, kid, I'm not here to hurt you and I didn't kill anyone," he replies, continuing his tactic of calm persuasion. "It's a long story that I clearly don't have time to get into, but I've been set up. And now I'm being Hunted for it."

Kale cocks his shotgun in a brash façade of bravado.

"He said don't move, asshole." But again, the hands brandishing the double barrel tremble, exposed by the quivering muzzle.

Clayton inches on unfazed, after all his dumb plan hasn't gotten him killed yet. Even slower still, he persists.

"The love of my life was just taken from me. Murdered, and all I could do was watch her last breath flee her body as I held her in my arms. My whole world is in fucking shambles. So, if you're going to shoot me, then just shoot me already. Otherwise, let me pass. Please, I don't have much time."

The two boys exchange anxious glances at each other as Clayton finally comes to a stop a mere foot shy from the mouths of their guns. He can tell they're conflicted. It's what he hoped for. Even in this new world's messed-up name of justice, getting one's hands bloody for a first kill is easier said than done.

He takes another step forward.

They counter by repositioning themselves and their sights at shaky attention, fingers wavering over the triggers like a prepubescent onset of Parkinson's. Another small step closer and Clayton's chest makes contact with the steel of their outstretched barrels.

"You guys don't want to do this," he declares, nudging the pointed barrels away with delicate fingertips like he's using the Force on two, rookie over-their-heads Storm Troopers. "Just let me go. Please."

The teens swap another despairing look between themselves. A whole conversation is told with just their eyes. Without uttering a single word, a decision is made. They have no intention to kill tonight, maybe ever. So, they lower their guns and step apart. Clayton seizes the invitation, sliding between them with his hands still up.

Once he's a few feet past the boys, he turns around and nods.

"Thank you," he says. "You guys did the right thing. Trust me."

Again, he takes off running into the jaws of night as the darkness closes in around him, swallowing him whole.

Fleet of foot, Clayton safely makes his way out of the cemetery hunting grounds and through the surrounding neighborhood. Within a few minutes, he's back onto the main city block. He removes one of the backpack straps from his shoulder, digging inside to grab the ballcap Jayson packed—a black trucker hat featuring a leather patch with an embossed steering wheel, the logo of Transport Brewery, Jayson's favorite local watering hole, coincidently just stumbling distance from his house.

It should blend in nicely.

As he wriggles it on and rounds the corner, his legs freeze like they've sunken into wet cement. Across the major intersection, it's like he's looking at himself in a skyscraper-sized mirror. Plastered for the whole city to see is a larger-than-life headshot of himself on an animated billboard with a giant OPEN SEASON: WANTED FOR MURDER flashing below his picture. He's seen wanted people on these billboards often over the years, but it hits differently seeing his own face.

Once he takes a moment to fully process the surreal reality of the situation, he tucks his chin down and lowers the bill of the cap, praying it's enough protection to conceal his alter ego from any prying eyes or facial recognition cameras scattered about the area. He can also hear the collective hum from dozens of patrolling drone propellers, prowling along the shrouded skies above. He gets in about five steps before the billboard screen cuts to a live recording of Klein, fresh on the scene at the convention center.

He does his best to keep an even stride and not look up.

"*Fellow citizens of Bannerton,*

*Tonight, we mourn a murder in our great city. The first in a long time within our dear community. And while we have, and must, remain diligent in our Hunt for Justice, tonight's particular death has me aghast. Shook to my very core. Earlier this evening, my own beloved daughter, Patricia Klein, was shot and killed before my very eyes. Murdered in cold blood at the hands of her own partner, Clayton Sparks. A man she loved. A man she trusted.*"

Clayton doesn't have to watch the feed to see that any morsel of sorrow Klein personally felt from the loss of his daughter has already perished, ensnared in a fresh web of lies. He talks about Trish's death using a heavy dose of emotional vocabulary, but there's no sincerity felt behind the hollow words.

The recording continues.

"*As head of The Hunt Initiative and a loving father, I address you all tonight, not only to plead for the justice of my daughter, whose spirit left her while I held her in my arms—the same way I brought her into this world. But to make you an offer. To sweeten the pot of righteousness. For the first time in Hunt Initiative history, I'm offering a reward for exercising our right—our civic duty—to ensure justice is duly served. I pledge $500,000 to the man or woman who brings me Clayton Sparks. Alive, preferably. Dead, if necessary. Let us mourn not what we have lost but celebrate what we have yet to gain. Let The Hunt begin.*"

The live recording ends and Clayton's wanted photo retakes the screen, now flashing the new bounty at the bottom of the image like an updated ticker feed. As if things couldn't get any worse—they just did.

Now he's not only on the run from die-hard Justice Hunters, he's on the run from anyone and everyone looking to cash in on a lucrative payday. He checks his watch. It's 10:36 p.m. He knows where he needs to go. But getting there isn't going to be easy, especially without a set of wheels. Trish's car is trapped at the convention center feeding grounds, and she had the keys, so that's no good. He can't take the metro because the fingerprint scanner will instantly detect him. And walking? Out of the question. It's too far and too dangerous with all the city's targeted surveillance.

Luckily, he knows a thing or two about how to jack a car. And here he thought his past life of crime would come back to haunt him. Maybe even kill him.

The reality is it might just save his life.

Clayton hoofs it south a few risky blocks just outside the heart of the city, sticking to side streets and dimly lit alleyways through the older, and consequently, poorer neighboring developments. Once he finds a strip of street dark and quiet enough to conceal his future misdeeds, he gets to work, checking every door handle on the line of parked cars that hug the curb.

Anxiously, he narrates the ride robbery with hushed car-to-car commentary.

"Locked."

"Too new."

"Locked."

"Way too new."

"Too Gross."

"Locked again."

"Will that even run?"

Finally, after what feels like fifty cars . . .

"Bingo," he whispers, gently cracking open the unlocked driver door of a late 90s midnight blue Jeep Grand Cherokee.

Maintaining enough discretion to camouflage his excitement, he quietly slinks into the sub-millennium SUV and wastes no time dipping into his bag of tricks and soon-to-be transgressions. Slinging his pack into the passenger seat, he unzips it, ruffling to find Jayson's gun and small pocketknife—an old-timey, grandpa-wielding blade with enough dinge on the steel that it looks as if it's been neglectfully passed down at least three generations or more. The edge is so dull that a cold stick of butter would give it a good fight.

Fortunately, the only sharpness he needs for this job lies in the acuity of his grand theft recollection. After all, he hasn't hotwired a car in nearly fifteen years.

Again, he uses the butt of the gun as a makeshift hammer and drives the knife into the ignition column while turning it like a key. He knows the piercing force will likely ruin the ignition cylinder, but he can't argue with its effectiveness, especially on cars manufactured before the millennium. He cranks the knife to the right, but the car won't turn over. Not a peep.

He sighs, cursing to himself under his breath. "Shit, so much for the easy route."

Method two is going to require a little more time and a couple more tools that he doesn't have on hand. But this Jeep is old enough and based on the assortment of blue-collar belongings that litter the back seat, including a worn pair of work boots, a grungy flannel shirt, and a dusty hard hat with an accompanying pair of safety glasses, he's betting there's a small toolbox somewhere in the trunk's floor storage.

He army-crawls over the cluttered backseat and peers into the open trunk space. It's even more of a mess than the rest of the car. Soiled blankets, more dirty clothes, random camping gear, and a dented blue and white six-pack cooler lay between him and where he needs to get. So, he digs, flinging everything over the back seat like a dog shoveling dirt in pursuit of its buried prize.

Once he can see a hint of the floor, he lifts up the under-storage pull tab and peeks inside. Dust explodes from its resting place, further polluting the dingy space in a haze of freckled light from the streetlamp across the road. It's nearly pitch dark inside the floor storage, but he can make out the spare tire, its corresponding jack and lug wrench, and a small black bag with yellow trim wedged in the corner.

"Bingo," he says, again.

Keeping his fingers crossed, he reaches for the bumble bee bag and unzips it. His struggle with the stiff zipper is a clear indicator that its contents haven't seen the light of day in years. Finally, he finagles it open, stripping away all the bite from its plastic teeth. Inside the dusty tote, he finds a set of rusty jumper cables, a dead flashlight, two sets of water-damaged flares, a rudimentary first aid kit, and a blue, eight-by-ten-inch roll-up tool case.

Reverently, he pulls apart the Velcro on the case. Tucked neatly inside the bare-essentials kit lies several core tools—pliers, wire cutters, a tire gauge, etc.—but his eyes light up when he spots exactly what he's looking for—a simple Phillips-head screwdriver.

A second wind floods his spirit. It carries a gust of something he hasn't felt in a while. Something almost foreign. The feeling of hope.

With the tool case in tow, he flings himself back into the front seat and gets to it, wasting no time taking out the screws from the steering column's top and bottom panels first. After all the screws are removed, he goes back to work on the plastic panel with the knife, peeling it apart like mechanical skin to expose the ignition cylinder and its corresponding cluster of cabled innards.

Studying the wiry guts in the soft haze of the nearby streetlamp, he identifies the two red battery wires responsible for distributing power to the car and a single brown wire connected to its starter. He rifles back through the tool case and fishes out the pair of wire cutters. A couple careful snips later and the two red battery lines are liberated from the cylinder.

It doesn't take long before his neglected hotwiring skills start surging back to him. Somehow still auto-programmed into his muscle memory like riding a bike. Or in this case, stealing one.

Next, he moves on to stripping the ends of the battery wires with the cutter. Once the plastic sheathing is removed, exposing their inner wirings, he kisses them together and twists. A jolt of electricity shoots life throughout the sleeping vehicle illuminating its headlights and dash lights, along with rousing the radio and several other of the Jeep's thirty-plus-year-old electrical components.

"Shit!" he shouts, caught off guard by the car's sudden attempt to stir from its parked slumber.

He's exposed himself now. The time to escape undetected, if it wasn't ticking already, is now racing toward the buzzer.

He double times the pace, stripping the brown starter wire with the same technique, only faster, and carefully touches the now exposed live end to the already braided pair of power wires. The new jolt from the electrical pulse sends a wake-the-fuck-up call to the snoozing spark plugs. He hears the crankshaft purr and turn but not all the way over.

He tries again, frantically muttering under his breath, "C'mon, c'mon."

It stutters, but it's still not quite enough movement. He starts to panic again as a wave of nervous sweat dribbles down from his scalp to his lips. Its saltwater disturbance tastes like desperation.

He tries a third time. Each audible plea growing louder with every cough from the ignition.

"Just start already, you piece of shit! Just fucking—"

*VROOM! VROOM!*

The car gives a drawn-out chug before finally revving to sustained life. He quickly grabs the wheel with purpose and applies a steady amount of pressure to the gas pedal.

"HA! Hell yeah," he lets out, in a hopeful hush.

Instantly, in a move that falls somewhere in the category of hasty but not reckless, he's on the move again.

About a quarter mile down the road, he calculates how long it will be until the jacked car is reported stolen. If everything goes right, which has been a far cry from today's ill-fated theme of events, it likely won't be called in until sometime early tomorrow morning.

Whenever Construction Carl tries to leave for work only to be greeted with the expletive-filled awakening of his car mysteriously not being where he last parked it. That means Clayton's got at least eight hours, ten tops; plenty of time to get to where he needs to go, then ditch the car.

Hurtling down the road, the needle on the speedometer teases the threshold of bending the law but not breaking it—just slow enough to avoid being pulled over, but fast enough to make the left lane feel like home. He passes a series of billboards lining the highway advertising his wanted picture and the reward money Klein anted up earlier. The price is up to $600,000 now, as if every hour he's on the loose adds another $50K to the appetizing pot. He bets it'll be well over a million by sunrise.

But morning is a long time from now, so it's best he counts his wins while he's still got them. A quick recap in his head tallies narrowly yet successfully escaping from a horde of Justice Hunters—not only once, but twice, tonight—safely ditching Jayson for his own damn good, and coming out of retirement to swipe a fresh set of wheels undetected. He thinks maybe his luck is actually headed for the better.

The comforting thought is short-lived.

Out of nowhere, he spots the red and blue lights of a checkpoint about a mile ahead. Four lanes of seventy-mile-per-hour freeway being siphoned into a single, strangled line of standstill traffic as Hunt for Justice patrol workers and the local Bannerton police ID every person and search every set of wheels choking their way out of town through the city's exit.

More bad fucking luck.

Clayton follows suit, merging over into the middle lane where cars are zippering in from left and right like a waddle of ducks failing to find the order of a single row. His palms immediately begin to clam up as he starts searching every corner of his mind for an intelligent way out, talking aloud to see if anything he's saying even remotely passes as believable.

"Shit, shit—fucking shit," he blurts, trying to shift his brain into gear. "Okay. They're going to ask for your ID first," he adds, starting a full-on conversation with himself.

"But of course, you can't give them your ID, can you?"

"Not unless you want a bullet in your forehead."

"Nope, hard pass." He shakes his head. "So then what?"

"Well, they'll probably stare you dead in the eye judging you with the guiltiest of glares and demand your registration."

"Right . . . exactly!"

That's when the thought hits him. He lunges at the Jeep's glove box and dives in, rummaging for any form of identification or paperwork he can find. He comes back with nothing but a bag of unopened potato chips, a tattered owner's manual, and a fat stash of random fast-food napkins.

But wait.

Tucked in the back, underneath a way-past-when asthma inhaler is a folded-up manilla envelope with the word REGISTRATION attentively chicken-scratched in all caps across the top. He snatches the neglected packet and can hardly wait to open it, quickly sliding his thumb under the no longer sticky flap.

Only inside it's like all the rest of his luck today, shit out of.

"You gotta be fucking kidding me," he balks and throws the empty envelope back inside the compartment, slamming the lid shut while that glint of hope takes yet another tarnished turn in the wrong direction.

"Another swing and a miss," he utters, and moves to the center console, lifting the armrest to find a work lanyard with a Dondlinger & Sons Construction ID badge for a "Timothy Phelts" inside. He studies the face on the badge. Other than the fact that Tim probably outweighs him by fifty pounds or more, with ten of those being carried in his blubbery cheeks alone, the resemblance is actually pretty close—age in the same ballpark, same dirtyish blond hair at a similar length, patchy facial hair, blue eyes.

"Holy shit, this just might work," he assures himself, going over the checklist in his head.

But he's going to need to sell it.

He reaches into the back seat pigsty and grabs a pile of Tim's work gear. He frantically puts the soiled flannel shirt and loose goggles on, swapping out the brewery ballcap for the hard hat.

Continuing the conversation with himself, he talks out the next sequence of events.

"Okay, so I've got an ID," he says, trying to focus on one detail of his fabricated story at a time. "It's not a driver's license but it's something to work with. What next?"

"Where are you headed, sir?" he asks himself, imitating the patrol unit.

"Where *am* I headed?" he repeats, hoping to form a better answer than the lack of one buzzing around in his attic.

"Umm, I'm working the graveyard shift, Officer," he continues, buying into his own lie one detail at a time.

"Yeah, yeah. We just broke ground on a new development out south by—uhh, out there by Pine Grove." The story further taking shape. "Yeah, the boss has been really riding us to get the site underway, and I accidentally left my wallet on-site—in my excavator. We've been busting our asses but we're already at least a week behind schedule. Gotta love those lax government deadlines."

Another thought zooms across his racing mind. He takes Jayson's backpack and empties the protein bars and water bottles onto the passenger seat.

He thinks aloud again.

"What next?" he asks, his mind going to a scary scenario he hadn't thought of. "Are they gonna fingerprint scan me? Because I'm fucked if they do."

He hopes it won't come to that. Anything but that. The thought dwells as he continues to reluctantly inch forward in line. Drawing parallels to the fact that it's the very same line his whole life now hangs on. He counts only a handful of cars ahead of him, but the rigor of the searches he's witnessed in waiting so far doesn't bode well for his already faulty confidence.

*What if they run the plates on the Jeep*? Again, thinking of the worst possible scenarios.

*Hopefully, my guess that it won't be reported stolen until the morning pans out and they'll discover it's clean.*

He edges closer to the front. Two cars idle between him and his possible fate. There's no turning back now. He grabs the gun from the open bag and places it in the driver's door cup holder. A last resort, just in case.

When he finally reaches the front of the line, he does his best to casually roll down his window as a stocky and stern-faced, seasoned patrolman waddles up to the vehicle. Clayton's heart pounds heavier and harder with the rhythm of the officer's encroaching steps. If he were attached to a polygraph machine, the needles would be ripping through the paper right now.

The officer reaches the Jeep's driver-side window and affirmatively places his hand on the open sill. Immediately, he asks for Clayton's driver's license—straight to business, the hell with any pleasantries. The prepped response spills out of Clayton's mouth just like he rehearsed. Better, even.

"Sorry, this is a bit embarrassing, Officer . . ." he confesses, looking over at the patroller's badge ". . . Thomlin. But I accidentally left my wallet in my excavator this morning. I took it out because I hate sittin' on that damn thing all day. Doc said it's not good for my back. Got a bad sacrum. I've been trying to lose weight to help relieve some of the pain, but I got that damn sweet tooth, you know? Of course, you would know, a little donut never hurt a cop, amirite?" he jokes, behind a full mouth of clenched white.

Only the jest doesn't land in person as well as it does in Clayton's head because Officer Thomlin's lips fail to even flinch.

"Ahem. Well, anyway, we just broke ground on a new state-of-the-art apartment complex out south in Pine Grove, and the boss has been riding the shit out of us to get the site underway. Working pretty much non-stop 'round the clock." He gestures to the pile of food and water surplus in the passenger seat. "I'm practically living out of this damn thing. Not even enough time to grab lunch most days. Although, I gotta say it's done wonders for the ol' waistline. Yeah, I may be here physically, but my mind—" Clayton makes a fluttering motion with his finger while whistling, "Well, it's anywhere but. Guess all work and no sleep will do that to you. But who am I kiddin'? I'm probably preaching to the choir right now."

Clayton puts the finishing flair on his bullshit story and sits back to see if the officer bought all of it, or any of it. If his heart could talk right now, he'd already be dead.

Officer Thomlin simply gives him another blank look as he cranes his neck through the open window to look around inside the car. He cases the backseat through the passenger glass and then reverts his attention back to Clayton, ready to speak but Clayton cuts him off.

"Uh, like I said, I don't have my license, Officer, but I do have my work badge. If you'd like to see that. And you can run my plates." He hands over the lanyard and ID to the officer, praying for the best. Officer Thomlin studies the badge with eagle eyes, hunting for anything awry. For Clayton, each studied second feels like an eternity. The officer's head doesn't move but his eyes finally resurface, peering up from the badge to give Clayton a twice over.

"You mind taking off your hard hat, sir?"

"Not at all. Forget I even have the damn thing on half the time," Clayton jokes, still fishing for that elusive laugh. A smile. Any fucking emotion from the robotic T-1000, but none is reciprocated. He combs down his hair to shroud as much forehead and face as he can.

The officer again goes back to scrutinizing the badge and his face. Clayton watches helplessly as Thomlin's eyes dance between the two. Back and forth, to and fro—like the tick-tock of a quick clock. Inside Clayton's chest, the muffled metronome begins to pound, raging like

*The Tell-Tale Heart* as his thoracic floorboards hiding the truth thump faster than a pair of African bongos. He's sweating profusely from the inside out, using every inch of fleeting cool he has left in his flushed body to stop from hyperventilating.

The officer finally speaks up, "I'll be back."

Clayton gives him a calm nod but exhales a giant gasp of desperation as soon as the officer turns away. The internal tension is anaconda-tight. He can feel his insides suffocating while his sweat glands continue to swell and spew like a sieve.

He wipes his brow with Tim's raggedy XL flannel sleeve, but it's instantly a sponge again. Watching hopelessly from the car he's just stolen, Clayton's eyes home in on every detail of Officer Thomlin's actions as he sits in his squad car and types with determined diligence on his MDC. A second female officer with short, auburn hair and an overcompensating walk approaches Thomlin's squad car. The two exchange a few words before they both turn their gaze directly at Clayton. He forces a smile back and then turns his head toward the windshield, watching them anxiously through his periphery with his best *Cool Hand Luke* impression.

Thomlin directs the female officer elsewhere while he makes his way back toward Clayton.

Foolish thoughts of escape enter his mind. Just flooring it won't get him far. They'd be on his tail in seconds—the chase over before it ever began. Then, he remembers the gun in his driver-side door. He reaches down and nestles its L-shape into a mirrored form with his left hand, flipping off the safety.

Officer Thomlin parks at Clayton's window yet again, his face as stoic as ever. He reaches his hand inside the stolen Jeep as Clayton eases the hammer back.

"Here's your badge back, Mr. Phelts," he says, passing Clayton the ID. "Sorry about the wait. Just had to run your name and tags. You're free to go."

Clayton fights with all his might to steady his quivering right hand

and accept the badge. With a slight hiccup in his voice, he responds, "Th-thank you, Officer."

Officer Thomlin nods and waves him on before turning around to engage the next car in line.

A pour of shock and adrenaline with a garnish of reprieve courses through Clayton like a shot without a chaser. He sits idled in disbelief, feeling like he just pulled off the impossible. He starts to roll up his window when Thomlin turns back around, his hand halting the pane.

"Mr. Phelts!" Clayton freezes.

"My old man worked in construction for Bannerton. Slaved away for nearly thirty years before he retired, so I get it. But don't forget your license next time. This is your only warning, all right?"

Clayton doesn't even realize it as his raises in a gesture of accord.

Then, he slides the car back in Drive and accelerates. Within seconds, the checkpoint scene is nothing but a distant memory in his rearview. The worst part is, it's not even the scariest encounter he's had—or expects to have tonight.

# CHAPTER 19

About an hour and a half past the close-call checkpoint, Clayton's stomach starts to growl. It's just after midnight; he hasn't had anything to eat or drink aside from a couple of fancy, unfulfilling finger foods and a roulette of alcoholic beverages several hours ago. He reaches across the passenger seat and grabs one of the protein bars. Freeing the stale peanut butter chocolate chip rectangle from its astronaut-inspired cellophane, he takes a bite. It tastes like chalk covered in thick wax paper.

"Ugh," he groans. "How do you eat this shit, Jay?"

Reluctantly, he takes another bite. He's so hungry, he doesn't care what it tastes like going down. This is a results-based dining session. Halfway through choking down the space food, he remembers the bag of potato chips in the glove box. He fishes them out and uses both hands to rip open the bag, careful to avoid a fried sodium confetti accident all over the front seat. They're just plain, boring potato chips but compared to the poop-dried protein bar, they hit the spot better than an inmate on death row's last meal. He knows it's a poor analogy for his current situation, but he doesn't care. He just keeps popping the salty coins into his mouth until the sodium overload hits.

He snatches one of the water bottles from the pile and twists off the cap. He's beyond dehydrated from tonight—all the alcohol, the running, the waterworks—they've depleted his internal tank. He just hasn't had a chance to notice. But when the rush of water hits his mouth, it's like fresh rain on the desert floor. There's no hesitation as he chugs the rest of the bottle.

On the quiet, late-night highway, the dotted lines blur into one while he passes the exit for Pierce Street. The surrounding suburban plains are all tucked in bed under a blanket of obscurity. Only faint lights in the distance from the occasional houses and pocketed towns break up the black backdrop. Even though he can't see anything, he's close.

As his exit looms, so too does the familiar rumbling sensation in his stomach. Only it's not hunger this time. It's unease. Everything he's gone through to get here tonight just might pale in comparison to his next move. Something he's been absolutely dreading since the crazy idea first crossed his mind.

He takes the next off-ramp and works his way through the lower south side of the quaint, outer Bannerton burb. He hasn't been out here in ages. Even still, the town is a spitting image of what it looked like a decade-plus ago.

The humble chapel on the corner of Hill Street and Vine still offers its curbside community bookshelf exchange. Only its free library selection is threadbare and more than picked over now. A little further down, the basketball goals outside his old elementary still rock the same chain link nets and concrete courts, plagued with a little more rust and cracks than he remembers. It's where he first picked up a ball, and the last place he ever played.

The school itself looks to have fallen on even harder times. Even under nightfall's curtain, the once lush landscaping looks to be nothing more than stretches of clumped dirt and sporadic patches of intrusive weeds. Several of its two stories worth of windows appear darker than others against the nocturnal canvas—either broken out or boarded up. And the Raider Elementary marquee out front seems to be supported by a makeshift two-by-four leg on one side. The unsteady rig serves as a crude interim solution for its current students and a less-than-stellar welcome for any future generation.

All of it is more than likely fresh fallout from cut district budgets inflicted by the nation's leeching legislation and a lack of community funding. In this new America, every available state dollar seems to funnel directly into the lined pockets of The Hunt Initiative and the One percent. Just another price people are willing to pay for the promise of justice. Or the fear of opposing it.

Clayton continues his childhood reunion tour passing by the old drive-in, an American relic perfectly preserved in the Polaroid of time. Its long-standing truss screen, a tad patchier and not so white anymore, along with only a handful of surviving speakers map the nostalgic gravel lot. It's where he lost his virginity when he was sixteen to Lindsey Gardner in the back seat of his dad's station wagon during a revival showing of *Halloween*. It was sometime in the fall, right around the actual holiday. Nothing like a babysitter-slaying serial killer in a white spray-painted William Shatner mask to really get the teenage libido going.

He remembers that once he finally found the nerve to make his move that brisk October night—the sex was great. Better than great, actually. After all, what first time for a horny, hormone-raging teenage boy isn't?

Done right or not.

Long or short.

Orgasm or none.

Doesn't matter.

However, his dad finding the used condom and half-empty bottle of Southern Comfort tucked under the back seat the next day—not so great.

Even further along his trip down memory road, Clayton spots the old corner ballpark off Coleman Avenue. It's the same rundown sandlot where he used to spend nearly every summer in his pre-teens shagging balls and every Friday night in his actual teens getting hammered. A few rows of sun-faded, pine bleachers still line the diamond's backstop. There's just a pinch more wood rot now, and nature grows wherever it pleases, blurring the line between a jungled outfield and an infested infield.

And finally, the Royal Pub at the far end of the drag looks to still be serving the same heavy-handed pours to the same drunken locals, likely reciting the same drunken stories about glory days long gone.

It's like the whole damn town was placed in one big time capsule when he left. Only the seal was somehow compromised, and Father Time got his greedy hands on the best of its contents.

He still can't believe he's officially here, back at his old stomping grounds.

His home.

And the ironic part is, it's the last place anyone will ever think to look for him.

It's been more than thirteen years since he last cruised these Midwest suburban streets. He left the day he was sent to prison, and he's never looked back. Even Klein, who wanted nothing to do with Clayton from the start or shared an interest in learning anything about him other than his criminal record, knows his disdain for this place—and the ties that were severed when he left. Especially, the way in which he left.

The Jeep's tires begin to work a little harder against the pavement as the car grinds to a slow stop. Discreetly, he parks across the street from an olive-green Cape Cod-style house with perfect architectural symmetry. He kills the headlights but leaves the car running.

The home's grass is freshly trimmed and patterned, just as

suspected. The landscaping, anal-retentively measured and manicured to a uniformed twig height across the decorative shrubbery. Not one flower in the bed wilted, or porch ornament askew. Although, the natural wood-stained shutters are a new touch from the old white ones. And the weeping willow out front still casts a lamenting lawn shadow from the dim embrace of the humming streetlight at the end of the block.

Seeing his parents' house again for the first time in over a decade—the place he used to call home—it all feels comfortably foreign. Like nothing has changed, but everything is different.

Clayton imagines a perfect scenario where he could walk up to the porch right now and ring the doorbell. Where his parents would rush to answer it, greeting him with wide smiles and loving embraces. Where they would all go inside and spend time healing old wounds and making amends for past sins and the countless arguments they created. That everything would be all right, like it used to be. Like it was when he was a kid. He pretends that for a moment he could just erase his past and start all over. He wonders if his parents would even recognize him now, having not seen or talked to either of them since he was sentenced nearly a decade and a half ago. That day, they made it abundantly clear that they wanted nothing to do with him. That his countless run-ins with the law and collective catalog of crimes had finally stacked the deck high enough against their willingness to forgive him. To love him. He recounts the last phone call home from prison, the moment he was disowned by his father and ostracized by his mother. He thinks, if they saw him now, what would they see? Their long-lost son? Or the criminal—a murderer?

But that long shot at happily ever after will have to wait. There's no time for a family kumbaya right now, or maybe ever, if The Hunt has anything to say about it.

The low rumble of the engine purrs as Clayton shifts the car back into Drive. The clock on the dash reads 1:18. His body craves sleep, but his mind knows better. He risked getting here for a reason. He can't back out now, even if he wants to.

There's nowhere else to go.

It's 1:40 a.m. by the time Clayton rolls up to the next stop on what's become his prodigal return. He disconnects the starter wire from the power cluster and the engine dies. Directly before him lies the vague frame of an old moonlit barn that houses an auto body shop. It may be the middle of the night, but he can see that some of the original red paint from its shadowy exterior—although chipped and faded—is still intact.

A modest one-story, ranch-style home lies detached just behind it about thirty or so yards away. It's hard for him to picture it now, but he grew up in that very garage learning everything he knows about cars—the legal kind and not-so-legal kind. They were some of the best years of his life, spent with some of his closest friends. So, why does he hesitate now? Why the apprehension?

*Just get out of the car*, he tells himself, his confidence in protest. *Just get out of the car and walk up to the door*. He repeats the scenario over and over in his head, trying to translate the thought into action.

Soon enough, the decision is made for him. The metallic slide of a pump action shotgun outside his window wakes him from the tangles of his after-midnight daydream of disinclination. The startling firearm alarm is followed by a male voice.

Its tone is anything but welcoming.

"Shop's long closed, asshole," the voice bellows as the long, steel barrel enters the open car window. "Now, hands where I can see 'em. Nice and slow."

Clayton raises his hands from the steering wheel into field goal pose as the man strategically opens the car door for him, maintaining the imaginary bullseye aimed at his chest.

"Now, slowly, and I mean slowly, shit for brains, like you're making love to Marvin Gaye, step out of the car."

Clayton does as he's instructed, moving his feet in baby-step decline from floorboard to concrete. Once he's fully birthed himself from the driver's seat, he receives a new set of commands.

"Now turn and face the car," the voice growls, while his arms continue to hold a steady mark with the boomstick. "And don't even think about lowering those palms."

Clayton's nose meets the roof of the Jeep as a set of hands vigorously pat and claw their way up and down his entire person. Rummaging under his ballcap, overturning pockets, digging into his socks and waistline—no crevice left celibate.

The man with the shotgun steps back and buries the muzzle of the gun into the soft patch on the back of Clayton's head.

"All right. Now who are you, and what the fuck are you doing here? 'Cause this ain't the yellow brick road and you sure as shit aren't in Kansas anymore, Dorothy."

Clayton shuffles his feet, baby steps again, pivoting to face his assailant.

"Well, you know what they say—" he turns and looks up, staring the man square in the eye, the outline of his face illuminated by the soft glow of a waning moon. "'There's no place like home.'"

The man's gun drops as fast as his jaw. His eyes brimming wide with disbelief as if he just accosted a ghost.

"—Clay?"

Clayton lowers his hands, removing the ball cap on their way down. He flashes a slight smirk in the name of peace.

"Hey, Toni . . ."

# CHAPTER 20

Antoni Rivera, the man responsible for sending Clayton to prison for aggravated assault—just shy of an attempted murder charge—glares at his unwanted guest with an emotional cocktail of disbelief and disgust, vigorously shaken with a shot of anger. It's a face he hasn't seen in more than a decade and thought he'd never see again. And if he ever did, a face that he wasn't sure what he'd do to the man it was attached to.

Antoni tilts his head at the ground and back at Clayton, making a ball inside his lower lip with the force of his tongue.

"Only my friends get to call me Toni," he instructs. "And last I checked, you lost that title a long time ago."

Clayton composes himself, easing away from the car to quip back.

"Yeah, well, last I checked I didn't have much of a choice in that matter, now did I?"

Antoni steers the trip down memory lane back to the present, his shotgun still at the ready.

"I've seen you all over the news," he confirms, pulling the neck of his shirt down to expose a gnarly scar that trails from below his jawline to just above the outline of his collarbone. "Looks like this time someone wasn't as fortunate as me."

Clayton takes another step forward.

Antoni holds steady with the shotgun, nudging him back toward the car with the enthusiastic muzzle.

"I didn't tell you to fucking move."

Clayton roars back, "Oh, for the love of god. Cut the shit already, Toni. We both know it was an accident. An accident that *you* started."

The after-effects from that previous emotional cocktail kick in, the shot of anger amping his rage. Antoni drives the bezel of the shotgun deep into Clayton's sternum, setting his back on a collision course with the hood of the jacked Jeep.

"Because you left us!" he shouts. "After all we'd been through together. You bailed on us, your family. Just like that. If you'd have been there from the get-go, Leo wouldn't have died. My little brother would still be alive."

A surge of equal rage floods Clayton's reflexes as he peels himself off the hood. He slaps the gun away from his chest and darts back to his feet. He's rehearsed this moment in his mind a million times over the years.

The things he'd say.

The way it'd go.

None of it has prepared him for the reality of the situation.

Fuming from the falsity of accusations, yet still aware he's being babysat by a shotgun, he treads timidly.

"It was *me* that told you guys not to go in the first place. That *I* had a bad feeling about it. If I hadn't changed my mind and shown up when I did, you'd probably *all* be dead and you know it! So, stop blaming me," Clayton pleads. "It's not my fault Leo's gone."

Antoni lowers the gun and takes a small step back. The anger on his face appears reflective, softening by the second. For the time being, the standoff seems to be neutralizing.

"And it's not yours, either," Clayton adds.

The remark triggers a switch in Antoni's head. His guard reports back to duty, stacking up mental bricks double-time. Deep down, he knows—and has always known it was his fault his little brother died that night. He's just spent so much time blaming everyone else that it's the lie he's come to believe. The lie he wants to believe. The truth is Clayton's right. He should have never gotten Leo involved in that drop in the first place. He failed at the one job a big brother has, and the pain, that swell of repressed emotion, all comes boiling up to the surface as he rears back the shotgun.

Before he can flinch, the butt of its solid wooden stock slingshots into the right side of Clayton's chin; the force temporarily relocating his jaw two inches to the left. In a split second, he drops down belly first toward the pavement faster than his unconscious hands can react to pillow the fall. Again, the right side of his face is acquainted with an unforgiving blow, this time courtesy of the concrete.

After the terrible first impression with Antoni's shotgun and less-than-stellar introduction with the ground, it takes a moment for the upstairs lights to come back on. Once the bulbs begin to flicker, Clayton crawls to all fours, checking the posture of his chin as part of the slow illumination process. It doesn't feel like it, but it's still intact.

"Ungh," he grits. "Guess I had that coming."

His eyes tilt up at Antoni who's resumed staring down the cross-hairs at him.

"So, what's next?" Clayton calmly delivers, smearing red across his hand from his ballooning lower lip. "You gonna shoot me, Toni? Go right ahead. But before you do, tell me one thing. Is it for the revenge you think I owe you, or are you planning to sell me out just for the money?" He spits a warm wad of bloody bar-bell-shaped saliva onto his former blacktop bed. "I'm just curious as to where your priorities lie."

Antoni jab-steps closer and jams the steel cylinder back into Clayton's chest.

"You almost fucking killed me! Your best friend," he shouts

through clenched teeth and an oxymoron of scowling sincerity. "You were like my other brother, Clay."

"It was an accident, Toni," Clayton barks back. "And we both paid for it, in different ways."

Antoni, seething over the locked-in sight of the shotgun, tests, "What did I tell you about calling me that?"

"Goddammit, Antoni, listen to me! You started that fight. You threw the first punch. And last I checked, *you* were the one who threw *us* through the garage window. You make it sound like I personally held the glass to your neck. Like I didn't get hurt in the whole fucked up situation, too. I spent over five years in prison. I lost my parents. I lost my friends." He forcefully gestures at Antoni. "I lost you."

He pauses a moment, scrambling to find his next words.

"Look, I'm sorry I wasn't there for you. I'm sorry about a lot of things. But I tried to save Leo, and I sure as hell didn't try to kill you. So, what's it going to be, Toni? You going to shoot me or forgive me?" Clayton asks, stepping closer and lowering his hands. "But more importantly, are you going to finally forgive yourself?"

Antoni hovers the shotgun in proper form, his finger buzzing the trigger like a losing game of Operation. His expression says it all as his eyebrows flip from a down-and-in furrow to an up-and-out arc, revving from anger to guilt in less time than a *Fast and Furious* ten-second car.

Then, like the slow and the steady, he lowers the weapon to his hips.

"So, did you do it?" he returns with his own question from left field. "Did you kill her like they say you did?"

The unexpected thought of Trish overtakes Clayton with an adrift memory—one of her working in their lone, spare bedroom turned art studio. He can't quite remember what she's painting, but it's vibrant. Full of color and life just like her. She's wearing his cozy sweatpants. The navy pair that she sneakily stole from his drawer, "accidently" spilled paint on, and then staked a claim as her own. She's just out of key, yet somehow still adorably singing aloud to every lyric of *Just Like Heaven* spinning on the background record player. Of all the thoughts buzzing around in his hive for a brain, he ponders how the littlest memories—the ones that are so often overlooked—tend to resonate the most.

He looks back at Antoni with his own oxymoron of a stare, stern but fragile.

"No more than I did you," Clayton finally answers.

Antoni raises the shotgun over his shoulder, holstering it while letting out a subtle snicker. He extends his hand toward Clayton, who looks at the gesture with waning remnants of uncertainty. The thought of being clocked across the jaw again doesn't do much to help relieve his hesitation.

Sensing the reluctance, Antoni emphasizes the olive branch attempt by curling his hand and rolling his eyes above a growing smile.

"Relax. I'm not going to hit you again—not unless you want another welcome home present."

Clayton grins in response, and they embrace like friends who haven't seen each other in more than a decade. Like long-lost brothers.

"All right, all right. I know you didn't come here just to make amends," Antoni says, being the first to break the Kodak moment but failing to conceal his newfound smile. "So, what do you need?"

Clayton sighs as he combs both hands through his soiled hair. "I don't even know where to begin."

"How about we start with getting you some food and some sleep? Because I gotta be honest, you look and smell like total shit."

Antoni turns around and starts making his way back inside the house tucked behind the auto shop. Clayton tags along close behind.

"I've got some leftover pasta and meatballs if you want, courtesy of the missus."

The sound of two pairs of feet walking in unison fades to one as Clayton stops dead in his tracks. Antoni notices the sudden abandonment of trailing footsteps and spins around in reciprocation.

"You coming?"

"Wait, I'm sorry. What? You're a married man?" Clayton asks, not even trying to hide his astonishment. "You're just going to casually glaze over that one."

Antoni just smiles and turns back around to continue walking.

He answers without looking back.

"It's been over ten years, Clay. You think you're the only one who's changed?"

"Well, no, it's just . . . I never pictured you settling down. I can't believe someone finally made an honest man out of you," he jabs.

"Settled down? I'm afraid so. And if me being married threw you for a loop, then you're really gonna flip when you meet my kid." He turns around right outside the front door to look at Clayton through crinkled eyes. "But I'm still working on that whole "honest" part. Which works out in your favor because I'm betting the help you need from me isn't exactly the legal kind."

Antoni reaches for the knob and opens the door. He steps inside, finishing his thought. "That's what you never understood, Clay."

Idling in the doorway, Clayton can only make out the faintest gray outline of his old friend consumed behind the pitch-dark panorama of the house's noir setting.

"Oh, and what would that be?" he asks, genuinely curious as to what a decade-plus of righting wrongs and self-reflection hasn't already taught him about his own scarred past.

"That once you're in the game, you're always in the game," Antoni continues. "There's no escape. No matter where you go or how long you're gone, trouble will always find its way back to you."

He can still hear Antoni's voice, but his silhouette has withdrawn into the dim oblivion.

"Well, that's cryptic," Clayton mutters, entering the house as the darkness swallows him whole. "Are you saying we're cursed?"

He hears Antoni fumbling around a few feet away from the door. Instantly, the black fog is cast away by the soft yellow glow of a cream-shaded lamp in the corner.

"What I'm saying is trouble is always out there. And if you were smart, you'd find it before it finds you."

They make eye contact in the light, finally seeing each other fully for the first time in thirteen years. Antoni is no longer the skinny, baby-faced teenage boy that Clayton remembers. He's a man now. His face has sprouted substantially more facial hair from their peach fuzz years, and his eyes look heavy, carrying a burden of pain tucked deep behind them. His back-then, high and tight fade has been replaced by a grown-out, slicked-back pompadour, and tattoos now serve as conjoined collages covering his chiseled arms from wrist to shoulder, like a collection of badges depicting enough life experiences for three men.

Antoni points to a cozy, oversized caramel-colored leather couch in the living room.

"Take a seat."

Clayton rambles over to it and plops down. The cool comfort consumes him whole. For the first time tonight, he feels safe, almost relaxed—aside from his throbbing jaw. Despite the decade-plus of bad blood, he feels back at home. He sighs a much-needed breath of relief and melts further into the worn-in, cowhide cushion.

Antoni opens the fridge and pulls out a large black cast iron pot. He reaches above his head, opening the white wooden cabinet to locate a bowl. He loads up the leftover dish and tosses the ceramic vessel into the microwave. After a couple of beeps, the bowl spins as 2000-plus volts do their job to warm the cold noodle mixture.

Antoni raises his voice over the hum to speak to Clayton in the living room.

"You know, I always wondered what would happen if we ever saw each other again." He snatches a fork from the silverware drawer. "How it would go. What I would say." He digs back into the fridge, wrestling two bottles of frosty Modelos from way in the back. "I gotta say, this wasn't exactly what I had in mind," he finishes with a self-serving chuckle as the microwave lets out a sustained, finishing beep.

"I always figured—"

But as he walks into the living room, he finds Clayton already passed out in a ball on the couch. He gently places the bowl down on the coffee table and grabs a knitted blanket off the back of the couch. Draping it over Clayton with a grin, he mutters under his breath, "Yeah . . . definitely not what I had in mind."

He walks over to turn off the lamp but pauses with his hand on the chain. He looks back at Clayton sound asleep.

"Welcome home, brother."

A little under five hours later, Clayton is progressively wakened by a myriad of morning senses—the dense aroma of fresh, fatty bacon and brewed black coffee hangs in the air; the sizzle of eggs chatters on the neighboring stove; and streams of sunlight pour in from the loose slits in the eastern blinds above him. He sits up on the couch and lets out an exaggerated yawn, but the relief is cut short by a sharp pain shooting from his swollen jaw. He massages his chin until it subsides. Somehow groggier now than before he crashed, the jury is still out on whether the extended power nap did him any favors.

He peeks into the hazy kitchen where Antoni is putting the finishing touches on breakfast.

"Well, well, look who's up?" Antoni jokes, as he slides the bacon off the skillet onto a paper towel-padded plate. "I see you still sleep like a fucking rock."

Clayton responds, rubbing his eyes. "I'm surprised I slept at all."

"The mind's a powerful thing, but it ultimately does as the body says. And last night your body was singing a lullaby." Antoni walks over to the round dining room table adorned with a floral linen cloth cover. He sets down two teeming plates of bacon, eggs, and toast.

"Come. Eat," he orders. "You need it."

Clayton stands up, staggering his way to the kitchen, trying not to yawn again for the sake of his jaw. He grabs one of the four mismatched dining chairs and scoots up to a prepped plate of piping eggs and bacon drenched in a hefty red drizzle of Sriracha sauce. He scoops a full fork of steaming scramble into his mouth and mumbles, "I see you still put this spicy shit on everything."

"That's because it's fucking delicious," Antoni defends, standing up against the blasphemy of his favorite condiment. "It's not my fault you have the spice tolerance of a toddler and the acid reflux of a geriatric patient."

"Yeah, well, forgive me for not wanting to pee out of my butthole every six-to-eight hours after I eat that crap."

They look at each other, shoveling in another round of collective bites, and share a touché laugh over mouthfuls of cheesy egg curds.

"Ouch." Clayton yelps mid-bite, rubbing his jaw with his free hand. "Should have had you make mine over easy." He takes another ginger nibble. "Extra easy."

"Yeah, sorry about that," Antoni slurs in between chews. "I got a little carried away with the emotions last night. If it helps you feel any better, I always imagined doing much worse to you."

Clayton brings another trepidatious bite to his mouth. Thankfully, the soreness from last night's blows seems to be fading more with each chew.

"Nope. That doesn't help at all, actually," he garbles, his mouth still full. "But at least you didn't really think about shooting me," he jokes, and looks over at Antoni who just stares blankly back at him, not blinking. His guilty eyes darting to hide intent.

Clayton's grin drops as the unswallowed protein hits the wrong passage on its way down. He coughs and a little scramble comes back up. He chokes it back down as hard as his bruised jaw will allow.

"Holy shit," he bellows, amid another series of smaller coughs. "You were really going to shoot me!"

"Whaaat? Noooo," Antoni says, hastily snapping into a crisp piece of bacon. "I mean, maybe? Yes. No. Well, I did think about it. Kind of. But only for like an instant. You know what? I don't know. Just shut the hell up and eat your breakfast, will ya?"

"You were really going to shoot me—" Clayton accuses again in shock, chipmunking a dose of unchewed toast in his agape mouth. "Weren't you? I can't fucking believe it."

Antoni delivers another slab of bacon to his lips along with a half-hearted reply. "But I didn't, though, so just drop it. Okay?"

"I just can't believe you really thought—"

"Oh my god, Clay! If you don't shut up about it in the next two seconds, I'll go grab the shotgun right now and follow through with it this time."

"All right, all right. Fine," Clayton retreats, plowing into another heap of eggs. "You don't have to get all touchy about it."

He waits a few seconds for the dust from the threat to settle. "I mean, it's not like *you* were the one that almost got shot or anything."

"Oh, for fuck's sake," Antoni shoots up from the table, rolling his eyes along with the rest of his annoyed self over to the kitchen island to top off his coffee.

"I'll be over here when you're ready to talk like an adult, instead of whining like a petulant child. All 'Aww, gee willikers, mister, I can't believe you almost shot me last night. Even though I was trespassing at nearly two o'clock in the morning and almost killed you the last time we saw each other,'" he mimics Clayton's bitching, complete with innocent hand gestures and an overly nasal tone. It's been more than ten years, but the impersonation is still spot on.

"Hmm, not bad," Clayton chuckles, finishing off his plate by accordioning the final stick of bacon into his already brimming cheeks. "Although your pitch is a little rusty."

After observing Clayton devour his plate like a stray dog, Antoni figures it's time to poke the fat elephant in the room and ask the question of the hour.

"Sooo . . . what's your endgame, Clay?" he asks over a concentrated sip of coffee, "Assuming you've got one."

"Endgame? Kinda poor word choice, don't you think?"

"Fine. Plan. What's your game plan, Clay?"

"Well—" Clayton says, swallowing his last gulp of breakfast. "First, we should probably get rid of that Jeep out front."

"Let me guess, stolen?"

"Yup."

"See, I told you."

"Told me what?"

"That once you're in the game, you're always in the game," Antoni remarks in between smug sips of more morning fuel. His priggish smirk blossoms into full-blown arrogance, perfectly framed by the self-satisfied smile stretched just above the brim of his mug. "Who would have thought?"

He passes the eye-rolling baton over to Clayton now, who relays his own annoyance and takes a drink of his untouched cup. The jaw-jarring jolt of beyond-bitter caffeine sucker punches his lips into an instant pucker.

"Jesus! What'd you brew this with, morphine and motor oil?" he shrieks, nearly spitting out the murky mouthful.

Antoni laughs as Clayton desperately reaches across the table and snatches a piece of remaining bacon from his plate to chase down the lingering pungency.

"It's my own personal brew," Antoni sniggers, polishing off the remaining swig in his coffee cup. "No motor oil in it, but god knows I've got plenty of it in the shop if I want to experiment."

"Ugh, it's like donkey-kicking each one of your tastebuds right in their individual mouths. I could get the jitters just smelling this shit," he gags, putting the mug back down. "Sorry, what were you saying before I nearly spewed my breakfast all over the table?"

Antoni leans in and pours himself another cup from the pot. A subtle flex that isn't lost on Clayton.

"Nothing, really. I was just laughing at all those years of us boosting cars—the very same reason you wanted out way back when if memory serves me correctly—and now it's come back full circle to save your ass. Gotta appreciate the poetic irony of it all."

Clayton gets up from the table to rinse his plate off in the sink. Opening the dishwasher, he changes the subject to something a little less ridicule-worthy.

"So, where exactly is this *family* you spoke of, again?" he inquires.

Antoni doesn't answer the question right away. Instead, he grabs his plate from the table and finishes the remaining bite of eggs, swirling the last forkful of gooey yellow into a heaping puddle of chili-based hot sauce. Casually, he wipes away the extra grease pooled in the corners of his mouth.

"Well, I sent Thad off to school before I whipped up breakfast, and Sonya left for work a couple hours ago. She gets up at the ass crack of dawn when she has to work her day shifts at the ER."

"Ohh, so she's a *nurse*, huh?" Clayton says in a humor-me tone. "And when did you two lovebirds meet exactly?"

Antoni snatches the eye-rolling baton back from Clayton's gazed grasp and dumps his own finished plate into the kitchen sink.

He knows exactly where this conversation is going.

"Yes, we met at the hospital if that's what you're getting at. She saved my life. Then helped me heal, in more ways than one." He gestures to the scar on his neck.

It's the first time Clayton has been able to see the wound clearly in the light—a long, pink horizontal mark tracing around the front of his Adam's apple just below his jawline above the collar bone. He doesn't know exactly how many stitches—and he's not about to ask—but it's easily double digits.

Maybe it's the feeling of being back home? Maybe it's bantering with his old best friend again? He doesn't know and he can't quite put his pulse on it, but everything seems too easy right now. Almost normal, like nothing's wrong. And nothing's changed.

"So, one might say, hypothetically, that I *helped* you meet your future wife?"

The humor-me question is returned with an ice-cold glare. "Nice try, asshole, but I'm not ready to let you off that easy."

"Eh, it was worth a shot," Clayton heckles, "Oh, wait, poor choice of words to use on someone with such an itchy trigger finger like yourself."

"Ha-fucking-ha," Antoni jeers and fills up a thermos with his motor oil coffee, polishing off the pot. "It's been so long I forgot you had jokes, Clay. Now get your shit together and meet me out front by the shop. We got a lot of work to do." He's halfway out the door when he looks back at Clayton and says sarcastically, "That is, if you even remember your way around a garage."

Clayton gives him a complimentary fuck-you finger and a nod as the door shuts. He dumps his one-sipped cup of cold coffee into the white farmhouse sink and takes a look around the place.

Antoni's house looks like the inside of an antique store meets car collector's wet dream. Old auto parts, including a random collection of vintage hood ornaments and a 1940s Chevy grill, hang above the cobblestone fireplace while other dated knickknacks like old tube radios, weathered leather boxing gloves, and sporadically placed vinyl records decorate the quarter's quaint shelves and walls. It's about one busy shelf shy of tipping the scale between passionate collector and straight-up hoarder.

Amid the hodgepodge of patinated furnishings, various plants and cursive wall art bring pops of vibrancy and a much-needed feminine touch to the abode, making the obsolete clutter somehow feel fresh and structured. And the few stray child toys that didn't make the cleanup toy bin give the house a true home feeling. A place that feels lived in. Loved in.

Outside, Antoni launches a tennis ball that's clinging to its last tuft of yellow fuzz tighter than a bald man's fleeting combover high into the air. Clayton watches as a beautiful German Shepherd eagerly retrieves it.

"Wow, a wife, a kid, and a dog? It's like *Leave It to Beaver* over here," he jokes, walking up to the chain link fence. "So, what's his name?"

"Her name—" Antoni corrects him, hurling the fetched ball sky high again, "—is Cleo."

"She's beautiful. And that's a good name," Clayton says, acknowledging, without mentioning, the nod to Antoni's deceased brother, Leo. "But I always thought you wanted a pit bull."

"Well, that's one of the things I've learned since you've been gone, Clay," Antoni answers after another toss. "You don't always get what you want. But things always seem to work out."

He moves on from the fence and heads toward the garage despite Cleo's puppy dog pleas for more playtime. His keys jangle as he works to free the heavy-duty deadbolt and open up the shop.

As Clayton enters the garage, it's like he's instantly transported back to his teenage years. Nothing has really changed, but it's not quite the same either. Through his older, wiser lens, the honest auto body shop by day—chop shop by night—that Antoni's father used to run still has the same old feel. Only now, the vintage car decorations that have always lined the garage's walls are juxtaposed with the most modern auto mechanic tools and industry tech that money can buy. The familiar waft of motor oil and gasoline permeates the place, flooding his nostrils with a heavy fueling of nostalgia.

"Smells better than your coffee in here," he jokes, walking over to a series of old framed photos.

Several pictures of Antoni and his father decorate the narrow strip of wall. There's even a photo of himself and Antoni rocking a pair of oversized, grease-saturated coveralls with their arms around one another. They can't be any more than twelve years old. Just a couple of baby-faced boys with their whole lives ahead of them.

He looks over at Antoni who finishes opening the third and final garage bay door.

"Man, this place hasn't changed a bit," he remarks, picking up a fancy new cutter tool from the nearest workbench. "Although, I do see you've upgraded."

"Yeah, well, crime evolves over a decade. Why work harder when you can steal smarter, right?" Antoni asks and flips on a series of overhead fluorescents. The rectangular panels illuminate in synchronized sequence across the space. "I've got the latest and greatest shady money can buy," he adds, pointing to various new machinery and technology around the shop.

Clayton sits back and watches the show-and-tell.

"That over there is a smart MIG pulse welder, this right here is a high-def imaging precision wheel alignment tool, and over there—" he points to a bus-sized booth with a series of vertical windows in the corner of the shop. "That's the Nova Verta. A top-of-the-line, temperature-controlled paint booth that delivers flawless coats, every time." He takes a jolting drink of coffee from his thermos. "See, I told you. She didn't *quite* make an honest man out of me."

"Damn, I guess not," Clayton laughs, peeking into one of the exposed windows of the empty paint booth. "And I'd add she's running out of time."

Antoni retorts, "Just go grab the car, funny guy."

But Clayton's attention diverts to the raised lift in bay one. He didn't notice it when he first walked in, but hoisted several feet in the air is a pristine cherry-red 1955 Chevy Task Force pickup.

"I'll be damned," he says, his eyes gawking wider than the gape of his mouth as he dashes toward the raised truck. "No way! Is this . . . Is this what I think it is?" he asks, pointing in the air like a hyped toddler.

"I was wondering if you'd remember," Antoni coyly answers, crossing his arms and leaning against one of the various tool cabinets like a proud father.

"Pfft. Remember?" Clayton scoffs. "I was with you the day you bought the hunk of junk," he adds, doing a bit of a double take while stepping back to re-admire. "Well, back when it actually was a hunk of junk."

Antoni laughs. "Hey, I was seventeen and poor. But at least I paid for her straight up."

"Only because you couldn't boost her," Clayton jokes, wasting no time stripping the honest statement down to the naked truth. "She didn't even run. Hell, I don't even think she had all four tires."

"True or not, I still bought her with honest money."

"Oh, I know," Clayton replies as he pans around the truck. "You spent every last dollar you had on her. And if my memory serves, quite a few of my dollars, too."

He shoots an accusatory glare in Antoni's direction. "So, this is what a decade-plus of TLC looks like, huh?"

"Yep. She's my baby. Totally restored from the ground up." Antoni admires, locking eyes with her headlights. "Last time you saw her, I still don't think I had her up and running yet, and she definitely wasn't much of a looker behind that thick layer of rust and those mismatched patches of faded turquoise. But I switched out the battery for something from this century, and removed the bumpers, fender, and all the tarnished door handles and window moldings. Of course, I flipped the rotted tires for some fresh dubs and shiny chrome rims, reupholstered the seats with original cowhide leather, scraped out the decayed door and interior trim for something with a little more flavor, replaced the floorboards—"

"Umm, I think you mean, *put in* an actual floor," Clayton interrupts. "I remember there being a huge, rusted-out hole on the driver-side floor. I used to joke about you having to Flintstone your ass wherever you wanted to go."

"Oh, I haven't forgotten," Antoni retorts. "That's when you started calling me Bamm-Bamm, like an Ass-Ass."

"Oh yeah, that's right," he agrees, with a commemorative giggle. "Guilty."

Antoni looks back at his hand to see what finger he left off counting on. "Anyway, where was I with the truck?"

"Somewhere between flirting and foreplay, I think," Clayton quips back.

"And I see you're *still* an Ass-Ass," Antoni jibes, moving around to the front of the pickup. "Oh, yeah. So, after I installed the new floor, I repaired the smaller hairline cracks in the windows and replaced all the panes that weren't salvageable. Then I got to work on the frame, which was really the only piece still in decent shape, luckily. I adjusted the axels and replaced the front and rear suspensions, swapped out all the dry, seventy-plus-year-old cracked belts, flushed out all the old fluids and build-up, and of course, the coup de gras, I completely rebuilt the engine and transmission—with a little help from Dad—and finally got this beauty up and running. Oh, and I took the Nova Verta's V-card by breaking it in for her first paint job," he concludes, tilting his head along with his eyes upward in a delayed afterthought. "Now that I think about it, it's totally fitting that I painted her cherry-red . . . anyway, she's my first true love."

"Wow. So, how does Sonya feel about you two-timing on her with an older love interest? And a piece of machinery at that," Clayton jokes. "How do you two . . . you know? Do you slip it in the exhaust or under the hood? Or . . . how does that all work exactly?" he continues, bobbing his right pointer finger in and out of the hole cupped by his left index finger and thumb.

"I know it's been a long time, but I just can't remember. Were you always this fucking annoying?" Antoni shakes his head, the hint of a smile hanging on his lips. "Like I said before. Just shut up and go grab your car, funny guy. We've got a lot of work to do."

A couple minutes later, Clayton pulls into the second open bay and kills the jerry-rigged starter. Antoni flips the switch as the car lift hums, working against the one ton of added gravity to raise the vehicle off the floor. He looks the Jeep up and down judgingly as it slowly rises.

"Really? This is the best you could boost?"

"It's not exactly like I had time to find the pick of the litter. You know, I had that whole running for my life thing to worry about."

Antoni walks to the driver's side to reach in and pop the hood. He peers over the exposed engine after shutting the door.

"Since you brought it up . . . you still haven't told me what really happened. You wanna talk about it?" he asks with his head buried next to the transmission. The whole scene feels like déjà vu to when they were kids. Boost cars and talk about life.

Clayton looks away at the question, he wants to tell him the story, and he will, but he's not quite ready to reopen that fresh wound so soon. He's still struggling to process the pain of it all himself, and so far, this has all been a much-needed distraction.

"Not just yet. Sorry, man."

"Fair enough." Antoni retreats willingly and grabs a large crescent wrench off the tool rack. He takes a seat in a futuristic-looking, ergonomic metal chair on wheels. He pushes a lever on the sleek cart's side, and the chair instantly folds into a flatbed car creeper. He glides under the Jeep like a kid on a playground slide, getting to work on removing the catalytic converter.

But Clayton can't hold back. Mentally, he's not ready to start talking, but his words and the lips that contain them say otherwise. Blame it on the grieving process.

"I loved her, man. More than anything. We were—" He feels a lump blistering in the back of his throat. He chokes it down hard. "We were gonna have a baby. I was going to ask her to marry me. I had it all—everything I wanted right in front of me. And now it's all gone."

There's a deliberate pause in the cranking chatter coming from underneath the vehicle. Antoni slides back out to face his friend just in time to catch the pain swelling behind Clayton's eyes, turning them to brittle glass. Consolation has never been his strong suit, or conveying really any emotion, in general, but he makes a valiant effort.

"I'm sorry about what happened, Clay. Truly. I can only imagine what it would be like if I lost Sonya," he continues, switching out the bit on his ratchet for a 19mm. "There's no telling what I'd do. Or who I'd want to hurt."

"Oh, I know exactly who I want to hurt," Clayton rebuts, as the grieving process quickly jumps from denial to the next logical stage—rage. "Her father. He's behind all of it. The bastard tried to bribe me and then have me killed. He's the one responsible for her. For her—" He struggles to get the last word out. To acknowledge that she's truly gone.

Antoni sits up on his creeper. He can sense the embers of the old, angry Clayton he knew all too well rekindling. Prepared to catch something rash, and most likely stupid, ablaze.

"Clay, listen to me," he cautions, putting the ratchet down. "I know you're hurting right now. Trust me. I've been there. But going after Simon Klein is suicide. There's no way to get to him without you getting killed first. Period. You're on the most powerful predator in the nation's Most Wanted list. I watched the latest news this morning while you were still asleep. Your bounty is up to a mill already and counting," he continues, picking up an oversized, red monkey wrench from the floor before sliding back under the Jeep to continue loosening bolts. "Hell, I'm surprised I haven't turned you in myself."

Clayton stares down at Antoni's protruding feet in earnest, his eyes still fragile, his voice serious. "And why haven't you exactly?"

There's a pregnant pause. Then a muffled voice trails from under the car, "Because no matter how much I wanted to blame you. To hate you. To hurt you." He slides back out, meeting Clayton's shattered gaze head-on. "You're still my brother, for better or worse."

Clayton wipes a trickle of moisture from his cheek. "Thanks, man. I owe you.

"Oh, you damn sure owe me," Antoni responds sarcastically, knocking the tension down a few pegs. "But if you want to thank me right now—" he tosses Clayton a second wrench. "Then take that and get your ass to work. That is, if you still remember how?"

Clayton and Antoni get to it. After removing the first wheel and reacquainting himself with the cordless impact wrench, Clayton finds his footing and the chop job becomes second nature again.

He finishes with the wheels, rims, and brakes faster than expected, then moves onto the air bags and aftermarket stereo—a nice JVC one with a big-ass nav screen. By the time they're all said and done dismantling the Jeep, Clayton won't have to worry about the vehicle being traced back to him, and Antoni is in the position to make a couple thousand or so in profit from the humble job.

Wiping his greasy, black-streaked hands on an oily rag, Clayton puffs contentedly and adds, "Not gonna lie, I've kinda missed that," he admits, admiring the level of mess on his palms and under his nails.

Antoni smiles at him. "Once you're in the game—"

"Yeah, yeah. 'You're always in the game.' Blah, blah, blah," Clayton cuts him off, finishing his recycled catchphrase. "Thanks, I got it already, criminal Mr. Miyagi."

"All right, then. So, what's next, Clayton-san?"

Clayton cranes his head around the room, peeping all the new gadgets and mechanical gear.

"Well, it's pretty simple, just not easy. I need to get off the grid. Disappear. And based on the surplus of state-of-the-art gadgets around this shop, I'd say you've got a bag of tech tricks hiding somewhere up those newly tatted sleeves of yours."

Antoni doesn't say a thing. He just pulls a rag from his pocket, wipes the grime from his own hands, and casually gets up from the creeper. He shoves the soiled cloth back into his pearl snap chest pocket and starts walking purposefully toward bay three. Clayton watches from across the room as Antoni hops down into the dugout, disappearing out of sight. A few seconds later, he hears only a shout from across the garage.

"You coming? Or you just gonna keep sitting there with that dumb look on your face and dick in your hands?"

Clayton shoots up from the stool like a sprinter off the block. When he gets to bay three, he peers down at his childhood friend with confusion pasted across his eyebrows, apparently, dick still firmly in hand.

"Uh, you gonna tell me what you're doing down there exactly?"

"Just hop down here already, Mr. Twenty-One Questions. You'll see."

Clayton does as instructed while Antoni hits a hidden button tucked just inside the lip of the bay's above-ground floor. Like an elevator jarring to life, the bay starts to lower farther below the receding concrete surface. About half a floor down, a heavy-duty, diamond-plated door with a fancy numeric padlock emerges into view.

Seconds later, the bay's secret lift comes to a halt. Antoni inputs a passcode. Six little beeps later, the lock releases, and he opens the door to the underground vault.

"After you, pal."

Clayton treads into the black unknown as a motion sensor illuminates the claustrophobic chamber with a flood of harsh overhead UV. His eyes dart around the cramped, ten-by-ten-foot steel space, their surprise bested only by his bruised jaw hanging in total disbelief.

Throughout the concrete cavity lies a stockpile of cutting-edge tech and black market contraband not just used for petty car boosts, but what look like heists and crimes of all kinds. At first glance, Clayton notices a few pairs of night vision goggles with unique, yellow-tinted visors he's never seen the likes of. He also glimpses a bin full of some sort of sophisticated tracking devices and what looks to be a beefy, safe-cracking mechanism atop the nearside workbench. On the far wall hangs a steel pegboard with hundreds of thousands of dollars' worth of guns, everything from hand pistols and shotgun varieties to more military-grade semi-automatics—even a couple sniper rifles.

And that's just the tip of the technological iceberg before him. He's surrounded by a perimeter of so much other illegal hardware that he has no clue what they do, or what they even are.

"Whoa—" he mumbles, finally able to tuck his jaw back in and find the right order of vibrations, "So *this* is what a decade-plus of chop shop money will get you, huh?"

Antoni grabs a sleek, aluminum briefcase from the adjacent top shelf while Clayton tries to get a grip on his ogling.

"I tried the honest route for a while, truly. Played it straight. But I couldn't make ends meet," Antoni says, lowering the case. "I haven't made a profit on the shop in years. Even with the side chop hustle, I can barely break even. I only keep it running because I love working on cars, and because my dad built it from nothing but the American dream. Whatever the hell that is these days? But this—" He motions to the bevy of covert military gear and surplus of other prohibited paraphernalia surrounding him. "This is what pays the bills now."

Still trying to absorb the top-secret lair full of 007-inspired contraptions, Clayton asks, "Don't tell me you're working for someone. Are you still running heists, Toni?"

"Neither, but thanks for the scolding," Antoni counters, placing the metal briefcase on the table. "Hate to say it, but it's a young man's game now."

"Then what the hell are you doing with all this gear?"

Antoni shakes his head and inhales.

"I'm just trying to keep up, man," he huffs. "I'm strictly a salesman now. Still maybe not the most legal of jobs, per se, but it's like I told you, Sonya hasn't quite made an honest man out of me yet." He signals to the space around him with the twirl of his finger. "I buy most of this stuff on the black market, and from a handful of local, loyal contacts I've built over time. Then, I turn around and hawk it right back at a decent margin. Perhaps not to the most law-abiding citizens, but it keeps the food on the table and me away from the actual action."

Antoni pops the metallic latches on the briefcase and swivels the open box in front of Clayton.

"Check these out," he insists, tweezing out a small glass vial—no bigger than a sample of cologne—with what looks like tiny clear capsules of petroleum gel floating inside. "These little guys right here are micro-tech silicon fingerprints. Or as I like to call 'em, *jellyfish*. Each individual pod contains intelligent microcircuitry that can connect to any Wi-Fi or Bluetooth-enabled device. They discreetly adhere to your fingertips and then scour police and government databases, finding a clean and suitable authorized print to emulate. Once the print is found, they adapt automatically, molding to match the unique maze of the chosen fingerprint's shape. You could get scanned in ten different places, and it'll look like a different person was there every time."

Clayton removes one of the silicon globs from the pods and inspects it closer under the bright overhead lights. Inside the gel, he can see an entire city of microcircuitry that almost seems to pulsate at his touch, like some kind of living biomechanical organism. Like a microbotic jellyfish.

"Incredible," he mumbles in amazement as he gently places it back inside the glass container.

Antoni closes the briefcase and grins. "Buckle up, buddy. We're just getting started."

He wheels around a metallic surgical table resting in the center of the room like a portable kitchen island. Reaching down low, he pulls out an odd combination device that looks like a fancier version of hairspray attached to a retail checkout scanner.

Clayton doesn't even bother trying to guess, "What the hell is that thing?"

"This odd-looking beauty is a latex facial recognition scrambler.

Got it from an incredibly questionable-looking Russian fellow who mean-mugged me the entire transaction harder than Ivan Drago ever punched Rocky."

"What's it do?" Clayton glibly questions. "Single-handedly defeat communism?"

"Close. But no. It does exactly what it sounds like it does. The canister is filled with an unbelievably thin and malleable liquid latex. You spray it on your face like you would sunscreen, and then you take the scanner and pass over the application," Antoni instructs, mimicking the actions. "It coats on clear and then the scanner scrambles the recognition pattern so even the most sophisticated cameras can't trace or track your face. It basically distorts their electrical signal, making it hard to lock onto any key facial features. You won't look any different physically, but to a surveillance camera—or a drone—you'll be faceless."

"Hmm, pretty cool," Clayton replies, and takes the scrambler from Antoni. He studies the device, turning it over in his curious hands. "What's this button do?" he asks, pointing to a little red knob on the backside.

"Oh, that? Apparently, it's also got some kind of retinal recognition capture feature. Very *Men in Black* but without the whole 'sunglasses or you lose your entire memory' vibe. I'm not entirely sure how it works actually, I haven't really had the chance to play around with that function quite yet."

"Really?"

"Nope. Not yet."

"Hmm, that's a shame. Why wait?"

Clayton pushes the button and a flash of neon red floods Antoni's vision, blinding him in the process.

"*Aargh*," he shouts, and staggers backward into the main gun rack, frantically patting his eyes. The metal pegboard of loaded firearms wobbles upon impact. "Fuck, that's bright!"

After a few deep eye rubs, followed by an involuntary blinking spree, his rods and cones slowly start to return a blurred vision of the room to his dilated pupils. Once he's able to see well enough, he snatches the scanner out of Clayton's hands.

"Give me that damn thing," he orders. "It's not a toy, man. I'm so glad I had to go temporarily blind for a useless capture of my retinas."

"Useless? Oh, I wouldn't say that. It was pretty fun for me," Clayton jokes.

Casting the scanner back onto the table and out of Clayton's childish reach, Antoni continues his second show-and-tell presentation, still blinking more than usual.

"Anyway . . . it's a handy tool to make it look like you were never where you actually were. Only problem is, it doesn't really work the same with people being able to ID you. After all, it still physically looks like your face."

"And I'm assuming you've got something else for that?" Clayton asks, entertaining the setup he just walked into.

"I thought you'd never ask." Antoni cashes in with a smirk as he grabs a probe-like device from another slim briefcase on the shelf, his compulsive blinking finally back to normal. "This little guy is an expression compressor, or as I like to lovingly call it, the *Mug Mangler*."

"Do I even want to know why it's called that?"

"I think your imagination can probably fill in the blanks, but I'd be more than happy to give you a firsthand demo."

"Yeahhh, I'll pass on that one," Clayton balks, looking around the room again, shopping the space with perusal. He takes in a neatly wound bundle of ultra-thin, bendable wires topped with what resembles little pearl snaps.

"And what about that bundle of black-looking noodles?"

Antoni turns, following Clayton's finger to the cable cluster. "Ah, those are flex cams." He walks over and grabs a roll off the shelf. "They're just as small if not smaller than the scopes used in advanced surgical procedures. They give a live video feed that can be patched into any compatible monitoring system via USB-C or Thunderbolt 3. Perfect for scoping and recording inside engines, safes, anything surgical or discreet—you name it."

"Very *Mission Impossible*. Got it." Clayton nods in approval. "And uh, all of those? Enlighten me on what all those are used for?" he asks, gesturing to the floor-to-ceiling bank of guns on the wall.

"Those?" Antoni replies, matching Clayton's stare. "Let's just say those are for plan B."

Clayton looks around the entire room one last time, scoping out a *Matrix*-style computer setup in the vault's southern corner. The sophisticated rig consists of three, twenty-four-inch monitors flanking a larger thirty-two-inch one, plus a spacecraft-inspired server with a rainbow of blinking LED lights. It looks like a miniature version of one plucked right out of The Hunt for Justice server room.

"And do I even want to ask what you need all that shit for? I mean, the armory wall and the hacker's wet dream—there's no way this is all part of your salesman act. What the hell have you gotten yourself into since I left, Toni?"

Antoni methodically places the flex cam bundle back on the shelf and drops his chin, his gaze sinking dozens of degrees by the second.

"After I got out of the hospital, I fell on hard times. You were gone, Leo was gone, and the crew was never the same. Then, to top it all off, my dad got sick. Colon cancer. A few months later, I lost him, too, and then I nearly lost the shop. To make ends meet and take my mind off one bad situation to another, I started boosting again with a new crew. And that just made my already bad situation turn to utter shit. I found out quick that these guys weren't interested in fishing in the kiddie pool, they were after the big prizes. Minor carjacking turned into major heists—corporate theft, bank robberies, drug running, arms and human trafficking, turf wars—you name it, they did it. And they didn't bat an eye. They were basically an organized crime syndicate."

"Wait. What crew was it?" Clayton probes, both hesitant to hear the answer and sensing Antoni's tentativeness to give it.

Finally, he stops faltering and spits out the name camping on the tip of his tongue.

"The DB88s," he whispers, flashing Clayton the corresponding tattoo on his left hand.

"Wait, DB88s? As in Desmond Baine's 88s? As in Desmond 'The fucking crime kingpin' Baine 88s?" Clayton shouts. His words echo off the steel walls in the confined space serving up a double dose of admonishment. "Jesus Christ, Toni, what the hell were you thinking, man? That's one of the biggest known crime syndicates around—it's a goddamn cartel.

"Don't you think I know that? Look, I wasn't thinking, all right," Antoni admits, the guilt evident in his eyes, his tone, his demeanor—each and every sense. "I mean, I knew what I was getting into. What was at stake. But it felt like I had no other choice."

"The hell you didn't!" Clayton continues his berating. "How could you be so stupid?"

"Those are big words coming from a man wanted for murder by The Hunt Initiative," Antoni sneaks in a low blow, and he knows it as soon as the kneejerk words leave his lips. "Shit. I'm sorry, Clay, I-I didn't mean . . . it's just . . . you tell me. What was I supposed to do? Sit back and watch my life continue to fall apart? Just let the thread keep unraveling before my eyes?"

"Better to be a spectator to its spiral than a contributor. You might as well have just grabbed that thread and took off running."

Clayton instantly realizes the harshness behind his own words. Low blow or not, Antoni's right. Who is he to lecture anyone about risky decisions? He couldn't even protect the one thing he loved most. And now he's the biggest prize prey The Hunt has ever pursued.

As the thought of eating crow catches up to his temper, calmer nerves start to prevail.

"Sorry, I just . . . never mind. So, how'd you get out?" he asks. His tone is a hint more cordial, a tad less chiding.

Still stewing in his own prison of shame, Antoni can't find the courage to look Clayton square in the eye.

"I didn't. At least, not entirely," he confesses, his gaze darting around the room. "After I paid my debts, I told them I wanted out. The jobs were getting more and more reckless. Sonya and I were expecting. I did what I thought was right and asked her to marry me. What I was unwilling to lose was so much higher than what I could ever gain." He finally finds the nerve to look at Clayton, his eyes transparent, assuming. "You can probably imagine how well that went over."

Clayton gives a subtle consoling nod. "What happened after you said you wanted out?"

"Well, I told Baine I would do one last job, then I was done. And surprisingly he agreed. But I should have known better. It was supposed to be just another routine job. Get in. Make the drop. Get out," he says, shaking his head, recounting the repressed details. "But the whole fucking thing was just a setup from the jump. Cops raided the place almost instantly. Five of us went in, I was the only one that made it out. Turns out one of the guys on Desmond's crew was working on the inside for the ATF. Desmond had his suspicions and sent us anyway. Like some kind of fucking test. As if we were cows to the slaughterhouse. Because he could. Because that's who he is. We were nothing but expendable hired hands to him. Mere pawns to move on his chessboard."

Antoni walks over to the computer setup and scans the screens. The top left screen is the largest monitor of the four. It provides a gridded view of security cameras mapping the entire body shop premises and perimeter of the house.

"That was nearly six years ago. I haven't heard from him since. I guess in a weird, fucked up way, he kept his word. Then again, there's a part of me that still thinks he's keeping tabs on me. I don't know, maybe I'm just paranoid. But at least I'm prepared."

"And you should be. A guy like Desmond Baine doesn't just forgive and forget." Clayton adds, peering at Antoni. His voice calm, but eyes still locked in full reprimand mode. "Once you're in the game, you're always in the game, right? Or don't you buy your own advice?"

Antoni directs Clayton's accusing gaze back to the wall of firepower, strategically organized from smallest shooters to biggest boomers.

"What do you think plan B is for?" he notes. "Look, I know all this doesn't fix anything I did or make up for what happened, but it's prepared me for what could happen. And that's the best I can hope for now."

The thought of the whole charade makes Clayton wonder how everything and everyone else in Antoni's life fits into the situation.

"Does Sonya know about all this?"

"Some. Not all," Antoni admits, adjusting the surveillance monitor. "She knows about everything before the hospital, prior to rehab. It's not exactly easy to hide a history of crime and violence from a nurse that's seen your health record. Cared for you in your darkest moments. But this room? All this stuff? Desmond Baine?" Antoni shakes his head, the guilt resurfacing as he shifts his gaze to the ground. "No. She doesn't know about this." He looks up, his eyes solemn yet stern. "And I need to keep it that way. I'd lose her if she ever found out. Thad, too."

Antoni checks his watch as if the thought that he's got somewhere else he needs to be just triggered in his mind.

"C'mon, it's almost time," he says, ushering Clayton back toward the door.

"Huh? Almost time? For what? What are you—"

"Almost time to introduce you to someone I'd like you to meet."

"Okaayy," Clayton drags, brushed with skepticism. "After you, I guess."

As they casually make their way back up the underground lift and through the autobody shop, he takes a fresh glance at the Jeep. It's hardly even recognizable, just shambles of what it was mere hours ago.

No wheels.

No doors.

No engine.

No trace.

Cleo prances over to them as they exit the shop, her sad and slobbery tennis ball in tow. She drops it at Clayton's feet and gives him a good wag, a strong indication her pleading eyes are quickly losing patience. He grabs the flap of neon-faded rubber and flings it. She tears off in hot pursuit across the yard just as a school bus pulls up to the house. The exit door slides open and a round-faced, little boy no older than five with jet-black hair steps off the bus in turquoise Chuck Taylor's, rolled-up gray jeans, and a blue and white striped pocket t-shirt. He takes off running at the sight of Antoni, and they meet in a cheerful embrace in the yard. Antoni bends down in one fell swoop, swirling him around in a tornado of affection.

As Clayton watches, his mind starts to drift to Trish and the lost prospect of being a father. He wonders what his kid would have looked like as a kindergartner. How life would have been as a family. How it all could have been—should have been. He can feel his emotions balled up in a lump in his stomach, choking their way to the surface. They recede as he hears Antoni call out.

"Clay," Antoni says, rubbing the boy's head. "I want you to meet Thaddeus, my son."

Clayton walks up to the boy in Antoni's arms, a smile masking his pain. He offers the child his hand.

"Hi, Thaddeus, it's nice to meet you. My name is Clayton."

Thaddeus studies him like a stranger from head to toe with the kind of curious wonder that only a child's innocence can possess. That early glimmer and inquisitive marvel everyone is born with, but ultimately loses as they grow up and become jaded by the world and let down by the people around them. As youthful imagination becomes nothing more than harsh reality, and hopes and dreams mere figments of a naïve and exploited subconscious.

The boy hesitantly extends his chubby little palm in return as Antoni directs him, "Thad, what do we say when we meet someone?"

Behind bashful eyes and an even shyer voice, he replies, "Nice to meet you."

Clayton slowly drops to one knee, meeting him at eye level. "So, Thad, how old are you, bud?"

The timid boy, still unsure about the prospect of an unfamiliar guest, hides halfway behind his father's stretched leg, bunching Antoni's pants into tiny denim handfuls.

Antoni laughs.

"Thad, tell Clay how old you are," he instructs, before rephrasing the command into a softer question. "Can you show him on your hand, please?"

Thad lets go of his father's leg with one hand and juts out five plump, little fingers in Clayton's direction.

Antoni looks down at Clayton, shrugging his shoulders, chuckling. "I don't know what his deal is, he's never this shy around new people. In fact, usually, I can't get him to put a sock in it."

Clayton just smiles in return, fabricating his own true feelings. He thinks just like a dog can sense a storm coming, maybe kids have their own unique sixth sense. Maybe it's that inherent sense of innocence, or maybe it's because instinct tells them trust is still a foreign concept. That life is about survival—and as new members of the human species, it's the one thing they should be wary of before time and experience catch up to tarnish it. In Clayton's case, he feels it's Thad's innate ability to sense trouble, to perceive deep down when someone is cursed, just like himself.

"Can't say I blame him," Clayton responds as he gathers himself back up to his feet. "He must have a good intuition, like how to spot a bad omen."

Antoni shoots Clayton a deprecating eye roll that says, "don't be so hard on yourself, asshole." That is if looks could talk.

"Daddy, what's an omen?" Thad blurts out, no timidness behind the kindergartner's inquisition.

"I can't get him to sit down and recite his vocabulary words every night, but he jumps at that one faster than a fresh plate of dino nuggets."

He messes up Thad's hair again as the boy wriggles.

"T, an omen is like a sign or a warning that something bad is coming."

Thad immediately follows up with the only logical response a child could give—another question.

"Is something bad coming?"

Antoni drops to one knee as Thad finally lets go of the death grip on his jeans.

"No, buddy. Nothing bad is coming," he assures him, followed by a kiss on the top of his buzzed head. "You've got nothing to worry about, okay? Now, why don't you go inside and do your homework, then you can watch some cartoons before dinner. Clay and I will be right out here if you need us, all right?"

Thad nods and takes off running toward the house as Cleo eagerly tags along, her tail happily helicoptering at the fact that someone is finally here to play with her. When his turquoise sneakers hit the porch, Antoni yells out, "And Thaddeus Leonardo?" The boy obediently whips around at the mention of his full name. "In *that* order—homework, then cartoons. If I come in there, I better not see any school papers in front of the TV. Got it?"

Thad turns around and gives his father a compliant little nod before entering the house.

"I swear that kid is too damn smart for his own good," Antoni says, returning to face Clayton "And too fucking stubborn."

"Well, stubborn—I can connect those dots—but that's not really the obvious one, is it?"

"Huh? What do you mean?"

"What I mean is, he clearly got all the smarts from his mother because they sure as hell didn't come from you."

"Yep, you're definitely still an Ass-Ass."

They share a laugh, and in that moment it's like they haven't lost a beat. Like they just picked up where they left off before the night that changed everything. As if all those years lost from not speaking, spent hating one another—now all seem like nothing more than an erased memory. A span of time that never existed. It's not funny to think about, but all they can do now is laugh.

# CHAPTER 22

It's a quarter past 7 p.m. and Clayton, Antoni, and Thad are all gathered around the kitchen table. Thad's working on the writing homework he got caught neglecting earlier for a sneaky opportunity to watch cartoons; Clayton's working on his third beer; and Antoni's working on dinner—a honey-glazed chicken risotto with sautéed asparagus au jus.

"Let me get this straight. The guy whose total diet consisted of nothing but chicken fingers and pizza growing up is now Gordon Ramsay in the kitchen?" Clayton confirms, utterly shocked. "Get the fu—"

But he catches himself as he looks over at Thad whose pencil is wagging along the page, practicing his capitalization. "—Funyuns . . . out of here."

"Funyuns, huh? Nice cover," Antoni adds, in between a pan toss of the green veggie sticks.

"Funyuns!" Thad shoots up in the middle of adding the second leg to his uppercase R. "Can I have some, Dad?"

"Sorry, buddy, we don't have any. Besides, dinner's almost ready." Antoni smiles as he samples a wooden ladle of the homemade honey glaze. "And yeah, Clay, it's true. I'm like Ramsay up in here but without the sailor mouth. Something that you could work on at the moment, apparently," he kids, drizzling a little more chicken stock into the glaze. "So, turns out, Sonya's a bit of a foodie. After the first few dates of her watching me pick everything off my plate, she just straight up refused to let me eat like a child anymore. So, I had to expand my culinary horizons. Now, I literally eat everything, and cooking it's even better."

Clayton takes a swig of lager from his bottle. "Wow. I've got to meet this woman. The one who tamed the infamous Antoni Rivera," he adds, using his free hand to frame an imaginary plaque in the air. "How'd you land such a catch, anyway?"

"He used a big rod with lots of bait," a sassy voice from the front door calls out, as a petite woman in dirty navy scrubs with a straw-colored ponytail and eggshell-steps strolls into the kitchen. Hard on the heels of a long, thirteen-hour ER shift, she wastes no time freeing the migraine-inducing, dome-tight hair tie on her head as her blond locks flow into cascading waves, crashing down atop her narrow shoulders. Each curl possesses its own unique shade of cresting amber and gold. "But I did try to put up a fight before he could reel me in," she says, shooting Antoni a wink. "Just about broke the line, too."

"Mommy!" Thad shouts out in glee while waving his homework proudly in the air. "Lookit, I did the whole alphabet by myself."

"Wow, good job, little man. I'm proud of you. But wasn't that supposed to be done *right* after school?" she inquires, cutting straight to the hard-hitting investigation questions like every good detective mother. "Looks like someone treated themselves to an early cartoon break again."

"Busted, buddy," Antoni confirms over the stove's sizzle.

Bouncing gracefully from one conversation to another, she strides over to kiss her husband.

"Mmm, yum, is that honey glaze?"

Antoni nods and meets her lips with his. He goes back to adding another patient cup of water to the simmering risotto.

Finally, Sonya turns her attention to Clayton.

"And you must be Clay, it's nice to finally put a face to the name. I'm Sonya," she introduces herself, still brushing out the knots in her hair with one hand while extending her other. "I've heard *so many* stories about you."

At her revelation, he whips his attention to Antoni, who's doing an admirable yet inconvincible job of pretending not to eavesdrop by oversalting the chicken breasts.

All this time, Clayton thought his old friend hated him. Blamed him for his brother's death. Believed that he intentionally tried to kill him the night they got into their scuffle. It turns out, he was just as stubborn as Clayton was. Reluctant. Scared to be the first to reach out and attempt amends. To swallow his pride and forgive. But that's the funny thing about men's pride, it's never there in the situations that truly call for it.

Clayton gets up from his chair and shakes Sonya's hand. He kindly smiles and says, "Well, remind me to give you the real stories then because who knows what kind of fabricated fairytales he's been feeding you." She laughs at the jab. It sounds warm, full of heart, like one of those genuinely contagious giggles that can light up a room. "Nice firm handshake by the way."

"What can I say, my daddy taught me right."

At the thought of hearing her fatherly lesson, Clayton is yanked out of Wonderland, up through the rabbit hole, and back into reality. He thinks about Klein, Trish, and The Hunt. What his next move will be and how he intends to do it. If he can even do it. But his nightmare of a daydream is quickly interrupted by Sonya.

"I'm gonna go freshen up real quick before dinner's ready. Pretty sure I have at least a quart of dried blood on my shirt and maybe just as much, if not more, urine on my pants. And I think a little vomit, or some other unidentified bodily fluid caked on my shoes. I honestly don't know. Sometimes ignorance is bliss. Gotta love the ER," she quips, and exits the room, disappearing into the shrouded hallway.

Clayton watches and waits for the closing clink of the bathroom door.

"Man, you hit the jackpot. I hope you know that," he whispers to Antoni in between congratulatory sips of beer. "I don't even know her yet, and I can already tell she's way too good for you. And the whole big rod and reel, bit. Was that a covert penis innuendo?"

"I have a penis!" Thad proudly proclaims over his eavesdropping. "But why's one in the window?" he asks, innocently studying the exposed glass panes for phallic remains. "I don't see it."

"Oh, for the love of . . ." Antoni chuckles. "Just go back to your homework, okay buddy? Dinner is in two minutes. And you—" He juts his mixing spoon at Clayton. "Just stop talking already."

Recovering from his series of laughs thanks to their personal episode of *Kid's Say the Darndest Things*, Clayton nudges again.

"So . . . ? C'mon. Do tell. I need deets."

But Antoni plays the *gentleman never tells* card, pleading the fifth with no response. Although Clayton can see him failing to conceal his smile as he finishes chopping up a stalk of cilantro.

"Why you sly S.O.B.," Clayton hails.

This time, without bothering to even look up from his paper for fear of being reprimanded again, Thad shyly asks, "What's an S-O-B?"

"Jesus, Clay, maybe I ought to have you teach Thad his vocab lessons, since he apparently absorbs literally everything you say." That's when the idea for a friendly little game crosses his mind. "Actually, yeah, Clay, do tell. What exactly is an S.O.B.?"

Clayton chokes on his mouthful of beer, nearly spewing warm fizz across the entire table, all over Thad's worksheet.

"Hrmm. Ohh, well, uh Thad, umm—guess I'm really doing this—an S.O.B. is . . . uhh, well, it's when you don't really like someone, you see, so umm . . ." He continues to fail miserably with his delivery, making more sound effects than forming actual words. "But it can also be a joke, too, you see, like uhh, among friends. You see it stands for son of a—"

"*Ohh*-kay," Antoni practically shouts, sparing any more casualties in the verbal trainwreck. "Dinner is ready," he adds, shooting Clayton another chastising glance.

"What? I wasn't actually going to say it," Clayton responds, wiping a dribble of suds from his upper lip.

"Just . . . both of you go grab a plate," Antoni orders, shooing them to the bar. "Good god, it's like all of a sudden I've got two kids to watch now."

Clayton and Thad both grab a plate and shuffle over to the counter, their hungry bellies leading the way. Clayton helps Thad make a small plate before heaping a hearty helping of risotto onto his own dish.

"Shit, Clay, save some for the rest of us," Antoni carps.

Thad's ears perk up from the table, risotto already coating his chin in a creamy soul patch. "Ooh, Daddy said a bad word."

"Well, well, well. Looks like we know who the real potty mouth around here is, sailor," Clayton piggybacks. "Perhaps you really are Gordon Ramsay, in more ways than just cooking. And I'm willing to wager that Thad's already been introduced to S.O.B.—among many other fun four-letter words."

With her hair still wet and fiddling with her earring, Sonya re-enters the kitchen just in time to catch the tasteful dinner conversation about various one-syllable vulgarities.

"What on earth are you two teaching my baby?" she grills, tilting her head to the side, finally clasping the second hoop. "Do I have three kids in the house I have to parent now? Don't test me. I've got plenty of soap to go around for all your potty mouths."

Clayton and Antoni's mischievous eyes meet. They snicker like conniving children. Just like when they were kids, growing up together and getting into countless bouts of juvenile delinquency around town before harmless pranks turned into criminal records. Before life got heavy, and in the way. When the world was all still fun and games.

Like the time they got the cops called on them for accidently setting fire to part of a new neighborhood development. Because what could possibly go wrong popping off October fireworks in a wide-open space full of tall, dead grass and piles of raw lumber? They fled the scene at the first wail of sirens, pedaling as fast and furious as their little nine-year-old, pyro-obsessed feet could push them.

Or, when they were eleven, and Antoni thought it would be funny to hit up the rich side of town and go streaking on the glitzy golf course. He called it a complimentary middle finger to the privileged. They made it all the way down the par four on hole five before clubhouse security caught up in hot pursuit. The only reason they managed to get away was because Clayton lured the trailing security cart over the hole's blind fairway right next to a big sand trap. Then, in a last-ditch, evasive maneuver, he veered, and they didn't. Their ride caught the sudden lip and barrel rolled into the grainy pit. Sand, grit, and chunks of golf cart flew everywhere. By the time it stopped flipping, its wheels were parallel to the sky still comically spinning.

Then, there was the time the two thought it would be fun to go out and shoot the paintball guns Antoni had just received for his thirteenth birthday. Once the pair were too sore from feeling the litter of stings from shooting one another, they decided to focus their assault efforts off the 8th Street Bridge that overlooked the freeway. It started out harmless enough, aiming for street signs and random underpass graffiti, but, eventually, it took a turn for the worse when Antoni shot at the oncoming traffic below. Because boys are stupid.

It was all laughs until he splattered the windshield of a car hauling at seventy miles per hour with a series of paintballs. Blinded by a smear of royal blue, the driver freaked out and slammed on the breaks, causing the unprepared truck directly behind to plow right into his rear end.

Luckily, no one was injured, but by the time the crunching of metal and screeching of burnt rubber stopped, six cars had piled up, completely blocking the westbound underpass. Although they took off running as swiftly as their size sevens could take them, they couldn't escape this one thanks to Clayton's nosy neighbor, Ms. Beverly, or as they used to call her, Ms. Beaverly. A befitting nickname due to the tectonic-sized gap separating her two-front, chiclet-sized teeth. They always joked that it looked like her teeth were throwing a middle school dance where all the boys lined up on one side of the gym, too afraid to ask the girls on the other side for a dance. She was a bitter, lonely old hag of a woman who used to get her jollies by berating them for skateboarding on the street or yelling at them for hopping their shared fence to retrieve overthrown baseballs.

As it turns out, on the day of their paintball pileup, Ms. Beaverly had been walking her mangy, red-mopped excuse for a dog, Ginger—a nasty-tempered little shih tzu, totally deserving of the repulsive-sounding breed name—around the block. Despite the boys successfully fleeing the scene, it wasn't before the Wicked Witch and her little dog, too, were able to ID them as the perpetrators.

Later that night, just when they thought they had made it out scot-free, yet again, there was an unexpected knock at Clayton's house. When his mom opened the front door, two fuck-around-and-find-out patrolmen in pressed blue uniforms stood humorlessly on the other side.

That was not a fun one for Clayton to explain to his parents. The beginning of the end, really. The irreversible start of the downward spiral where they claim everything started to go wrong. Before the grand theft accusations and juvie hall. Before the aggravated assault and battery charge that put him behind bars. Back when he was just a kid trying to be a kid.

The four sit down for dinner together, relishing the good food and even better company. After several failed attempts from Sonya to get Clayton to regale her with embarrassing stories about Antoni as a kid, he finally caves much to Antoni's chagrin.

He tells her about the streaking at the golf course in junior high, which comes as no surprise to her. What does come as a shock, however, are the shits he had taken in the cups on holes twelve and fourteen's greens the next time they revisited that same uppity golf course at night.

"Wait, *shits* . . . plural?" Sonya exclaims. "As in multiple? Bahaha, how's that even possible?"

But Antoni doesn't even try a defense. He just takes a swig of beer, crosses his arms, and hangs his head in dread.

"Never underestimate the disgusting potential of a teenage boy, Sonya," Clayton remarks. "Remember that when Thad hits puberty."

"Gross," she sneers. "And that's coming from a nurse who gets doused with literally every sort of bodily fluid anytime I walk into work."

"Ohhhh, I'm just getting started," Clayton laughs and continues, nostalgically narrating the time Antoni got vomited on at the movie theater because the girl he was dating had just come down with the flu.

"Sonya, I kid you not, I could hear her dry heaving from two rows back," he says, reenacting the retching sound. "But Antoni was so persistent, so determined to kiss her because it was like their third date, and he hadn't sealed the deal yet. We'd been giving him so much crap about it, that he didn't even care she was on the verge of yakking. So, he just kept leaning in for the kiss. Closer. And closer." The more detail he recites, the more vivid the recall becomes. "But before she could push him away or get up to excuse herself, she just upchucks, and I mean Up. Chucks. It goes all over Toni's face, his chest, into his lap, the floor, the people in the row ahead of them, even the person's handful of popcorn on the next armrest over, literally everywhere—you name it. Like a scene out of a raunchy comedy or *The Exorcist.* Just absolutely vile."

In between uncontrollable laughs, he finds enough control to continue the story.

"Then, and this might be the best part, the whole row jumps up, parting from the gag grenade that's just been dropped as she continues her spewing spree all the way down the aisle to the exit. Leaving a trail of barf shrapnel everywhere. Retch getting on and in everything—shoes, laps, candy boxes, popcorn buckets, sodas. No one and no snack were spared in the puking process. And I don't know what this girl had eaten, but it glowed neon yellow under the backlight of the movie screen with all sorts of indiscernible chunks and undigested pieces glistening in the projector light like some kind of toxic cottage cheese. She ran out of the theater so fast, so embarrassed. I don't think she ever talked to Toni again. At least, I never saw her again."

Clayton peers at Antoni who's shaking his head in reprehensible recollection, eyes buried deep in his guilty hands.

"What was her name again? Something Reynolds, right? Like Megan or Morgan?"

Antoni cinches his eyes even tighter, puckers his lips, and releases his forehead from his hand. It's shame, and every form of it.

"It was Molly. Molly Reynolds," he mutters, beyond disgraced. But a choked-away smile can't hide itself from sneaking across his lips at the absurd amusement behind the childhood story. "Yeahhh, I'm pretty sure she moved away like a month after that incident," he confesses like a clenched teeth emoji. "We dubbed that night the 'Upchuck at the Uptown.' God, I still feel awful to this day for that."

Shocked, but with a smile stretching from ear-to-ear, Sonya playfully slaps her husband across the arm. "Oh my god! That's so awful. You literally made a girl move away? Jesus, Toni, you guys were terrible."

Clayton, trying to contain himself, speaks up.

"Sonya, that's not even the worst of it."

He faces Antoni with a devilish look, his upper lip curling into a sinister smirk like the Grinch Who Stole Humility.

"Does she know about the wet bet?"

Antoni tilts his head and shoots him a desperate look of

hopelessness. His eyes pleading. "No, and you better not or I swear to—"

But he can't finish his sentence before Sonya throws her eager hand over his mouth, silencing him mid-threat.

"Shhh, you don't get to talk right now. You made a poor, sick girl move away," she whispers, placing her index finger over the Cupid's bow of his lips. "Go ahead. Spill it, Clay."

Clayton goes on to tell the tale of the time he happily lost twenty dollars because he had bet Antoni that he wouldn't piss his pants in the middle of freshman English class. In near tears from laughing so hard, he recounts every rich detail about how mad Mrs. Kornigan was when Antoni casually stood up in the middle of her lecture on the symbolism in *Ethan Frome,* or some other self-reflective load of literary crock from the turn of the century, with his khakis soaked all the way down on one side from crotch to ankle and just calmly asked if he could be excused. Then, even after his verbal berating in front of the entire class, he had made it a point to walk by Clayton's desk on his way to the principal's office and coolly collect his hard-earned Jackson.

"I'm not lying, Sonya. He casually strolls up to my desk, literal urine dripping off his shoe onto the classroom carpet, and says, I quote, 'Should have made it thirty.' Then, he winks, snatches the twenty from my hand, and struts out. I nearly fall out of my desk laughing while the rest of the class doesn't know whether to join in or be absolutely appalled." Clayton leans back in his chair, finishing off the remaining gulp of beer in his bottle. "I'll never forget the look of utter disbelief on Mrs. Kornigan's face that day. She probably had taught high school for thirty years prior and at least another ten years after, and I can guarantee you, she never had another ninth grader piss themselves in the middle of class. Let alone willingly."

Despite the overwhelmingly dire situation at hand, Clayton can't help but think the laughter from reminiscing feels good, almost therapeutic. Like a prescription of nostalgia and a hefty dose of endorphins are just what the doctor ordered. To shed tears not associated with sadness or remorse. To feel like there's something still worth fighting for. Worth living for.

He tries to regain his composure in between heavy chest heaves, only to lose it again when he hears Sonya snort. Even Antoni can't help but join the laugh track, even if it is at his own expense.

Shaking his head in embarrassment, Antoni gets up and paces to the fridge, signaling the others for another round of beers. As he brings three cold ones back to the table, the comedy club has cooled down to nothing more than a couple of diminishing giggles. Clayton's tone regains its senses, remembering the severity of the situation he's in and that he's put them in by simply being here.

He looks at Sonya with sincerity as he accepts the fresh bottle from Antoni.

"Thank you two for this. For helping me," he says popping its cap. "I . . . I don't know what I would have done. Where I could have gone. I'd probably be—"

Dead. But he can't bring himself to say it aloud.

Sonya cracks open her fresh beer, returning the sincerity with a dose of her own.

"Hey, you're Toni's friend, but more importantly, you're an innocent man, Clay. You're more than welcome here."

"Are you sure? Are you really okay with me being here?" Clayton asks after a crisp gulp. "The last thing I want to do is put you all in danger."

Sonya takes another generous drink and slowly lowers the bottle back to the table. She looks at her husband, then at her son, who's moved on from doing his homework to finishing a piece of double chocolate cake in front of the living room TV. A fat piece with extra frosting that he's successfully gotten more of on his face and shirt than in his actual mouth.

"Clay, why do you think I became a nurse?" she queries, pushing her beer to the side.

Clayton replies, "I-I . . . um, don't know. Why?"

"Because I truly wanted to help people. And yeah, I know how beyond cliché that sounds, but I still believe I'm doing that every day I wake up and walk into that hospital. The idea that I'm actually making a difference, even if that just means one person. And sure, some days—okay, most days—it's hard. Really hard. And it sucks. And people are assholes. And I question whether it's all worth it for my mental health. But then, I think about all the patients I've cared for—those I've helped walk again. Breathe again. Not have to fight alone again." She reaches across the table, putting her hand on Antoni's thigh. "Helped love again. I didn't just take an oath to care for people. I followed my dream and I'm not about to quit on that now," she concludes, taking another drink as she slides back into her seat. "So, you're more than welcome to stay here. As long as you need."

Clayton follows her lead by leaning back in his chair, taking in the moment, the touching monologue, and the horrid road less traveled it took to get here.

He raises his bottle in a toast.

"To friends."

He looks to Antoni; their eyes meet in a mutual exchange of gratitude. Of appreciation almost forgotten and long overdue.

"To family," Antoni adds.

They cheers their respective bottles, clinking a three-way toast. Clayton takes a modest swig and wipes his mouth with his sleeve. He slaps his free hand on Antoni's shoulder as he too finishes his post-toast drink.

Facing his guest, Antoni apprehensively clangs the bottle back down onto the table. He can sense there's something Clayton's been putting off telling him. The *real* reason why he's here, perhaps. The plan that he's strategically been hiding behind a day full of reminiscing. And he's not ready to hear it. Because he's not ready to re-lose the friend that took him so long to get back.

Clayton slowly starts to rise from the table like a party guest who's hesitant to be the first one to leave. The tentative words soon follow.

"While I truly appreciate everything you've both done and are willing to do, we all know I can't stay here. It's just not safe. For anyone."

Antoni tries to stand and interject, but he's cut off by Clayton who tightens the grip on his shoulder, easing him back down.

"I have a plan," he continues, doing his best to reassure. "And before you tell me how dumb it is. Just hear me out, okay? So, I know that—"

*DING DONG!*

The doorbell echoes throughout the house like an amplified record scratch before Clayton can utter another word.

# CHAPTER 23

DING DONG! The conversation killer rings again.

Cleo zooms into the kitchen letting out a series of howling barks followed by a low, lengthy growl. Clayton instantly lowers his drink and raises his guard, exchanging a grave look with Antoni across the table. Sonya watches like an innocent, third-party bystander as the two switch gears from laid back to on edge in the span of a second-long ding dong.

Clayton is the first to break the tense silence.

"You happen to be expecting anyone, Toni?"

Antoni slowly rises from his seat mid-reply.

"No. And anyone invited here knows better than to ring the doorbell." He shoots a glance at Sonya and Thad to gauge the temperature of their mounting panic. They can both sense something is awry but have no clue what's going on.

"Babe, I need you to take Thad and Cleo and go to the basement right now. Lock the door and don't let anyone in unless it's me," Antoni commands, as he slides over to the kitchen sink, flings open the cabinet underneath and damn near reaches his full arm up inside until it comes back out with a pistol in tow. The surprised look on her face clearly states her total ignorance of the fact that there was a firearm tucked above the cleaning supplies this whole time.

"Now, Sonya," Antoni repeats.

Sonya grabs Cleo and Thad, who are both growing progressively more concerned by the second, and makes her way to the basement door. By the time she gets there, Thad's eyes have glossed, and he starts to cry, his tears turning Cleo's aggressive growls into consoling whimpers. Sonya tries to calm them both down, but her hushes just make his wails and Cleo's howls climax. What was just a nibble of worry is now consumed by full-on horror.

"Toni? I'm scared," she says, clutching onto Thad, her protective arms draped around his shoulders like a superhero cape.

"Don't worry, babe. Everything is going to be okay," Antoni assures, pointing to the basement door. "Just get down there and stay put. Don't come back up here no matter what you hear. Understood?"

The doorbell rings a third time. The uneasy jingle resonates throughout the house again, cranking up the tension to a 9.9 on a ten-point scale.

"But Toni, what if—?"

"Now, Sonya!" he erupts, not out of anger but urgency. Realizing he's just tipped her tension scale to an eleven, he tries again with a calmer approach. "Baby, please, you need to get downstairs right now. There's no time for questions."

Sonya is quickly losing the battle against her nerves as distress digests her from the inside out. Her once confident composure has all but been replaced by a frantic damsel in distress demeanor. Her lips are trembling, fighting against the involuntary shake to form words, but nothing comes out. Reluctantly, she opens the basement door, and the three of them disappear down the flight of stairs.

Antoni rushes over to the silverware drawer in the corner and rips out the plastic divider, casting the brass utensils onto the granite countertop in a cacophony of vibrating clanks and clings.

The doorbell rings a fourth time, and Clayton dashes to the

window above the sink. With a reverse pinch, he splits a small diamond-shaped crease in the drawn blinds, but it's too dark to see anything outside and the nosy streetlight that lit his arrival last night shows no trace of illuminated intrusiveness now.

Still chucking the drawer's remaining utensils across the kitchen, Antoni jimmies the oak box until the bottom board on the tracking system loosens. Finally, he pries it off, revealing a loaded handgun clip tucked inside. He slaps the eighteen-bullet cartridge into the magazine chamber and tucks the semi-automatic pistol into the back of his pants.

Silently, yet aggressively, pointing toward the kitchen dimmer switch, he gives Clayton a gesture to kill the lights as he inches toward the front door.

Clayton flips the switch and grabs a butcher knife from the counter's neighboring cutlery block. Now that the level of light inside and outside is synchronized, he tries again to peek through the blinds but he still can't discern anything in the shadowy abyss.

When Antoni gets to the front door, he's careful not to expose too much of his body against the slab of bolted hardwood. He unholsters the pistol and checks the peephole. Only there's nothing to see but fuzzy darkness on the other side of the tiny fish lens.

Someone clearly doesn't want to be seen.

"Yeah?" he finally says, fortifying his voice. "Who's there? Awfully late for a house call, ain't it?"

There's a long, unsettling pause before a response muffles its way back through the reinforced front door.

"Hello, sir. Good evening," a pleasant voice replies, although slightly difficult to make out. "We're here to share a message from our Lord and Savior. Do you have a few minutes?"

Antoni's silhouette, lit only by the dim glow from the outside moonlight, motions to Clayton who's watching suspiciously from the foyer entryway.

He whispers, "Back door. Check it."

Clayton nods and navigates his way through the dark, foreign space to the rear of the house like a bumbling ninja in the night.

Back at the front door, Antoni rests the back of his head against the wall adjacent to the entrance, running through the next series of plays in his head. He picks the best-offense-is-a-good-defense route and goes with it.

"Sorry, just a bunch of sinners in here content to burn in hell, so you can take your Lord's salvation elsewhere. Piss off, now."

He can hear a group of men aggressively whispering among themselves on the other side of the solid mahogany slab. They're too stifled to make out completely, but he can depict at least three distinct tones in the exchange. The multiple voices cease as one of them speaks up.

"Salvation is justice," the outside voice responds, dropping the friendly Bible salesman pitch. "Now open the fucking door, Rivera. We know Sparks is in there."

"Gentlemen, gentlemen—where did the manners go?" Antoni goads, mainly to buy Clayton more time, but in part, to further instigate them. "I'm sorry, fellas, but I think you've got the wrong house."

He backs away slowly from the door, still talking. Still buying time. "Because if you're looking for salvation, you sure as shit aren't gonna find it here." Crouching to his knee, he continues to work his way down flat onto his stomach. In an army crawl pose, he trains his gun on the peephole just about head height. "Now, do me a favor, yeah?" he asks rhetorically, adding an extra beat for good measure. "Take yourself and the other mouth-breathers out there with you and get the fuck off my porch."

Then, nothing but hush.

The long pause of still, unadulterated quiet is brutally interrupted by a barrage of thunderous artillery. Large wood splinters and a storm of bullets rain inside the house as the front door is ripped to shreds one hole at a time. A few deafening seconds later, the bombardment abruptly stops. The recaptured moment of calm is broken again as the remnants of the entrance are forcefully kicked in by a large shadowy figure dressed in all black. He's closely followed by another man decked head to toe in darkness, like death incarnate.

They funnel into the home's smoke-filled entryway in a single, calculated line of coverage. Antoni pops off two concentrated shots striking the first shadow in the chest, then the head. He drops dead instantly. The second silhouetted figure attempts to retaliate, but before he can aim down to squeeze the trigger, Antoni unloads another charge between his eyes. His black stocking cap acts like a sponge, filtering the exit path of the lethal impact like red wine spewed from a spray bottle. Its crimson mist paints over the moon's distant waning glow, adding thousands of new red dots to its scarred surface. He joins his partner on the floor, dropping his gun along the descent.

Antoni catches a glimpse of the man's limp hand as it unfolds before him in the glint of lunar light. DB88 is tattooed across his index finger.

Moments later, another wave of gunfire showers the exposed entry, flooding in from where the front door used to be. Antoni rolls from the foyer into the kitchen, bracing himself against the refrigerator for cover. He readies his gun, resting his trigger finger over the curved metal lever.

Looking down, he notes the same DB88 tattoo on his own hand.

Desmond Baine's 88s crew.

His old crew.

Meanwhile, on his obscure route to the back door, the boisterous orchestra of fireworks from the front of the house consumes Clayton's undivided attention, and he ducks for safety behind the couch. A tick later, the back door is demolished in a single blast by a stout silhouette toting a tactical shotgun.

Clayton crumbles to the ground for cover, ears ringing, while his equilibrium fights for every morsel of balance and clarity it can scrape together. As the shadow enters the house, it spots him on the ground writhing in discombobulation. It raises its scattergun for the kill, but Clayton musters enough coherency to blindly swing the butcher knife in his hand faster than the figure can pull the trigger. The flail from his back carries enough force and bite to cut right through the man's exposed Achilles. The gruesome slice sounds like someone slapping a plastic grocery bag with an open hand, but it's nothing compared to the blood-curdling scream that follows.

Clayton quickly finds the way to his feet—unsteady, but upright—and punts the shotgun out of the downed man's arms before he can think twice about using it again. He follows that kick with a barrage of heavy heels to the man's mask, only stopping the unconscious pummeling to dive for cover when he feels a rifle shot hiss too close for comfort above his head. The fatal bullet just inches from its opportunity to splatter his gray matter against the slow-turning blades of the ceiling fan.

Luckily, his dive lands him in the direction of the vacant shotgun. With even quicker reflexes and a presence of mind fueled by pure adrenaline, he grabs the smooth-barreled boom stick and turns around just in time to unload a scattered shell on another inbound assailant. The intruder flies back several feet from the point-blank blast, taking down the Golden Age-shelved portion of Antoni's vintage radio collection with him.

The fleeting victory doesn't last long as a new shitstorm of bullets hails in from the drywall and windows, blistering throughout the back of the house. Clayton bear crawls beneath the windowpanes for the kitchen as fast as his elbows can scurry while glass shards and chunks of sheetrock cut through the room every which way.

Slithering into the heart of the house, he hears Antoni yell out among the scathing sound of strafed fire. "Clay, you all right?"

He slides across the kitchen's hardwood floor on all fours with a sarcastic answer locked and loaded.

"Oh sure, I'm fucking hunky-dory." But the incessant blasts swallow his next words, making them inaudible. "Are you good?" he mutely reciprocates, flipping the dinner table over for added coverage.

Contributing his own select shots and their accompanying clamor to the heavy exchange, Antoni shouts back, "What?"

"I said—" Clayton pauses as an eager bullet carrying enough force splinters its way through the overturned tabletop, barely missing his elbow. "Fuck!" he yelps out in response.

"I know!" Antoni hurls back. "This *is* fucked."

"Huh? I . . . No—" Clayton hollers in return as another slug buries itself into the wood.

"I KNOW!" Antoni again yells back. "That's what I *just* said," urgently combating confusion with agitation.

"What? No! Not I know. I said—" but Clayton stops, realizing this useless exercise for the hearing impaired is like trying to carry on a conversation at a rock concert, only over bullets instead of distortion. "Ah, fuck it."

"I already said *that*, too!" Antoni barks, as he rattles off a couple more targeted shots from behind the fridge. Visibly confused, he looks toward Clayton who returns a shotgun blast of his own from around the fragmented dinner table.

Finally, there's a small break in the shootout, leaving the shambled room around them ringing out in an audible cloud of gun smoke.

"BTW, I'm *also* all right," Antoni issues cynically, ruffling the fresh blanket of quiet. "Thanks for asking . . ."

In no hurry to warrant his current annoyance with another fumbled response, Clayton just scowls from the safe side of the splintered tabletop.

Finally, he pipes up. "Are you shitting me?"

"Huh?" Antoni shrugs, totally oblivious. "About what?"

"I've only been trying to ask you that for the past two goddamn minutes."

"Oh," Antoni says, his misdirected sarcasm now devouring crow. "I couldn't hear you."

"Yeah, no shit, Sherlock," Clayton replies, "Captain Fucking Obvious over there."

"Oh, I'm *sorrrry*," Antoni apologizes, not a hint of remorse. "Did you want me to ask them to turn it down? Or maybe we can request they bring silencers next time? Better yet, just make it a goddamn knife fight."

"Pshh. Whatever, man," Clayton shrugs. "How many did you get anyway?" he asks, switching the subject to something much more pertinent to their current situation. "I dropped two in the back."

"Make that four," Antoni adds. "I got another pair at the front door."

Slowly, the gunfire starts to pick back up like a swelling snare drum gaining tempo. A few isolated beats here and there turn into a drum-roll bevy of constant artillery, rumbling the walls and rattling the floorboards. It may be mid-September, but it sounds like the Fourth of July as Antoni and Clayton quicken the pace of planning their next move.

"We've got to lure them away from the house into the shop," Antoni instructs, returning a few shots of his own, keeping the assailants honest. Clayton follows suit with a couple dispersed shotgun blasts. He checks the chamber, less than a handful of shells remain.

"Damn, I'm almost out," he yells, under a desperate look at Antoni across the kitchen.

"Me, too," Antoni chimes in, inspecting his clip.

"Okay," Clayton agrees. "I think plan B sounds pretty damn good right about now."

The remaining icicles of glass hanging from what's left of the kitchen windows come shattering down as two more of Baine's crew crash into the home's galley. Antoni and Clayton both take cover behind their respective home furnishings as the spray of assault rifle rounds rip through the cupboards and pantry, splashing remnants of chevron-tiled backsplash across the entire room.

Antoni turns around from the fridge and opens fire to draw their attention his way.

One of them is foolish enough to take the bait.

Stalking toward the stainless-steel appliance, the intruder empties his rifle to ensure Antoni stays helplessly pinned in place. When the firing stops, Antoni turtleheads his neck around the cold locker, craning to see the man frantically reloading—his window of opportunity closing just as quickly as it opened. Before he knows it, instinct takes over and he pops up from coverage. With one violent pull, he flings open the top freezer portion of the fridge door, striking the man in the head with a forceful pendulum of solid steel momentum. The assailant staggers back dazed, affording Antoni just enough time to squeeze off two rounds center mass. The body drops, crashing into the farmhouse sink on its way down. A smear of red streaks the glossy white porcelain, mapping his lifeless path to the floor.

The commotion draws the attention of the other intruder who now has a clear shot at an exposed Antoni. But Clayton reacts faster than he can pull the trigger, skidding one of the dining chairs across the floor with a fierce kick. The assailant topples over at the knees while physics goes to work.

He tries to scramble back up to one knee, but it's too little, too late. Antoni sees a wide-open headshot and pulls the trigger. The man's neck slingshots his skull backward as a spatter of blood and bone fragments paint what's left of the pantry door. The red and white peppermint-swirled chunks gradually run down the shattered wood like the first raindrops on a virgin window. He hits the ground, and a stream begins to pool, drowning Thad's capitalization homework that's been strewn about all over the hardwood floor in a dark crimson pond.

"If we're gonna move, we've got to do it now," Clayton urges, his rushed tone matching the chaotic climax of the moment.

Antoni peaks at the front door for possible exit number one, but immediately starts taking relentless fire.

"Well, we're sure as shit not headed out the front door," he confirms, and shoots a measured glance down the hallway toward the master bedroom, then back at Clayton. "I've got an idea," he yells, checking his magazine again. "Cover me, then follow."

He takes off without another word while Clayton unloads a few rounds of forgivable cover fire. It's just enough breathing room to safely shuffle from the kitchen past the foyer before tumbling into the hallway. He returns the favor as Clayton makes his own mad dash and dives for the hallway.

Just as the two clamber to their feet, another wave of 88s piles in from the front and back doors, as well as the busted-out kitchen windows. Through the sheer number of incoming men, the probability of escape starts to exponentially decline as the friends now find themselves completely surrounded with almost no ammo and no available exists. Over the roaring volley of encroaching gunfire, Antoni leans in, practically shouting into Clayton's ear from mere inches away.

"Bedroom window! Go, now!"

Under siege, they sprint down the hall. Within seconds, the master bedroom door is battering rammed open by the joint effort of their shoulders. They spill in headfirst from the momentum.

Clayton is the first to spring to his feet. "Fuck. How many do you think there are?"

Antoni, a little slower to get up and slightly gassed, responds between weighty exhales, "If I had to guess, around twenty? With the six we've already taken out, there's maybe fifteen or so left?"

Clayton checks his ammo; he's got three shells left.

Antoni does the same. Five rounds remain.

"Listen, Clay, if I don't make it to the shop—"

"What? Don't talk like that. We've got—"

But his interruption is immediately returned.

"Just shut up and listen! We don't have much time," Antoni continues, his hefty breathing doing its best to replenish his nervous lungs. "I know you're planning on going after Klein. I think it's a dumb fucking plan, but god knows I can't stop you. Hell, I might not have to if we don't make it out of here alive. But I know you came here for help, and—"

The two duck behind the plush California King as bullets spew through the bedroom door, shredding the down comforter into feathered confetti.

"—I'm glad you did," he adds with a slight delay in his words. "If something does happen to me, the code to the bay lift is 080690. Take whatever you need."

Wrinkles spread across Clayton's forehead and his pupils dilate. With earnestness in his voice, he asks, "You used my birthday for the code?"

"Yeah, yeah . . . now's not the time to get all sentimental." The gunfire growing closer, louder. "And Clay? I'm sorry."

Amid the absolute shit storm they're trapped in, Clayton finds himself in a sudden rainbow of emotions. Confusion takes center arc. "Sorry? For what?"

"These men," Antoni replies, a heavy weight of guilt pulls his gaze to the floor. "They're Desmond Baine's 88s crew. My old crew. When I was first initiated, I told Baine who I used to run around with back in the day. What jobs I pulled, who was in my crew. Like some kind of criminal resume. He must have remembered your name and somehow put the two together after you became wanted, thinking you'd come back out of desperation or something. I don't really know. But I'm sorry."

Urgency regains the bow's limelight as Clayton's confusion dissipates. Booms from the hallway gunfire continue to mince the master bedroom into a snow-covered feather wonderland.

"Now's not the time for sentiment or coming clean. How were you to know?" Clayton places his hand on Antoni's shoulder. "Right now, our priority is don't die."

Antoni nods and points to the bay bedroom windows.

"It's the only way out."

Staring past the navy curtain at the glass cove, Clayton shakes his head.

"Why are we always crashing through glass?"

"Chalk it up to that whole being cursed thing," Antoni mocks, crouching into a sprinter's stance. "You ready for this?"

Clayton exhales a hopeless chuckle. Reluctantly, he matches Antoni's readiness.

"Just watch your neck this time, all right?"

An inadvertent smile cracks Antoni's pursed lips. "Still an Ass-Ass. Have I said, 'Fuck you' lately?"

"Nope," Clayton replies, ducking as the bed's backstop of decorative throw pillows joins the demise of the down comforter, bursting into cotton snowfall from the avalanche of bullets. "But now's as good a time as any."

On a rushed count of three, Clayton pops off a targeted shotgun blast. The scatter of pellets makes quick work of the window as shards of glass sprinkle and sparkle in the freed moonlight. The two take off in full gallop, diving headfirst through the shattered bay, thankful for every centimeter of uncut grass that pads their landing on the other side.

Without hesitation, they roll up to their feet as soon as they feel the turf, providing cover fire in opposite directions with what little ammo they have left.

"Clay, go! I'll cover you."

With Antoni trailing close behind, Clayton accelerates toward the shop, emptying his last round on the double-paned glass door. Cracks weave like spider webs across the reinforced glass, but the buckshot doesn't break it. He swivels the shotgun around, placing his right hand on the rib and his left near the muzzle. Then, in one fluid motion, he swings the gun like he's going for the fences. The compromised glass doesn't stand a chance against the second assault. Pebbles of crystallized sand disperse all over the concrete beach.

Inside the shop, there's only one goal in mind as they race for their lives to bay three. They don't even make it halfway across bay two before a blitz of artillery forces them to take cover behind the jacked Jeep's freshly chopped-up remains.

"Shit, I'm out," Antoni announces in between bouts of uncontrolled, out-of-shape breathing, and over the once again consistent uproar of bullets. "You?"

Clayton yells back, "Same."

"Dammit," Antoni groans, surveying the area for anything at his disposal. "Guess we're gonna have to skip ahead and get a little creative with our plan."

Hugging the empty shotgun like a child's teddy bear, Clayton shakes the Jeep's incoming glass fragments from his sweat-laced hair.

"You never said anything about a plan C!"

"You're right. Think of it more like plan B2, then," Antoni says, as he frantically pops open the gas tank lid and removes his shirt. The tattoos on his arms extend throughout his body, blanketing his chest and back in a texturized black and gray mural. Clayton catches one on his shoulder that has Thad's name and birthday inked in cursive.

"Clay, grab one of those tires," he orders, pointing to the stack of four eighteens they removed just hours earlier. Clayton cautiously snakes to the end of the Jeep to grab one while Antoni jams his shirt into the open gas tank like a haphazard sleeping bag being forced back into its reluctant sleeve.

Seconds later, he pulls the sopping shirt out from its gasoline bath. The unleaded perfume numbs his nose. Taking the tire from Clayton, he wrings out the shirt, soaking the entire outer rubber circumference in the fragrant fuel. Once he can't squeeze another drop from the fabric, he plunges it back into the tank, marinating the absorbent cotton in a second gas bath. Again, he yanks the soaked shirt out, this time wedging the dripping top into the tire's inner liner.

Digging deep into his front pocket, he returns with a gold Zippo. "When I toss this, run like hell for bay three's bunker. Got it?"

"What about you?"

"Don't worry about me. I'll be right behind." Antoni shoots a glance in the opposite direction at the series of bay lift panels. "I've got another idea. Now you ready?"

Clayton nods as he gets back into track stance.

"Wait," he interjects at the glimpse of metallic sheen from the car creeper still tucked beneath the Jeep. Reaching below the undercarriage, he grabs the reclined flatbed on wheels and clutches it like an eager kid would hold a sled while gazing downhill after a fresh snowfall.

"Okay. Ready."

One flick of the Zippo's flint and an orange teardrop bounces nimbly atop the chamber's wick. Upon contact with the tire, the rubber immediately bursts into a perfect ring of layered red, orange, and blue.

"Now!" Antoni shouts, chucking the fiery donut like a discus toward bay one where several of Baine's men have stationed their last stand. It lands at the feet of the closest intruder, holed up behind one of the portable steel tool cabinets. Gasoline from the saturated shirt inside the tire's liner splashes out onto his black cargo pants, sprinkling a surge of rising flames onto his combustible cotton cuffs.

Within seconds, the man is ablaze from the entire waist down as the wildfire continues to climb higher, rapidly consuming his torso. The rest of the men just stare in horror, helpless, as their comrade flails his arms in a desperate attempt to put himself out. But the blustery movement only feeds more oxygen into the spreading blaze as it engulfs his chest and ultimately devours his head, like a dragon feasting in reverse.

He fights it for as long as he can, but it's no use. Layers of torched, charcoaled cloth fall to the ground, exposing burned skin as black as the material it just replaced. No amount of stop, drop, and roll can save him now. By the time the other men have a chance to pat him out with soiled shop rags, he's already choked to death on the surplus of carbon monoxide. His crisp carcass lays motionless on the concrete floor still smoldering as the rest of the fire slowly flickers out.

The burning man reenactment gives Clayton enough time to dive onto the car creeper. Keeping low and out of the line of fire, he sails seamlessly across the shop floor until the front wheels catch the lip of bay three, forcefully flinging him to safety inside the greasy dugout.

Simultaneously, Antoni makes a run toward the bay lift panels in the middle of the shop's north wall. He punches the red kill button on bay one, and instantly, the lift holding up his restored 1955 Chevy Task Force comes slamming down onto the concrete floor like a three-ton elevator cut loose. The gunfire ceases as two of Baine's men who were using the bay for cover violently collapse under the collision. Clayton watches the whole scene play out from afar as their backs accordion in on themselves, and their limbs and joints fold and snap in all the wrong places like writhing flies after being swatted.

Upon impact, a handful of surrounding men dive out of the way for cover, affording Antoni just enough window of calm to join Clayton for momentary safety.

By the time he slips into bay three, Clayton is already inside the bunker fast at work. He's made a dent in the gun wall, as several of the weapons now lie sprawled across the center table. Without saying a word, Antoni joins the assembly line and gets to work loading the queued arms cache.

Between his feverish grabbing and dropping, Clayton glances over at the security system in the corner. He does a double take when he spots a man just outside the body shop entrance wearing a starched, white tailored suit, juxtaposed with the other men in head-to-toe black. Only it's not the choice of contrasting colors that grabs his attention. It's what—or who—he's holding that arrests him.

"Toni," he says, pointing to the screen. "Look."

Antoni shifts his focus from rapidly filling magazines with bullet clips to a total stalemate as the grave reality of seeing his wife and son hits like a slow-motion shot to the brain. It takes only a handful of seconds before the initial shock quickly morphs into its next emotional state: sheer rage.

He snatches a shotgun off the table and throws an assault rifle around his shoulder for backup. Clayton grabs his arm as he steamrolls for the exit.

"Toni, wait," he pleads. "That's exactly what he wants. We need a plan."

"There's no time," Antoni barks, ripping his shoulder out of Clayton's grasp. "They've got my family up there!"

Clayton knows it's too late, that there's no stopping him. So, he does the only thing he can and grabs a pistol off the table.

On the short ride back to surface level, Clayton looks to his friend, but the pleading gaze isn't reciprocated. Antoni just stands in the corner, wrenching his shotgun barrel with a clench that could turn its steel into dust. Before the lift even fully reaches the top of the bay, Antoni calls out at the top of his lungs, dwarfing the gunfire.

"BAINE, let them go!"

An abrupt cease-fire is ushered by none other than the kingpin himself. Once the commotion dies down, he responds with an all-too-familiar arrogance Antoni hasn't missed.

"Rivera. It's been a long time, huh, pal?"

Baine looks lustfully at Sonya who's openly weeping while clutching Thad tight.

"Looks like you've been busy, Toni—a wife, kid, house . . . dog. Well, there was a dog. Ferocious little thing. Even managed to take out one of my men before we put her down." He needlessly adjusts the collar on his jacket. "You've got yourself quite the little cozy setup here. What else have you been hiding from me for the past five years?"

"Fuck you, Baine, just let them go. They've got nothing to do with this."

"Oh, but on the contrary, they have everything to do with this. You see, I don't want them. I don't even want to hurt them. I'm a dealer, Toni, not a murderer. Well, at least not entirely. That's always been more of a gray area for me," he admits maniacally, reassuring himself. "What I do want, however, is your little friend over there."

He begins pacing back and forth fully comfortable in the position of power he's set up for himself.

"You see, after I saw the news that a man named Clayton Sparks had found himself in the middle of Bannerton's largest, most renowned Hunt to date—for killing the daughter of the founder himself, no less—and that for the first time there was a bounty for justice—a staggering 1.2 million-dollar reward to be exact. I thought to myself, 'Now, where have I heard that name before?'"

Baine pauses and strokes the dark, finely manicured hair on his chin, perfectly acting out the part of big bad boss—ready to turn his forthcoming villainous monologue into a blown-out, one-man show.

Sonya attempts to wiggle free from his grasp during his intermission, but he's able to tighten the noose of his arm around her neck.

"Not so fast, darling," Baine says, shortening the leash on his clutch. "Now where was I? Ah, yes, the name Sparks. It sounded so familiar. Like something from the past." Baine pulls out a cigar from the inside pocket of his linen sports coat and tucks the wrapped stick of pressed tobacco firmly between his cocky lips. "Then, I remembered a story you once told me of a kid you used to run around with when you were young. Until you two had quite the falling out. The story behind how you got that nasty scar on your neck."

He strikes a match, kissing the dry-leafed tip with the open flame until a cloud of smoke masks his devilish grin. "And that's when it 'sparked'—for lack of a better word—a revelation. Desperate times call for desperate measures. And what if? Just what if he came back here? Back home. The prodigal pal, desperate to make amends and ask for an old friend's help."

He breathes in a monstrous fume and exhales; the stream of white smolder bullishly escapes from his flared nostrils. "And here we are. In a bit of a predicament, I must say. Lucky for you, you have a choice. A rather simple one, really. To give up your past." He points in Clayton's direction. "Or lose your future," he proposes, stroking a stream of tears from Sonya's eye.

"Go ahead, honey, call out to your man," he orders. "Convince him to make the right decision."

Sonya pulls her face away, snuffling her tears back in the process. Staring her captor square in the eye, she rears her head back and spits. The weighty mixture of snot, tears, and phlegm lands with an audible splat against the stubbly crater of his smug dimple.

"Fuck you, you pussy," she snarls.

Unamused, Baine slowly raises his hand to his face, cupping his fingers. He combs the loogie from his facial hair and flings it to the ground with a flick. The dimple reappears along with the sinister smile it's attached to.

"I've got to admit, Toni. You picked a strong woman. I guess it's up to you to see what kind of man she picked in return. Give me Sparks, now, or say goodbye to your family. It's that simple."

Antoni rests his forehead on the barrel of his gun, eyes clenched shut, racking his mind for a way out. Any semblance of a plan that involves everyone he loves escaping safely. But the longer he thinks, the quicker he comes to the realization that happy endings exist only in fairy tales. And his story—his life—is nothing but a cursed nightmare.

He is the bad omen.

Not Clayton.

Him.

Baine continues, "I told you, Toni, that I'd always be around. Did you really think I didn't know your whereabouts? What you've been up to all this time? When you became an 88—" he jests, displaying the tattoo on his own hand. "—You gave yourself to me. I *own* you, your life, and everything in it. It's all mine, Toni."

Antoni lets out a deep sigh. It's the sound of desperation and it's worsening.

He chooses his next words carefully.

"Only my friends call me Toni, asshole."

Maybe not too carefully.

"Ahh, there's the fiery Rivera I remember," Baine coyly responds. "Well, Toni, it's a good thing we're former friends then, now, isn't it?"

Clayton can't help but sit there powerless, watching the inner torment on his friend's face from the moral debate slowly consume him from the inside out. He's the reason Antoni's in this position in the first place. It's exactly why he ditched Jayson when he had the chance. Trish is already gone. He doesn't want anyone else he cares about to get hurt. He's made his decision. And his time is up.

"STOP!" Clayton shouts.

Without an ounce more of thought, he stands straight up with his hands in air and starts to crawl out from behind the safety of bay three's pit.

"Clay, what are you doing?" Antoni begs, trying to pull his friend back down to shelter. "You don't have to do this—"

"It's me you want, right, Baine?" Clayton shouts over Antoni's pleas, surrendering himself to the cause. "Well, here I am," he reveals, slowly walking across the garage. "You can have me. Just let them go."

With his arms shaped in a conceding Y gesture above his head, he looks around the shop and counts at least seven of Baine's men remaining. Every premeditated step closer feels like one closer to death.

A random memory of Trish and him at the beach floods his racing mind, growing in detail with every trembling tread. The whiplashed sunset. Her black hair shining in the day's golden hour, reflecting an almost blue sheen. The ebb and flow of high tide washing away the day's sandcastles and the traces of their footprints from their walk along the white sandbar. He wishes more than anything that he could go back to that moment right now and stay there, forever.

Baine starts puffing on his cigar in a more celebratory fashion with each surrendering stride. His smirk conspicuously failing to hide his overt narcissism as his soon-to-be victory casually walks itself over to him in defeat.

He's got what he came for. Nothing else matters now.

"You've got what you want, Baine," Clayton emphasizes, just before crossing bay two. "Now just let them go. You don't need them."

"You know, you're right," Baine replies, his eyes slit with sinister intentions. "I don't."

He brings back the hammer on his pistol, but before he can leverage enough pressure in his index finger to squeeze it, he feels the serrated pinch of a set of fangs dig into his fleshy forearm.

Cleo clamps down with all the life she has left, cranking his arm as she fights for balance on her injured backside. The heroic struggle doesn't last long before Baine regains control and flings her off. She yelps as she hits the ground before him, and in one short burst, a single gunshot rings throughout the otherwise silent room. It echoes across the concrete structure prolonging the horror of the moment. Clayton doesn't have time to react, he only watches helplessly as Cleo collapses to the floor. This time for good.

The solemn but serendipitous sacrifice buys Sonya and Thad enough time to flee Baine's grasp, but the escape leaves them vulnerable—stuck in the middle of the garage's dead zone—halfway between Antoni and Clayton, and the rest of Baine's crew.

"NOOO!"

A primal cry rings out from behind Clayton as Antoni bum-rushes forward in a reflex of rage, fueled by total desperation. He unloads a series of strategic shots with his newly equipped assault rifle, taking down two more of Baine's unexpecting men before they can seek shelter or return fire. Clayton reaches behind his back and pulls out his pistol, capping off two short bursts. A third 88 drops from the precision.

In the heat of the sudden scuffle, Baine and his crew dive for any form of instant cover while exchanging their own greeting committee of heavy gunfire. The resumed tug-of-war leaves Sonya and Thad openly stranded in the crossfire—all alone amid the complete chaos. With nowhere to run, maternal instinct kicks in and she drops to her knees, blanketing her son—using her own body and unconditional love to shield him from the explosive opera.

With total disregard for his own life, the same one he's spent the last twenty-four hours running for and doing everything in his power to protect, Clayton races into the fray for the marooned mother and son. Antoni follows behind leaving a trail of bullet casings in his wakeful wrath.

Clayton calls out for Sonya to run to him, but she can't move.

She can't even hear.

Dodging an onslaught of life-ending lead that a cursed soul has no fortune to survive, Clayton dives toward Sonya and Thad, tackling them in a selfless, sacrificial gesture. As they connect with the ground, two small arms with surprising strength find themselves around his neck as another set of slender hands take his arm. He pongs his head around in a do-or-die search for the closest bit of cover as Antoni aids in the improvised rescue mission, providing a wall of timely cover fire.

A well-placed headshot finds the exposed forehead of another 88 crouching behind a stack of tires by bay one. The satisfying pop drops him into the unsteady heap of rubber as a couple loose donuts roll off in random directions.

Sprinting for safety again behind the chopped-up, and now shot-up indigo Jeep, the three make it all the way to the SUV's hood before Clayton feels the searing force of hot metal pierce the flesh and bone of his left shoulder blade. He crumbles to the ground just in time to safely pass Sonya and Thad over to Antoni.

Lying sprawled on his back, the speed of the moment decelerates to slow motion, and the barrage of gunshots turns into nothing more than muffled static from the malfunction in his basic motor skills. He looks up at the moonlight seeping in through the skylight above and another memory of Trish illuminates his pale, fuzzy thoughts—the exact moment he realized forever was meant to be with her.

It was just a night like any other. Nothing special. No big event. Trish was sitting outside on their apartment patio swallowed up in one of his old flannels just staring into the nighttime haze. Probably drawing artistic inspiration from the subtlety of life and the unanswered beauty surrounding it. He can still picture it exactly. How the city glow kissed her olive skin and cooled her rosy cheeks, softly lighting the wonder in her face. The air was crisp, and a calm breeze was singing, giving her hair reason to dance. Her smile sparkled brighter than the stars.

It's only a memory, but it's so vivid he can almost reach out and touch it.

Touch her.

Feel her all over again.

Slowly, the stifled shots begin to crescendo again, breaking through the static bliss as his construct of time catches back up to the moment. When he finally snaps to, he looks up to find Antoni dragging him behind the Jeep to safety.

"Clay? Clayton? You there?" Antoni beckons. "You're hit, man. Are you okay? Say something."

He can see Antoni's mouth moving, but he can't make out any sound behind the muted words. Antoni leans him up against the driver's side door. The sudden gravity from the upright action causes him to wince in pain.

Antoni keeps yelling and, finally, the volume of the hushed shouting starts to slowly rise, matching the motion of the jittery lips it's coming from.

"Stay with me, Clay," Antoni orders, as the double treatment of senses takes root. "Are you good? Talk to me, man!"

"Ye-yeah, I'm okay. I think," Clayton shudders. "We gotta get the hell outta here."

But despite his return to reality, he can clearly see the opposite answer already branded in Antoni's ember eyes.

"I'm not leaving. Not yet. I've got a score to settle," Antoni says without hesitation. "Take this and keep an eye on Sonya and Thad."

Before Clayton can even react, he feels a hefty metal object take the shape of his cupped hand.

"I'll be right back," Antoni adds, lunging forward, but his path is obstructed by a gentle grip upon his bicep. He looks back anticipating Clayton trying to stop him, but he's met by Sonya's soft, entreating gaze. Her eyes wide and scared. Her voice trembling just like her body.

"Toni, please don't go," she pleads, cinching Thad tighter to her chest. Her shirt damp from the river breaking his levee. "I'm so scared."

"I know. And I'm so, so sorry, babe," Antoni apologies. The sincerity rushed but genuine. "But I have to end this now, or we'll never be safe. There's so much I have to tell you. That I will tell you. But I can't right now. Everything is going to be all right. Trust me." He reaches behind his back and returns with another pistol tucked into his waistband. "Here, take this. Just in case. Shoot anyone or anything that isn't me."

And without another word of fabricated reassurance, he's gone.

Clayton struggles to get back to his feet as Antoni re-enters the fray. The organic wiring of his audio and visual component cables has resynched, but he's still searching for a controlled sense of feel. On unsure Bambi legs, he finally makes it all the way upright. Just in time to offer the bare minimum of cover fire for Antoni, who blindly pushes toward Baine and his remaining four henchmen. Surprisingly, Clayton's able to clip one of them in the flank before his legs give out, but the gap between both sides begins to close as Baine's men push forward on Antoni, who's stuck in the middle of it all. Fresh out of ammo.

He takes refuge behind an adrift tool bench in no man's land as thick gunfire riddles the stainless-steel cart with a cluster of deep but non-penetrating indentations. Desperation quickly ensnares his thoughts once again, and the belief of no way out cinches its grip even tighter around the fraught thought.

For Clayton, unscripted instinct sets in along with his recalibrated motor functions. He searches his surroundings and spots a second car creeper a few feet away. A plan begins to seed in his head, but his actions react faster than the full thought can blossom.

Before he knows it, he's gliding across the floor toward Antoni's tool bench. The heroics offer enough of a window to distract Baine's men from Antoni, who quickly grabs a torque wrench from atop the worktable and sprints toward bay one.

He cuts the corner, dipping behind the double-stacked tire rack—just out of the stationed intruder's periphery—and violently swings the chrome bar down against the man's outstretched arms. His gun skirts across the ground into the open floor before he can even see what hit him or fully register the pain of his freshly fractured forearms.

The single blow seamlessly morphs into a combo as Antoni spins around 180 degrees, bashing him across the face with the force of his full momentum. The crunch of the intruder's skull reverberates throughout the length of the elongated wrench; the direct blow caving in his entire cheek, shattering his eye socket. He drops like a rag doll, unconscious—more than likely dead—before he even hits the ground.

Antoni's gaze instantly shifts to Baine, whose blown-out pupils indicate his upper hand is quickly losing the higher ground. He takes off running for cover behind his two remaining men. One of them turns to meet Antoni's advancement with a series of hurried bursts, but he closes the distance quicker than his assailant can accurately aim. With another vicious swipe of the torque wrench, he knocks the assault rifle and its cluster of kill shots off target.

Seconds later, the two entangle in a back-and-forth grapple with both men fighting for prime position. After a short tug-of-war for who wants it more, Antoni gains enough leverage to dictate the struggle courtesy of a bear hug wedged underneath the man's armpits, locked in with the wrench pinned behind his back. He curls the tool with every bit of might his biceps can muster. Every ounce of added tension sinks into the man's diaphragm, cutting off the air supply to his lungs, rendering them useless.

But he doesn't have the luxury of time to wait for the man to finish gasping for air on his own. So, he decides to take time into his own hands and expedite the passing process.

Antoni rears his head back as far as his neck can take it and begins violently swinging it like a wrecking ball from shoulder to shoulder, battering the man's wheezing orifices with a barrage of heavy headbutts. Fresh splotches of glistening crimson instantly appear underneath the assailant's nose and lips.

Clayton briefly watches the brutality unfold before turning his attention to the last assailant who's lining up a clean shot at Antoni's exposed back.

He yells, "Toni, behind you!"

Digging his head into the enemy's left shoulder, Antoni turns and spots the gun taking aim from his periphery. In a move of epinephrine-fueled brute strength, he lifts the man off the ground and flips him around just in time for use as a human shield.

The series of shots season the man's flesh as pockets of red discharge splatter out like the blue paint balls on the 8th Street Bridge when they were kids. His body seizures from the jolt of every incoming thud.

The torque wrench clangs to the concrete floor as Antoni reaches down to the bodybag's waist and unholsters his 9mm pistol. Discarding the tenderized meat shield to the ground, Antoni empties several unanswered shots into the lone henchman who's fazed after accidentally neutralizing his own comrade. He falls back dramatically into Baine's open arms. His white suit jacket is now smudged like marbled peppermint.

Incandescent with white hot berserker rage, Antoni turns to his former employer, seething with a hatred that epitomizes *if looks could kill.* He doesn't say a word. He just stares, steadies his gun, and pulls the trigger.

*Click.*

He tries again.

*Click.*

And again.

*Click.*

Sensing the fortunate procrastination of his survival, Baine raises his own gun to meet Antoni's primal gaze. His shit-eating grin returns at the sight of once again gaining the upper hand.

"Tsk, tsk. So close, Toni," he remarks. "But it appears you're empty. What a shame." His grin now fully stretched from ear-to-ear into his patented, sinister smile. "Ready to be reacquainted with your little brother, Toni?"

The sound of a metal hammer cocking back echoes in Baine's eardrum as the bezel of cold steel brushes against his temple.

"Fuck you, asshole."

Sonya's index finger twitches, and a second later, Baine's smile is turned upside down as his body topples over itself on its descent to the ground. A fresh cigar falls out of the inner lining of his jacket pocket. The tip dipped in the encroaching pool of red as if it were lit.

Sonya holds her executioner pose, vacantly staring at the smoking barrel in shock—lifesaver turned lifetaker. Antoni scurries over and removes the gun from her quivering hands. The couple look at each other in silence. No words. There's no need to talk. Their faces say it all—the horror and the relief. The quiet exchange is interrupted by the sound of a child's voice in between bouts of sniffling.

"Mommy? Daddy? Is it over?"

They drape their arms around his back and pull him close, overwhelming him in a protective familial embrace. In between a trio of synchronized sobs, Thad points and shakily asks, "Is Cleo okay?"

Antoni follows the tip of his son's finger to the motionless body of the dead German Shepherd. In that exact moment, he can't contain himself. The adrenaline from the shootout has faded, and the somber reality is all that remains. He doesn't know what to say. Or how to even say it. He just holds his son and wife, rocking them back and forth like the flux of tears streaming in waves from his eyes.

Over by the Jeep, Clayton slumps to his knees, his wounded shoulder follows suit in a delayed reaction—limp and lifeless like a wilted flower. The gun falls out of his ginger grip as he crumbles to the floor.

Even in their paralyzed emotional state, the reunited family notices the commotion. Antoni totes Thad in one arm while leading Sonya with the other, and they crawl over to Clayton. Sonya immediately examines the threat of the wound, applying pressure around his collar bone to help slow the bleeding.

"Toni, get me a clean towel or something," she orders, as he runs to grab an unsoiled rag from one of the tool benches. She quickly rigs up a makeshift sling and carefully props Clayton back up to help with circulation. He groans and winces throughout the entire linear movement.

"How do you feel, Clay? Can you move it?" Sonya asks, a new level of confidence breaking through what was pure panic just minutes ago.

"Ermm, yeah. I think I'm all right," he responds shyly, while moving his shoulder in small circles. "Argh, that stings."

"Clay, we can't stay here. There's no telling if more of Baine's men are on their way or if Klein knows your whereabouts," Antoni divulges, helping steady his friend. "Another Hunt party could show up any minute. Do you think you can make it to your feet?"

Clayton sits, momentarily swaying in and out of a battle with consciousness. His entire shirt is soaked in shiny, syrupy crimson. Even his fingertips resemble a leaky faucet, dripping blood one steady drop after another. He looks at Antoni kneeling beside him, and the moment is again replaced by another memory of Trish.

She's sitting cross-legged, like always, on the floor in her studio as he walks in with a not-too-thrilled-to-be-picked-up Scout tucked under his arm. The faint smell of roasted garlic has followed him down the hallway and into the room. He does his best to delicately step around her painting supplies that haphazardly litter every vacant bit of hardwood space.

Genuflecting, he kisses the top of her head to tell her dinner is ready. She returns the affection with her own kiss before teasingly dabbing the tip of his nose with a paintbrush caked in red acrylic. Her ornery smile, infectious as ever. He dwells on that smile as long as he can, almost certain he can still hear the warm sound of her ensuing laugh. Scout runs off, totally unamused by the shenanigans, and the two engage in a playful paint fight that ends in them making love on the studio floor, covered head to toe in a rainbow of paint, forgetting about dinner and everything else.

Because in the heat of that moment, nothing else mattered.

"Clay, do you hear me? Clay, can you get up?" Antoni presses.

Clayton blinks and the memory fades as the urgency of the moment fast forwards his flashback.

He looks up at Antoni.

"Huh? Yeah, I . . . uh, I think so. Maybe a little help?"

Antoni and Sonya give him a hand and together they all make it to their feet.

"We gotta move fast. We'll take the old Chevy," Antoni says, as he moves over to the shop desk to grab the keys.

"Antoni, he's bleeding a lot," Sonya cuts in with valid concern. "We've got to get him some help."

"And where would that be exactly? It's not like we can take him to the hospital, and we can't stay here any longer."

"Well, let me at least see what I can do. Just hold on," she urges, and runs off to the shop's office for the first aid kit.

"Wait," Clayton responds. "I need to get some supplies from your bunker before we go."

Antoni immediately stops searching the desk for his keys and turns toward Clayton.

"For fuck's sake, Clay, you're not still planning on going after Klein, are you? I mean look at yourself, you can barely even stand. Hell, look around you at what just happened. We're lucky to even be having this conversation. What's your endgame here?"

"How about a life? A future?" Clayton counters with his own rising rebuttal. "I know it's crazy, but it's the only way I can get myself out of this mess, to clear my name, and hopefully take down Klein in the process. Otherwise, it'll just be a new group of people hunting me down. And another after that. And another, assuming I even make it that long. That's not a life, Toni, and you know it."

Conjuring all the strength he can muster, Clayton shuffles over toward Antoni and puts his hand on his shoulder.

"There's more that you don't know about Klein. Things I haven't told you yet. About him. About his wife. About The Hunt Initiative. I've got a plan; you just need to trust me. But I can't do it without those supplies or—" Ignoring the surge of pain in his shoulder, he stares Antoni square in the eyes. "Without you."

Antoni doesn't need to probe any deeper to know there's no stopping him. It's in his eyes. His tone. His body language. He either goes alone, and likely dies alone on a suicide mission, or he helps an old friend try to prove his innocence. To get his life back. And maybe, just maybe, they stand a chance.

Sonya arrives just in time with the first aid kit to witness the end of the exchange.

"Toni?" she implores. "What's going on?"

But deep down, she already knows. She's known since the moment Clayton showed up at their house.

She can tell by her husband's slouched posture and deliberate lack of eye contact that he's already made his choice without her. She could fight it, and probably win, but then she might as well just let Clayton bleed out right here. Because there'd be no point in saving him now to just patch him up and send him off to die later.

Antoni's eyes finally find the courage hiding behind their optic nerves to meet hers, and without a word, she hangs her head and nods. He returns the gesture and takes a deep breath, lowering his head as if he's already regretting the decision he's made.

"All right, Clay," he utters under a reluctant exhale. "What's your plan?"

# CHAPTER 24

"Argh," Clayton grunts while flinching.

"Hold still, will ya? I'm almost done," Sonya orders, as she threads the last suture on his exit wound. "There, finished."

"Unghh," Clayton whimpers through gritted teeth. "I feel like you were back there forever. At least way longer than in the front."

"That's because I was. Luckily for you, the bullet's exit somehow missed your heart and major arteries, but its impact managed to shatter a decent part of your scapula on its way in."

She picks up the tweezers from the small auto parts caddy acting as a makeshift medical tray and shows him a tooth-sized sliver of ivory stained in read smears.

"Is that why it hurts so damn much?"

"Well, yeah, you got shot, Clay. And it hurts so damn much because I removed about five other pieces that are just as big, if not bigger, than that one. Your shoulder and arm are going to hurt like hell once you get some of the feeling back, especially since I don't have any actual painkillers to give you. Just these few extra carprofen that we got for Cleo when she broke her leg last year."

At the mention of her name, Clayton looks over to the motionless mound of black and brown fur across the garage. He catches Antoni doing the same. His friend's helpless gaze doesn't last long before he wanders off to one of the shop's locker units and pulls out an all-purpose car cover. As he walks over to the body of his dead dog, he orders Thad, who is still visibly and justifiably shaken up from everything, to look away.

Antoni kneels to the ground next to Cleo, who's resting in peace on a blanket of blood from her execution wounds. Then, like making a bed for her eternal rest, he slowly pulls the car cover over her.

Clayton watches the whole sad scene as a spectator, and the fresh memory of holding Trish's lifeless body in his arms floods his thoughts. No matter how many memories he has of her, that one will forever be his last.

"Clay? Clay? Clayton!" Sonya's calls snap him back into the moment, his mind a fragile rubber band being stretched in too many directions.

"Huh?" he mutters.

"Focus," she instructs. "I need you to take two of these and do your best to take it easy on that arm. Put this sling on. It should help with stability and take the pressure off that ball joint. I got the bleeding under control, but those stitches . . . well, let's just say they're not my best, but they should do. I didn't exactly have the right tools on hand, and they're rushed."

"Speaking of rushed, we need to get the hell out of here, and fast," Antoni's hardened voice regains the conversation. "Like now."

"Sonya, do you have family nearby?" Clayton asks, as he gingerly slides his shirt back on.

"Yeah, my cousin lives—"

But Antoni is already on it.

"Sonya, I'm going to drop you and Thad off at Sloan's. I need you to go back into the house and grab whatever you can fit for him and you into an overnight bag in the next three minutes. We're out of here in under five."

She removes the surgical gloves, freeing her hands from their rubbery confines. The blue colored latex, which is streaked in rich red lines of coagulated blood now exudes a more purple palette.

"But Toni, how long—"

"Babe, there's no time, just go!" Antoni barks, immediately realizing the harsh tone isn't doing the already stressful situation any favors. Even Thad takes notice of the strict uptick and runs to hug his mom's side. "I'm sorry. I didn't mean to . . . I just need to get you two somewhere safe, right now. So, go do it now, please."

She doesn't put up another ounce of resistance, or even say anything in return. She just nods, kisses Thad on the top of his wiry head, and jogs off back to the house.

Thad, who's now been left behind by his main source of nurture, looks to his father through furrowed brows. One representing confusion, the other fear.

"Hey, buddy," Antoni says softly, taking a knee to meet his son at eye level. "I know you're scared right now. And that's okay. I am, too. Fear is natural. There's nothing wrong with being afraid. But right now, I need you to be strong, okay? For me. But more importantly, for your mom. Think you can do that for me?"

Slowly, Thad's eyebrows start to unwrinkle as the pep talk takes root in the space of flesh between them.

"Can you be my strong little man?" Antoni adds.

"Mm-hmm," the little boy mumbles in response.

"That's my guy." His father smiles. "Now do me a favor, go hop in the truck, okay?"

Thad nods and books it for the vintage pickup, which still has the corpses of two men trapped underneath its suspension.

"And Thad?" Antoni says, as his son's tiny strides come to an abrupt halt. "I love you, buddy. Don't ever forget that, all right?"

For the first time tonight since they were attacked, the boy regains enough of his cheery childhood spirit to conjure a small smile.

"Love you, too, Dada," he replies and finishes his dash to the truck.

Antoni diverts his attention back to Clayton, who's inspecting the faint red blur that's starting to peek through his fresh bandages.

"Clay, gameplan time," he says. "I'm going to take Sonya and Thad to her cousin Sloan's. They're about a twenty-minute roundtrip. In the meantime, grab whatever supplies you need from the bunker. And stay there until I get back, just in case more people show up looking for trouble. The main monitor is linked to all the cameras I have around the perimeter of the place, and it's a reinforced steel room surrounded by several feet of solid concrete. No one's getting in there without an invitation."

He examines Clayton's arm, studying the wound and the makeshift shop towel sling.

"Just take it easy in the meantime and wait for those pain meds to kick in. When I get back, we'll figure out our next stop. Look for my truck to roll up on camera, and you'll know it's safe to come out."

He extends his hand to pat Clayton on his good shoulder.

"And Clay? Be careful."

"You too, man. Good luck," Clayton returns the sentiment, as Sonya scurries back into the shot-up shop with a stuffed duffle bag that's making every tooth of its closed zipper work extra hard for its bite. "Keep them safe."

In less than twenty seconds, Antoni, Sonya, and Thad all pile into the truck. They're officially out of eyesight in less than half that amount of time.

Moments later, Clayton again finds himself riding the lift down to bay three's bunker. He inputs his birthday into the electronic door code and gets to work loading up his own duffle bag with anything and everything he can grab, relevant or not—a pair of night vision goggles, the steel briefcase with the micro-tech fingerprints, the facial recognition scrambler, a bundle of flex cams, and as many guns as it takes to define "for good measure."

With the bag brimming full of tech gear and enough weapons for a small army, he plops down in front of the computer to watch the cameras. For once tonight, everything looks calm. Nothing out of the ordinary catches his attention aside from several motionless DB88 bodies randomly strung about the property.

He continues to survey the surrounding aftermath when he feels his eyes start to tug at their lids in a protesting plea for bedtime. Before he knows it, he's caught in a losing battle against blood loss and adrenaline fatigue as his eyeballs roll back to tuck themselves in for the night. The room wobbles for just a second, and before he's even aware, he's out.

The next thing he sees is the blurry image of Antoni shaking him awake.

"Clay? Wake up! Clay? You can't fall asleep!" he shouts, his vigorous shaking now escalated to aggressive slapping. "Shit, you've lost too much blood. Sonya said we shouldn't have left you alone."

After a handful of smacks, he finally comes to.

"Wh-what h-happened?" Clayton mutters groggily through slit eyes. "You're back already? Where's Sonya . . . and Thad? Are they okay?"

"Whoa, one thing at a time, buddy. Everything's fine. They're fine. You passed out from loss of blood, again. I figured something was wrong since you didn't come out when I pulled up," Antoni says, pointing at his truck on the surveillance screen. "We've got to fix you up real quick and get you some fluids. You able you follow me?"

"Yeah," Clayton responds confidently. Only his body doesn't quite see it that way.

He doesn't even have the strength or the equilibrium to get up from the chair alone. His legs instantly buckle as he tries to stand, but Antoni catches him before he hits the ground.

The next several minutes are more or less a blur—a semblance of weaving in and out of incoherency than anything else. He remembers taking the lift back up to the garage, but somewhere between the shop and the house, he lost consciousness again. When he comes to for the third time, he's lying down sprawled out on the bench seat of the old Chevy.

Antoni notices him slowly stir.

"Hey, welcome back, buddy."

Softly, Clayton speaks, "Wh-what happened? Where are we?"

Antoni transfers his attention from his muzzy friend to the dotted yellow lines before him. A sigh of relief seems to lessen the pressure on his solemn expression.

"You passed out again when I got back to the shop."

Clayton struggles but eventually works his way to an upright position on the wide black-and-white, two-toned bench seat. He looks at his shoulder and notices it's been rebandaged and placed in a more sophisticated sling than his makeshift towel rig.

"I managed to rebandage you up a little while you were out. Hope it's not too tight. It's also not as pretty as the impromptu stitches Sonya did, but lucky for you the bullet went all the way through. She said it just missed clipping your aorta by an inch but did a number on the lower portion of your shoulder blade, remember? It's gonna be sore as shit, but you'll be just fine. You did lose a lot of blood though, so just take it easy for a little while, okay? Oh—" Antoni reaches into the duffle bag between them and hands Clayton a water bottle and some beef jerky. "Drink up and eat this. You need to hydrate and replenish your blood sugar levels. It'll help you get your strength back."

Clayton fumbles the bottle in his first attempt to twist off the cap, clearly exposing his lack of brawn and dexterity. After watching him struggle again on try number two, Antoni snatches the bottle and unscrews it for him. Clayton steadies the open container with both hands and takes a huge gulp. The roof of his mouth feels like sandpaper before the water washes away the dry grit. He gasps after nearly chugging the entire bottle.

Wiping his mouth with a new, clean shirt sleeve, courtesy of Antoni's closet, he asks again, "Where are we going?"

Antoni gives him a tiny grin before answering his question with another question, "Well, I was hoping you could tell me. You're the man with the plan, remember? Right now, I'm just keeping us on the move."

Clayton places his hand on his forehead as if to jumpstart his brain into rethinking properly again. He winces as he repositions himself. He thinks he knows what he needs to do, but he hasn't had the chance or the clarity to put everything into chronological order. He obviously can't go straight for Klein right now. He has nothing to go on and that would be a suicide mission, especially in his current shape.

His flickering memory then catches light, latching back onto the mystery surrounding Rebecca Klein's ghost file and his last conversation with Jayson. He recalls Jayson's guess at cracking the made-up location, somewhere in Westport, but he doesn't remember the actual address listed on the file. Worse yet, he doesn't have his phone to reference the picture of Rebecca's file to get it—thanks to Jayson tossing it out the car window. That's when he remembers Jayson took a picture of his picture with his own phone, and he's got Jayson's phone in the backpack.

Leaving Antoni high and dry on his question about what they're doing and where they're going, Clayton begins aggressively rifling through the duffle bag. Tossing things left and right.

"Hey, hey! Remember when I said to take it easy? Well, that ain't it."

But Clayton ignores Antoni's precautions and continues digging through the supplies until he locates Jayson's backpack.

He rips it out of the duffle and instantly unzips it.

"Are you gonna tell me what the hell you're looking so enthusiastically for, or are we already onto the twenty questions game portion of the trip?"

But seconds later, Clayton finds what he was frantically searching for, proudly showing it to Antoni while brandishing a smile.

"This! I found it."

"Wow . . . a phone. Cool. What about it?" Antoni's eyes dart back and forth from Clayton to what dimly lit portion of the road his sixty-plus-year-old headlights ineffectively reveal.

"What? No. I mean, yes, it's just a phone, but—" Clayton stutters, his mind still oxygen-deprived and slow to process. "It's what's on the phone that we need."

"No offense, Clay, but I think that maybe you need to pass out one more time. You know, just to get your mind right because I'm still not tracking, buddy."

"Okay, just hear me out—"

Clayton sighs at the thought of having to recount the entire story of the events that got him here. The wounds surrounding Trish's death are still fresh, but he has no other choice. Antoni has already lost so much to be here. And he's risking everything he has left to help him see it through. So, Clayton dives in. He tells his friend about the bribe from Klein, about Marco and the server room, the missing file info, and the bogus address on Rebecca Klein's report. He recounts the horrors that happened at The Hunt Initiative Anniversary party—how he found out about Klein's secret plan to take him out, the details surrounding Trish's death, and how he barely escaped with his own life. Ultimately, he finishes playing catch-up with the story of how Jayson might have cracked the whereabouts of the mystery address and that's where they need to go. At least, he thinks it is. After all, it's not like he has any other leads.

"So, you're telling me that Rebecca Klein wasn't killed in a hit-and-run?"

"No, I'm not saying that. What I'm saying is that there's more to her death than what her phony file indicates or, in this case, doesn't. And this place—this mysterious fucking address—is the key to finding that out."

"But why? She's dead and has been for what, like over twenty-five years? What's it even matter at this point?"

"That's exactly what we're going to find out."

Antoni studies Clayton.

His friend's unwavering resolve is enough to slowly peel away the layers of his wall of skepticism. For as long as he's known him, Clayton has always been a rash person, but his instincts have more than made up for his impulsiveness. After all, it was Clayton who saved him and the rest of the crew all those years ago when Leo was killed. He told them not to go. That he had a bad feeling about the drop that night. And if Antoni had just listened to what Clayton had to say back then. If he had just trusted his friend, instead of following the cash, he never would have gone on that job in the first place. And Leo would still be alive today.

"All right then, man. I'm in," Antoni says, committing to the charade of events for better or worse—likely the latter. "So, where in this Westport are we headed?"

Clayton holds up the phone, giving it a little shake.

"Like I said, that's exactly what we're going to find out."

Once again, Clayton finds himself in the familiar situation of waking up to Antoni staring at him. At least this time it's by his own accord, not from passing out. As he rouses from his voluntary spell, his eyes open but everything remains blurry and delayed, like some kind of out-of-focus lag, or fog. For five disorienting seconds, he wonders where the hell he is. Again.

Slowly, he straightens up from leaning against the window to see the moon hovering in the distance over Bannerton. Countless buildings and offices in its sprawling downtown are still lit up, creating a starry skyline below the real one. The city's spangled twilight makes him think of Trish, and the first time they went camping together early in their relationship.

He remembers how insistent she was that they sleep under the gaze of the galaxy, not the polyester confines of a tent roof. It was also the first time they made love. Laying there afterward, with her warmth wrapped in his arms, and two sets of legs tucked into one sleeping bag, he remembers picking a shooting star in the sky that night and wishing for it all.

If he didn't know the danger that the quiet city ahead had in store for him, he'd relish the beauty in this poetic moment. After all, his wish came true.

"How'd you sleep?" Antoni says, yawning himself.

"Errm," Clayton groans, clearing his throat and his mind. "Like shit." He adjusts his injured arm through gritted teeth. "But I suppose some shut-eye is better than none."

"Yeah, sorry about that. She may be a looker, but I can't vouch for the comfort of this classic beaut. I don't think luxury had been invented for trucks yet."

Clayton places his hand on the back of his neck and moves his head from side to side. A Gatling series of pops traverse his spine, instantly relieving some of the stiffness. Antoni was right, his shoulder is sore as shit, and taut, but it moves and he's still alive.

Clayton takes Jayson's phone out of his pocket and touches the screen.

Antoni looks over at the awakened device. "It's probably been long enough, yeah? Surely, it's enabled again." His gaze moves up to Clayton. "You've really got no other ideas for what the passcode could be?"

Clayton looks down at the six-digit lock screen. He's tried everything he can think of, but none of the obvious have worked—Jayson's birthday; his start date at The Hunt for Justice, which he didn't have high hopes for in the first place; the date Jayson lost his virginity, 11/03/02, which he's still mortified by, yet slightly impressed that he not only knows it but remembered it. He's even tried the all-too-easy 123456. Nothing but failed attempt after failed attempt.

"No. It could be anything," he concedes, and tosses the phone back onto the seat in frustrating defeat.

"Damn. If I'd known you needed to crack a phone, I could have brought some hacking software. But it's back at the bunker, which I'm sure by now is swarming with feds and Hunt for Justice representatives. So that's definitely a no-go."

The thought gives Clayton one of his own.

"What about your other contacts?" he asks, nodding in the direction of Bannerton. "You've got to know someone in the city that could help, right?"

"Sorry, man, I don't do biz in Bannerton. Too heavily monitored," Antoni dismisses, and shakes his head. "And even if I did, these are the types of shady characters and lowlifes that would turn you in, in the blink of an eye. Or just shoot you on the spot for a quick payday. Either way, not good for you."

And just like that, Clayton's momentary sliver of hope fades as quickly as it flickered.

He searches his thoughts for any other inclination. Any possible clue for what Jayson could have used as a passcode. The options are limitless, so he starts with the only thing he can think of—replaying the events at Jayson's house after Trish's death.

Still fresh in his head, he thinks back to the kitchen table littered with random papers and other junk, but nothing notable stands out. Just some little leaguer headshots, a stack of unopened bills, and a black, briefcase toolbox. He moves his mind to the living room and scrolls through the pictures hanging on the wall.

Reluctantly, he recalls the one of himself, Trish, and Jayson at a past New Year's Eve party, but again nothing password-worthy there—just another trip around the sun. What about Jayson's parents' forty-fifth-anniversary cruise trip? Maybe, he thinks, but he has no idea what year the picture was taken to subtract forty-five years, let alone the month and day to solve that textbook story problem. His brother's college graduation? Possibly, but not likely. Clayton knows Jayson's always been proud of his brother, but graduating college wasn't *that* big of an achievement. After all, Jayson's whole family are college grads, even if his own community college degree is at the bottom of their higher education totem pole.

And that's when it hits him like a line drive.

The picture of Jayson coaching his nephew's little league team. The new season's scattered headshots on the kitchen table. Almost every time they hang out, even at work, Jayson brags about his nephew, Curtis.

"Curtis hit a home run the other game. Curtis has the best arm on the team. Curtis aced his science test." Curtis this and Curtis that, always. He loves that kid as if he were his own. The two are practically inseparable.

Antoni watches as the gears in Clayton's head start to turn, his demeanor cranking from complacent to contemplative.

"You on to something?"

"Maybe." Clayton puts his index finger up in an attempt to stifle any further interruption. He turns to face Antoni, who has seemingly forgotten that he's driving with his eyes clearly focused on the phone and nowhere on the road.

"Toni! Watch where you're going, man."

"Huh? Oh, shit," Antoni flinches as the truck swerves from the shoulder back between the blurred dotted lines.

"This is all for nothing if we crash and die," Clayton adds.

"Sorry, man. My bad," Antoni admits, steadying the wheel. "So, what are you thinking?"

Not entirely sold on the idea himself, Clayton breaks down his loose theory to see if maybe it holds any validity in Antoni's mind.

"All right. So, Jayson coaches his nephew's little league baseball team. And he's always going on about how proud he is of the kid, fully relishing the role of the cool uncle."

"Okay?" Antoni responds, clearly unimpressed. "What are you trying to say?"

"What I'm saying is that the passcode could be his nephew's birthday. Our ticket to getting into this damn thing," Clayton emphasizes, waving the phone like a madman.

With his eyebrows furled high, competing for space on his scrunched forehead, Antoni shoots Clayton a look of trepidation.

"That's a great theory and all, Clay, but there's just one problem. Do you happen to actually *know* his nephew's birthday?"

Clayton's optimism crawls underneath the bench seat.

Fuck.

Antoni's right. He doesn't know Curtis's birthday. Not even a single number in the six-digit date. But the more he thinks about it, adding up certain life events that coincide with his birth, the closer to the answer he might be able to get. And that's worth more than a try. It's all they have *to* try.

"No—" Clayton gives in.

Antoni expels a weighted sigh upon the surrender further slumping his already glum gaze.

"But I might," he finishes.

Antoni's head springs back up at the slightest hint of likelihood. Keeping his eyes glued to the road this time, he prods for more details, somewhat hopeful but still overly skeptical.

"Not to burst your bubble again, man, but you're being super vague."

The timeline inside Clayton's head starts auto-filling the gaps around Curtis's birthday in chronological order. He says them aloud to see if it all makes as much sense in reality as it does in his still foggy mind.

"Okay. Well, Curtis is playing coach pitch, which if my memory serves me right, that's ages five to seven, yeah?"

"Uhh," Antoni does the quick math in his own head, agreeing, "That sounds right." He continues with added emphasis, "Yeah, because Mick Chroner's dad was our coach, remember? And a few years later in middle school, we caught him shopping in the adults-only section at the local video store, rocking a healthy pile of X-rated VHS tapes in his soon-to-be creamy hands."

"Oh shit, that's right, Coach Chroner the Boner," Clayton chimes in. "How could I forget such porn gems like *In-Yee-Anus Bones and the Temple of Poon* or *Blown in 60 Seconds*?"

"Total cum classics." Antoni arouses a response. "Although, I was always fonder of his choice of Horror & Whore porn. Scary sexy hits like *I Know Who You Did Last Summer* and *Wet Dreams on Elm Street*."

They both share a reminiscent laugh, thinking of a time in their lives when life was just living. Just kids being kids. No responsibilities. No cares to speak of. Just best friends with their whole lives still ahead of them. Hopeful lives that didn't include serving time in prison or suffering a life-threatening injury. Futures that didn't revolve around deaths of loved ones or being caught in the middle of a full-fledged manhunt.

Clayton snaps out of the throwback trance first.

"Anyway, I know Curtis isn't five because he's past kindergarten. So that means he's either six or seven, and I want to say seven because this is his second year in the league. So that would put his birth year sometime in 2017, right?"

"Okay, so maybe we've got a year. Now, what?" Antoni remarks, his tone still chalked full of skepticism. "We're still missing a month and a day. That's two-thirds of the passcode, bud. Endless combinations."

"You're right," Clayton admits, only his confession still holds an inflection of optimism. "But I know his birthday is right around Labor Day because Jayson dipped out of last year's float trip to take the whole team on a birthday trip to the Negro Leagues Baseball Museum downtown."

"All righty, *now* we're getting somewhere," Antoni says, matching Clayton's hopeful tone. "We've got a tentative year and month. We can just trial and error it until we get the day, right?"

"Not if you want to continue being locked out of the phone again, we can't?"

"Sure, we can. You get six failed attempts before it locks you out, right?"

"Yeah, six failed attempts disabled it for a minute last time. Seven was five minutes, eight was fifteen, and lucky number ten had us down and out for a full hour."

"Okay, then just start on September 1st, 2017, and work your way up to Labor Day. It's always the first Monday in the month, right?"

"Yeah."

"Then that gives us a pretty good chance to get it right before you're locked out again. Of course, that is if you are in fact right about any of this ridiculous guessing game."

Clayton picks up the phone from the seat and taps the screen. The black rectangle wakes as the lock screen reappears. He inputs 090117, but the screen shakes and the phone vibrates from the all-too-familiar failed attempt. He quickly tries again, 090217. Again, the screen rattles with the incorrect passcode.

Agitated and losing confidence, he confides "Fuck, I'm starting to think I might be wrong about this whole birthday thing."

He tries 090317, but again the screen shakes, almost taunting him at this point. Beyond frustrated, he hastily types 090417.

Shake. Buzz.

Then, 090517.

Shake. Buzz.

Finally, he punches in 090617 on his last attempt before he's locked out again. Only this time, there's no accompanying shake or buzz to antagonize him. Just a coveted unlocking sound and a home screen filled with multiple rows of apps.

Blinking hard to confirm his victory, Clayton's excitement emanates in delayed jubilation.

"Holy shit, it worked. I'm in!"

Antoni nearly veers the truck off the road again just to witness the triumph with his own eyes.

"Hell yeah! Whoa—" he shouts, correcting his course as the rumble of the road's shoulder not so subtly reminds him to keep his shit between the lines.

The jerk causes Clayton to whiplash against the truck's remodeled door before he can fully brace himself. The unexpected impact carries enough force behind it to jostle the phone from his grasp and onto the floor.

"Damn, man, should I drive?"

"Sorry, I got excited," Antoni apologizes. "My bad."

"Guess it's a really good thing you got these floors replaced after all, huh, Bamm-Bamm?"

"Wow. Really?"

"Just calling it like I see it."

"You really are an Ass-Ass," Antoni groans, pushing the grin that's crawled across his face away. "Just pick up the phone and tell me where we're headed, will ya?"

Clayton grabs the ejected phone from the floorboard and locates the photos app. He opens the recents library. Right there—the last picture in the camera roll—is the address for the mysterious location.

He shows it to Antoni.

15276 Westport Sq., Suite C
Bannerton, IL 60411

"Jay, you better be fucking right about this," he mutters under his breath, as the pickup continues its nocturnal descent back into the fray of the city.

Jayson takes a deep breath and knocks on the closed office door. A salty voice with zero fucks left to give barks back from the other side.

"What."

It's not even a question just a statement.

Jayson reaches down for the knob and twists it slowly, hoping every millisecond of procrastination will help ease the monumental ass-chewing he's about to receive on the other side.

When he enters, he spots Rickers sitting behind a tiny desk, littered with cluttered stacks of strewn-about files and tattered remnants of junk food wrappers from the breakroom's vending machine—candy bars, potato chips, donuts—the works. Come to think of it, Jayson's never actually seen Rickers eat a real meal at work for as long as he's been here. And judging by his doughy physique and the pigsty of an office—more of a glorified broom closet than an actual office, really—he's pretty sure his boss couldn't tell a pot from a pan if it hit him in the face. Hell, he's probably never eaten anything in a shade of green or that even remotely resembles a vegetable in his entire life. In fact, Jayson wouldn't be surprised to find out that Rickers's actual home address is The Hunt for Justice.

He has no kids.

No spouse.

No hobbies.

No life.

Unless one considers eating copious amounts of highly processed, preservative-rich, cellophane-packaged junk food a hobby. He's practically married to his work, which is evident in the fact that he's always the first one to the office and the last one to leave. As if deep down he's afraid to be alone. To exist by himself. If he wasn't such an absolute dick, Jayson would almost feel sorry for him.

Spread out among the desk's chaos, Jayson can count at least four used coffee mugs with brown stained rings so old they're sprouting a healthy collection of fuzzy white and blue mold. The rest of the armpit of a room is unfurnished, aside from two mismatched, rudimentary chairs placed across from the desk. Minimal decorations adorn the beige walls and unlevel shelving. In fact, the only thing hanging on the wall is a lone framed certificate of achievement. It reads:

*A Pledge to Uphold Justice*
*We proudly acknowledge Reginald J. Rickers, Head of Security for The Hunt for Justice, with this certification of achievement for his continued excellence in the field.*
*Awarded this day of February 16th, 2007*

The plaque is topped off with Klein's illegible signature and The Hunt Initiative seal in the bottom right corner.

Jayson almost breaks down laughing upon reading the plaque, forgetting that Rickers's first name is Reginald. He's so used to everyone calling him Rickers, including Rickers himself, that a first name—anything to make him more human, more like a real person—doesn't seem to exist.

He recalls back to when he and Clayton first started at The Hunt for Justice. They were in orientation together, and one of the other new hires in their group, a cocky class clown type, openly called him Reggie in front of the whole class as a harmless gag. Rickers instantly paused the training and took him out into the hall. None of the muffled yelling was audible, but the impact was felt throughout the entire room.

In fact, that's the first time he and Clayton ever talked. They couldn't help but lock eyes with one another and joke about the situation, only to feel sorry for the guy who failed to show up for work the next day, or any day after that. He got his ass chewed so bad the first day that he quit on the spot.

Jayson reaches for one of the two open chairs and begins to sit.

"I didn't tell you to sit, Moore," Rickers counters, halting him from taking a load off. Jayson awkwardly stands back up from a half squat. Without even looking up from his pile of disarray, Rickers asks, "Where is he?"

Slightly confused, but more so playing dumb, Jayson replies with his own question. "Where is *who*, sir?"

With one fell swoop, Rickers drags his pudgy arm across the disaster on his desk, flinging papers, pens, and wrappers into the air like feathers from a bird that's just been rifled out of the air. All four coffee mugs shatter in a cascading impact with the opposing wall, speckling the off-white paint with a peppering of penicillin. The staggered smashing is dramatic but effective.

"I'm going to give you one last chance, Moore," he says, removing his gun from its holster and placing it on the freshly cleared table. "Where is he?"

The time for playing dumb has come to an abrupt end. Fucking with Rickers is one of Jayson's favorite past times, but even this is further than he's ever seen Rickers take a threat. Normally, it's empty warnings of "putting a foot up your ass"—or, really anything that involves your ass—but this, this doesn't feel like an empty threat anymore.

Jayson glances down at the gun. It's not pointed in his direction, but Rickers is still holding it while staring bullets from across the table at him.

He meets Rickers's gaze, gulps, and then whimpers, "I don't know, sir. Honest."

"What do you mean you don't know?" Rickers fires back. "He got away on *your* watch. Javorsky's patrol car was found at the cemetery just a few blocks from *your* house. The two of you are thick as flies on shit, and you're just going to sit here and tell me 'I don't know, sir'? I know you helped Sparks escape, Moore. Now where the hell is he?"

Jayson shifts his weight, shuffling his mounting anxiety from side to side, but Rickers doesn't flinch. He just stares steadfast and starts tapping the tip of his gun against the top of the desk.

Jayson sighs.

"I couldn't just stand there and let him be killed for something he didn't do, sir," he confesses. "Something he wasn't even tried for. I got him to safety, and then, he ditched me. He told me it was too dangerous for me to keep helping him. I have no idea where he is. I haven't heard from him since. That's the whole truth, honest."

"I fucking knew it," Rickers responds, marching around the empty desk. The sound of castaway papers crunch and crinkle below his heavy T-Rex stomps. "I should have known better than to have you and a rookie escort your little butt buddy away." He leans against the opposite side of desk, brandishing the gun cross-armed in his lap. The power move causes Jayson to take a step backward. "The only reason I don't shoot your ass right now for Hunt Initiative interference is because technically—" There's a visible pause in his delivery, almost anguish behind his next words. "—you were doing your job."

Jayson doesn't fully register the comment. He just blinks and mumbles the most intelligent and poignant response he can muster.

"Huh?"

Rickers elaborates, "When I sent you and Javorsky to take Sparks away, you were following Hunt Initiative protocol. No accused murderer is released to The Hunt until a jury of his or her peers convicts them. That's the law. Always has been. Klein bent that ruling in this case because the victim was his daughter and emotion got the best of him. But you weren't aware of that because you had already escorted Sparks out of the convention center when he made that decision." He takes a deep breath and reluctantly continues, "So, it would seem that based on the situation you were dealt, you did nothing wrong . . . correct?"

Rickers's words stumble out, but the pain of articulating them is visible and audible in the tight-jawed delivery from which they came.

Jayson can't help but stand, completely stunned. He searches his mind for the right words, but it's as empty as Rickers's newly unfurnished desk.

"Look, I may be an asshole, Moore. But I'm an asshole who believes in upholding the law as it stands. To the full extent." Rickers gets up, wading his way back to his desk chair through the sea of papers, broken porcelain, and vending trash, still toting the gun in his hand. "That's your story and if anyone asks, that's exactly what you tell them. Nothing else. Got it?"

Still at a loss for what to say, Jayson just stands and nods.

"Good. Now get the hell out of here, Moore. I'm tired of looking at you."

Finally, Jayson finds the right thing to say. The only words that seem appropriate for the moment.

"Yes, sir," he mumbles, as he turns and heads for the door.

"Oh, and Jayson?"

He whips around at the unfamiliar use of his first name. Something Rickers has never done.

"This is your one *get out of jail free* card. Based on a technicality. If I find out you're lying to me or that you've been in contact with Sparks in any way—" He waves his gun in the air. "—I will happily shoot you myself. Justice is coming for your friend. There's nothing you can do to stop it. Don't try me, Moore. Is that clear?"

"Crystal, sir."

Jayson reaches for the handle and exits. As the door shuts behind him, he leans against it and thinks about Clayton, hoping his friend is still alive. Wishing there was anything he could do to help him.

He already has more than he knows.

It's just after midnight by the time Clayton and Antoni roll up into the West Bottoms district. At one point in Bannerton's early years, this historic place brimmed with life and excitement. The idea of a fresh start led to the hustle and bustle of hopeful, entrepreneurial ventures that the Industrial Revolution would usher in during the decades to come. Situated in parallel with the up-and-coming railroad port, the West Bottoms was a major metropolitan area in the growing town's infancy and the economic engine many thought would drive the city's future forward.

Anchored by the biggest livestock exchange in the Midwest, thanks to its central location, the West Bottoms was the prime distribution hub for cattle, hogs, and horses around the nation. And although livestock was the area's flagship product, other industries like agriculture, baking, furniture warehouses, and household goods also saw years of persistent prosperity. Even the massive Union Station that was built to support the area's tidal wave of commerce and exchange was considered the largest train hub west of New England during its construction.

But all that "what could have been"—that future of hope—came and went well over a century ago. The Great Depression was the tipping point. The airport up north was the final straw.

All that remains now are the remnants of what was and what never became. Giant, empty warehouses clutter the area like desolate haunted mansions, housing ghosts of the city's forgotten past. The buildings' signs and paint are beyond worn from a century of neglect, and the stacked factory floors have more busted windows than functional ones. Piles of rubble are strewn about the streets outside of buildings like trashcans continually ignored for garbage day pickup. Union Station ceased operation and closed down more than forty years ago, and with it, so did the city's entire interest in the area. Looking at it all now, no one would ever guess it was anything more than a tarnished slum the city was keen on hiding. Even the homeless don't bother coming there. At one point in time, this place had immense opportunity, but that better future died and was buried decades ago under the tombstone of progression.

"Umm . . . Clay, you sure about this?" Antoni asks, weaving the truck in and out of the piles of rubble beneath daunting shadows of empty, multi-storied factories.

Clayton doesn't respond immediately, but that doesn't mean he's not thinking the exact same thing. He pulls out Jayson's phone and checks the address again—15276 Westport Sq., just like the last time—as if he doesn't have it memorized by now. Like somehow reading the numbers over again and again will suddenly spur the destination out of thin air amid all the surrounding desolation. But alas, there is no magical arrow pointing from above that says, "This is the place. You are here. Congratulations."

To further complicate their needle-in-a-haystack search, none of the century-old buildings seem to have any addresses, and none of the roads seem to have any remaining street signs. And even if they did, there are no functioning lights outside the dim beam of the truck's headlamps to even see them by. It's total darkness down here.

"Just keep your eyes open, it's got to be around here somewhere," Clayton says confidently, although his mind is anything but.

The truck pulls down a dark, unidentified side road where nothing but the soft glow of a haunting crescent moon and sixty-year-old pickup lights fight to break through the pitch black. In true wasteland form, only the grumbling crunch of gravel beneath the tires can be heard. If the area could be any eerier, it wouldn't take much.

"Clay, I can barely see a damn thing. Maybe we should turn back around? Try another route."

But Clayton doesn't want to turn back around. He can't. Back there, there's nowhere to go. No one to go to. He's in the presence of company, but he's never felt so alone. And that growing island of isolation—the feeling of being Hunted—is starting to make him question if all this is really worth it, especially now.

"No, we've got to keep going," he urges, his tone fighting hard to reassure his uncertain words. "It's got to be here. It has to."

Antoni releases a small sigh.

He looks over to his friend anxiously searching for any indication that they're on the right track or even in the right place. Anything at all to show a glimmer of progress. Any hint of hope that this place so eagerly once offered, back then and right now.

"Clay, man, I know you want to find this place and get to the bottom of whatever the hell is going on, but maybe it's just—"

But before Antoni can finish pleading his case to leave, Clayton goes wide-eyed and yells, "Toni, look out!"

Stuck somewhere between mid-consolation and inattentiveness, Antoni can't bring his eyes back to the road in time as the truck comes face to fender with a large pile of antiquated cinder blocks. Stems of rebar jutting out like rusty tentacles trap the vintage vessel in a malicious snare. Like a kraken from the deep, dark sea. The truck comes to an abrupt stop upon impact on the paved ocean and the shoulder-flinching crunch of a head-on collision is followed by the hiss of thirty-five pounds per square inch slowly escaping the driver-side front tire.

"Fuck!" Antoni shouts, pounding his palm into the steering wheel. In a series of quick, deliberate movements, he leans down, pops the hood, swings open the solid steel door, and hops out of his seat. Clayton cranks the passenger window down in a pathetic attempt to survey the damage done from inside the truck.

"How bad is it?"

Antoni hoists the heavy, solid steel domed hood as steam and smoke escape the engine's sinuses like fresh smolder from a dragon's nostril.

"Even if the radiator and engine are okay, which is a big fucking if, I don't have a spare tire on board because I just took it out to air it up the other day. Just my fucking luck."

The hood slams back down, and Clayton's seat shakes as he feels the added aggression behind the violent impact reverberate throughout the rest of the truck.

"Dammit! What are we going to do now? What's our next brilliant plan, Clay? We don't know where the hell we're going, and now, even if we did, we have no way to actually get there. We can't even see anything out here in this fucking wasteland." Antoni brings his hands up to his head, yanking his hair in frustration. "How did I let you talk me into this shit storm of a plan again?"

"Toni," Clayton says cautiously, as he steps out of the truck, doing his best not to crack any of the eggshells surrounding his friend. "It's going to be okay. We'll find a way. We've just got to—"

"Oh, cut the bullshit, Clay. We're screwed and you know it," he adds and stomps off around to the bed of the truck, diligently digging in the back for something that Clayton can't quite make out. He feels a gentle hand on his shoulder, and the hostile scrounging lulls to a softer rummage. From behind, a tender and apologetic voice carefully makes its way to his ear.

"Toni, I'm sorry. About this, about Cleo, your home, endangering Sonya and Thad—everything."

Antoni stops searching the back, but he doesn't turn around. He just keeps his head down, focused on the bed of the truck. Within seconds, Clayton can feel a slight tremble start to pulsate in his friend's shoulders, traversing his entire body in erratic, abbreviated waves. A moment later, faint sniveling can be heard as Antoni attempts to wipe the shallow accumulation of tears away before they can fill the bottom of his eyelids like a cup that's passed when.

"Don't try to stop it, man. Just let 'em out," Clayton reassures, through a grasp of added pressure on his friend's shoulder. "Trust me. It helps," he adds, thinking of how Jayson helped him grieve as he broke down in his kitchen. "I know."

"Cleo's gone, man. My house and garage are beyond fucked. The truck's busted. And more than that, I almost lost my family tonight. My entire world—everything that means anything to me."

"I know, man," Clayton reassures. "I'm sorry to have put you, Sonya, and Thad through all this. It's all my fault. I should have never gotten you involved in any of this."

Antoni takes in a couple of short sniffs.

"No, Clay. You didn't do this. I did. It's time I take responsibility for my own actions. This is all *my* fault. Desmond Baine was my doing. My curse to bear. And I brought those sins upon my family. It was just a matter of time." He looks up at Clayton through reflective eyes. "And I'll never be able to forgive myself for that. And I won't blame Sonya if she doesn't either. That is, if we even make it out of this mess alive."

Clayton doesn't know what else to say or do, or if he should even say or do anything. So, he just strengthens his grip on Antoni's shoulder and lets his friend ride it out. The déjà vu moment of helpless empathy transports him back to another memory of Trish.

He remembers his arm draped around her shoulders as she openly wept on their apartment couch, reading a letter in the mail from her

Nani. Rather than call or text each other, the two used to handwrite letters to one another like old pen pals. Clayton always thought it was the cutest thing because for one, he never knew his grandma, so it was sort of his way to experience the wholesomeness of having one by living vicariously through hers. And two, Trish used to read the letters aloud. Multiple pages of cursive notes jammed front to back with endearing small talk about the weather, old acquaintances she'd run into at the grocery store, trips to the nearby casino with her church girlfriends, and adorable misspellings of common words like "restraunt" and "loose" instead of "lose." It was like something of an age gone by, and he loved the simplicity of her stories and the passion with which she told them.

In this particular dispatch, Trish had received some tear-jerking photos of her mother. Old pictures of her mom at a pumpkin patch, smiling while cradling a sweet baby girl dressed in a puffy orange jack-o-lantern sweatshirt. The baby no more than a year old. Apparently, Trish had never seen these photos of herself and her mom before, and her father didn't have but just a few childhood photos of them together to share as it was. So, when she read the accompanying letter where her grandma talked about how much her mother loved her and how excited she was to celebrate the holidays together for the first time as a family, Trish couldn't hold back the waterworks.

Clayton remembers holding her on the couch that day, wanting to say something that could instantly cure her emptiness. Anything that would help take away a lifetime of not knowing her mother. But as he sat there holding her, there was nothing he could do. Anything he should do, other than just hold on.

So, that's what Clayton does. He keeps his hand firmly planted on Antoni's shoulders just like he held Trish. Just like he wishes, more than anything, he could hold her again now.

Antoni eventually turns around to face Clayton. Even in the darkness, his eyes retain a certain glassy quality, reflecting what exists of the waning moonlight above. He returns the gesture of putting his own hand on Clayton's shoulder as he struggles to let the right words escape.

"Clay . . . I think—" he mutters, squinting into the dim distance.

Clayton moves to intercept his distracted gaze, urging him with his eyes to get the words off his chest.

"Go ahead, man. You can say it," he presses. "Just let it out. It'll help."

Antoni's eyes focus, shooting Clayton a confused look back. Then, another quick peek past his friend's shoulder into the dark nothingness.

"No, Clay . . ." he shakes his head and wipes his eyes as if nothing happened. "15276."

"Huh?" Clayton counters with his own mystified glance into the black unknown.

"15276 Westport, right?" Antoni clarifies the question.

"Uh, yeah," Clayton answers, still confused about what the address of the make-believe location they're searching for has anything to do with the current sentiment of the moment. "What about it?"

"I think . . ." Antoni says, again squinting. "That's it. That's the place," he insists, pointing past Clayton's ear.

Clayton's head instantly swivels, following his friend's finger to the inconspicuous and dilapidated building on his six.

"Holy . . . shit," Clayton stutters in total disbelief, as two white grins crack the bleak look and feel of the moment. "That *is* it."

# CHAPTER 28

Vague remnants of the numbers 15276 adorn the unassuming building, partially obscured by untamed vegetation running rampant up the cracks of the aged brick like wild vines. The building itself looks to be part of an old manufacturing plant, composed of crumbly red slabs that almost turn to powder at the touch. Nothing about the shape of the place gives any indication that it's a functional address, whatsoever.

Clayton strides over to the door, his anticipation pressing for the answers he hopes will follow. He tugs on the steel handle sprinkled with varying hints of rusty, Rorschach-like blots.

It doesn't budge.

"Shit. It's locked," he quietly shouts.

"Did you really expect it to be that easy?" Antoni ridicules, as he studies the daunting stature of the abandoned-looking structure.

"Yes? No? I don't know. I mean, look at this place. It's a total shithole. Guess I figured getting in wouldn't pose much of an issue."

Antoni casually strolls up to the front door, shooting his friend a smirk before responding, "It may look like just a shithole, but it's a shithole with state-of-the-art security."

"Huh? What do you mean?" Clayton responds, failing to see what Antoni is getting at.

"Look to your left, at that keypad."

Clayton diverts his attention to a small electronic lock system hidden behind some more weeded overgrowth. A steady red light faintly blinks illuminating an ominous and highly advanced-looking digital keypad with an accompanying two-by-four-inch touchscreen functioning as a fingerprint scanner.

"Oh, shit," he says, studying the intricacies of the smart lock—a formidable opponent way above his weight class.

Antoni piggybacks, "Yeah, that's definitely not original to the building."

"Can *you* crack it?" Clayton asks, in a tone that sounds more like a challenge than an inquiry.

Antoni shoots his childhood friend an accusatory glance. No words are needed as the follow-up question "Who the hell do you think you're talking to?" is firmly stated in his stare.

"I mean, I just . . . this isn't like the car locks we used to jimmy as kids." He tries to save himself from the shame of underestimating Antoni's skillset, but before he can finish stuttering over his trip down grand theft memory lane, Antoni walks off toward the truck, disappearing into the night's void without saying a word.

Clayton can hear him faintly fumbling around in the pickup bed for a moment, then, silence. Seconds later, a concentrated beam of light cuts through the overwhelming darkness, nearly blinding him. His pupils contract and then dilate as they fight to refocus against the black backdrop.

Antoni's person catches up with his shadowy figure as he re-enters Clayton's limited bulb of view.

"Hold these," he commands, handing Clayton a small flashlight and what looks like a credit card reader with some random color-coordinated cords and stray wires sticking out of the back. "And try to keep the light steady. The doctor is about to operate."

Clayton watches as Antoni goes to work. He starts by attaching a tiny magnetic remote with a circular digital screen to the lock itself. It clings to the metal keypad with a satisfying clang. Once in place, he attaches a series of wires from the odd-looking card reader in sequential order to the remote: black first, red second, and white last. After ensuring everything is properly connected, he pulls out a small, rectangular-shaped glass card. At first glance, it looks like any ordinary credit card, just transparent.

By now, Clayton's fascination has got the best of him.

"What the hell is that thing? Looks like a futuristic credit card."

Antoni doesn't look up or miss a beat tackling the task at hand.

"Yes and no," he replies, sliding the crystal-clear card across the reader. "It's a hotspot-enabled database identification card. Or Hot D.I.C. for short."

Clayton immediately bounces the light from the card reader to Antoni's face. He flinches in the blinding process, chastising, "Ah, what the hell, Clay? I told you to keep the light still."

Moving the light out of Antoni's eyes to under his own face, like they used to do as kids trying to scare each other with ghost stories under a blanket fort, he shoots him a furrowed look.

"Hot D-I-C? *Really*?"

"Yeah, what about it?"

"You really never thought to sound that one out, huh?" Clayton accuses, steadying the light under his chin. "You're walking around calling it a "Hot Dick" for short, bud. You know that right?"

Clayton watches as the eureka embarrassment brightens the white in Antoni's eyes. Somehow, someway, he's clearly never thought to put the two together.

Shaking his head and smiling loudly. "I'll take that as a *no* then," Clayton adds with a laugh.

Still trying to sound out the shame in his head, Antoni replies, "Damn, I really thought I was being clever with that one, too."

"Yeah, ri-DICK-ulously clever," Clayton snarks.

"Oh, fuck you."

"Yes, please. So long as it's with that card."

The two friends pause, staring at each other in the ominous loom of the flashlight. Silence consumes the conversation, but it's fleeting as combined laughter erupts, shattering it mere moments later. After an unexpected but welcomed bit of emotion that isn't loss or sadness, Clayton brings the conversation back to the task at hand.

"All right, okay," he starts, trying to regain his composure. "So, what does your hot dick do exactly?" Still stifling chuckles like a prepubescent boy.

"Well," Antoni carefully chooses his words, making sure he doesn't refer to it by that name ever again. "The ID card and reader connects you online to the system's database that it's linked to. In most cases, it would be things like specific bank ATMs or gas station pumps, so you could pick up the personal card information of the person who last used it. It filters out all the rerouting and security checks, searching for the correct sequence of numbers, and then links them to the ID card. Making it imitate—"

"The person's credit card," Clayton jumps in, completing Antoni's sentence.

"Bingo. But in this case, we're not interested in stealing someone's bank account or credit card info. We just want the lock code sequence." As Antoni continues explaining his latest pursuits in becoming king of the tech theft game, the tiny remote attached to the lock begins to filter through a chain of numbers. One at a time, single digits start to rapidly scroll through in individual columns before settling into place. After ten or fifteen seconds, three numbers have already been accounted for with what looks like five slots to go.

About a minute later, all eight numbers have settled into place in their individual windows.

"All right, so we've got the code," Antoni says, as he plunges back into his duffle, pulling out a familiar, small metal briefcase. "Now, give me your hand."

Timidly, Clayton obliges and surrenders his left hand to Antoni, who grabs it and sprays his thumb with some kind of clear-coated adhesive.

"What's that stuff?" Clayton asks, but he's instantly shushed by Antoni who has gone into full concentration mode.

"It's imperative that you do your best not to move right now. If I misplace one of these micro-tech silicon fingerprints even a tad, it can ruin the whole print. And these jellyfish ain't cheap or easy to come by."

Clayton steadies his hand the best he can as Antoni meticulously adjusts the silicon mold until he feels the placement is adequate. Then, he pulls out a small electronic device about the size and shape of a smartphone. Within seconds, the gelatinous mold and the microcircuitry inside begins to take shape, adhering perfectly to Clayton's thumb.

"Wait, how does it know who's fingerprint to mold to? This isn't how you explained it earlier," Clayton diffidently asks.

"Ahh, Clay, you've been out of the game for too long, man. So much to learn, young grasshopper. These things aren't just one-trick ponies. But technically, in this instance, you're not wrong. It's not working like I told you earlier, but I'm glad you were paying attention," he says, inspecting Clayton's thumb. "Instead, I've programmed it to create a generic print template. Think of it like a blank fingerprint canvas. So, now when you press your thumb up to the scanner, it'll pick up traces from the last person's prints. If it can recreate at least a seventy percent match to whoever scanned in last, then it's smart enough to reconstruct the rest of the print to about an eighty-five percent success rate. More or less."

"Wait, wait, wait. Hold up a sec. I may have gotten a *C* in Algebra back in high school, but I know basic math. Neither one of those numbers add up to one hundred percent. Are you're telling me this might not even work?"

"Ye of little faith, my friend. Have some trust in your old pal, Toni. I've had pretty good results with these so far."

"And you would define pretty good as what? Like nine out of ten times?"

"Eh, more like six. Give or take a half percent."

"What?" Clayton shouts, nearly flinging the silicon mold from his finger. "Sixty percent! That's worse than your failing grade score average back in school."

"What can I say? I was understimulated. Besides, look at me now," Antoni says, posturing a puffed chest and matter-of-fact face. "Now, stop worrying and just put your damn thumb up against the scanner. Nice and slow-like."

Reluctantly, Clayton raises his hand toward the scanner on the keypad. About halfway there, he stops and looks at Antoni.

"What if this *doesn't* work?"

Antoni takes a deep breath in, followed by a long, drawn-out sigh.

"Oh, you know, the usual. A lock system this sophisticated will surely trigger a silent alarm, and the building will probably go into total lockdown mode. We'll most likely get caught as authorities flood the scene in record response time, and well, I'm sure your imagination can take it from there, being the nation's most-wanted man and all."

"So, the worst possible scenario? That's all you had to say. Could have just left it at that," Clayton retorts as he resumes, cautiously extending his thumb toward the scanner. Upon contact, he can feel the tiny technology going to work like some kind of intelligent biomechanical microorganism, concaving and convexing to copy the pad's desired print.

"Yeah, kind of wiggle it up and down and side to side a little. That can sometimes help get more of a complete match," Antoni instructs, while making the motion with his own thumb.

After just a few seconds, a digital image of a fingerprint begins to appear on Antoni's device. Building and constructing itself from the inside out in real time using a network of squiggly lines. The image creation finally comes to a stop as the screen reads: *Match Success 73%.*

"Bingo. We should have enough of a match. But just keep your thumb there for a little bit longer while I finish up."

Clayton strains his neck to see what Antoni is doing on the screen, but with his thumb essentially glued to the scanner, he's simply left to his own oblivious devices. The seconds feel like minutes as his shoulder wound starts to ache and his hand begins to cramp. His doggy painkillers are wearing off.

A moment later, the light on the lock flips from blinking red to solid green. The door's series of electronic-driven deadbolts simultaneously clink, making a satisfying lock release sound as they nestle into their disengaged resting places.

Basking in the fresh air of newfound optimism, Antoni shoots Clayton a smirk amid the flashlight's beam.

"Voilà," he brags. "Maybe I should've been our class's valedictorian. ValedicToni!"

"Can you even spell that word?" Clayton quizzes.

"Pfft, yeah. V-A-L . . . touché."

"Thought so." Clayton reaches for the door. Before he can open it, Antoni quickly snatches the handle.

"Not so fast," he says, blocking Clayton's path inside. "We have no idea what's behind those doors. If this rusted-ass and totally unassuming factory can have a digital smart lock as advanced as the one I just cracked, then I'm pretty sure it's got a few more tricks up its sleeve inside. We gotta be careful."

Antoni bends down and puts all the used lock-hacking gadgets back into his duffle. His hands reappear with a pair of night vision goggles, the same ones Clayton scoped out back at the shop's bunker earlier.

"Here, put these on and flip the switch on the right side three clicks to the right," Antoni instructs, extending a set to his friend.

Clayton slides the goggles over his head, doing as told until they're snug. He powers them on with a single flip of the switch and instantly his vision is transported to accompanying fields of green and black. He surveys the surrounding area briefly, and it's safe to say that the forsaken factories and buildings that compose the West Bottoms don't look any more welcoming in night vision. But at least he can actually see them now.

He looks toward Antoni, who is just now putting on his own pair of goggles. He can see his green-tinted mouth moving.

"Clay, are you on the third setting?"

Clayton reaches back to the switch and feels two more clicks. In the blink of an eye, the green and black night vision lens switches to a black and gray system with radiating areas of white. He looks at Antoni, who resembles a silvery red illuminated blob of light.

"Whoa, is this infrared?"

"Thermal infrared night vision to be exact," Antoni responds as he slings the duffle over his shoulder. "This place isn't the only one with a few tricks up its sleeve."

Clayton extends his own hand in front of his eyes, slowly waving it back and forth. He's mesmerized by the various layers of temperature—white hot in the center accompanied by dimmer rings of grayish yellow, orange, and darker black on the outskirts, like some kind of heat sensory bull's eye.

"This is super cool," he gushes with childhood wonder, like a boy who just unwrapped a shiny new toy at Christmas.

"Clay, focus," Antoni responds, bringing his friend back to earth.

"Right, sorry," he says, putting his hand back down to his side. "So, why the infrared?"

"I don't want to take any chances with this place. For all we know, there could be trip lasers and other security systems inside that we can't see with the naked eye. But with these—" he points his white-hot glob of a finger to his goggles, "We'll have the upper hand. Just in case."

"Whatever you say Double 00 Mission Impossible."

"Mock me now, buddy. But you're going to thank me when I use the explosive chewing gum to save our asses later."

"Oh, does it have a dumbass, homoerotic name like hot dick, too?"

"Hot D-I-C!" Antoni hisses in a failed attempt to plead his case. "Shit. I'm never going to live that one down, am I?"

"Not a chance."

"Figured. Oh well, you ready for this?"

"No, but let's do it."

The two breach the factory entrance as the front door slams shut behind them. Both jump from the boisterous clang. Instantly, track lights on the floor illuminate, lighting a narrow, linear path forward. Clayton looks back to Antoni, whose head is making arcs around the room, studying the surrounding area.

"Hmm. Must be on a motion sensor," he infers.

"Speaking of sensors . . . how do we know we're not being recorded on surveillance cameras right now?" Clayton asks, afraid of the answer.

Antoni replies, "Don't worry. I haven't seen any."

"And how exactly are you so sure about that, MacGyver?" Clayton queries, turning around. "This room is huge."

Antoni reaches up his glowing hand and taps Clayton's goggles. A faint heat signature trails behind the subtle movement.

"These things are formatted to detect a variety of wavelength sources outside of just infrared. They can pick up microwaves, radio waves, X-rays—and in the case of surveillance cameras—light and ultraviolet waves. So, if there were cameras in here, I'd have detected them by now."

"Wow. Okay," Clayton says, assuredly. "These things really do have it all. Do they transform into a gun? Or maybe a jet pack?"

"No, but they do have a pretty cool *shut the fuck up and focus* function on them that I'm considering using."

"Geez. Noted," Clayton says, zipping his mouth shut.

About fifty feet straight ahead, another door appears out of the vast chamber's obscurity, dimly lit by the surrounding track lights against a sea of nothingness. It too appears to have some kind of locking mechanism, based on the slow flashing red light on the panel next to it, which appears white as chalk through their goggles. The rest of the room consists of starch brick walls; however, these rust-colored slabs appear new in comparison to the exterior's bricks eroding to dust from four generations of oxidized wear and tear.

The lit path ahead resembles one of those theme park funhouse bridges within a spinning chamber. It has a raised metal catwalk with security railings and all. Underneath the carnival walkway appears to be a glass floor structure. Beneath the thick layer of glass, it's difficult to tell, but it seems to go deep.

"Jesus, could they have gone any more suspenseful with this secret agency vibe?" Antoni whispers behind Clayton.

"You mean the brushed metal floating floor tiles and motion-activated LED runway lights aren't enough for you? I'm just hoping the lock at the end of this yellow brick road isn't some kind of state-of-the-art optical scanner. Something tells me even you don't have a ridiculous gizmo for that trick."

"Really? You better knock on some wood for jinxing us with a comment like that."

"I would—" Clayton scans the futuristic chamber. "If I could actually find some."

When the two arrive at the door, Antoni briefly studies the lock mechanism.

"What's the verdict?" Clayton asks, watching the gears behind Antoni's goggles turn. "Do we need some kind of mechanical eye to open sesame?"

"No, actually, this should be an easy one," he replies without breaking his concentration from the door's lock. "You still got the silicon microprint on your thumb?"

Clayton looks down and verifies that it's still attached. With so much stimulus unfolding around him, he almost forgot all about it.

"Yeah, it's still there, somehow."

"Perfect. They tend to become even more adhesive and durable with time," Antoni says, as he digs into his bag of tricks, once again pulling out the small, screened hacking device. "Go ahead and press your thumb onto the pad just like you did at the front door. Once the silicon solidifies, the print does, too. If we're lucky we should just be able to use the same print."

"Should? You know for being some high-tech criminal mastermind, you're not instilling a whole lot of confidence in me to step up to the plate."

"Well, for starters, I never said I was a mastermind. You did. I'm just a dealer, but I should probably know how the merchandise works, right? After all, inquiring customers want demos. And you know what else? For being a former criminal, you've kind of turned into a little bitch. Now, shut up and put your finger on the scanner already."

"I'm sorry, would you like me to continue where I left off with that scar on your neck?" Clayton quips, grudgingly placing his finger on the lock pad.

Before Antoni can continue with a well-timed rebuttal to the back-and-forth bickering, the light on the security panel blinks green and the door latch releases.

He waves his arm in an ushering fashion. "Bitches first."

Clayton reaches for the handle.

"Cute. I was going to say assholes second, anyway."

He attempts to step into the next room but feels a grip tighten around his bicep.

"Clay, just be careful. For real."

He gives Antoni a subtle nod and takes his first step into the great abyss. Unlike the corridor behind them, the new space doesn't activate any motion sensor lights. Through his goggles, the room looks like some kind of black-and-white sci-fi cathedral. As unassuming and lifeless as the outside of the building looked, the inside resembles something out of a spaceship, beaming with dormant activity.

An embankment of sleeping monitors panel the upper portion of the room like digital wallpaper. Underneath the connective screens, massive servers line the lower walls. Their paparazzi of flashing lights flicker like Morse code while the middle section of the room is divided into multiple rows of high-tech cubicle setups. The assorted computer desks are cluttered with used coffee mugs, random electronic devices, haphazard stacks of papers, and other random folders full of files that look beyond classified. It's like a scene out of Area 51, minus actual alien life. Or any life, for that matter.

In the center of it all, hangs a sizable four-sided, non-functioning jumbotron setup. Something straight out of Wall Street's playbook. The two-story ceiling rig is accompanied by its own stream of ribbon monitors that wrap its entire square perimeter, like a ticker that would run the latest stock trends and point shares. Upstairs, even closer to the jumbotron action, the room is split into two large glass spaces. One side appears to house a sophisticated boardroom with smart whiteboards and a grand conference table. The other side looks like additional office spaces for whomever or whatever oversees this place.

"Um. What the actual fuck is this?" Clayton says aloud.

"Eloquently put, man. Took the words right out of my mouth," Antoni adds, slowly lowering the duffle bag to the floor, processing the overstimulation surrounding him. "This must be some kind of command center. I guess for The Hunt Initiative?"

"Possibly, but I think it's something more than that. If back there was the yellow brick road, then we just found Oz," Clayton replies and removes his goggles to see if his eyes are deceiving him. But his natural sight is just pure blackness, save for the faint illumination of the bordering server lights like stars in the night sky.

"Well, all right then, Dorothy," Antoni adds. "What's next?"

Clayton locates a light switch on the adjacent wall next to an illuminated EXIT sign. He prepares to take a first step toward it, when again he feels Antoni's hand grasp his bicep. Only this time it's his wounded arm and the grasp packs much more fervor. The jolt of pain drops him to his knee.

"Ahh, what the—?" he grimaces. "Watch the arm, man."

Easing his vise-like grip but not totally letting go, Antoni helps Clayton climb to his feet. The contrived gesture detains a lingering sense of seriousness.

"You can let me go now, man."

The controlling grasp is soon followed by a new, grave tone in Antoni's voice.

"Don't. Fucking. Move."

"Huh? Why? What are you talking about?"

Antoni takes the goggles out of Clayton's hand and shoves them back over his friend's eyes before aggressively swiveling his head in the right direction. No more than two feet past where he was about to step, Clayton discovers an intricate matrix of trip motion sensor lasers that grid out a large chunk of the main floor.

"Oh. Shit," Clayton lets out.

"Yeah, oh shit, indeed," Antoni responds, finally letting him go. "You just about walked right into it."

Rubbing his throbbing shoulder, Clayton asks, "You think you can disable them?"

"That depends," Antoni says, scanning the corners of the room. "I'd need access to the central security source, and something tells me we don't have time to go play hide 'n' seek."

Clayton surveys the floor, studying the ebb and flow of the faint white lasers. The grid intersects, weaving in and out from one another like a rippling ocean carrying an infrared tide.

"Fuck," he mutters.

"Again, eloquently put, man."

Clayton thinks for a moment. He's come too far, gone through too much, to just give up now. He looks at Antoni and realizes that it's not just about himself anymore. He's not the only one who's lost something. He knows he has to find a way to make this right. Whatever that means. Whatever that may take.

"What if we could get to one of those computers? Could you hack it then?" Clayton asks, pointing to the cluster of computer stations in the center of the room.

Antoni takes a break from haplessly scouring the area for another route.

"Mmm, possibly. But I don't see how we're getting around this laser maze to test that theory out."

Clayton knows it's a shit idea before he even has time to think it all the way through. But in the past twenty-eight hours, when was the last time not thinking a plan all the way through has stopped him? Barely escaping from one dire situation just to end up in another seems to be the only solution forward so far.

Antoni would tell him hopscotching his way across the trap floor to the first desk is absolutely out of the question. So, he figures why bother asking a question when the answer isn't what he's looking for in the first place. Without any further hesitation, Clayton finds his pattern in the matrix and makes his move as the laser grid ebbs to the widest part of its cubed intersection.

One step in, and it's now fight or flight.

"Clay, no!" Antoni shouts at the sudden suicide attempt.

But it's too late, he's committed now.

Two steps in, he can see the squares closing in on him, fast—even faster than his half-baked plan anticipated.

Three steps in. There's no turning back.

Four steps in and the intersection of lasers sizes up his leg, ready to eclipse his calf at any second.

Five steps in, there's no choice left but to jump and pray for the best before the grid crisscrosses over his ankle, triggering whatever alarm it's programmed to.

Clayton explodes, launching off his back left foot, but midway through the leap of faith, it's evident he's not going to make it all the way to the desk. He's going to have to settle for its cubicle wall and pray that its aluminum finish is sturdy enough to support the heft of his weight and the momentum he's about to throw at it.

The smooth, metal divider is cool and surprisingly slicker to the touch than expected as Clayton's fingers make slippery contact with the pseudo-wall. He curls them around the cubicle's upper edge to form a constricted clench—an aptly named death grip for the grave situation he's just landed himself in.

With nothing but one functional shoulder and the tips of his fingers for support, his feet dangle hopelessly off the ground, hovering dangerously close to the incoming laser mesh. Slowly, with every joint of his knuckles taut white with tension, he pulls himself up to the top of the divider wall just before his toes can trip any part of the hovering matrix of beams. Safely atop, he's suddenly thankful for all those dreaded years of routine prison pullups.

Trying to catch his breath in between bouts of rushing adrenaline, he hears Antoni call out from across the room.

"Remember when I called you a little bitch earlier?" Antoni shouts, his voice accompanied by the sound of genial relief and a smile. "I was wrong. You're just fucking crazy."

Clayton gives Antoni a thumbs up and a return smirk as the consequential outcomes of what could have happened with his less-than-stellar plan slowly dissolve in his racing mind.

Up until now, he's nearly forgotten about the bullet that shredded his shoulder. But after the courageous charade he just pulled, the physical exertion on the fresh wound has caused a shooting pain to light up every nerve ending in his left arm. A throbbing ripple effect works its way from his shoulder to his hand, stabbing its way from muscle to muscle on the plummet down. He takes a moment to grit through the discomfort, but quickly casts aside any remnants of his stupid shenanigan or its painful aftertaste when the computer on the desk recaptures his attention.

Again, he hears Antoni shout from the doorway.

"Just so we're clear, I'm not doing any of that," he says, shaking his head while the goggles follow left to right. "Hard pass."

"You'd never make it anyway," Clayton hollers back from atop the desk's island of safety. "I played every sport imaginable with you, remember?"

"Oh?" Antoni probes. "And what's that supposed to mean?"

"It means you might as well have been born with two left feet, Graceful."

Antoni takes a moment to gather a worthy comeback, "So you're fucking crazy and *still* an Ass-Ass. I guess time really doesn't change people."

"Aww, don't be bitter. You can challenge me to a game of one-on-one later if it'll make you feel better. Right now, we've got to figure out how to hack this thing," he says, swiveling to face the computer. "Can you walk me through it?"

"I don't know, probably, but that's like asking a blind man to solve a puzzle. I need to visualize it to know what I'm working with."

"But it can be done, right?" Clayton asks, clearly avoiding the gray answer in search for the black-and-white solution to the situation.

"Doable? Yes. Time-consuming? Absolutely."

"Well, let's start with step one then. Which would be—?" Clayton asks helplessly from across the room.

"How about turning it on, genius?"

"Right."

He fishes around the back of the smooth, metal tower for the power button. Feeling for the switch, he flips it and boots up the drive.

Just as the computer begins to wake, a muffled slam from the heavy front door in the corresponding chamber resonates throughout the hushed space. The room's bare surfaces and vaulted ceilings serve as the perfect echo receptor, effortlessly pinging the entrance vibration across the large brushed steel, glass, and concrete space like a three-way game of audible Pong.

"Shit! Someone's coming," Antoni whispers out loud from across the room.

In a scrambled act of panic, Clayton searches for cover. There's just one problem. He can't touch the floor because of the trip lasers, so he does his best to improvise, scrunching behind the desk's cubicle wall as best he can.

Antoni hisses from afar at his failed attempt of *hide* and seek.

"Clay, I can see your ass hanging out from here."

Frantically, Clayton responds in his own aggressive whisper, "Just shut the hell up and hide."

"Where?" Antoni asks sarcastically. "I can't move any more than two fucking feet."

"Just—"

But Clayton's rebuttal is cut short as the keypad behind the secondary entrance sounds off. A short sequence of beeps is followed by the clank of a metal locking mechanism and a corresponding hiss as the door opens.

Antoni takes cover, as much as a sitting duck stranded in an open pond can, by side-stepping as far to the left of the door frame as possible. Just careful enough to avoid tripping the floor alarm. Within seconds, a third, uninvited party joins them in the room.

The looming presence is accompanied by a soft, female voice that cuts through the airy silence like a dull knife through thick tension.

"*Patricia*, enable lights please."

At the sound of the command, Antoni rips off his goggles while Clayton instinctively shoots his head up from behind his cubicle. Not a minute since her death has he not had Trish somewhere on his mind, but hearing someone else say her name sends a rush of memories back into his thoughts. The only reason he snaps back to the moment is because the former darkness is consumed by a flash flood of bright fluorescence, causing his goggles to zap him blind like a bolt of lightning to his pupils.

As light engulfs the black space, the woman instantly catches a glimpse of Clayton frantically flinging off his goggles. Before she can get out a reflexive scream, an imposing hand overtakes her mouth and pulls her back. She hears a metallic click by her ear as the bezel of cool steel graces her temple.

She freezes, dropping her handbag and thermos to the floor. Coffee flees from the casted container, caffeinating the porous concrete below.

The clamor of fallen belongings is followed by a gruff set of commands.

"Don't move. Don't make a sound. Nod if you understand."

The woman does exactly as she's told, shelving her stride and silencing her lips. Calmly, she moves her head up and down. The rest of her body trembles in place.

Stranded on his cubicle island, Clayton aggressively rubs his eyes to help them finish readjusting from the unexpected bout of blindness. Still fuzzy, he looks over to see a blurred Antoni holding their unwelcomed guest at gunpoint.

Out of pure instinct, he yells across the room, "Toni, don't! Put the gun down."

But Antoni doesn't heed the order. He only pushes the gun's muzzle harder into her temple. Tightening his grip around her waist in the process.

"She hasn't done anything. If she knew we were here, there'd be Justice Hunters breaking down the door already."

"I don't care. It's not safe," Antoni barks back. "We should just take care of her now before it's too late."

Sensing that a bad situation is about to get worse, Clayton's mental reflexes kick into play.

"Wait," he spurts, still voluntarily blinking his eyes some. "Maybe she can help us."

Antoni catches himself subconsciously dropping his guard at the thought, so he quickly readjusts, positioning the gun's barrel perpendicular to the woman's face.

Clayton continues, trying all the tricks to talk his friend down.

"Look, we need computer access, right? Well, maybe she's our ticket in."

Turmoil bubbles in Antoni's thoughts, but deep down he knows

Clayton is right. This could be a blessing in disguise. Get what they need now and figure out what to do with her later. After all, a single unarmed woman pales in comparison to another house raid or herd of Justice Hunters.

Hesitant, he slowly lowers the gun down to his side, but only after he makes sure she fully understands the gravity of the situation she's walked into.

"I'm going to release you, but if you try anything . . ." he repeats himself again for good measure. "Anything. I won't think twice about putting one between your pretty little eyes. That clear?"

The terrified hostage nervously nods her head as Antoni lets her go. She staggers forward a couple of steps and quickly gets to work wiping away the accumulation from her eyes. It's a futile act, but the recouping gesture helps her regain a semblance of control in her otherwise powerless situation.

Turning back around to shoot a disdainful glare at Antoni and a semi-thankful one back at Clayton, she finds her words. They pour out in a string of questions.

"Who are you? How did you guys get in here? What do you want?"

Antoni tries to respond, but Clayton cuts him off from across the room.

"Toni—" he raises his hand to emphasize the interruption. "Let me."

Clayton diverts his full attention to the startled woman who has somewhat regained a handle on her irrepressible trembling.

"You know who I am, right?" he asks, gently meeting her gaze from across the room.

It's a face she doesn't need to study twice. She's seen it plastered all over the news and on every city block for the past thirty hours straight.

She answers him with compliant eyes and a subtle nod as she bends down to pick up her spilled belongings.

"It's okay. We have no intention of hurting you. I promise."

Clayton tries to assure her, raising his hands in the air as an added peace offering. "Contrary to what the news is saying about me, anything you've heard—" he glares over in Antoni's direction as her eyes follow. "Or what impression my shoot-first-ask-later friend might have given you, none of it's true. We just need to get access to your computer database," he adds from the edge of the desk, glancing down at the floor to where the matrix of laser beams nearly Jaws'd his leg. "And maybe some help with the security system. I'm kinda stuck over here."

The woman takes a deep breath in and steadies her exhale the best she can through anxious lungs. Collecting herself, she brushes back her auburn hair and tucks the bangs of her tight bob behind her ears while nudging her cat-eyed rims flush atop the bridge of her button nose. At first glance, Clayton's best guess is that she's on the shy side of twenty-five. Her innocent, round hazel eyes, youthful face, and timid demeanor all give off the appearance of someone who'd likely be carded before any order of alcohol, and quite frankly, before entry into an R-rated movie.

She shrugs her bag back over her shoulder, readjusts her green field jacket, and tugs down on her knee-high plaid skirt. All insignificant actions to buy herself some needed reprieve and exhibit a little self-reassurance as she studies Clayton from afar.

She hinges on the moment, holding her gaze for a few delayed beats before speaking.

"*Patricia*, disable security protocol for F1. Authorized user: Norse, Kara, 14687."

Instantly, a low hum reverberates throughout the quiet space before quickly dissipating. Clayton gingerly lowers his foot to touch the floor, toes first, as if testing the surface temperature of a pool.

Nothing happens.

Slowly, he shifts the bulk of his weight backward as his heel plants itself onto the ground.

Still nothing.

After a matter of seconds, he's standing with both feet firmly rooted. Tense at first gait, then more relaxed with each uninhibited step taken toward greeting Antoni and their unexpected guest.

"So, Kara, is it?" he asks.

"Yes," she replies, short and to the point. Her apprehension still soaring.

"Well, Kara. It's nice to meet you. I'm sorry it had to be under these circumstances." Cognizant enough to give her ample room upon his approach, Clayton doesn't waste any more pleasantries. "As you can see, Kara, we're in a bit of a predicament here, and we could really use your help," he explains, studying her eyes. "Will you help us?" he asks coyly, almost pleading versus demanding, unlike someone in control of a hostage would sound.

Kara peers deep into his eyes. They're dark and shrouded, full of hurt, but there's a softness to them. A glint of honesty that against all her better judgment puts her at a surprising sense of ease in an overwhelmingly uncomfortable situation.

She struggles to find her verbal footing.

"I-I . . . okay. Yes. I'll help you."

"Perfect," Clayton says, as he marches back over to the center desk, motioning to the only awake computer. "But first thing's first. Should we be expecting anyone else to randomly surprise us through that door anytime soon?"

Kara shakes her head. "No, it's just me on the night shift tonight."

"Okay, good. Second thing, the security protocol that you disabled—did it shut down the video feed on these cameras?"

Again, Kara's head moves. This time, a delicate nod.

"Yes, it shuts down the sensors and the entire feed. Well, all security except for the door locks."

"Great. Thank you. Okay, third and most important thing, I need to see everything you can find on Rebecca Klein," he insists, patting the top of the monitor while dragging out the desk chair for her.

"Rebecca Klein? As in Simon Klein's deceased wife?" she responds with squinted pupils behind her thick frames and puzzled head tilt.

"Precisely," he confirms.

Still cautious, Kara takes a small step forward but changes course when she catches a glimpse of Antoni readjusting the gun tucked above his belt.

Clayton catches the apprehensive scenario play out.

"For Christ's sake, Toni, will you just relax already? You're scaring her."

But Antoni remains stoic and responds begrudgingly.

"You just worry about what you got to do, and I'll worry about what I got to do, all right?"

He unholsters the pistol wedged in his waistband, "Screw it. I'm going to go case the place and make sure we're not *actually* going to be expecting any other surprises." He turns and stares Kara square in the eye before exiting. "No offense for not believing you, kid. I just don't trust you."

He marches off as the door slams shut behind him.

Clayton shakes his head and returns his attention to Kara.

"Sorry about him. Toni means well, he can just be a little—"

"Dickish?" Kara interjects, turning Clayton's sentence into her own Mad Lib.

"Uh, well, I was actually going to say intense, but yeah, he can definitely be a dick, too."

"Tell me about it," Kara responds, again taking a small step toward Clayton now that her main source of apprehension has left the room.

"Yeah, he . . . well, we . . . have lost a lot in this whole mess," Clayton justifies, as the words strike home, and his eyes begin to sweat. The sincere perspiration involuntarily makes her loosen her guard even more before the alarm in her head sounds off for foolishly trusting a wanted murderer.

Clayton takes notice as she regains rigidity in her posture, halting the stride of her advancing steps.

"Look, Kara, I'm sorry that you got involved in all this. I truly am. But for what it's worth, I didn't kill my girlfriend. I don't care if you believe me or not. I would never do something like . . . like that. I loved her more than anything. And, I know it probably sounds crazy, but I believe there's something hidden in her mother's file that may help me clear my name. But I don't have the luxury of time to explain it all right now."

Kara mutes the alarm wailing in her head and tentatively accepts the seat next to him at the computer. As she slowly reaches her hands out to log in, hovering her fingertips just above the keyboard like a computer savant about to perform her administrative opus, she pauses.

"How do I know you're telling the truth? How do I know you just won't shoot me after I help you?"

Clayton pauses at the blunt question. It's the most she's said since they met less than five minutes ago at the not-so-great first impression of gunpoint.

He surveys the delicateness of her face, her thin lips and piercing eyes, seemingly probing his mind and its intentions. In all honestly, he's quite taken by her overall composure. So, in an effort not to mistake complacency with confidence, he does the best he can to reassure her that this isn't a situation he wants to be in any more than she does.

"You don't. You'll just have to trust me. Just like I have to trust you that we're not currently being recorded by those cameras. That there isn't a squad of Justice Hunters setting up a perimeter outside right now waiting to ambush us when we leave here," he says, pointing toward the exit. "Speaking of here, what the hell is this place exactly? And why doesn't it seem to exist on any map or GPS?"

Giving her response a designed delay, she waits for her eyes to finish their cross inquisition of his. Once they've traced over the innocent sprawl of his fragile iris and peeked into the dark truth behind their reflective pupils, she responds.

"This place is a failsafe. A data backup for The Hunt Initiative."

"And that requires a nonexistent address and state-of-the-art security?" Clayton adds, emphatically.

"Well, there's a lot of sensitive material in here. Tons of liable PII."

"PII?"

"Personally Identifiable Information," Kara replies. "Everything from police records, patient data, third-party claims, and a whole lot of other government intel used to create the building blocks for The Hunt Initiative. Loads of private citizen information with some of the highest clearance. It was also used to serve as the central command center when The Hunt Initiative was in its infancy."

"So, you're telling me that all this—the servers in this building, the computers, everything here—are data duplicates of the servers in The Hunt for Justice building?"

"No," Kara answers, detecting a hint of skepticism in his sea of thought. "This place doesn't house the data duplicates of The Hunt for Justice servers."

At the sail-stealing words, Clayton's diaphragm goes into paralysis, robbing him of his ability to breathe.

"These *are* the original files," Kara continues. "The duplicate files are created here, processed, and then most are routed to The Hunt for Justice and its servers. All the raw files are housed here, including classifieds and the ones that haven't been vetted yet."

"Vetted?" He jumps at the conspicuous word.

"Processed and duplicated." She shoots him a guilty look. "And in some rare instances, edited."

The feeling of finally getting somewhere takes root in Clayton's mind as he continues to probe deeper, "Who else knows about this place?"

She replies innocently, "What do you mean, exactly?"

"I mean, who the hell else knows about this place? Because by the sound of it, it's like this place was made not to exist for a reason. And it's starting to sound like it's a pretty shady reason," Clayton accuses, his tone growing louder and more agitated at every revelation.

"I don't really know," Kara responds, her trepidation mounting to match the ascending attitude of his agitation. "I've only been an employee here for less than six months. They don't tell us much, and the limited info we do know is confined to lengthy NDAs that we're sworn to uphold. We usually work in single, sometimes double shifts, with the explicit instructions not to release any information about this place to the public, hence, its nonexistence. Not that I would even know enough to really tell anyone anything, anyway. My job is to just cleanse the data and sort through the code, fixing any corrupted, incorrectly formatted, or incomplete data sets."

Kara takes a moment to gather the caboose on her train of thought.

"Outside of the handful of data analysts, like myself, that work here, I don't know who else knows about this place other than maybe Hunt Initiative cabinet members, and of course, Mr. Klein himself. I was told when I started that this was his creation in the first place."

Clayton suppresses his rising anger, shaking off the initial impulse to scream at the mention of Klein's name and his newfound list of shady undertakings. He turns away from Kara and starts storming back and forth, thinking out loud.

"Why would Klein create a top secret, duplicate data storage facility that only he and maybe a handful of execs know about? Why the public charade?"

Just then, the main door opens and Antoni strolls in. He appears to have cooled off from his shoot-first-ask-later moment of machoism from earlier.

"We're in the clear," he updates, looking at Clayton. "There's not a soul out there."

Clayton shoots a look at Kara and cracks a grin, "It appears I *can* trust you. Good to know. Thank you."

Without realizing it, she smiles in return before quickly catching herself and averting her attention back to the computer screen.

"So, umm, my turn," she says.

"Hmm?" Clayton mutters, confused.

"Well, I answered your questions—" she states with a surprisingly poised matter-of-fact intonation. "Now, it's my turn to ask some."

"Yeahhh, I don't think you're quite grasping how the whole hostage situation works," Antoni cuts in, flashing his pistol. "We don't have to tell you shit."

Again, Clayton counters his bad cop versus good cop, or in this case, bad captor versus good captor motif for a lighter approach.

"It's all right, Toni. Let her ask whatever she wants. I think we at least owe her that for helping us."

"Pshh, whatever," Antoni scoffs. "Go ahead then, kid. Shoot."

"Interesting choice of words," Kara digs, and looks at Clayton. "Does he ever think of just talking and not shooting?"

"In your case, kid, no. Every time you open your mouth my index finger gets just a little itchier."

"Toni—" Clayton interrupts again before the trigger talk can squeeze any more tension into the conversation. "Please."

He shoots a stern look over at Kara through crinkled eyes and pursed lips. It's enough to say something similarly diplomatic without saying anything at all.

"Kara, what do you want to know?" he continues.

"Well, for starters, how did you find out about this place? And why exactly am I looking up a dead woman's file from nearly thirty years ago?"

Clayton takes a deep breath in and exhales. He doesn't want to get waist deep in all the shit he's been through over the past thirty hours and counting. But she was honest with him. Now, it's his turn. Whether he likes it or not.

Reluctantly, he dives in, rehashing the abridged story of Klein's bribe, the server room, the blank file that led him here, Trish's death, and any pertinent tidbit he can think of in between. It's the second time Antoni has heard the story, but the first for Kara, who is sitting on the edge of her seat like a theatergoer, bracing herself for the next jump scare in his real-life horror movie.

When he finally finishes delivering the onslaught of revelatory information, Kara inches back into her chair, not sure where to begin processing the story overload.

But there is one thing that she does know. She believes him. She doesn't exactly know why or how, but she does. She has since the moment he removed his goggles, and she saw the hurt buried deep behind his eyes. That heavy burden being cautiously carried in the sincerity of his gaze like brimming baggage because there's no way to leave it all behind.

"Wow," she finally says with an empty expression that doesn't quite match the joyous word choice. "That's . . . a lot to process."

She gets up from the desk as her chair slowly rolls away. Aimlessly, she paces like the thoughts bumbling around in her brain. With her focus directed to the floor, she adds, "I'm sorry."

Clayton's nose folds and his eyes slit.

"What for?"

"For Trish. For you. For everything. No one deserves all that."

Choking back his feelings, doing his best to suppress all that emotion for what seems like the fiftieth time since he's been on the run, he nods in return.

"Thank you."

Antoni, who has been a distant observer during this circle-of-trust breakthrough, finally chimes in, in the only way he knows how. Abruptly and aggressively.

"I hate to be the one to ruin this kumbaya moment. Actually, that's a lie. I don't. But we're currently caught somewhere between a rock and a hard place right now. Sitting on a powder keg atop a dumpster fire, overlooking a pickle wedged between a hammer and an anvil. Up to our ears, drowning in the middle of a thunderstorm without a paddle. So, pick your favorite shit-out-of-luck analogy and maybe we can actually get back to the task at hand, yeah?"

"Oh, right," Kara jumps. "Sorry."

She grabs the rogue chair and slides back to the desk.

Within seconds, she's clacking away at the keys, hurriedly inserting her login credentials. She pounds Enter and she's in. Not sparing another second, she inputs a series of keyboard control shortcuts that somewhat resemble the shapes of chords played on a piano. They're all but lost on Clayton.

Before he even knows it, she's pulled up the mainframe database with an open search bar for *KLEIN, REBECCA N.*

The name auto-populates on the screen, and she hits Enter again. The file loads as she pulls up the document for him to see, but that same feeling of wind fleeing his sails quickly returns.

The file looks just like the document back at The Hunt for Justice building—empty field after empty field.

No statement from the responders on the scene.

No time or cause of death.

No autopsy report.

Nothing but a blank slate affording zero insight into Rebecca Klein's death. It's an identical file to the previous one, right down to the bottom of the document where the familiar unauthorized access and this place's mysterious address appear.

Clayton is dead in the water, again.

"Dammit!" he shouts, as he slams his hands on the desk startling Kara who flinches at the force of contact. "It's the same fucking file as before. There's nothing there."

Clayton storms away with his head in his hands.

"Hmm. This doesn't make any sense," Kara responds after a second look, studying the file a little closer.

"I know," Clayton responds in defeat, rubbing his forehead as if trying to wipe away the failure of the moment. "It's another goddamn dead end."

"No," Kara says, inching her eyes closer to the screen. "Well . . . yes, maybe that, too. But that's not what I'm talking about."

Flopping into a beaten pose upon the floor, Clayton feels a sharp, stabbing ache reverberate in his shoulder and shoot down his arm. The adrenaline of breaking into this place and the thought of finding answers had numbed a lot of the gunshot's pain, even keeping the stinging aftermath of his heroically stupid jumping escapade at bay. But now, with his hope all but gone and nothing but despair left to grab ahold of, he begins to feel the searing ache from the unattended bullet wound.

"Ugh, what is it then?" he asks her through gritted teeth, rubbing his raw rotator cuff.

"Well, you're right. At first glance, it looks like nothing but a blank file, right? Just Rebecca Klein's name and some frivolous personal information."

"Yeah, there's nothing there. Tell me something I don't already know."

Sensing his less-than-subtle desperation, Kara cracks a smile, and for the first time since their initial meeting—again, one that began with being held at gunpoint—she starts to feel at ease. Like an ally versus a hostage.

"Well, there's nothing there to *you*, maybe," she continues. "But not to me. This file has been tampered with."

"Kara, I already know that," Clayton says, throwing his head back in defeat, exposing his Adam's apple. "For the hundredth time, that's why there's nothing in it."

"See, but that's where you're wrong. You just aren't looking in the right place. It's encrypted."

Clayton feels his body move before his mind can tell it to do so. He jolts back up as if his feet have minds of their own and rushes over to the computer as fast as his thinking legs can carry him.

"Hold on. So, what exactly are you getting at?"

Kara jabs her pointer finger at the bottom of the monitor.

"This address, the one you successfully cracked to find this place, has an embedded link attached to it. I didn't notice at first but after I did a couple of "href=" search shortcuts, I was able to view any hidden links embedded in the file."

Kara clicks to maximize a separate window on the desktop.

"And this is what turned up when I clicked on it."

Clayton's eyes scramble to frantically read every new detail on the uncovered file before him. It contains everything about her death that was missing before, including the police report of the accident, which like Trish had told him was a car-related hit-and-run. Only the more he reads, the more apparent it becomes that the report is full of holes and contradictions.

Eager to get in on the newfound action, Antoni leaves his post by the front door to join them at the computer.

"What's it say?" he asks, trying to peer over the backs of their concentrated heads.

Clayton holds up his finger, signaling him to wait so he can finish the last couple of lines. Once he's done, he turns around and takes a seat atop the desk, staring vacantly across the room with an unresponsive gaze.

"Uhh, Earth to Clay," Antoni says, waving his hand in front of his friend's aghast face.

But Clayton's empty gawp doesn't flinch as his focus blurs past his friend through fogged eyes.

Antoni moves his head to meet Clayton's vacant vision. Again, he asks, "Dude, what'd it say?"

Clayton's eyes finally find the right combination of rods and cones as he regains focus.

"Everything. And nothing," he theorizes, turning to look at Antoni. "None of it seems to make any coherent sense."

"What do you mean it doesn't make sense?" he asks in a bout with confusion. "You're not making any sense, man."

Clayton walks away from the desk and begins pacing parallel next to it. He jets his eyes back and forth from floor to computer screen, trying to piece together disjointed remnants of the story.

"It says that Rebecca Klein was killed in a hit-and-run, but the time of day and location don't add up. What was she doing in a podunk Missouri town when she was killed? And the time of death . . . they have it marked at approximately 1:20 a.m. And the way they describe her wounds—" He walks back over to the computer to read the medical examiner report's line verbatim.

"Victim appeared to be erect upon primary impact suffering a spiral facture of the lower left leg, originating just above the knee, most likely from vehicle's front bumper. Victim was also found with a vague tight-knitted imprint on the upper left thigh, indicative of trauma from a vehicle's headlight. Conversely, the victim also appears to have an additional primary impact, multiple compound fractures throughout the ribcage, indicating the victim may have been recumbent prior to being rolled underneath the vehicle upon secondary impact with the ground. Tire tracks appear to be of similar make and model, but evidence is not conclusive enough to distinguish if these primary impacts are two isolated incidents or from the same singular vehicle. The former would indicate a possible accident while the latter could suggest a potential homicide."

Clayton finishes reading and turns to look at Antoni.

"Potential homicide? It says right here that she was hit twice. What kind of accidental hit-and-run driver tries to run over someone twice? That just doesn't add up. It all seems a little too odd, don't you think?"

"I don't—" but before Antoni can refrain, he's cut off by Kara whose eager curiosity beats him to the punch.

"Maybe she was visiting family in the Show Me state? She could have had one too many drinks and accidentally crossed the street at the wrong time. Then *BAM*!" she says, and slams her fist into her palm. "Hit-and-run. Then, moments later, *BAM* again!" This time even louder. "She's hit a second time by another car because it's late, dark, and she's lying in the middle of the street," Kara wildly regales while looking them both square in the eyes.

Antoni and Clayton leer at her then back at each other with identical eyebrows cocked in appropriate WTF positions.

Feeling the looming aftershock of their reverberating judgment, Kara sits up in her seat, improving her defensive posture.

"Hey, I'm just throwing out ideas," she says, tossing her arms in the air. "I'm involved now. Remember that whole hostage-slash- kidnapping situation?"

Antoni shoots her a look as a smile slowly widens his lips.

"Oh, so you're making jokes now?" he asks, nodding before averting his attention to his friend. "You know, Clay, I'm kinda beginning to like this girl."

Kara blushes from the surprise compliment as she leans back in her chair, searching for anything to take the attention off her. Shyly, she focuses her gaze back to the computer screen.

The hint of a furled unibrow peeps above the top bar of her glasses.

"Hmm, that's weird."

"What?" Clayton asks, leaning back over her shoulder for a closer look.

Kara points to a spot on the file where something should be but isn't.

"It doesn't look like they have her autopsy report on file. Just the medical examiner report from the scene. That's a little weird."

Antoni responds, "Why would they have conducted an autopsy if she was clearly killed in a hit-and-run? Isn't that cause of death enough?"

"Yes. And no," she replies, adjusting her glasses and crossing her legs. "You see, every alleged murder and manslaughter case that occurred once The Hunt Initiative started required an autopsy report, regardless of motive or accident. It was one of the government's ways of ensuring that the cause of death was in fact a form of homicide. Kind of like a checks and balances system for the due process."

Clayton butts in, "Yeah, but Rebecca Klein died before The Hunt Initiative was ever even a thing. Trish used to tell me that her mom's death was a large part of the reason her father created The Initiative in the first place. As a sort of way to cope. To help those who had lost a loved one find closure or justice, or whatever the fuck you want to call it."

Kara bites her bottom lip and widens her eyes.

"You're right, but if her file is in fact accurate, and Rebecca Klein was hit and killed in Missouri, then an autopsy report would have been mandatory for two reasons. First, because of the peculiar time of death and nature of the wounds. I mean, you saw the report, 'potential homicide.' And second, and this is the real kicker, Missouri was among the twelve states that made autopsy reports part of official legislation thirty years ago when the nation's murder numbers were skyrocketing—you can thank St. Louis for that one. The Hunt Initiative had nothing to do with it."

"Okay, that's great and all, but then where's this required autopsy report you speak of?"

Kara exhales and twirls around in her chair. She shakes her head while her fingers blur across the keyboard.

"You guys really are lucky that I showed up, you know that?" She peers at them from over her shoulder as her fingers continue to glide across the keys with ease. "Hate to say it, but you two noobs would have been caught with your pants down without me."

Clayton gawks, his mouth speechless as a burst of laughter from Antoni cuts the silence.

"Yep, it's official. I'm starting to like her," he says through uncontrollable chuckling. "You always this much fun in hostage situations, kid?"

"Oh, this is nothing," she retorts with a smirk, turning back around to navigate a series of clicks. "You should see me at parties, when I don't have a gun pointed at my head."

"You just can't let that one go, can you?" Antoni asks, as his smile flatlines.

"Would you?" she replies.

"Let it go? No. Bitch about it less? Yes."

Finally, Clayton's words catch back up, interrupting their banter session.

"Okay, wait. Are you telling me you can find her autopsy report?"

"Find it? I've already got it," Kara says, as she swivels the computer monitor toward Clayton and Antoni. "It was pretty simple really. I just had to cross reference Rebecca Klein's file from the database with her Missouri death certificate report. From there, I could access the state's public autopsy records. The rest, well you're looking at it."

Clayton's teeth flash a beaming smile from the monitor's unexpected horizon of hope. Two things he hasn't done much of in the past day and a half—smile or hope.

He looks at Kara with admiration. The shy, timid girl he just met has seemingly transformed into a confident and sassy woman who refuses to take any shit from her former captors, especially Antoni, right before his eyes. Apparently, she just needed a little murder mystery to bring out the Hyde to her Jekyll.

"You're amazing, Kara! Thank you," he reiterates his sentiments with a bear hug that catches her off guard. She stands there paralyzed in the unexpected embrace, like an anxious person on camera unsure what to do with her arms. She settles for an awkward pat on the back.

"Yeah, well, I have pretty good people instincts. Kind of a like a sixth sense, really," she mumbles, her face still scrunched in the crook of Clayton's shoulder.

He releases her, and she works to regain her composure.

"There was something about you that just felt . . . raw but sincere. Like, I could feel the pain you've been through. I could see it all in your eyes from the first moment I looked into them. Even yours," she adds, nodding toward Antoni.

"Mine?" he asks, surprised. Pointing to himself for clarity as if there's a fourth party in the room.

"Yeah. I could tell you weren't really going to shoot me."

"Oh?" he scoffs. "Is that so?"

"It is. Whether you admit it or not."

But Antoni doesn't rebut back. He just lets out a defeated laugh to fill the void of words he doesn't possess.

They all share a brief moment of gratitude before Kara dives into reading Rebecca's autopsy report out loud.

**Autopsy report for** *Rebecca Nicole Klein*
**Eyes:** Green
**Hair:** Blond
**Weight:** 125 lb.
**Clinicopathological Correlation**
*Cause of death of this thirty-one-year-old female is hypovolemic shock due to internal bleeding. Multiple internal organ hemorrhage with primary injury to liver and spleen. Additional injuries include left femur FX with femoral artery laceration leading to profound hemorrhage and hemodynamic collapse.*

*Victim was allegedly crossing the street and was struck and killed in a hit-and-run accident. The body was found in the middle of Nieman Road in downtown Shermer, Missouri at the end of fresh skid marks.*

*A quick examination of the body revealed severe, critical contusions to the thoracic and abdominal cavities as well as extensive injury to the left leg. The top and back of the head also appeared to suffer secondary trauma likely from blunt force from the ground upon impact.*

"That's it?" Clayton asks, confused. "That can't be it. There has to be more, right?"

"Afraid not," Kara replies, delicately delivering the bad news.

"No. There has to be another link or something else embedded," Clayton pushes.

"Not this time," she confirms.

"Sorry, Clay," Antoni adds. "Doesn't sound any different than the medical examiner report. Just looks like normal injuries from a hit-and-run to me. Maybe there really is nothing here," he concedes.

He reaches out to place his hand on Clayton's good shoulder.

"You tried, man, I think it's time to move on. We need to focus on getting you out of town. Somewhere safe where you can lay low."

"Wait!" Kara shouts, interrupting the touching moment. "Look down here at the toxicology results."

Clayton and Antoni both turn in unison to home in on the small section at the bottom of the report.

**Toxicologic Studies**
*Blood ethanol level: < 50 mg/dL*
*Blood drug screen via gas chromatography/mass spectrometry: 63 ng/ml of Acepromazine*

Clayton's eyes go wide as a solar eclipse of black engulfs nearly every available space of blue in his surrounding iris.

"Acepromazine," he mutters aloud. Sounding it out again and again like it's a spelling bee competition. Something about that name rings familiar for some reason, but he can't quite put his finger on why. "What is that?"

"Don't know," Antoni pleads.

Kara spins around to meet Clayton's goggle-eyed gaze.

"It's a type of tranquilizer used for large animals," she says without missing a beat.

Antoni fires his own cock-eyed glance her way. One that fully infers his surprise as to why in the hell she knows that.

She takes notice of the silent judgment.

"Growing up, my grandparents had a farm outside the city that I used to spend summers at as a kid. They would use acepromazine on their horses when they needed to treat an ill mare or clip a rowdy stallion. With that dosage level, combined with the amount of alcohol content in her system, it's a wonder she was even coherent, let alone able to function enough to be walking down the street like the report states."

Triggered by Kara's story, Clayton's mind reels back casting the puzzle pieces into place. As the full picture gains clarity, he remembers why acepromazine sounds so familiar.

He thinks back to his face-off with Klein. The one in his office where he attempted to bribe him out of Trish's life. Amid all the emotion of that heated exchange and the haunting visual of countless stuffed animal heads plastered to the wall, Clayton recalls an open container of acepromazine tranquilizers meticulously laid out on the bookshelf by the door.

"Holy shit," he says under his breath.

"What?" Antoni asks.

"I know who killed Rebecca Klein," he adds, as he turns his dazed expression toward the other two.

"Really?" Kara chimes in, no longer trying to hide the escalating eagerness in her tone. "Who?"

"Her husband."

Wait! You're telling me Simon Klein, the man so opposed to murder that he created The Hunt Initiative in the first place, killed his own wife? That same Simon Klein? No way. Not buying it." Kara shrugs in disbelief. Shocked as if she'd just been told that God himself committed the murder.

"Actually ran her over? I don't know that. I can't be a hundred percent sure yet, but I know he definitely had a hand in the strange circumstances surrounding her death," Clayton confirms.

Antoni breaks his role as dialogue bystander and rejoins the conversation. "I believe you, Clay, I really do," he butts in. "But what's your proof? People are going to need proof."

"I saw a box of acepromazine in Klein's office. Not even two days ago, when the asshole was trying to slip me a blank check to disappear," Clayton describes. "It was right there on his fucking bookshelf, in plain sight."

"I just . . . I can't believe that Simon 'The Face of Justice' Klein would ever kill his own wife," Kara chimes in, still hung up on the contradictory nature of it all. "I mean, why? It literally goes against everything he stands for."

"Yeah? Well, it didn't stop him from planning to get rid of me," Clayton counters.

"Huh? What do you mean?" she probes.

"Look, when I told you all those things earlier, those were just the CliffsNotes. What I didn't tell you was that at The Hunt's anniversary party, just before Trish was killed, I overheard Klein talking backstage to his head lackey, some guy named Marco. I was on the other side of the door, so I couldn't make out all of it, but it was something about getting rid of me. Disguising my death as a home robbery gone wrong. I guess since he couldn't buy me out, he was going to take me out. Anyways, I heard Marco say he'd organized an ambush party to wait for us to return home that night . . . only that never happened, obviously."

"Wow," she replies, stripping any remnants of delight from the contrary choice of word. "What a hypocritical piece of shit," she adds, as her previous disbelief is washed away by an ensuing wave of anger after hearing Clayton's firsthand account. "I can't believe I'm working for that two-faced asshole. Gross."

"So much for those people instincts of yours, huh, kid?" Antoni mocks. "Sixth sense, my ass."

"Oh, bite me already. Like I'm just supposed to know about all the shady things the most powerful man in the world is doing behind everyone's back?"

"I mean, he is your employer, is he not? This whole top-secret database is his doing, and you work here. Sorry I'm not sorry that I find it kinda hard to believe you didn't know what you were getting yourself into when you took this gig."

"Don't get it twisted, Toni," Clayton cuts in, trying his best to deflect the misplaced blame. "Kara's not the bad guy here. Klein is. And he's got everyone fooled and aimlessly believing his bullshit for far too long. Hell, I've been at The Hunt for Justice for over a year now, dated his own daughter, and had no clue just how big a pile of shit the man truly is. He's pure evil, and we've got to take him down. It's the only way to stop all this."

Feeling like the sudden tug of emotion is tipping the scale of level-headedness, Antoni jumps back in as the voice of reason that nobody asked for, but everybody needs to hear.

"Well, I hate to be *that* guy, again, but that's still not evidence, sorry, Clay. At least, not enough to go on to actually prove anything to anyone. It's just hearsay. Speculative accusation," he states, tossing his helpless hands up in the air. "I mean, what are we supposed to do with that info? Like really? Tell me. Just hop in a car and drive down to buttfuck Missouri to ask some random townies about the mysterious death of a woman that took place here more than twenty-five years ago?"

He can't even make it halfway through the entire thought before guffawing from its absolute absurdity.

Only Clayton doesn't join in. Not even the slightest hint of a smile. He just deadpans his friend with stoic doe eyes that say it all. An insistent face Antoni's all too familiar with but hasn't seen since childhood.

"Ohhh, no! Nope. Not happening," Antoni repeats, vigorously shaking his head. "Hell, no. Don't even think about it, Clay. It was just a fucking joke."

"But, Toni, what if?" Clayton engages.

He walks over to Antoni, his hands open and palms up, pleading his case.

"Wasn't it you who told me it's best to find trouble before it finds you?" Clayton swings, sucker punching him with his own advice. "Well, I'm ready to go find it because I'm sick of running from it."

Antoni stands stunned. Speechless, like a mouthy know-it-all who was just forced to eat their own words. It tastes like raw chicken.

"C'mon, Toni. What do we have to lose?"

Sensing this conversation is headed in a landslide of terrible direction, Antoni plucks out the remaining feathers from the crow wedged in his mouth and attempts to squash the dumb idea avalanche before it can snowball into anything even dumber.

"Hmm. Let me think real quick. How about for starters, our lives?

Clay, it's a ridiculous, far-fetched wild goose chase across the Midwest. Your face is on 'Wanted' billboards everywhere, and there's only so much night left as every drone in the metro is out scanning the sky right now, eagle-eyeing for you. There's huge prize money up for your head, which gives this particular Hunt an even bigger incentive than ever before. Oh, and not to mention. Just a small, teeny-tiny little detail. We don't even have a fucking car."

Just then, a subtle jingle is heard.

Clayton and Antoni turn in unison toward the source of the chime to find Kara dangling a set of car keys with a smirk smugly plastered across her childish face.

"But I do."

Antoni tosses his head back and sighs.

"And to think, I was just beginning to like you, kid."

"Don't worry, looks like we're about to have a whole road trip to work on that," she jokes, as her smirk blossoms into a full smile.

"Wait. Hold up," Clayton replies. "Let's take a step back here. Kara, what makes you think you're coming along?"

"Uh, well, for starters, it's my car."

"No, I mean what makes you think I'm willing to put you in danger?"

"Seriously? Were you not here just a half hour ago when Clyde sans Bonnie over there had me at gunpoint?"

Antoni quips back, "Seriously, kid, you're losing brownie points fast."

"Guys, enough!" Clayton shouts, dousing another flare-up of hemorrhoidal hijinks. "It's not happening, Kara. Period. Thank you for everything you've done so far, but there's no chance in hell that you're coming with us. I'm sorry. End of discussion."

"Well then, I'm sorry, too," Kara says, as she sits up in her chair, suspiciously reaching her hand underneath the desk.

Clayton's eyebrows cock, an arc of confusion rainbows across his forehead.

"What? Why are you sorry? What are you talking about?"

"I'm sorry because I guess now I'm going to have to push this emergency alarm button underneath my desk."

Antoni scoffs, "She's bluffing, man."

"You willing to gamble your life on that?"

Clayton asks, "You're telling me you've had an emergency alarm button under your desk this whole time?"

"Umm, yeah. This place has motion sensor floors for Christ's sake. Why would an emergency alarm button be out of the question?"

"Well, it's official," Antoni asserts, shaking his head. "You're fresh out of brownie points and back on my shit list."

"Okay, everybody just relax for a second," Clayton butts in. "Can you both do that, please?"

He looks directly at Antoni first who gives him a reluctant nod, and then at Kara who still has her hand underneath the table.

"Oh, I'm totally relaxed," she says. "But my fingers are getting kinda heavy, if you catch my drift."

Over the past thirty-plus hours, Clayton has managed to evade a swarm of Justice Hunters, not only once but twice, a surprise home invasion by one of the most notorious gangs in the entire region, and not to mention, locate and break into a mysterious and heavily secure private records building without getting caught or killed. To overcome all of that, just to be bested by a single, unassumingly harmless kid who looks like she's not even old enough to vote. He can't believe it.

He knows it's a terrible idea. Beyond terrible even. But the barrel of ideas is getting awfully low, and all that's left now are the scraps of stupidity stubbornly stuck to the bottom. He shakes his head and inhales as he brings his hand up to pinch his forehead.

Unfortunately, he's not dreaming.

"Shit," he exhales. "Where are you parked?"

# CHAPTER 31

"Yesss," Kara shrieks, yanking her hand out from underneath the desk in a mini fist pump.

"You guys won't regret this," she adds, and runs over to hug Clayton. He doesn't acknowledge the eager embrace. He just stands still with his arms glued to his sides, dumbfounded.

"Won't? I already do."

"Un-fucking-believable," Antoni adds, rolling his eyes harder than a marble run playset. "We're fucked. Totally and unequivocally fucked."

"Oh, lighten up, will ya? Besides, I can help you guys out. I'm handy with a computer and, as you already know, I'm pretty cool under pressure."

Grasping her shoulders sternly with both hands, Clayton finally peels her Velcroed arms off him.

"All right, all right. Let's get a couple things straight first. This isn't a field trip, Kara. This is my—" He looks over at Antoni who's still in disbelief that he, too, has been had by an unassuming party of one "—our lives at stake. I'm literally being hunted right now by the worst possible person you can be hunted by and his entire flock, and yet somehow, some way, it's even worse than that because there's a bounty out for my head, and it's only growing by the hour. So, if you're coming with us, you need to do exactly what we say, when we say it. And if it gets bad, know when to bolt. Understood?"

Kara draws the curtains on her enthusiastic showcase as her spirited performance shifts to a more dramatic third act. The staged sincerity is almost believable, but her peek-a-boo smile is still blatantly visible through a set of botched pursed lips.

"Of course. What you say. When you say it. And bolt if things get bad," she repeats, using her fingers to emphasize her registry of the three direct orders. "Got it."

Clayton lets her go and shakes his head once more in disbelief as he looks to Antoni for any form of validation.

"Don't look at me," Antoni scoffs. "I was against this whole shit show of a plan from the get-go. Just for the record."

A soft, tentative voice cuts in from their periphery.

"Actually . . . it was your idea, technically speaking," Kara says through a gritted grin. "I mean, if we're being totally honest, you did bring it up first. Remember that whole buttfuck Missouri monologue?"

Antoni shoots her a dead-eyed glare. Its emotional vacancy even takes Clayton by surprise.

"Keep it up, buttercup. At this rate, I'm bound to throw your ass outta the car window before we even reach the highway."

"Geez, someone's touchy," she counters, rolling her eyes. "I was just saying."

"Oh, and that's another thing," Antoni adds with an accusatory two-finger point in her direction. "If you don't stop rolling your damn eyes around in those ridiculous hipster cat-framed glasses and flashing that smug smirk at how pleased you are with yourself, I might just glue 'em in place and duct tape your mouth shut."

"*Mrrrawr*!" she growls in tandem with a clawing gesture. "Well, paw-don me. Sounds like someone's got the cat by the tail. But you know what I really think?"

"I don't care. But I have a feeling you're going to tell me anyway."

"I think—"

"Fuck, I knew it."

"I think you got the bark of a dog but the heart of a puppy. If you were really going to hurt me, you'd have shot me when you had the chance. But much like your innocent cohort over there," she says, nodding in Clayton's direction, "You're both genuinely good guys despite what your reputations may show . . . and it eats you up inside knowing that I know that."

Antoni poises himself for a witty rebuttal, but he's left open-mouthed, cat fully hanging from his tongue. He can't remember the last time anyone other than Sonya has so fully called him out on his bullshit. He thinks back to growing up with Leo and the brotherly banter they used to hurl at one another incessantly. Just a constant 24/7 rag fest that usually ended in Leo shutting up before he got shut up.

After a few seconds, he wrangles the metaphorical claws from his tongue as a large grin begins to tug at his upper lip.

"Touché, kid." He nods in respect. "Maybe you can actually be useful."

He averts his attention over to Clayton who's been a silent observer during his verbal depantsing.

"All right, then. What's the plan, meow?" he asks with a quick wink back at Kara, receiving her full pun approval.

Clayton knows he hasn't thought this all through yet, that much has already been made apparent. But, in an effort to not look like he's totally making this up as he goes, he says the first obvious thing that comes to mind.

"Well, for starters, we should find out exactly where Shermer, Missouri is and what would have drawn Rebecca Klein to go there nearly thirty years ago."

Another random thought enters his head, piggybacking his previous idea. He turns to Kara.

"I know she wasn't from Missouri, so she couldn't have been visiting family. She was born somewhere on the West Coast. It's why Trish said she never really got to see her grandparents growing up." Clayton looks back at the computer. "Kara, did Rebecca's file say anything about where she went to school? Or any breadcrumbs to help us trace her back in time?"

Kara swoops back into the desk chair, pulling her file back up with a series of calculated clicks. She scans the document with her finger until it comes to an abrupt stop.

"What?" Clayton readily asks. "What's it say?"

With a sigh, "University of Bannerton," she replies, and returns to scanning the screen.

"Damn. Swing and a miss," Clayton groans in response. "Of course. Couldn't be that easy, right?"

"Actually. Maybe, it is," Kara pipes back up. "You were right about her family being from the West Coast. Says right here that Rebecca was born in Bend, Oregon in 1964, a small town about 150 or so miles southeast of Portland."

Antoni, right on cue and with his patented pessimism and cynical charm, butts in.

"And that helps us how, exactly?"

Kara dramatically clears her throat. The guttural sound carries a hefty dose of sarcastic undertones that say more than any words could.

"Well, maybe if you'd let me finish—" she adds.

Antoni takes a retreated step back and mimes zipping his lips.

"Thank you," she continues, tossing in a nod and a pleased grin. "Now, like I said. She may have been born on the West Coast, but according to this list of addresses on file, it looks like her family moved around a lot when she was younger. Any hot guesses on where one of those might have been when she was sixteen?"

"Shermer," Clayton answers, mirroring her grin with a sly smirk of his own. "Well, I'll be damned. Looks like we're headed to buttfuck Missouri, after all," he finishes, and slaps Antoni on the shoulder.

"Perfect. So, we're looking for a needle in a haystack in the middle of a wild goose chase for our lives, all while playing babysitter," Antoni remarks with two thumbs up. "Solid plan. What could possibly go wrong?"

Despite his friend's thick double coat of cynicism, Clayton feels a growing sense of optimism for the first time since he's been on the run. He may not have gotten the answer he was looking for by coming here, but bit by bit the picture is becoming clearer with every new added piece to the puzzle. He knows the true character behind Klein, and he's on a mission to prove it to everyone else. Not that he has much of a choice—only the fact that his entire life depends on it.

"Okay, if we're going to do this, we need a concrete plan. And we need it fast," Clayton says, as he reverts to pacing the room aimlessly. "Kara, how far is Shermer from Bannerton?"

She quickly pulls up GPS on her phone, typing in Shermer's whereabouts into the search bar.

"Looks like a little over four hours."

"Okay, so that's the fastest route. What about alternate routes? Anything to keep us away from big towns and major highways? You know, away from hunting eyes, rogue drones, and obvious checkpoints."

Her thumbs make a couple of adjustments on the phone screen before she answers.

"Looks like we could get out there in just under six if we avoid the interstate all together and stick solely to backroads."

"Sounds like the scenic route will have to do," Clayton says, snapping a picture with Jayson's phone of Rebecca Klein's autopsy report. "In the meantime, see what all you can find about Rebecca Klein's family during their time there. They clearly weren't there for long since they ended up back west sometime after her college graduation yet before her death; but they had to have made some connections while they lived there. After all, it's a small town, and if I've learned anything about small towns in my life, it's that everyone knows everyone else's dirty secrets like they grow on some kind of indigenous gossip grapevine."

"Yeah, there's no such thing as clean laundry in a small town," Kara adds in affirmation as she deletes the search history on the computer log and reactivates the security system timer before signing out. She swipes her car keys off the table but on their descent back into her bag, Antoni snatches them out of the air.

"Hey! Those are mine."

"Correction. They were yours until you decided to pull that cute little alarm stunt," he disputes, pocketing the keychain. "So long as you're with us, you'll be keeping the backseat company. As in, your ass doesn't leave the seat unless one of us says otherwise. That crystal?"

"But I . . . that's not . . . ugh, fine. Whatever," she yields. For the first time since being held at gunpoint, Kara is again speechless much to Antoni's amusement. No witty comeback. No Cheshire grin. She just rolls her eyes again and slings her bag over her shoulder, making it a blatant point to not break eye contact with him throughout the silent tantrum. Clayton turns to face the disgruntled duo who are now childishly engaged in an impromptu no-eye-blinking contest.

"Umm . . . so are we ready to go or do you guys need another minute of passive-aggressive eye contact?"

Neither one of them respond, so Clayton continues.

"Okaaay, then. I'll take that as good to go. Kara, where exactly is your car? I don't recall seeing a lot when we got here. Then again, it was dark as shit, and I couldn't see anything, so—"

Hesitant to be the first one to break the staring contest, she replies while maintaining laser beams at Antoni.

"It's in the parking garage underneath the complex."

"Of course, it is," Clayton grumbles. "Let me guess, just another discreet security measure that comes with the job? I guess a place can't really cease to exist if cars are parked outside of it for everyone to see."

He shoots a panning look around the place aimlessly searching for any EXIT sign to indicate said parking garage. No such luck.

"And the secret garage would be in which direction exactly?"

This time Kara flinches as her eyes accidentally scan to the right in unison with her pointer finger.

"Ohhh, you lose," Antoni heckles.

"Dammit!" Kara laments, as she stomps the floor and balls her fist. "That's not fair. I was distracted."

"Hey, I don't make the rules, kid. I just win the games. Sorry, not sorry," he taunts with the douchey flash of a grade A, schoolboy grin and fluttery eyes that scream better luck next time.

"Well, this is going to be fun," Clayton mutters while admonishing them both with an agitated glare. "Am I seriously going to have to deal with babysitting you two for this entire car ride? I feel like I can already count how many times I'm going to have to say, 'Don't make me pull this car over.'"

Already marching toward the exit, Antoni turns around to face Clayton.

"Hey, you showed up at *my* door, remember? This was all *your* idea. You get what you get," he rebukes, opening the unmarked exit door that leads downstairs to the parking garage. "So, are we going, or are we just gonna sit here with our fingers up each other's asses?"

Clayton shakes his head, suppressing the hint of a smirk.

"It's good to know that after all these years, you've still really got that whole being an asshole thing perfected."

"Yeah, I know. I had to settle for good looks over a charming personality."

Kara follows behind Clayton, aimed and ready for one last jab.

"You sure about that?" she swings, as she walks past. "I don't think your math is mathing because neither of those add up.

"Maybe? Maybe not? But I am sure that your ass *plus* that back seat is gonna *equal* best friends," he cracks, using his hands to gesture a name in the air like it would appear on a marquee. "'Backseat Bitch.' Has a nice ring to it, don't you think? Now, get a move on it."

Kara gives him the finger without turning back around. He grins and gives the room one last look before shutting the door.

The three unlikely accomplices proceed down a similar metallic hallway to that of the front entrance guided solely by dimly lit LED lights until they reach a nondescript elevator shaft. In their hasty steps, Antoni notices a few strategically positioned surveillance cameras adorning the corners of the walls above them. Their lights are blinking, indicating the security measures are fully back online.

"Uh, should we worry about those?" he asks, pointing toward the ceiling as the trio continue to slink down the corridor.

Kara looks up without stopping and responds, "No."

Clayton takes notice of one of the cameras above as he passes by. Its blinking light pulsates in rhythm while its glossy black lens pans, seeming to track his steps in real time.

"Are you sure, Kara?" he adds.

"Positive," she says, looking back at Clayton to see the worry painting his face. "Every camera in this joint is a recording, not a live feed. No one ever looks through the footage unless there's a cause to do so. And since you geniuses didn't trip any of the other security measures—still shocked, yet impressed about that one, myself—there's no reason to be alarmed. Just ignore them," she assures, motioning to the elevator twenty feet ahead. "We're almost to the garage."

Leading the pack, Kara makes it to the lift first and jabs the call button. Within seconds its shiny brass outer doors part to reveal an old, industrial-like freight elevator complete with its original accordion-folding black metal gate. The barred walls are rusted and flaking large chips of paint, but the inner machine's steel braided cables look as brand new as its polished exterior.

"I know. It doesn't really fit the whole sleek, state-of-the-art interior like the rest of the place. I guess this was a meat packing plant back in the early railroad days, and they decided to keep the original elevators. Probably because it was already big enough to move all the servers and tech junk inside, but also because this thing will continue to function long after we're all dead and gone. They just don't build them like they used to."

"Gee, thanks, Tour Guide Kara. What are you, like nineteen going on menopause?" Antoni snarks from the back of the line.

"I'm twenty-four, thank you very much," she replies, holding the door to the lift open. "And judging by how slow you move and all the shit you talk, I'd guess you're wearing a pair of soiled Depends under those jeans?"

Clayton whips around and shoots him a "gotcha" face.

"Pshh. Whatever." Antoni secedes. "Let's just go already."

"After you, Grandpa," she adds, fanning the flame for one last burn.

They all step into the elevator cabin and Kara punches the only option available.

DOWN.

The large freighter rumbles and squeals momentarily as the combination of fresh cables and old pulleys labor to lock into gear and proceed on the chosen path of descent. After a short ride, the lift comes to a similar screeching halt, and the cage doors slide open to reveal an even drabber parking garage.

"And this charming space, a.k.a. the parking garage, used to serve as the plant's makeshift slaughterhouse." Kara exhibits, redonning her docent voice while stepping out of the cabin. "Super comforting to know that you're actively parking in a space where large animals used to get butchered on the reg. As if dark and desolate parking garages weren't terrifying enough for unaccompanied, young women."

"Quite quaint, really, if you ask me. Just close your eyes and you can almost smell the bacon-to-be," Antoni jests, as he pulls out the car keys from his pocket. "Now, let's see what kind of wheels we're working with here. I picture you as a Ford Fiesta kind of gal. You know, not quite an SUV but not really a sedan either. Something cute, somewhere in between, and trés chic, of course. Ooh, like maybe a Mini Cooper. That'd be very basic B of you and totes on the nose," he teases and clicks the lock button on the fob.

Taillights illuminate in the near corner of the garage accompanied by an aggressive horn honk. It echoes throughout the century-old cement structure. Antoni stops dead in his tracks as the keys jangle subtly by his side. Parked not more than thirty feet in front of him is a pristine, jet-black 1985 Chevy K10 Silverado.

As soon as he can finish wiping the drool from the corners of his grease monkey mouth, he blurts out, "Holy shit, this is your ride, kid?"

"Yep. I'm just a country girl who decided she loved tech at an early age. Guess you can take the gearhead out of the country, but you can't take the country out of the gearhead," she responds, admiring her vintage black beauty.

She looks over at Antoni, who is still trying to fold his tongue back into his mouth.

"Oh, I'm sorry. I believe you were in the middle of saying something extremely sexist and stereotypical about my 'girly' taste. Did you want to finish, or—?"

But before she can complete her comeback, Antoni is already nose to paint, inhaling every beautiful inch of the classic truck before him.

"Caramel leather bench seats. Flood lights add-on. Beautiful black pearl body paint. Six-inch Rough Country Lift Kit." He pauses a second and looks back at the key fob in his hands. "You even installed an aftermarket locking and remote start system. Hot damn, kid, you're just full of surprises, aren't you? Maybe I underestimated you," he finishes, looking back at Kara who is standing cross-armed and slightly slouched on one leg, enjoying every second of Antoni boner-spewing over her ride.

"Yeah, well . . . guess you can't judge a book by its cover. Plus, it doesn't hurt that this job pays stupid well," she responds, as she opens the door and drops her bag under the lone, extended bench seat. "Oh yeah, and so much for riding backseat, huh, bitch?" she adds, her grin the biggest it's been since they met.

Antoni takes a step back and ogles Kara with the same level of affectionate admiration he just flaunted for her vehicle.

"Well played, kid. Well fucking played." He flings open the driver's side door. "I guess you'll just have to settle for Middle Seat Bitch then. Now, get your ass in the car, and let's make like a shart and skidasshole out of here."

Moments later, the vintage Silverado pulls up to a towering iron gate leading out of the sub-garage. In the shade of the encroaching twilight, it looks like just another industrial remnant of the old factory, but upon closer inspection, the welding looks too sophisticated, and there's no accumulation of reddish-brown oxide infiltrating the corners of its barred pattern.

Antoni shifts the truck into Park once he's parallel with the exit keypad, an advanced lock with a digital display that would confirm any suspicions about the gate being a modern add-on.

"Another one? Jesus, it's like Fort Knox up in here," he says, cranking the handle to lower the driver-side window. "Do you have to give a pound of flesh to get in and out of this place?"

"You have no idea. Just keep the window down, Starsky, and let Hutch handle this," Kara says, as she digs into her bag and pulls out a badge attached to a short blue lanyard.

She leans over Antoni from the middle seat as a nose full of lavender and cream perfume permeates the cabin from her sudden movement. Reaching out from the manual window, she scans her badge and inputs a short PIN, most likely her employee ID number. After the machine successfully registers the two authentications, an automatic retinal scanner attachment extends from a slot inside the device to scan her pupil. The red beam moves up from her cheeks, then back down from her forehead. There's a short pause, then a loud click as the fortified iron gate leading outside the garage swings open.

"Open sesame," she mutters, as she settles back into the center seat.

Clayton chimes in, "Next stop, Shermer."

But his uptick in mood is as fleeting as it was welcoming when an overlooked thought enters his mind.

"Hold up," he halts, grabbing the wheel. "Are people going to notice that you've just up and left, Kara?"

She looks at him and shakes her head, unfazed.

"Highly doubt it. Like I said, we work in shifts, rarely with more than person at a time, and half of the time the person in the shift before ours is already gone by the time the other gets here. It's kind of a weird system, but that's why no one was home when you two showed up. You guys were lucky, really. You just missed the person on the last shift by half an hour or less. And I've gotta say, anyone else wouldn't have been nearly as trustworthy as me, especially Bryce."

"Who the hell is Bryce?" Antoni asks.

"The neckbeard that worked the shift before mine," Kara elaborates. "Real peach, that guy."

"Yeah, well no surprise there," he adds. "Has anybody ever met a cool Bryce? Like, ever?"

It's not a failsafe response, but Clayton's satisfied enough with her answer. He pulls out Jayson's phone, unlocking it with the passcode of his nephew's birthday. Apps populate the screen as he clicks on the Maps icon and inputs "Shermer, Missouri" into the vacant address bar. He leans over to Kara, and she adjusts the directions to the backroad route she calculated earlier. The GPS animates to display an approximate distance of 376 miles, just under six hours of drive time.

"All right. We've got about six hours until we get to Shermer. Of course, it's not going to be that easy. I'm sure my face, and possibly Antoni's now, will be plastered on every major billboard along the way, with facial recognition scanners and droves of drones working the skies overtime to spot a match. Not to mention we're headed straight for the danger zone—small-town America—where everyone and their dog has a readily available stockpile of firearms and a misplaced patriotic duty for blindly supporting any cause they get to use them on."

"Like The Hunt Initiative?" she adds.

"Exactly," Clayton responds. He reaches into his bag and pulls out the Mug Mangler. "If we're going to do this, we've got to be smart about it. No unexpected plays. No hero shit," he says, shooting an emphasized over-the-nose glance in Antoni's general direction. "Are we all in agreement? There's far too much that can go wrong, and I'm pretty sure I've used up any and all remnants of luck that I may have possessed."

Directing his next question at his friend behind the wheel, he asks, "Toni, how many uses will this scrambler give us if we get in a pinch?"

Antoni glances over at the short, rod-like device in Clayton's hands. From across the truck, it could easily pass as an electric razor sans the actual razor part.

"Well, if we'd have had more time, I could have grabbed some extra power capacitors, but as it stands right now—one, maybe two shots. But—"

He averts his attention back to the moonlit road, carefully

navigating throughout the dilapidated West Bottoms with the sun still sound asleep underneath the silhouetted blanket of rundown factories before them.

"—Let's just hope we don't run into a situation where we actually have to use it," he finishes.

Kara, who is seeing the facial scrambler for the first time, takes the device from Clayton.

"Why not? What even is this thing?" she asks curiously, studying its sleek, matte black finish. "It looks like a taser. Or, like a sex toy . . . on steroids."

Without taking his eyes off the road, a grin grows across Antoni's lips.

"Yeah, well, I definitely wouldn't recommend using it for personal playtime. Not unless you're into defying gravity like the cooch of an eighty-year-old hysterectomy patient. But if that graphic of aged roast beef doesn't paint the picture well enough for you, and you're still wondering why it looks eerily like a taser, then be my guest and give it a whirl. Otherwise, I'm happy to fill you in."

Kara doesn't actually answer, but the tag team of confusion and horror on her face says more than any words.

Antoni continues anyway out of sheer personal amusement.

"Okay, so imagine having to tase yourself, but right on the soft underbelly of your chin. Its nickname isn't the Mug Mangler for shits and giggles. There's nothing quite as painful as jolting your own face and brain with what feels like enough amps and electricity to power a rock concert. Now, imagine doing that same thing a few inches just below the belt. Does it still look like dildo you'd like to rodeo?"

At the revolting revelation, Kara drops the taser back into the bag like it's an active grenade ready to detonate at any second. Clayton moans in anguish, as if he can feel the voltage coursing through his skull.

"Yeah, let's label that one *last resort*," he says, rubbing the skin under his chin.

"So, what other kinky torture devices did you guys bring on our little road trip?" Kara asks with an extra pinch of sarcasm as she uninvitingly digs through the bag of tech trinkets on Clayton's lap.

"I don't know. Just a few other random gadgets and tech, and whatever else was in the box labeled 'Freaky Foreplay' under your mom's bed," Antoni cracks with a nudge of his elbow. "Does she need a Rug Mangler, I mean Mug Mangler, to add to her collection?"

"Ew. Just. Gross. That's beyond nasty, even coming from an uncivilized ape like yourself," she responds, shuddering off the comment like a bad chill. "But you know why boxes like that exist for women in the first place, right?"

Still relishing the lingering snickers of being overly pleased with himself. "Enlighten me?"

"Because men like yourself can never get the job done right. But hey, let's leave my mom and your inadequacies out of this. Shall we, Peewee?"

Antoni doesn't say a word. Physically, he can't. His dropped jaw is too busy tap dancing on the roof of the steering wheel to use for any witty comeback.

Meanwhile, Clayton tries his best to suppress the surge of incoming laughter with sealed lips, but the tail end of an initial chuckle sneaks out through his nose and triggers a loud snort.

Antoni turns his gaped gaze from the road to his cackling cohort who's no longer trying to hide his amusement. Within seconds, Kara joins in, adding her own series of uncontrolled giggles and sporadic snorts into the comedic mix. Before they know it, the entire truck, even Antoni, is brimming with hilarity.

After a sufficient reprieve, Clayton interrupts the laugh fest.

"So, what do you guys think we're going to find in Shermer?" he asks, in between fading chuckles, trying to get the conversation back on track. "Where should we even start?"

As the remaining giggles slowly subside, an elongated silence resonates loudly throughout the confines of the truck's limited cabin space. Kara breaks the quiet moment of contemplation first.

"If it were me in your shoes, I'd probably do a basic internet search for Shermer to see what I can find out about the town. We know we've already scrounged every bit of information about Rebecca Klein and her parents from her personal record, which wasn't much to begin with, but that doesn't mean more information doesn't exist out there somewhere else. Maybe even right under our noses," she says, sliding a laptop out of her canvas bag. "For starters, do you know what Rebecca Klein's maiden name was? That will give me a jumping off place as we work our way further down this rabbit hole."

"Shit," Clayton mutters through gritted teeth and clenched eyes. "I think her father's name was Carl. Maybe?"

He digs deep into the basement of his mind. That crypt of an area where meaningless grade school subjects like long division, religious studies, and cursive writing go to die because they're so seldomly relevant to everyday life. Coincidently, it's also the same vault where people who are bad with names instantly bury their forgotten first impressions as soon as they make them.

"And her name was . . . it was—dammit," he concedes. "I'm pretty sure it started with a *C*, too. At least I think it did. I definitely can't tell you their last name. I never actually met them when Trish and I were together.

Kara flings open the lid of her laptop, uncoiling her power cord before plugging in the charger to a built-in USB port hidden behind the truck's cigarette lighter. Antoni notices and chuckles under his breath.

"Of course, you've rewired the electrical system to equip your classic ride with more modern luxuries." He nods in approval. "Pretty cool, kid. I'm almost impressed. Almost."

Kara smiles, taking the half-assed compliment to heart. It's further reflected in the subtle flush of heat across her stained alabaster cheeks.

"Well, if that almost impressed you, then maybe this will push you over the edge," she contests, opening a search bar and typing in 'Rebecca Klein + Shermer, Missouri. "I've got Doc equipped with a high-speed mobile hot spot," she adds, pointing to a little black square underneath the glovebox.

"Doc?" Antoni asks, confused.

Kara replies, "Yeah, Doc. That's its name. You know, Doc Brown from *Back to the Future*? Real old, cult classic film. Came out in 1985, same year this beauty was made. Probably when you were like my age or something."

"Wait. How old exactly do you think—"

But before Antoni can finish, Clayton interjects.

"So, Kara . . . what'd you find?"

Within a matter of seconds, she's already pulled up several pages worth of search engine results that pinged hits for Rebecca Klein. She clicks on the URL atop the list and begins scanning the page. Only the biography seems to skip her birth and adolescence almost entirely, focusing the bulk of her life around her relationship and marriage to Simon Klein, founder of the revolutionary Hunt Initiative. There's no mention of her maiden name, her parents, or her origin story. But there is a photo of her and Klein at the top of the page, dressed in their best at what looks to be some fancy charity gala. At a glance, Rebecca appears to be in her late twenties in the photo, which would put her right around the same age as Trish.

Clayton studies the picture, and instantly, the first thing he can't help but notice is the spitting image between mother and daughter. Rebecca shares the same mirrored almond skin under dark, beautiful flowing hair, complemented by a few elusive strays adorably wandering free from the corralled rest. Her soot-black eyelashes, round lips, and defined cheekbones imitate Trish's model-like appearance with seemingly little effort, but with a few more freckles peppered throughout. She even has the same tender ocean-blue eyes—a welcoming gaze which radiates an unexplainable yet familiar comfort inside of Clayton.

Everything about their resemblance is so close it's almost uncanny, even down to the tapered chin and slight hook of her upturned nose.

And for a split second—a fleeting moment in time—Clayton forgets that he's not actually looking at a photo of Trish. That he's never even met the person behind the familiar face staring back at him.

Grasping onto a memory that was never his in the first place, his eyes continue to scroll over the picture, but halt when they spot a familiar ring on Rebecca's left hand. The very same pearl ring Trish wore the night of the anniversary party. The night this all started. The last time he would ever see her alive.

The reminiscent anecdote abruptly dissipates as Kara closes the page and clicks the next search result down on the list. It's the same deal. A rinse-and-repeat article solely focused on highlights of her life and time associated with Simon Klein. It's as if her entire existence was just a steppingstone in her husband's biographical rise to the top.

She tries another link.

And another.

But each discouraging click down the search reveals no helpful details surrounding her life before the couple met.

"Wow. Talk about straight, old, white, wealthy male privilege," Kara scoffs. "I can't seem to find anything of relevance on her. They're all just about him."

Unbeknownst to her, Clayton's been quietly reading every redundant result over her shoulder the entire time. Every article dead end swelling his anxiety, piercing enough holes to sink his patience.

"Another new article, same recycled story," Kara continues.

Finally, Clayton's festering unease gets the best of him.

"Just try the next one!" he snaps, stabbing his index finger at the fifth link down. "There's got to be something about her somewhere, right? I mean, hell, she can't just not exist before Klein got ahold of her."

But the next link is just another lost cause.

"Sorry, man, but it sounds like she's a ghost," Antoni softly taps in across the cabin for an admonished Kara. "As if Rebecca Klein's entire former life was simply deleted and then cut and pasted across the entire web in some lavish internet plagiarism conspiracy."

"Shit," Clayton bellows and shoots up in his seat. "I was hoping we'd have *something* to go on by the time we got to Shermer. But it looks like we're going to have to keep running into every situation blindly. Guess we'll just have to hope for lightning to keep striking the same goddamn place."

"But . . . lightning never strikes the same place twice," Antoni adds, confused.

"Ding, ding." Clayton shrugs. "Exactly."

"Actually, that's just a myth," Kara interjects, crashing the deserved downer fest with misplaced logic and bad timing. "Lightning can and often does strike the same spot repeatedly, especially if it's a tall and isolated object."

Antoni pipes up next to her.

"Oh, okaaay, Doc Brown," he mocks. "Why don't you just go back to setting your industrial strength electrical cables on the courthouse clocktower now and let George and Marty talk?"

"So you *have* seen it?" Kara replies.

"Of course, I've seen it!" Antoni barks back with a snub-nosed bite. "It's fucking *Back to the Future*! Everyone's seen it! It's a goddamn cinematic classic!"

With one *W* under his belt, he diverts his attention back over to Clayton, hoping to go a perfect 2–0 with a second dose of harsh reality.

"And, Clay, just to be clear. When you said, 'running into every situation blindly,' did you actually mean stupidly, totally unprepared, caught with our pants down and our cocks out, freely pissing against the wind? Just a couple of naïve pee-stained man-children trying to figure out dick basics through trial and error?"

"Wow . . . um, thanks for that visual. Definitely didn't need it," Kara shutters, attempting to delete the image from her memory through a couple head shakes. "Now, if you can put the penis analogies back in your pants so we can actually get back to the problem at hand, I have an idea of how we might be able to get some more info on her background."

Antoni shrugs. "I'm just saying, it's starting to smell an awful lot like a porta potty up in here."

Ignoring his friend's stream of piss-poor pessimism, Clayton perks up in his seat at the hopeful news. "How do you mean, Kara?"

She looks at him and then over at Antoni, who has retreated to focusing his attention on the road ahead as it slowly but surely reveals more of itself with every approaching minute toward dawn.

"Okay. So according to this census search, Shermer has less than 8,000 residents. That's a really small town, right?"

"Uh, yeah, I guess," Clayton responds, waiting for the lightning to restrike. "So what?"

"Well, as someone who came from a small town herself with a similar-sized population, there's bound to probably only be one high school in the whole town. If I can hack into the school's online directory and access her record in their database, I should be able to pull up information on her maiden name, parents' names, address, phone numbers—the works. And that should give us the ticket to get into contact with them . . . assuming they're still alive."

"Really?" Clayton exclaims. "That's great. Let's do it then."

"Well . . . there is just one *small* problem," Kara delivers shyly, attempting to be as gentle as possible before dropping another disposition bomb.

But Antoni is already ahead of her, laughing aloud before she has the chance to speak her peace.

"What?" Clayton probes, confounded by the unexpected burst of humor he's not privy to while Antoni's giggling grows uncontrollably louder and more maniacal.

"What's so fucking funny?" Clayton demands.

"You want to tell him, kid, or should I?" Antoni asks, in between bouts of fading snickers.

"I don't give a goddamn who tells me, but someone better spill it soon before I start pistol-whipping people for answers," Clayton threatens, picking up the gun from atop the dashboard.

Kara places her hand on Clayton's shoulder in a feeble attempt to calm him down. She's already dreading the words about to come out of her mouth.

"The problem is—" she shoots a dagger-filled glare at Antoni, then a delicate gaze back to Clayton. "I can't hack into her file from my laptop."

"So, you're telling me you can't *actually* hack it?" Clayton clarifies.

"No. I didn't say that."

Still a little slow on the uptake.

"Okay, what exactly are you saying then?"

Realizing this passively painful back and forth is getting them all nowhere fast, Antoni interjects. "She's saying the only way we can hack into Rebecca's school file is to physically break into said high school and access their computer database firsthand."

"Wait! What? How's that the only way?" Clayton replies, shoulders shrugged, palms to the sky. "I mean, doesn't that seem archaic? Like, don't we have the tools to hack in remotely?"

Kara closes her laptop, bringing the device into an embrace against her chest. It's a subtle display of comfort in an otherwise uncomfortable situation.

"Yes and no. It's archaic in the fact that because it's a small town, it's very likely that the school's servers are on the premises, not remote-hosted. And because of that, it makes it a heck of a lot harder to hack into, especially since I don't have access to my proper rig."

Clayton slingshots his head from Kara to Antoni, shooting his friend a pleading glance for support.

"Toni, can you—?"

But he's already shaking his head.

"Nope. Hate to say it, man, but she's right. Our best bet, like it or not, is getting into that school somehow, someway."

Clayton sinks back into his seat, slow and dejected. He tilts his chin up, fixating his gaze directly on the truck's roof above—as if it's a hopeful place where contemplation just dwells and solutions to problems are ripe for the picking.

Antoni looks over at his friend, and for the second time since his return he sees just how rough he really looks. He's been on the run for the better part of forty grueling hours now. Nearly two days of being taxed to his limits physically and emotionally, not to mention being shot in the shoulder, and he's starting to wear the despair on his fatigued face and in his defeated demeanor.

"Hey Clay, I know this is probably the last thing on your mind right now, but I think you could use some shut-eye, man. You've been through hell the last couple days. A little power nap could help you recharge a bit," Antoni says, looking over at Kara. With his eyes not so subtly conveying concord, he continues, "The kid and I can take it from here, right?"

A little delayed, she gives him an understood nod and replies, "Oh, yeah. Definitely. We'll wake you up when we get closer to Shermer. According to the GPS, we've still got about five hours to go so you've got plenty of time for some—"

But as they both turn to face him, they see he's already halfway there with his eyes scrunched shut and head faintly rattling against the passenger window.

# CHAPTER 33

"Nope. Not a chance, kid. There's no way in hell that *Back to the Future's* time machine is a cooler car than KITT from *Knight Rider*."

Taken aback by the automotive blasphemy she's just heard with her own side mirrors, Kara rebuts, "Ugh. Your argument is so invalid before it even began that I literally don't know where to start. But let's look at the facts, shall we? Fact number one, and the only one I need to wreck your case. Can KITT time travel?" she asks with zero intention to let Antoni answer. "Umm, gee let me think, Doc. That would be a noooo."

"Yeah, yeah. All you've got is the overplayed time travel argument," Antoni retorts, unamused. "That's it! That's the only thing. Might as well just call it Blah, Blah, Blah to the Future."

"That's all I've got because it's all that matters," she pushes. "It trumps literally Every. Thing. Else."

Back on defense, Antoni instantly decides a hefty dose of mansplaining will work better at getting his point across.

"God, I'm so over that one-dimensional argument bullshit. You wanna talk about the facts, kid? Then let's talk about the facts, because

KITT had cool shit in spades. He was equipped with state-of-the-art artificial intelligence and could even speak for fuck's sake. He was a crime-fighting crusader with bullet proof armor and thermal resistant coating who could drive himself using an advanced CPU. He had turbo boost thrusters, as well as anamorphic and etymotic equalizers. Hell, he could even smell using an atmospheric sampling device mounted on his front bumper. Oh, and let's not forget, he was a sick, murdered-out 1982 Pontiac Trans Am. Not a fucking DeLorean, perhaps the biggest automotive reject. Of. All. Time."

"Wow, do you even hear yourself half the time? What are you like the honorary KITT Wikipedia page owner? Founder and sole, sad member of the I Heart KITT fan club since 1980-whatever? Jesus, I passed out at etymotic—whatever the hell that is—from the geek speak you just threw at me, like a soft pillow begging for a nap." Kara makes a series of snoring sounds before jolting herself awake. "Oh, and I'm sorry, but last I checked didn't Pontiac go out of business like over a decade ago? Meanwhile, Doc's DeLorean was powered by a freakin' plutonium-fueled nuclear reactor. Now, that's some cool Superman-level, Kryptonite-type shit."

"Hraaaarhh," Antoni fakes a yawn. "Oh, sorry, were you done, or should I just crash now and put us all out of our misery already?"

"I'm not, but I'm pretty sure your argument is," Kara coolly replies in a subtle attempt to one-up his arrogant nonchalance.

"HA! Not even close," he shrugs, readjusting his hands on the wheel and the comeback in his head. "Where do I begin? First off, I thought you were supposed to be some kind of smart nerd, but I guess you're just one of those snobby, wash-your-hands-and-turn-the-page types. Think, McFly, think," he eggs her on, knuckling his own forehead. "Etymotic, for your information, is the ability to hear by using specifically engineered technology," he defines, using his own ear as another visual aid. "Something you're in dire need of in this argument, BTW. And second, you want to talk superhero shit, kid? Okay, then KITT was basically the equivalent of the fucking Batmobile!

You can't get any cooler than that. You just can't. But go on, let's hear your uneducated rebuttal. I could use the laughs."

Kara frees herself from the corner ropes and wastes no time parrying Antoni's verbal shots with a well-placed counter of her own. One she's had plenty of time to rehearse in her head during his droning monologue.

"How dare you spew such superhero sacrilege. Maybe a poor man's version of the Batmobile, but let's face it, KITT isn't even on the same playing field as the Caped Crusader's vigilante vehicle. Just a wanna-be. Nothing more than a value-brand knockoff," she reprimands. "KITT . . . even the name is dumb. Nothing strikes fear into villains' ears like being pursued by a car called KITT. KITTen. KITTy cat. OMG, soooo *fur*-ightening."

Antoni takes aim, ready to fire back another poised shot like a pop culture game of automotive battleship. Just trying to poke enough holes in the validity of the other's argument to sink it. But he finds himself at a loss of words. He opens his mouth, only nothing comes out.

"What? No response? KITT didn't teach you how to speak? I thought that was part of its whole shtick," Kara fires back. It's a well-aimed shot, right on the mark and he knows it.

Battleship hit.

He scans her pugnacious posture. She's ready for the bell to ding and cue the next round. Then, a smile slithers across the lower half of his focused gaze, and a subtle laugh escapes him.

"What's so funny?" she retorts, her verbal guard still in striking stance. "KITTy cat got your tongue?"

Battleship sunk.

Antoni steers his attention back to the road where the surrounding views are still cast in the shade from a sun that's sleeping in. But just on the brink of the distant horizon, the thinnest sliver of swirling pink, purple, and orange begins to peek, backlighting the clouds like billowing layers of cotton candy.

"Oh, it's nothing. You just—" he starts but pauses as his gaze falls back over to her. "You just remind me of my little brother. We used to argue about dumb shit like this all the time. He was just as delusional as you with the whole DeLorean time machine debate. It was his favorite movie, and he always wanted a DeLorean. It was his dream car much to my dismay."

Kara adjusts herself on the middle bench seat. "I feel bad for him. Growing up with little Toni must've been exhausting."

Antoni shoots her a look of warning.

"What? Can give it but can't take it?" she accuses.

"No," Antoni responds, his eyes momentarily fixated on hers and not the road. "Only my friends can call me Toni. And you're not there, kid. Not yet. You gotta earn it."

"Wow, didn't take you for the sensitive type," she sasses before grabbing the water bottle in her bag, apparently parched from all the arguing. "I'm surprised you didn't put your brother out of his misery growing up with your terrible debate skills and overall cheery disposition."

The previous spunk from Antoni's gaze quickly falls to the wheel. The unintentional words hit him like a punch to the chest, knocking the wind from his lungs and the words off his lips. After a moment spent recovering from the unexpected blow and ensuing emotional hemorrhaging, he finds three words to accompany his regained breath and thought.

"But I did" slips out.

Instantly realizing what he just whispered aloud was intended as part of his own inner dialogue, he looks over at a puzzled Kara. "I mean, I didn't put him out of his misery, but it's my fault that he's dead."

The expression on Kara's face immediately drops from playful banter to grave sincerity. Verbally paralyzed from the cat that got her own tongue, she starts throwing out apologetic phrases hoping one will take hold.

"Antoni, I'm so sorry . . . I didn't know. Or mean anything by . . . I shouldn't have said . . ."

"It's okay, kid. I know it was an accident," he assures, cutting her off before she stumbles through more of her profuse apology. He clears his throat and swallows, pushing the rising lump back down. "Truth is, after Leo died, I never really talked about it to anyone. I spent the longest time blaming everyone but myself for what happened to him, most of all Clay," he admits, motioning to Clayton who is still passed out in the passenger corner. "We got into a big fight and one thing led to another—" Antoni trails off, inadvertently rubbing the scar along his neck as she takes notice. He catches her gawking at the mark and quickly lowers his hand back to the wheel.

"Ahem, anyway . . ." He clears his throat again before continuing, "We didn't talk to each other for a real long time. In fact, we hated each other. I wanted to kill him."

Hanging onto his every word with the most gracious of ears. "Is that how you got that scar?" Kara gently presses, "What happened exactly, if you don't mind me asking?"

He shifts uncomfortably in his seat.

"Well, kid, that's a long story."

She looks ahead. There's nothing but an endless road of blurred white and yellow lines and rise-and-shine green pastures passing by in front of them.

"All we've got is time right now," she says, pointing at the GPS route on the phone resting against the dashboard. "Well, three hours and thirty-three minutes of time to be exact."

"Sorry, kid, but there isn't a car ride long enough to tell that story."

"C'mon, tell me. Pleeease?" She ditches the gentle approach and goes straight to tiptoeing around begging. "Who knows, it might even help you cope."

Antoni snickers at her cute psychological attempt to bait him into talking. He contemplates how he would even approach a story that he's only ever recited to himself. Slogged and suffered through in the confines of his own head. He quickly concludes that there isn't a right way. There never is when emotions of that magnitude are involved.

"Okay, kid. You want storytime, then listen up," he says, as he recounts all the events that led up to what happened, painting a picture of the deal gone bad. How he was a naïve and arrogant kid from the streets looking to make a name for himself. That Clayton tried to be the voice of reason and tell them the whole deal was a setup from the get-go, but he wouldn't listen to him. How that night, and Leo's death, changed his life in every way a life can be changed—for better and for worse.

He goes on about their fight, and how he tackled Clayton through a window and wound up nearly slitting his own throat in the process. How he got hospitalized and had to eat liquid meals through a stomach tube for weeks, going to months of rehab to slowly regain his ability to even talk while Clayton got sent to prison for thirty-three months for aggravated assault. Both ultimately suffering their own personal hells as a consequence.

"I completely fucked up our relationship because I was just so angry at everyone. At the world. At myself. And I took it all out on the only other brother I ever really had," he continues, motioning to Clayton who stirs momentarily before rolling back toward the windowsill. "It wasn't bad enough that I was responsible for losing my little brother, but then I went and lost my other one in a fit of self-pitied rage. Never stopping to think that without Clay showing up like he did, against his own will and better judgment, that I'd probably be dead, too. We'd all probably be dead." He doesn't say the next thought out loud. He just thinks it, and the verbal aftermath is all Kara hears. "I should be dead, not him," he whispers under a deep breath, and heavy sniff.

Playing the role of sympathetic listener to a tee, Kara spots a break in the story to interject and bring everything back to a more positive note.

"You two seem okay now, though, right?"

Antoni swipes his left index finger across the upper part of his beard's mustache, making contact with his nostrils and their accrual of salted sorrow.

"If you'd have asked me that question two days ago, I'd have laughed in your face and told you piss right off. Like I said, I wanted to kill him. But this Hunt—this whole fucked up situation—it's oddly brought us back together after more than a decade. And even though it's literally the shittiest of possible circumstances, it somehow feels like old times again, as strange as that sounds. And although both of us have changed . . . a lot, it still feels the same. Like we didn't drop a beat. Like he's still my brother."

Kara turns her gaze back to the open country road and takes a deep breath in before sighing it back out.

"I wish I had what you guys have," she says, and anxiously tucks her hair behind her left ear, like her own personal nervous tick. "I was an only child growing up. And I know it might be hard for you to believe, *buuut* I didn't exactly have a lot of friends." She looks down at the floorboard, again tucking her hair back on the other side, "Or, like, any friends, really."

"Reaaally? A charming personality like yourself?" Antoni jokes, but he's quickly met with a pair of middle fingers and a scowl of unamused proportions.

"Hey, c'mon! At least I was nice enough to hear you out," she whines, shoving his shoulder and then tightly crossing her arms. "You can't even let me finish. Or did they not teach you manners out on the streets?"

"Sorry, you're right, kid. Shutting the fuck up now. Go on."

Kara gives him a hefty helping of tentative side-eye before she continues.

"All I was going to say is, I think it's really admirable what you're doing. To be there for him—after everything you've both been through, after all this time—for something literally as do or die as this. That takes a special bond and not everyone can say they have that. Or have ever had that. That's some *Fast and the Furious* ride-or-die type shit."

"What can I say? 'You don't turn your back on *family*,'" Antoni mumbles, butchering an overly dramatic Dom Toretto impersonation.

Kara laughs so hard that a sharp snort causes Clayton to stir next to her. She takes notice and brings her engine volume back to a reasonable rev.

"When did those movies become superhero flicks anyway?" she loudly whispers. "I mean, they were stealing TV/DVD combo sets in the first film. Now they're taking cars into space and saving the world. Like, WTF?"

"Oh yeah, no, they absolutely lost their goddamn minds with that franchise, but at least the cars are still cool. I'd probably give my left leg for his 1970 Charger," Antoni jokily states.

"Eh, I don't know. It's slick and all, but even I have to admit that KITT is a cooler ride than Dom's Charger."

"Don't tell Clay this, or let it go to your head, but you're all right, kid." He gives her a playful nudge with his elbow.

Kara returns the compliment with a smile of her own and a flutter in her eyes. "What can I say, somebody once told me that I have a charming personality."

Antoni nods in approval.

"Well, at least we learned one thing about each other. Something we can both agree on," he says, as he focuses his attention back on the wheel. The sun firmly above the horizon, illuminating the road and welcoming a new day—a new opportunity.

"What's that?" Kara asks.

"That the Batmobile is the coolest movie car of all time."

A grin stretches, climbing up toward her left ear. "You're goddamn right it is," she agrees, arching her eyebrows in a breakthrough effort to test the waters. "Ton—"

"Nope," he cuts in with a finger wave and a head shake. "I said you were all right. I didn't say we were friends. But nice try."

"Fair. But there's still plenty of car ride left to win you over. In the meantime, I'll take the small wins when I can get 'em. For all I know, the next thing you're going to try to tell me is that *Gone in 60 Seconds* is a better getaway movie than *The Italian Job* or something asinine," she says with a laugh.

Antoni's smile flatlines like the sprawling Midwest road ahead of them.

"Kid, I will literally throw you out of this goddamn car."

The Silverado continues its trek beyond the neighboring suburbs of Bannerton deeper into the surrounding countryside. Where the plains stretch on like oceans of lush grass, and the hills like waves of wrinkled earth. Doing their best to stick to backroads and routes off the beaten path, the three eventually reach the Missouri state line. As if the constant fear of running into a possible border checkpoint or facial recognition scan wasn't enough, a new hurdle always seems to find its way onto their path.

"Shit! You didn't tell me we were almost out of gas," Antoni remarks, looking down at the fuel gauge needle tickling the last hash.

"Oh, well excuse me. I wasn't exactly planning on an across-the-state *Mission Impossible* road trip when I stumbled into work this morning," Kara snarls back. "Not to mention, this vintage beast doesn't exactly get hybrid mileage in the first place."

Woken by the sudden spat that's quickly escalated, Clayton sits up in his seat and rubs the clarity back into his eyes. For a fleeting moment, he imagines that if he just presses hard enough, he'll actually wake up in his apartment bed with Trish sound asleep next to him in his arms. As if this whole situation has just been one prolonged nightmare. Nothing but a bad dream. But much to his disappointment, the only sight he sees when he reopens his eyes is the endless road before him and the familiar sound of Brother and Sister Bear bickering beside him.

"I'm sorry, maybe the next time you decide to randomly kidnap someone and steal their car, you should make sure they have a spare gas tank handy."

"Kidnap? Steal? Seriously? Kid, it was all your idea to come in the first place. If anyone kidnapped anyone, it's you when you pulled that little panic button stunt, forcing us to bring you along. Trust me, if it were up to us, the only seat your ass would be firmly planted in right now is your desk chair."

"Oh, yeah, sure. Blame it on the victim. Real patriarchy of you."

Partly because his shoulder stings like hell from the worn-off pain meds, but more so because his head aches even worse than his shoulder, Clayton sounds off.

"Hey! HEY! That's enough," Papa Bear roars. "Can you two just get a fucking grip already?"

The boisterous banter between Antoni and Kara comes to a record-scratching halt. They both sheepishly look at Clayton like a couple of siblings that were just threatened to have the car pulled over.

"Look, we're already in way over our heads," he continues his scolding. "We don't need to be going at each other's throats all the time on top of it, all right?"

Kara and Antoni exchange woeful looks at one another like chided children. After reluctantly swapping silent apologies, they both stare out their respective windows in opposite directions.

Clayton sits up and grabs the phone from the dashboard. Just over a couple hours to go until they reach Shermer.

"Okay," he says, taking a deep breath in an attempt to bring some semblance of order to the current chaos. "Did I hear that we're running low on gas?"

Antoni flips him a salute from across the way. "Aye, Captain. If we don't stop somewhere in the next few miles, then we'll be hoofing it to Shermer."

"Shit. All right, then. How far is the next—" But he looks up just as a sign that reads Food & Fuel 5 Miles comes into clarity. Pointing at the blue and white marker, he indicates their next destination. "Well, guess that answers that. Do we have enough gas to make it there?"

"Yeah, but—Clay, you sure about this?" Antoni probes. "We may be a long way from the city, but it's technically a highway rest stop. Bound to be full of people from all over. People who may recognize you from the news, billboards—you name it. There might even be a drone convoy this far out."

Clayton massages the back of his neck which also hurts like hell thanks to the most uncomfortable car nap of his life.

"I know. But it's not like we've got the luxury of another option. I'll just stay low in the car, and you and Kara can grab gas, freshen up, and do whatever else you've got to do," he says, dragging his ball cap over his eyes. "Just do me one favor, yeah?"

"Sure," Kara replies like it's a no-brainer.

"Name it." Antoni chimes in.

"Can you make sure to get yourselves something to occupy your mouths, so I don't have to listen to your bitching for the rest of the trip?"

# CHAPTER 34

A few quiet minutes later, the pickup pulls into the nearby rest stop. The game plan is simple. Antoni will pump the gas. Kara will run inside for a few essentials. They'll both take quick bathroom breaks, all while Clayton lays low in the truck, out of sight from any prying eyes, human or machine.

In theory, the plan should work flawlessly. After all, no one knows what vehicle he's driving or the fact that his reservation for one has turned into a party of three. For once, it feels like everything is shaping up to be smooth. Maybe a little too smooth.

Antoni parks at the farthest pump on the west side of the gas station and kills the engine. The marquee for the old roadside convenience store reads Gas & Goods, but the sign's prime has seen far better days. The red paint is so faded from decades of scorching country sun and prairie gales that one of the *O*'s and the *S* in Goods have all but faded away.

"Gas & God, huh? I guess if the halo fits," Antoni says to himself, as he steps out of the truck and reaches as high above his head as he can while standing on his tippy toes. The full body stretch immediately alleviates hours of sedentary sitting from his stiff back and cramped legs.

Bending over now, his eyes catch an old wooden billboard across the road on the other side of the gas station. It reads REPENT NOW & BE SAVED OR REGRET IT FOREVER.

"Jesus, I know we're in the heart of Christian country, but man, this is a whole new level of Bible-thumping down here." He reaches back into the cab to grab Jayson's phone off the dashboard. "Damn, not even one bar," he murmurs, tossing the device back onto the bench.

Kara slithers out from the middle seat and hops down.

"I'm afraid God, guns, and glory is the only 3G you're going to find out here," she says amid her own mini-calisthenics routine.

Antoni reaches into his back pocket for his wallet. After a couple anxious pats on his left then right cheek, he looks up unexpectedly and shoots Clayton an appropriate come-to-Jesus look.

"Uh-oh," he mutters behind clenched teeth, frantically checking all his remaining pockets, pieces, and creases like an overly eager TSA pat down.

Kara turns around at the distress to catch him doing a variation of the Macarena. She shakes her head out of pity while letting out an unimpressed chuckle.

"So, let me get this straight. First you kidnap me, then you steal my truck, and now you're making me pay for gas and goods?"

"Still not a kidnap. Didn't steal your truck. And it's Gas and God, actually," Antoni corrects. "According to the sign at least. I mean, it would be the Christian thing to do. I'm sure there's a pertinent parable out there or some shit about giving to those in need. And darlin', I'm needy. When in the Bible Belt, right?"

Kara spins back around from the momentum of another hefty eye-roll and starts to stroll inside, still shaking her head between steps. "Unbelievable," she sighs, as she no-look tosses a small wad of cash at him from over her shoulder. "And on the second day, God made it rain."

Antoni just stands there with his palms up, as the bills flutter down to his feet like confetti. He bends over to pick them up one at a time, shooing Kara and the situation out of his mind with the flick of a wrist and raise of a finger.

"You'd never have guessed it based on the timid girl we first met, but that kid is a fucking firecracker," he says mainly to himself but loud enough for Clayton to hear, as he grabs the pump handle and selects diesel.

"She only gets to you because she *is* you," Clayton mutters from an excessively slouched position inside the truck. "You've only known her for a few hours. Just imagine what it was like every day for me growing up with you."

"Oh, I'm sorry, but exactly what part of laying low implies blabbering your loud mouth?" Antoni counters, jamming the nozzle into the tank.

As the fuel begins to flow, he takes a closer look around the rest of the rest stop. Most of the trucker pumps are occupied with giant semis, but the general public pumps are mostly barren, aside from a minivan with a family of five most likely passing through on vacation and a small hatchback filled with disheveled luggage and a brimming laundry basket, probably a Bannerton University student headed home for the weekend.

"Coast looks clear," he says discreetly, sliding the pump back into its holster. "I'm gonna head inside and take a leak. Any snack requests?"

"Why? You plan on buying them with the money you don't have?"

"For the love of—as if the kid wasn't bad enough . . ."

But the rest of Antoni's rant goes inaudible the farther he gets from the truck. Clayton sniggers under his breath as he grabs Jayson's phone off the seat. He tries to pull up a search on Shermer, Missouri, but he can't get a strong enough signal to connect to the web even though the GPS is still running.

"Damn, Toni was right. Zero bars," he mutters to himself, as he slides Kara's laptop out of her bag, remembering her hotspot.

A quick online search shows that Shermer, Missouri is home to the

Stags, the lone high school in the tiny town. Built in 1941 to help educate Shermer and the neighboring towns' growing farm population, the 3A high school originally served students in grades ten through twelve, but incorporated ninth grade into the curriculum in the early '80s when it also became classified as a 4A school. In the late '80s and early '90s, the institute was quite the stereotypical small-town sports mecca, winning a series of football and basketball state championships. The kind of *Friday Night Lights*-type of school that happily dumped all its funds and attention into new football helmets, stadium lights, and jock straps rather than ever sniffing the idea of improving the curriculum, raising teacher salaries, or even fixing the air conditioning.

Crazy enough, all those championships and the school itself might not have ever come to be had the building not survived being struck by an F3 tornado in the spring of 1977. Fortunately, the twister's damage was only severe to the gymnasium, which was rebuilt shortly after, of course. Because sports make money.

Clayton continues reading up on the history of the high school, but he can't find anything special about it—at least nothing that stands out. No prominent figures came from it. Taught at it . . . anything. It's just another cornfed high school in another podunk farm town in pass-through America.

He reaches back across the seat for the phone and despite fluctuating between one bar and no bars, he's able to successfully plug in directions for the school. It's just over an hour and forty-five minutes away on what looks like the northeast edge of town.

As he studies the whereabouts of the high school and the surrounding destination, there's an unexpected knock on the window.

Startled, he fumbles the computer off his lap, sending it crashing onto the floorboard. Through the window, he can see what looks like an old, homeless drifter clanging his smudged change jar against the glass. Written on the container is an absolute grammatical nightmare of a note: "2 UGLY TO STRIP. 2 STOOPID TO STEEL. ENYTHING 4 HELP. GOD BLESS U!"

After a delayed moment of hesitation, Clayton reaches across the truck's cabin to crank the window down, being extra cautious to not reveal too much of his face.

The backwoods drifter looks like a cross between a legit redneck and a trying-too-hard hipster. His beard is patchy and unkempt, and his face leathery and cracked from the dry, sun-bleached country he's aimlessly wandered over the years. The hair sticking out from the bottom of his stocking cap is an oily matted mess, just like one would expect, but his black hoodie and cargo pants combo looks like something Clayton would see on any one of the college students back in Bannerton. The only difference here is this poor son of a bitch isn't wearing the wardrobe ironically, and the mileage on his faded cowboy boots looks like the better days they've walked were more than a couple decades ago.

"Spare some change, sir? I'm out of gas," the homeless man mumbles from his limited stock of teeth still intact.

Upon even closer inspection, this old man may not actually be an old man at all. After a more careful study, he looks to be only a handful of years older than Clayton, which makes him think what kind of sad life this guy has struggled through to end up here of all places, looking like this. After all, this man came from a family and at one point might have even had one of his own. What happened to him? Was it drugs? A mental disorder? The product of military recycling? A culmination of too many bad life decisions? It's all a chilling realization and Clayton doesn't fail to notice the possible parallels to his own undoing.

"Sorry, man, no change here. Good luck and God bless, though," he calls out, quickly tucking his head back behind the arbitrary cover of his collar and ball cap as he cranks the window back up.

"P-please, mister," the man begs, as he firmly plants both hands on the top edge of the rising glass pane. "Anything helps." His persistence growing more apparent and less welcomed by the second.

"Sorry pal, no tengo dinero," Clayton repeats, his tone sharper and patience shorter. "Goodbye now."

But the man doesn't seem to get the hint.

"Just a little change. Th-that's all," he pursues with his fingers still clamped on the window, preventing it from rolling up any further.

For Clayton, this game of "Hear what I'm saying, but don't listen to me" is really starting to wear thin, and it's getting the best of any remaining calm and cool he has left.

"No means no, man. Now get lost."

And just like that, Clayton notices a mental switch flip on in the drifter's head, reflected in the fresh focus of his glazy, discerning gaze. He squints his beady, wrinkled eyelids and cocks his leathery head ever so slightly. "D-do I know you, m-mister?" the man asks, accompanied by a new accusing tone.

"Nope. Not likely," Clayton coolly replies, trying to maintain composure over his outer expression, while inside his heart revs between expedited beats. "Bye now."

He starts to turn the window crank again, but the man's death grip continues to make it a losing battle.

"No, y-you look familiar. I-I've seen you before somewhere," the man mutters through chunks of missing teeth and years of probable drug-abused gums. "I kn-now it."

Any remnants of composure that Clayton had left are now officially gone.

"Look man, I don't know you. I don't want to know you. We've never met. Now let go of the window, and get the fuck out of here before I actually do decide to introduce myself."

Only the threat falls flat.

"Y-yeah, I know your face," the drifter persists. His voice growing more certain by the second. "You look like that guy—"

"Hey! Hipster hobo! Get the hell away from my truck," an aggressive voice calls out a short distance away.

The vagabond turns his attention toward the command as Clayton sees Antoni come into view just over the hood of the pickup.

Still holding onto the window, and now pointing at Clayton inside, the man responds to Antoni's aggressively approaching steps, "Hey, I think I know this guy. I've seen him somewhere. On TV!"

Antoni reaches into his pocket and pulls out the remainder of Kara's small wad of cash. Forcefully, he hands it to the determined derelict upon approach.

"Here's thirty-five dollars, now get the fuck outta here before I have to take it back and tell you again not so nicely. If you catch my drift . . ."

Delight fills the man's eyes, instantly and wholly taking his attention away from Clayton like a laser-focused kid tearing through the intricate wrapping job of a large, shiny Christmas present. He stumbles off without breaking eye contact with the green bundle, counting and recounting the chunk of change to make sure his delirious sight isn't deceiving him.

Antoni watches the man stagger away, ensuring that he's beyond earshot before turning to Clayton through the cracked window.

"I'm gone for five fucking minutes, and you've got your own personal hobo fan club? You gotta be more careful, man," he lectures. "Half of the homeless people in this country have smart phones and shit. This isn't some glorified *Thelma and Louise* movie chase. This is The Hunt!"

"You don't think I know that?" Clayton stresses, raising his voice in defense while jumping up in the seat before realizing it and quickly slouching back down. "I was just trying to act normal and get him to leave, but the asshole wouldn't drop it."

"Wouldn't drop what?" a raspy female voice asks, as they turn to see Kara approaching, arms full of pit stop essentials. Not wanting to get into it any further or cause any alarm, Antoni just opens the truck door and gestures her way. "Damn, kid. Took you long enough. What were you pooping or something?"

"Huh? No, I was—"

"Speaking of, hurry up and get in the car so we can make like diarrhea and get on the run."

"Geez, rip my head off, why don't ya? I was just grabbing more drinks and snacks like you told me to," she counters and slides across the bench to the middle seat. "And would it kill you to use some normal departing analogies? I don't need to think about the grossness of shitting every time we have to leave in a pinch. Which I have a feeling is going to be often."

The door slams shut as Antoni hops in, slips the key into the ignition, and gives it a hard twist.

"You know what else you can do with a pinch?" he asks, batting his eyes to ante up the sarcasm.

"Ugh, I set you up for that one," she replies, tearing open a stick of beef jerky while giving it a disgusted, on-second-thought look. "I feel like I'm trapped at a really nasty frat party."

"Sorry, kid, but you're here, and you've only got yourself to blame," Antoni says, as he snatches the opened jerky from her hand and takes a chomp.

"Now, let's make like a fart and blow this shithole," he adds through a mouthful of processed, dried-up beef product. "Mmm, teriyaki. So good."

A little under an hour and a half after their close encounters of the hillbilly-kind, the unlikely three enter the home stretch to Shermer. Clayton checks the phone's GPS. Their destination has an ETA of eighteen minutes. He looks out across the Midwest prairie before him, and the lush view of sprawling countryside sprinkled with vibrant wildflowers travels as far as his eyes can see. Not a mountain, hill, or even slightly raised mound of earth in sight.

Looking to his right, he spots a giant pasture full of grazing cows, mostly black Angus, but a few white Charolais peppered in the mix. What was once a mahogany stained pallet fence stretched across the infinite blur of green acreage is now nothing more than a splintered railing, distressed and neglected by the lack of nurture from Mother Nature and ticking spell of Father Time. As he turns to his left, he's met by an abandoned barn absent more roof than it currently possesses. Nestled next to the dilapidated dwelling rests a rickety old pump-jack in a zombified state. By the decayed look of it, the rusted-out oil well hasn't drilled a fresh drop of black in decades. The vastness of the plains should make him feel open and free, but he only feels exposed and out of his element. Behind the anxiety of what they may or may not find here, his only solace now is that this isolated road leading up to Shermer resembles something out of a Robert Frost poem. This is his "Road Not Taken." He only hopes he's made the right choice.

"No traffic for a few miles is a good sign," Clayton says, as he lays the phone back on the dashboard. "Should be there in about fifteen or so."

"Speaking of, did we ever actually establish a game plan for when we arrive?" Antoni says, popping another jalapeño potato chip into his mouth. "Or is this about to be an audition for *The Three Stooges*?"

"I hate to say it, but I've got to agree with Ton—I mean, *Antoni* on this one," Kara clarifies.

He nods and offers her a chip from his bag.

"What's our plan of attack?" she finishes mid-crunch.

Clayton turns and finds both of them staring at him with their mouths full, like a couple of pathetic puppies begging for a command in hopes of scoring another treat. He shoots back a side-eyed glance in between two big chugs of water.

"Huh?" he whimpers, wiping the excess dribble from his chin. "I hate to disappoint you guys, but I'm not a fucking breaking-and-entering criminal mastermind here. It's not like I'm a pro at this or anything." He twists the cap back onto the bottle. "That would be Toni's department."

The doe-eyed favor is reciprocated toward Antoni as both Clayton and Kara turn in unison to implore their driver for an impromptu strategy of *X's* and *O's*. Clayton digs his hand into the bag of potato chips, shoveling a handful of spicy crisps into his own mouth.

With the spotlight now beating down on Antoni, he responds, "Whoa, selling illegal tech doesn't make me some kind of expert at breaking and entering."

Clayton replies, "No. But one could argue that your high school rap sheet fits the bill rather nicely."

"Ahem," Toni gargles, regaining his poise and focus. "That was a long time ago. And besides, the only school I ever broke into was our own, and that's only because I knew every nook and cranny in the place."

"That's funny," Clayton replies.

"What is?" Antoni responds.

"That you were ever actually at school long enough to know it in such vivid detail," Clayton jokes.

"You can color me shocked," Kara adds.

"Ouch. That hurts, guys," Antoni retorts, sarcastically placing his right hand across his heart. "True. But hurtful."

Gathering his thoughts, he continues.

"However, if I were to revisit the expulsion-worthy workings of my prepubescent criminal past, I'd start with a quick case of the joint. See if we can locate the administrative office, which by my guess would be fairly close to the main entrance. In a school this size, that's where the computers and servers will most likely be. But we don't want to case the place for too long because then we'll just look suspicious."

He pauses a moment to think, patting the steering wheel in hopes it will drum up the rest of his masterplan.

"The good news is this car blends into our current scenery pretty damn well. The bad news is small towns have locals. And locals are not only territorial, but they're also nosy. They can spot the unfamiliar like it's part of their homestead civic duty. So, I'm thinking we go the gymnasium route. We'll park off the road behind anything we can find about a hundred yards or so away and hoof the rest on foot. Best-case scenario, the gymnasium will have a good ol' fashioned padlock we can easily break. Most likely scenario, a touchpad that I can bypass. It'll just take a little more time."

"Not an expert at breaking and entering, huh?" Clayton jokes.

"I never claimed to be a pro, but I didn't say I was an amateur, either."

"Ooh, do you have an InteliHack Card?" Kara jumps in. "I've read all about them. Although, they're apparently not as untraceable as hackers and authorities initially suspected."

Antoni shoots an agape look at Kara, doing his best to blatantly wear the level of insult on his expression.

"Do I look like a two-bit, IHC-using chump to you, kid? You insult me. I've got TalCom silicon micro-tech fingerprints in my bag right now," he boasts, pointing at the duffle on the floorboard underneath her feet. "Not that we'll even need them here. I'll probably just use my black market password scanner to trigger a brute force attack and pick what's most likely a simple PIN combination."

"Aww. All that big boy tech and you're not going to bust out your Hot Dick?" Clayton jabs, failing to conceal a gotcha-grin from across the bench.

"Wait, what?" Kara asks, ears perked.

"Nothing!" Antoni snaps back, shooting Clayton an *another word and I'll kill you* look as he quickly changes the subject. "Forget about it. All I'm saying is, it should be an easy day at the office." He gives Kara a final accusing glance. "This is the big leagues, kid. Try to keep up."

"And what if it's a padlock, criminal Houdini?" Kara snarks. "Do you have some fancy schmancy 007 laser cutter gadget that my simple mind can't fathom?"

"Don't be ridiculous, kid, if it's a padlock, well . . ." Antoni points to the gun tucked in his waistline. "I've got a tool for that, too."

"You're right, I forgot. It's been a few hours since you've had the chance to pull the trigger on your shoot-first-ask-later mentality."

"Well, I'm more than happy to do a reenactment right here, right now for you," he sneers and unholsters the pistol. "Now, if you'd both please shut the hell up, I can get back to the plan. Where was I again?"

"I don't know," Kara replies. "Something about popping one off or busting out your Hot Dick. Suspiciously phallic, either way."

"Oh my god, it was just a stupid naming oversight," Antoni shouts, power-gripping the steering wheel. "A harmless acronym, okay? OKAY!"

Clayton can't hold back the uncontrollable snickering coming from his side of the truck.

"All right, all right," Kara responds, putting her hands up in surrender. "It was just a question, no need to rip my head off about it." Smiling, she continues, "I mean, what you do in your spare time is none of my business."

"Dammit, kid! One more word about it, and you're going to test the safety theory of tuck and roll at sixty miles per hour."

Kara concedes and doesn't say another word. She just hunkers down into her shoulders and reemphasizes peace with her hands in the air. Only her compliance doesn't last long because she just can't help herself.

She leans over to Clayton and whispers, "You're gonna have to give me the deets on that one later."

"For sure," he whispers back and winks.

Unable to fully hear their hushed sidebar, Antoni calls out, "Do you two assholes want to hear the plan or not?"

"Yes, yes, sorry," Clayton replies. "We're sorry . . . right, Kara?" He gives her a slight nudge with his elbow.

She flinches forward. “Oh, yes, very sorry. Please continue your master plan,” she pleads, pursing her lips together to fight off the hint of a perming grin.

Antoni throws them the kitchen sink of dirty looks.

“*Ahem.* As I was saying, once we get into the gym, we can work our way through the building to the office. Like I said, most likely it’s near the main entrance. Make sure no one turns on any lights or trips any potential alarms from opening random doors. We need to be deliberate about our route. If you see an alarm system, tell me immediately, and I’ll bypass it. Once we get to the main office, it should be another simple lock, either a deadbolt or some sort of outdated pin pad, most likely. Inside, we’ll locate a computer and get to work hacking, pulling up anything we can find on Rebecca Klein’s file and her parents during their time here: contact information, background checks, their current whereabouts, anything and everything that could help us. I may need to look at their server room if we run into issues with security or firewall. I just hope this school is advanced enough to have switched to electronic records by now, including files for retroactive students. After all, it’s been nearly forty years since Rebecca was a student here. That’s far from recent.”

Antoni makes a hard left turn, skidding onto a lazily groomed dirt road.

“If everything goes according to plan, we should have the information we need to move past go. Just remember, once we get what we came for, we gotta pull outta there like—”

“—OMG, save it!” Kara cuts him off mid-sendoff. “I really don’t need another charming ass or whatever analogy.”

“You know what? You’re right, I’m sorry,” he emphasizes. “That one’s too easy. I’ll let you use your own imagination to fill in the blank.”

“Gee, thanks.” She shrugs, completely unenthused. “You’re like a child, yet somehow worse, you know that?”

“Learn to like it, kid,” he fires back with a smirk. “But seriously, what analogy did you come up with? Tell me. Since we're in the heart of Redneckville, I was gonna go more situationally sexual with 'Pull outta there like white trash and their definition of birth control,' but I was also leaning toward 'Playing Jenga on a first date, so she knows how good my pull-out game is.' I mean, you can't go wrong with a classic, am I right?"

Kara just stares at him, utter disgust hinging on the inflection of her arching eyebrows.

"God, you're vile. You do know that, right?"

Clayton just shakes his head, hiding the slightest smile as he looks down at the phone. They're just under three miles out from the school but based on the condition of the dirt road they're currently on, you'd never suspect there was any hint of society or form of intelligent life for another hundred miles.

The truck grinds along the loose gravel, kicking up bigger pebbles and chunks of topsoil along the way while trailing an earthly fog of tan and gray behind it. After another mile down the dusty road and cosmic sea of open nothingness, the GPS displays a right turn onto Main Street. Antoni follows the route and within a matter of seconds, as if from out of left field in the absolute middle of nowhere, the desolate dirt lane turns to pavement just ahead of a quaint small-town strip.

A splintered and off-kilter wooden sign that reads SHERMER, MISSOURI, POPULATION 7,951 hangs atop a period piece windmill lacking several blades on its rusted rotor and the faintest whiff of a fresh coat of paint . . . really any hint of TLC, whatsoever. It's the perfect welcome doormat to a relic of a town forgotten ages ago—a blip in time and space across the surrounding galactic grassland.

Their first reintroduction to supposed civilization in over seventy miles is a surprisingly updated and massive tractor supply store. It's selling John Deere everything, proudly indicated by the abundance of green and yellow machinery and signs with the iconic leaping deer silhouette plastered everywhere. It's plain to see where the town's limited income comes in.

Just past the lawn and fawn headquarters, no more than a hundred feet up the old downtown drag, lies a hometown bank called Shermer Savings. Its beige brick façade dates it back to the '50s, maybe early '60s. But now, its post-war clay color choice has not only fallen out of favor but looks to be falling apart all together.

Across from the outdated bank stands a five and dime retailer called Stockman Trading. The local outlet features a variety of western clothing styles, including bedazzled-ass jeans and pearl snap everything, along with other random farm town essentials in its old cowtown window display. Lots of hokey, homemade signs that nod to "Faith & Family" adorn the transparent nook in every tacky which way imaginable.

Beyond Stockman's is a run-of-the-mill dive bar called The Giddy Up. Other than the lit neon nodes on its clichéd domestic beer signs, it's a relatively discreet watering hole marked with an X-paneled barn door that also serves as its main entrance. Just outside, several half-empty beer bottles and smoked-to-the-butt cigarettes from last night's last call litter the sidewalk landing.

Toward the end of the block, just catty-corner, a classic-looking diner called Louellen's emits a lip-smacking fried aroma that's more than enough to tempt every cock-a-doodle-dooer with the slightest hint of an appetite. It's the kind of quaint, frozen-in-time comfort food café that's customary for every small town to congregate at for daily breakfast, especially on Sundays, and then return to for lunch and loitering right after church. And speak of the devil, at the far end of the street, atop a small hill just past a vintage, turquoise and pink solo-screen movie theater called The Armour, resides a pristine cathedral perfectly sun-kissed in the spotlight of heaven's rays. It's a divine image that serves as the ultimate heavenly reminder for exactly where they are.

God's country.

Based on the lack of people out and about and the early roll call, Louellen's looks to be the only place on the main strip that's even open. And judging by the amount of gray and white heads peppered throughout the restaurant, it appears to be the old-time regulars getting after their early-bird specials.

"Mmm . . . I could totally go for some home-cooked chicken and waffles right about now. Slathered in enough syrupy, sugary goodness it could give me the 'betes from just looking at it," Kara moans, literally drooling at the mouthwatering thought. "My stomach hasn't stopped rumbling since we left the truck stop. Apparently, a bag of chips and stale beef jerky sticks—that *somebody* kept stealing—weren't enough to do the trick."

Antoni shrugs off the accusation and lets out a big, meaty belch.

"I hate to deprive you of your Type II fix, Kara, but we've got a job to do," Clayton replies, squashing her buttery breakfast banquet hopes and dreams.

"But . . . but what about after we're done at the school? Can we feast then?" she says in a pleading tone. "I've heard it's not productive to play detective on an empty stomach."

Clayton starts shaking his head before the words even come out. Eventually, they sync up.

"Once we've got what we need from the school, we're out of here. No use sticking around and drawing any unnecessary attention to ourselves."

"Umm . . . from the looks of it, I think this whole town missed the memo on the latest Hunt," she replies, gazing out the window and pointing out the overwhelming desolation of idle, country life at its finest. Like some rural version of a still-life painting.

"Hell, looks like they missed the memo that it's the twenty-first century," Antoni adds, easing up on the gas pedal to match the sudden and drastic drop in speed limit.

"Right?" Kara continues, "I mean, there aren't even any digital billboards broadcasting live coverage. I don't see any vehicles patrolling the streets. No copters or drones overhead. Nothing. Just the choir of crickets and cicadas in the distance.

"Don't judge a book by its cover, Kara," Clayton rebuts. "As a small-town farm kid, yourself, you more than anyone should know that it's Bible Belt towns like this one that were the biggest proponents of passing The Hunt Initiative in the first place. Too many people with guns and regrets, and nothing—or no one—to use them on."

"Ugh," she grunts, tossing her head into the backrest. "I know. I'm just getting hangry. I get irritable when my blood sugar drops too low."

"Not to pile on the implausible syrupy short stack here, but I could definitely throw down on some biscuits and gravy myself," a soft voice from the other end of the truck mutters, under breath.

Clayton shoots a condemning look over at Antoni.

"Oh god, you too, now?"

"Hey, I'm just saying, we've been on the run for more hours than my exhausted mind can count. I could literally pass out behind the wheel right now. A little food could help us refuel and recharge," he pleads his case. "You know I hate to agree with the kid, but I think she might be right. This place looks like the ghost of Shermer past with no signs of present or future anywhere."

Clayton looks at Antoni, who stares back with puppy dog eyes. He turns toward Kara who's sporting an even sadder expression while rubbing her stomach.

"Fuck," he groans, knowing that inevitable defeat is in his imminent future. "I'm literally being Hunted right now, but it's you two who are going to be the death of me, you know that?"

A resounding cheer emanates from inside the truck as they pass the church at the end of Main Street. Nestled at the bottom of a tiny valley in the distance, they can see the high school. They've finally made it to their destination and hopefully one step closer to some answers.

After a loop of casing the school grounds for the best point of entry, the three settle on the attached gymnasium. The cylindrical arena is conveniently tucked behind the central building's primary entrance and just far enough off the main road as to help conceal the looming misdeeds of their forecasted felony. They find a small patch of evergreens about a hundred yards off the premises and park. The staggered pines don't offer perfect coverage, but their in-season foliage should be dense enough to shield the vehicle from any suspecting cars that may pass by. The fact that it's a weekend further alleviates the added threat of any unwelcome guests, and it doesn't hurt that it's the Sabbath either, where morning mass will hopefully serve as an obligatory distraction for the majority of locals.

Clayton and Kara hop out of the truck and silently scuttle up to the fieldhouse. They congregate by the gym's set of locked double doors while Antoni trails just behind with the duffle. Strutting up to the entrance, the flash of a white picket fence lines the acreage between his earlobes.

"Well, well . . . I'll take 'What is a simple PIN lock for five hundred please, Alex?'" he boasts, unzipping the bag and pulling out his password scanner to perform a remote, brute force entry hack. The numbers of the gym's PIN quickly spin on the scanner as each successful match lands and locks into its designated slot like a lucky 777's pull on a trip to Vegas. After a few seconds, all six numbers are aligned on the scanner, and Antoni manually punches them into the touchpad. The red light on the digital lock flashes yellow and then green as the door's latch releases. Clayton gingerly pushes one of the double doors open as Kara powers on a flashlight from the bag and disappears inside the dark sports cathedral.

"VRUMMMUMMMM FVICH," Antoni sounds, as he flips his accompanying flashlight on behind her, waving the saber of light side to side in the dust speckled darkness.

"You're such a dork," Kara quips.

"Takes one to know one, kid," he responds, and turns to face her in the shadowy abyss, his flashlight illuminating the lower half of his face. "Much fear I sense in you."

"Ugh. It's 'I *sense* much *fear* in you,'" she corrects. "If you're going to quote it, at least get it right, Jar Jar."

"Guys!" Clayton softly yet aggressively whispers. "Focus, please."

"Ahem . . . right, sorry, man," Antoni says, as he regains a grip on the task at hand and the severity of the situation. "Game faces on."

Once they're all inside, the door shuts, extinguishing all but a few slits of the outside light. All that can be seen are a trio of beams bouncing off the white brick walls and the basketball court's glossy wooden floor. Other than a few high windows spilling in tablespoons of sunshine and a couple of red EXIT signs on both ends of the court, the space is completely dark. One thing that is faintly visible in the infiltrating rays above are a series of banners hanging like cloaked phantoms in the rafters. Clayton shines his light up to reveal the plethora of past state and regional football and basketball championships won during Shermer's host streak in the '80s and '90s that he had read about, as well as a few softball titles sprinkled in the mix.

Kara and Antoni simultaneously look up to follow the sports

spotlight. The nearly two-decade run is pretty impressive, but there seems to be a major drop off in winning anything after the millennium.

"Hey, you think Rebecca was part of any of those championships when she was here?" Kara whispers, her voice calm, yet anxious at the same time. "She'd have graduated some time in that era, right?"

"No clue," Clayton responds. "Trish wasn't much into sports. She was an art kid, so my gut says no, but who knows. Let's just keep moving." The eerie feeling of the old dark gym mixed with the fact that he really has no clue what the hell he's even looking for exactly are finally starting to sink in. "The faster we're out of here the better," he adds, avoiding a stray rack of basketballs on the court's sideline. He shoots his attention to Antoni. "Unless you want to try your luck at that game of one-on-one?"

Antoni looks back at Clayton.

"As tempting as embarrassing you would be, I think I'd rather do what we gotta do and just get the hell outta here. This place is starting to give me the creeps," he responds, and continues to make his way toward the court's series of far south exits. "I vote for what's behind door number three. Based on the school's layout, my guess is that the administrative office is through this door and maybe a right turn or two down the hall."

There's no objection from Clayton or Kara as the group holes up at the third door. Antoni checks around but doesn't notice any alarm systems mounted on the wall or in the surrounding area, so he tugs down on the handle and is happily met by no resistance as it slides open. Outside the door is a small foyer, but the organization of the limited space and the amount of reflective glass displays give the corridor a larger feel than it actually is.

Against the far wall are additional glass cases loaded with shiny metal trophies of all colors, shapes, and sizes, along with medals, ribbons, and tons of past Shermer athletic team photos. Kara shines her light on the opposite wall and notices it's covered with mismatched frames of what look like prom pictures from classes of yesteryear. She walks over to the wall, shining her light up and down the staggered images as her eyes flicker back and forth with the wavering beam. Each prom photo shows the entire senior class, anywhere between seventy to eighty students along with their corresponding dates and a small description of the prom theme and class year. Starting with last year's class, she methodically makes her way down the wall, one decade, one Midnight in Paris and Under the Sea theme at a time until she finds herself four decades down with no more wall to spare.

"Hey guys, check this out," she says not breaking eye contact with the decorated wall.

The men make their way over, matching her gaze at the end of her bobbing flashlight.

"Do we know when Rebecca graduated exactly?" she asks, slowly probing the light over various photos as if one of them will randomly illuminate with her answer as soon as the beam hits it.

Clayton has no clue. He attempts to do some simple addition in his head but doesn't have a number with which to start. He can't remember from her file when she was born, just that it was in a small suburb of Oregon.

Antoni speaks up, "It was sometime in the early '60s, right? Like '62 or '63, I thought."

"No, it was definitely later than that. It had to be like '66 or something," Kara challenges with a useless combination of confidence and cluelessness.

But none of them can remember for sure and searching a decade's worth of pictures for a young face they don't know is an exercise in productive futility, a luxury they haven't the time or energy for at the moment.

"Forget it. Let's just stick to the plan and find the admin office," Clayton says, as he backs away from the wall, followed by Antoni and eventually a very reluctant Kara, who's still hopelessly scrutinizing the bank of photos with every fleeting step.

Carefully, the group make their way out of the atrium through the adjacent double doors. Not only are they not locked; they're not even shut. The lucky, uninhibited path leads them directly down a long hallway outlined with forest green lockers and a gauntlet of closed classroom doors. Even in the dim obscurity, the tiled floors are just as reflective as one would expect a recently mopped school floor to be. Shiny and mostly white, with colorful, interlocking cubes randomly sprinkled throughout—reminiscent of a popular education style long forgotten.

"Ugh, I feel like I'm right back in high school hell wandering through this place," Kara says, as she tilts her flashlight toward the ceiling. "They even have the same cheesy, played-out spirit banners."

Hanging above their heads as they trek through the quiet halls are large hand-painted banners with clichéd pep rally phrases that say, "BUCK BAYFIELD," "HOOK 'EM HIGH, HORNS," and "MESS WITH A STAG. GET THE HERD."

"Ah, c'mon, kid. Where's your school spirit?" Antoni jokes, as he looks up.

"As a smart kid without any friends—"

"You mean *nerd* without any friends?" he jumps back in, cutting her off, his smile vaguely evident by the ray of his flashlight.

"I mean this," Kara responds with a lone middle finger beaming in his direction. "I couldn't wait to graduate. So, this is literally my nightmare," she adds, followed by her own sarcastic cheer. "Give me an H-E-L-L, come on guys what's that spell?"

Antoni looks back, lightly chuckling to himself, "I'm sure there's a set of pompoms somewhere back in the gym if you really want to get into it."

Clayton piggybacks, "Could've fooled me. You sure you weren't part of the cheer squad, Kara?"

"Please, don't encourage him." She shrugs and continues forward.

By the time they arrive at the end of the hall, they can see the main entrance. And just to the right, like Antoni said there'd be, lies a door with a plaque on it that reads ADMINISTRATION.

"Boom," Antoni brags. "Called it."

The trio approach the door and find a similar touchpad to the one just outside the gymnasium. After a couple minutes, Antoni cheats it open, and the three enter the faculty room. In the center of the bleak space is a pod of low-walled cubicles, each adorned with their own assortment of kitschy keepsakes and personal photographs. The room itself smells of over-roasted coffee thanks to a caffeinated musk firmly trapped inside the stale furniture and asbestos-insulated drop ceiling from school week after school week of administrative binge-perking. After a quick room scan, Clayton immediately notices the pungent culprit—a scorched coffee pot in the corner likely set on constant brew just so the staff can get themselves through each day's bookend bells. To the left of the charred carafe is an old water cooler that looks as if it were plucked straight out of a generic corporate America breakroom, circa 1978. Next to the groovy watering hole are a couple of round, white laminate four-seater lunch tables and a beige pleather loveseat whose cushions are beyond faded from its share of constant up-and-down ass traffic. On the opposite side of the room lies a wooden counter with two shuttered box office-like windows. A service bell sits atop its glossy maple counter.

"This area looks familiar," Antoni says, as he approaches the box office. "I spent more time at a window like this getting doled out detentions than I can count."

"Nooo," Kara quips, as she takes a seat before one of the computers in the center pod. "You? An adolescent asshole? I'm shocked."

"Hey, last I checked it takes a rebel *and* a nerd," he says, pointing at Kara, "to make up two-fifths of the Breakfast Club. Or do you want to play the social outcast? You're perfect for either reject role."

More interested in finding answers than flinging banter, Clayton pulls over a chair from the neighboring cubicle and sits down next to Kara.

"How long do you think this will take?" he asks, but his attempt at a casual delivery fails to hide the inflection in his anticipation.

"Well, once I get past the login password, it shouldn't take too long to hack into the mainframe and pull up the student record log."

But sensing the rise in his anxiousness, she decides it's probably best to set some realistic expectations.

"Clay, I . . . I've got to tell you before we do this that it's still a long shot. Antoni was right when he said they may not have electronic student records here. It's a small town, after all. And even if they do, there's no telling how far back those records will go."

Clayton takes a moment to wrap his head around the discouraging info download. She's right, and he knows it, even if he doesn't want to fully accept it. But his eagerness wins out, pushing the doubt aside. He's come too far. Been through too much to be pessimistic now. Because if this doesn't work, what will? There is no plan B. No next step. He's at the end of his rope with nowhere to go but a long fall down.

"I know, I know, just do it," he says, shrouding the thought. "I've got a good feeling about this."

Instantly, Kara gets to work on the keys, clicking and clacking her way past the login password and onto breaking into the school's main infrastructure. Just as her and Antoni expected, the school's files aren't remote-hosted, which would have made this little hacking journey an exercise in futility had they not come here. Luckily, the school is current enough to have their digital records housed in on-premises servers, but not advanced enough to truly know how to protect them from prying eyes. Why should they? It's a small town after all. Why would anyone ever think or have the need to break into Shermer High School's database?

After a few minutes of easy sailing, Kara runs into a snag.

"Hmm, that's weird," she mumbles under her breath.

Clayton's attention sidetracks from the screen to her, "What's weird?"

"Well, I'm in the main system, but it's not giving me clearance credentials to access the directory. It seems to be requiring an additional intranet password, which I figured would have been auto-linked to their network."

Antoni's ears perk up from across the room. Straying from his lookout post, he joins them at the computer.

"It's their firewall," he says, hovering between Kara and Clayton.

"Firewall?" Kara responds confused. "Why would it be their firewall? I'm already in their system. Past their firewall."

"Yeah, I know," he says in agreement. "What I'm saying is we can get around the additional system password if we hardwire directly into their servers. We can set up our own web-based proxy on a private network and that should give us free access to the unauthorized intranet."

"And we circumvent the whole need for a password altogether," Kara completes his thought. "That just might work," she continues, as a grin starts to form.

"Of course, it will. I've just got to find their server room," Antoni boasts, looking around the admin space, stopping his gaze on a narrow door in the far corner of the office. He scurries over to the closet door where he instantly feels warmth trickling through the shuttered bottom and a subtle hum permeating from within.

He reaches for the knob, but it doesn't budge.

"Damn, it's locked," he softly shouts.

"Oh, I thought you had a tool for that?" Kara says mockingly, as she eyes the gun tucked into Antoni's pants. "Go ahead, blast it off, hot shot, and risk taking out the servers as well. That'll be fun on Monday when they walk in and see a nice bullet hole in their closet door."

"Or, even better idea, I could just shoot you," Antoni retorts. "Put yourself out of my misery."

While the two do what they do best, Clayton takes the matter into his own hands, literally. He knocks over a mug on the desk filled with random office supplies and begins untwisting a couple of the scattered paper clips. Casually, he gets up from his seat and heads for the closet, gently pushing a still jawing Antoni aside. Sliding the set of unraveled clips into the keyhole, he starts wrestling the knob and its inner workings. After several seconds, the lock makes a faint click and the handle loosens. Kara and Antoni hush their squabbling and stare open-mouthed.

Clayton turns to Antoni and lifts the chest flap on his friend's shirt. He tucks the broken paper clips into the welcoming pocket and closes it, giving an added pat for good measure.

"It's been a while, buddy," he says through tilted lips. "But once you're in the game, you're . . . how's the rest of that stupid saying go again?"

Antoni returns the favor with a grin of his own.

"Damn, I forgot how good at that you were." He laughs and cracks his knuckles. "All right, looks like we're back in business."

He takes out a small thumb drive from his bag of tricks and plugs it into one of the USB ports on the small tower of servers. He makes his way back over to Kara and the two begin hashing out their plan to circumvent the intranet password using a private web proxy. After an initial failed attempt to connect the proxy to the web server due to a TCP connection timeout, they manage to adjust the LAN settings and renew the DNS and IP to successfully access the school's intranet and supporting digital database. Within a matter of minutes, they've successfully pulled up the record log for every Shermer High student over the past ten years.

"So, how far back can we go?" Clayton asks, wasting no time as Kara clicks on the arrow for the next page of results.

"It actually looks like they've done a decent job of cataloging their previous student records," she says, scanning the first wave of results. "So far, I'm able to access at least the last fifteen years. Let's see what the next few pages show."

Another couple arrows over and class results as far back as the early 2000s start to populate the screen. After another few clicks, they're followed by results from the '90s and the late '80s. Clayton's eyes swell from anticipation as former student name after older former student name appear before his eyes.

And that's when he spots it. One name that sticks out from all the rest. The one they came all this way to find.

| **Name** | **Class** | **Gender** | **DOB** |
|---|---|---|---|
| GOULD, REBECCA NICOLE | 1982 | Female | 02/08/1964 |

"Holy shit, there she is," he exclaims, jumping up from the chair to poke at the computer screen.

But as Kara goes to click on her file, the sound of distant beeps from the main entrance's touchpad draws their attention. It's followed by the synchronized creak of a set of well-worn door hinges flexing.

"Shit," Clayton whispers emphatically. "Someone's coming. Hide!"

The trio take cover wherever they can find it and as quickly as their reactions allow it. Kara smashes the X at the top of the records page but there's not enough time to put the monitor to sleep as she ducks under the desk. Antoni shuts himself in the server closet, and Clayton makes a dash for the box office counter only to find that the door inside is locked. A chilled panic starts to consume his nerves before he feels a hand reach out and grab his ankle from beneath the core of cubicles. He takes the physical cue and drops under the desk for cover, doing his best to avoid entangling his wounded shoulder in the mess of intertwined computer cables on his way down.

A second later, the hallway leading from the main entrance is illuminated by a cascade of outside light followed by a squabbling dialogue between two women.

"So, I told him, 'That's not how this works, Braiden. You can't just give me a blank tardy slip with a random signature on it and no explanation as to why you're late and expect me to just accept it, no questions asked. I wasn't born yesterday,'" one of the voices says.

"I swear, these stupid little shits have either gotten exponentially dumber over the years or we're just failing miserably at an alarming rate as teachers," the other female voice responds. The two share a squawking laugh that teeters on the cusp of a cackle.

Their unwelcomed comedic relief screeches to a halt as the familiar beeps of an even closer touchpad fill the room's quiet void. A reinforcement of chills shudder throughout Clayton's body as the door to the administration office creaks opens. Then, a subtle click is heard. Instantly, a flood of overhead fluorescence engulfs every shadow of obscurity from the corridor's nooks and crannies.

From underneath the pod of cubicles, Clayton can only see two pairs of shoes. A suggestive set of suede navy heels belong to a woman with skinny calves and a not-so-shy pantyhose line. The other set are black ballooned dress flats with distressed seams, fatigued from doing their best to fight against a thick set of encroaching elephant calves.

Amid all the commotion, Clayton can feel his ribcage pounding, banging against his chest like a swelling timpani drum. One wrong move. One sound. And they're screwed.

"Hmm . . . that's strange," states the wearer of the risqué stilettoes. "That computer screen is on, and the chair is out."

"Ugh, again? How many damn times do I have to clean up after Andrea?" says the woman with tree trunk legs in a short-breathed rasp, as she waddles her way over toward the desk Kara was just sitting at and currently hiding under. The chair probably still warm to the touch.

Clayton feels a hand reach out and grab his, squeezing it with tremendous pressure. He looks over to see Kara every bit as terrified now, if not more than when they first met and Antoni held her at gunpoint.

Without missing a beat of her gossip, Large Marge turns off the computer monitor and pushes the chair back in under the desk. Kara feels the nudge from one of its wheels and does her best to give way, practically rolling into little spoon position in Clayton's arms. She looks back at him for what to do, but he just holds up a finger over his mouth.

"I'm getting really tired of playing mama bear around here," Cankles continues to bitch. "Sometimes I'm surprised she's responsible enough to even wipe her own ass without help, let alone shape the minds of our youth. Guess that's just what we should expect from little Miss Big City Priss."

"None of these fresh teacher grads have any accountability," replies Heels in a nasally tone. "They're almost as shit for brains as the dumbass students."

The voices begin to grow distant from the cubicles as the women work their way over to the box office counter.

"Shoot! Do you have your keys on you, Rita?" asks the skinny-legged woman in an even higher pitched whine this time. "I must have left mine in my classroom desk."

"God, Jeanie, sometimes you're just as bad as Andrea, you know that?" Rita scolds. "Come on. Follow me."

Seconds later a set of keys can be heard jangling as they struggle against the spring-loaded innards of the deadbolt. Finally, the door opens. Clayton watches from underneath the desk as the two pairs of contradictory feet disappear into the neighboring office.

"We gotta go," he whispers, giving Kara a shove. "Right now."

The two quickly and quietly crawl their way out from underneath the quartet of desks. Antoni notices them emerge from behind the grated closet door, and he, too, carefully turns the handle to exit the makeshift server room turned hiding spot.

Together, the three tiptoe their way toward the faculty exit, being sure to avoid making any sound louder than the muffled conversation of the ladies in the neighboring box office. Once they safely spill into the hallway, their heels reacquaint themselves with the ground as they enter a full sprint back toward the gymnasium.

"Go, go, go," Clayton murmurs, empathically waving his hand forward.

The same stretch of hallway that took them over a minute to walk down initially is conquered in less than a ten-second sprint. But as they reach the door to the atrium, they find it locked from this side.

"Oh, for fuck's sake," Antoni hisses, as he reaches the door first. He drops his bag onto the glossy floor and goes digging for his scanner again. But their hurried situation becomes horrifyingly hastened when the overhead hallway lights flicker on, one at a time, in a thumping wave of encroaching illumination.

"Toni, hurry it up, man," Clayton urges, piggybacking the anxious command with an aggressive finger twirl.

"No shit, Sherlock," Antoni retorts, rattled. "What do you think I'm doing, playing with myself over here?"

Kara tries to open one of the close by classroom doors for cover, but it too is locked.

She tries another.

And another.

No such luck.

"Um, guys, not to add to the panic fest, but we're running out of options and time here," she trembles, shaking another stubborn doorknob.

Clayton takes note and attempts to open a series of classroom doors on the other side of the hallway. Again, no such luck. That's when he remembers the paperclip lockpick he tucked into Antoni's chest pocket.

He turns to his flustered friend who's still working on bypassing the keypad.

"Toni, hand me the lockpick I gave you."

At the far end of the hall, Clayton watches the door to the administration office slowly creak open, followed again by the women's gossip-heavy banter.

"Hurry!" he adds.

"Forget it, Clay," Antoni hostilely whispers, wiping the perspired panic from his forehead. "There's not enough time."

"Toni . . . they're coming out now," he hisses back.

"C'mon. C'mon . . . almost there. Just a little more—got it!"

Finally, the last digit locks into place and Antoni punches in the code as fast as his bumbling fingers allow him. He grabs the handle and swings the door open. He and Kara pour into the atrium as Clayton, who is now just as exposed as the women standing at the opposite end of the hall, hastily joins the two, shutting the door with as much swift hush as his trembling hands can conjure.

"Quick! Back to the truck before they realize we're here," Clayton orders and darts for the gym exit. But before he can implement a hastened buddy system for fleeing the scene, Kara wanders off to the wall of framed prom pictures. Her AWOL maneuver takes Clayton and Antoni a moment to realize she's not behind them.

"Kara, what the hell are you doing?" he yells under the weight of his nervous breath. "We gotta go, now!"

"I want to see what she looked like," Kara responds, studying the picture that's dated Shermer High School Prom, Class of 1982. "Get a glimpse of who she was."

"Kid, we don't have time for this shit," Antoni reinforces. "Get your ass over here and let's go." But Kara doesn't budge. She just stands there staring at the picture.

With his calm already gone, Antoni's patience is next to go. "Goddammit, if I have to come over there and get you—"

Without wasting a moment more to consider it, Kara grabs ahold of the photo with firm hands. Wrapping her fingers around the underside of the frame's curvy bezel, she rips it clean off the wall with one hard yank.

Shocked, Clayton reacts by spouting the only logical thing he can think of in the heat of the moment.

"Kara, are you fucking crazy?"

But she doesn't answer. She just tucks the framed photo, along with the small chunk of drywall that came with it under her arm and rushes to join them at the exit. The men follow behind her until the trio are back outside the gym, right where they started. As the gymnasium door shuts, the touchpad sounds, locking the double doors behind them. They make another mad dash to the truck in silence, scanning all around for any other surprise visitors while Antoni fumbles to get the keys out of his pocket and unlock the doors.

Finally, with everyone safely inside, accompanied by an orchestrated symphony of heavy breathing, the engine revs to life and the pickup peels out from behind the grove of trees back onto the main drag as fast as the vintage set of wheels can carry them.

After about sixty seconds of silence, what feels like an arbitrary enough timeframe for everyone to catch their breath and slow the flow of adrenaline surging through their bodies, Clayton slams his fists into the truck's dashboard three times. Only this isn't Oz, they were never in Kansas, and he's not wearing magical red slippers. Although he wishes it were all just a dream.

"Fuck! Fuck! Fuck!" he shouts in unison with the flurry of punches. "We were there! Right fucking there. Just a click away. Now we're back to square one with no answers. No clues. Nothing," he finishes carping and snatches the stolen prom photo out of Kara's hands. "Nothing but this useless class picture at some dumb *Great Gatsby*-inspired prom."

The elicited fright from their narrow escape fades almost as quickly as it came, but the unescapable fury lingers as he studies the photo—the gala-themed attire jolting his right hemisphere with a fresh memory of Trish the night of the anniversary party. He remembers how perfectly that white, backless dress hugged every curve of her body in an enticing embrace. How her blush lipstick accentuated the already lush contours of her desirable lips. How he'd long to kiss them again. Hold her again. To hold—but that sweet memory is overtaken by the last image he has of her. Cradling her lifeless body helplessly in his arms. Her white dress soaked in damp glistening crimson, still warm to the touch. And her eyes. Her beautiful blue eyes a pale, frozen hue of gray like a cold and lifeless lake in the winter of his soul.

The flashback simmers just below the surface until it finally boils over. And in the heat of the moment, he rears his fist back once more and strikes the frame. The eruptive force of pent-up anger shatters the glass, bloodying his knuckles in the second stage of the grieving process.

He digs his red-streaked hand into the fractured frame—not heeding the shards that remain tucked into the border like hungry fangs—and rips out the photo. His fingers feel the sting from the glass bite even more as they exit. He doesn't seem to care about the physical pain, just the emotional anguish of a nightmare he can't seem to wake up from. Tossing the smashed frame out of the passenger window, he hands the liberated picture back to Kara.

"Here's a worthless keepsake," he dismisses, as she timidly accepts it. Slowly turning away, he stares off into the countryside in silence to dwell in his continued torment, skipping stage three's bargaining step and going straight into four's depression. Kara opens her mouth ready to attempt some solace, but she feels a hand pull on her left shoulder. When she turns, she's met by Antoni's soft gaze and shaking head. She sinks back into the middle seat, gently folds the photo in half, and stuffs it into her bag.

For the next few minutes, the dejected trio remains completely silent aside from some audible belly growls over the hum of the road. They've reached the end of the line, and failure is all they have to show for their sacrifices. Antoni finally musters up enough courage to say what their stomachs are all thinking.

"I know this probably isn't the right time. I don't know if there *is* a right time. But I think we could all use a little pick-me-up right now, and that diner is just down the road. What do you guys say?"

Kara is the first to respond with an eager, but not too eager, head nod and cool accordance. "I'm in," she squeaks. "I think we could all use a recharge."

"Sure. Fine. Whatever," Clayton grumbles, as he maintains his aimless gaze out the passenger window. "I really don't care anymore."

About two hundred yards up Main Street, the truck makes a left turn into Louellen's parking lot. The lot itself is about twice as full now as it was when they passed it earlier on the way to the high school. Antoni parks away from the crowd of cars and both he and Clayton shuffle out first, leaving Kara in the truck as she forages for something underneath the bench seat. She finally locates what she was looking for and pulls out a grungy Green Bay Packers ballcap.

"Here, thought you might want a little alter ego boost," she says, handing the hat to Clayton. "It was my ex's favorite. Real winner that one was. And the sad thing is—well, other than our entire relationship—is that I don't even like baseball. I think I kept it just to spite him, as petty as that sounds."

"Nuh-uh. Nope. The sad thing is, you think the Packers are a—actually, you know what, forget it. That's just too easy." Rather than crush Kara's underhanded meatball out of the park, Antoni settles for taking his base and continues walking toward the front door shaking his head.

"Sure. Why not add insult to injury?" Clayton murmurs, as he begrudgingly accepts the hat and slides it on.

Kara looks at him confused.

"What did I do? I don't get it," she whispers to Antoni, as they all pile up at the door. "Did I miss something?"

"Far more than you know, apparently. You see, we're born and raised Illinois boys. That makes us Chicago diehards by nature. Hometown pride and all that. You just gave him our archrival's hat," he enlightens her, as he reaches for the pull handle. "Oh, and just to save you, and myself for you, from any future embarrassment, Green Bay is a *football* team. You know, oblong ball, no bats, lots of tackling. Whole different sport, kid."

The inside of Louellen's is exactly as expected. It's like the owner picked up a 1955 copy of *Stereotype, Inc.* magazine and selected every product from the old, small-town USA diner catalog kit. Everything from the black-and-white checkered tile floor and corner, neon jukebox spinning classic 45s to the vintage collection of Coca-Cola posters lining the walls and mushroom top bar stools—all adorn the space like individual items from a golden-aged time capsule. Even the waitresses look like they're headed for a sock hop after work in their retro-inspired poodle skirts and button-down blouses. But among the type-cast décor of decades long ago, there are flashes of originality.

None of the tables' chairs or sprinkling of booths seem to be fully matching sets, and there's an entire shrine lit up in another corner of the restaurant full of trophies and framed pictures dedicated to the Shermer High School sports hall of fame. Like the banners hanging in the gym's rafters and the entirety of the café itself, none of it appears to be from the twenty-first century.

Clayton's outdated scan of the place snaps to a halt when he hears a friendly twang from his peripheral.

"Howdy there, y'all. How many this morning?"

He swivels to find a cheery woman staring at him from behind the hostess stand. Unlike the waitresses, she isn't wearing a throwback poodle skirt or a makeshift bouffant. She's dressed in a form-fitting black t-shirt and a bedazzled pair of bootcut jeans that she probably snagged from Stockman's across the street.

"Uh, three, please," he mumbles, as he tilts his head back down, trying to avoid any further eye contact.

"Certainly. Right this way, please," she responds with a warm smile and a heartland wave for them to follow her lead.

On the way to their table, they pass by a handful of elderly Shermer couples, who have probably made eating breakfast at Louellen's a Sunday tradition for the past thirty years. Saddled up at the bar sit three scraggly bearded gentlemen who look anything but gentle, decked out in differing patterns and shades of camo. They aimlessly stare at the lone tube television hanging in the corner, which is of course tuned into the latest news about The Hunt.

Through the kitchen-order window carved out behind the small bar, Clayton catches a glimpse of the cook—a big burly man with a 24/7 resting hard-ass face, and a giant, blurred pinup tattoo on his boa constrictor of a forearm. A quick first glance places him as possible ex-military. And based on his gruff demeanor, yet high productivity, it's a good chance he's the owner of the joint. Although he sure as hell doesn't look like a Louellen, so it must be a family business.

"Here we are," the hostess says, gesturing at the table before them in the corner by the jukebox. "Will this be okay for y'all?"

Clayton recedes to the back of the booth behind Antoni as Kara takes point and replies, "Yes, ma'am, this will be just fine. Thank you."

"You're most welcome," says the hostess, as she lays the menus down on the table. "Your waitress will be Annie, and she should be with you momentarily."

The trio orchestrates an unenthused "Thanks" in unison as the host walks back to her stand. Kara immediately reaches for the menus and passes them out with the speed of a professional poker dealer.

"OMG, I'm starving," she gasps, as she pries open the laminated menu, outmuscling the smattering of syrup and jelly residue working like glue between the pages. "How bad would you guys judge me if I ordered chicken and waffles *and* the eggs benedict with asparagus . . . plus a side of bacon . . . and maybe an extra biscuit?"

"Well, I'm about to go HAM on the biscuits and gravy, a veggie omelet with a side of sausage links, and one of those big-ass cinnamon rolls over there in the display window . . . that I have zero intention of sharing. So, you won't catch my fat ass passing any judgment," Antoni responds still eye fucking the rack of fluffy pastries. "What about you, Clay?"

But Clayton can't stop thinking about anything other than how close they came at the high school. The *what if* of it all. Just a few more seconds and everything could be different right now. He could be learning what Rebecca Klein was doing in Shermer the night she died, who she was with—literally anything to get one step closer to the truth. But he's here, at a podunk diner in BFE getting nowhere in the middle of nowhere.

"Clay?" Antoni shyly asks again. "What are you getting, man?"

"Huh? Oh, umm, I don't know. The number one, I guess," he answers apathetically.

Antoni puts his menu down and looks at his friend from across the table. Despite the excitement surrounding his appetite, his sincerity is evident.

"Look, Clay, I know the school didn't pan out. I'm sorry, man. Maybe we can try again tonight?"

"No, we're running out of ti—"

"Howdy, folks," interrupts a fourth and foreign voice. "My name is Annie, and I'll be taking care of y'all this morning."

Annie looks down at the three unfamiliar faces seated before her through caked-on turquoise eye shadow framed behind a set of ornate, thin-lensed bifocals with an ungodly matching eyeglass chain. They all look up to greet her, but none of them can find the words to respond to her unexpected arrival.

"Ahh, some fresh faces, huh? How exciting! Well, welcome to Louellen's," she says, immediately sensing the obvious group deflation. "Looks like y'all could use a little pick-me-up. Should I get three coffees goin'?"

A depressed nod sweeps the table in synchronization.

"Perfect! I'll be right back with a fresh pot then," she replies. Her energy as sizzling as the dye job on her fiery winter hair, like January embers still burning bright despite their old and cold, dire spirits.

Annie shimmies away from the table as her skirt sashays with the sway of her diamond hips. Antoni looks around to make sure no one is eavesdropping and then circles back to the topic at hand.

"All I'm saying is, we don't have to give up yet. We can try again later. Maybe tonight, a little after sunset or—"

Clayton rips the wrapper off his straw and aggressively plunges it into his ice water. The cubes kerrang off the side of the curved glass with an audible clang.

"Don't you get it, Toni? We're already too late. The bounty for my head is growing by the hour. Maybe even the minute. There may not be a tonight to go back to, and I'm no closer now than I was twenty-four hours ago to uncovering any concrete answers. This is the end of—"

"Okay, my Shermer strangers," Annie says behind a hint of provincial twang, as she startles the group once again. "Three coffees for three newbies."

She places the mugs down on the table without losing even a hint of curl or charm behind her Cheshire smile.

"Now, I know I'm probably biased, but I think our coffee here is the best. Better than any of those big city chains, if y'all ask me. Star-*what*, amirite?" she nervously jokes.

But as she looks down, she sees the lack of reciprocated energy and retreads her statement, slightly dimming her level of peppy shine.

"Then again, nobody did ask me," she says through a forced laugh and drops off some extra cream and sugar packets for the table. "Sorry, we don't get a lot of new folks around these parts, so when we do, I tend to gab. If you couldn't already tell. Kinda like I'm doing right now. So, what brings y'all to Shermer anyhow?—" she solicits, but simultaneously seems to catch herself in the act. "And see, there we go. Just like that I've done it again, my apologies. Y'all are probably hungry, so I'll just hush now and take your order."

She digs into her apron and fishes out a small, bedazzled pen and pad. "So, what can I get y'all?"

Kara orders her buffet line of breakfast essentials rivaled only by Antoni's massive all-you-can-eat feast, and finally, Clayton's meager number one. Annie writes it all down into her small server pad and then waddles off to another table where a couple of old-timers are reading what are sure to be exhilarating and drama-filled stories from the embarrassingly thin local newspaper.

Again, Antoni waits a few moments to make sure their private conversation stays that way before probing Clayton further.

"Tell us what you want to do, man," he nudges, manipulating his head movement in an attempt to cut off his friend's defeated daze. "We've got your back."

But Clayton's eyes are anywhere but locked in as he despairingly takes a sip of his coffee and proceeds to sink back into the booth. He draws a shallow breath in and slowly exhales as a pocket of steam from the mug shrouds his face. Placing his cup back onto the table with an overly dedicated diligence, he finally looks up and makes eye contact with Antoni.

"You want to know what I really want?"

"Yes! Tell us, please."

"Fine. Right now, I just want to sit here and not think for a minute," Clayton continues, nestling the back of his head into the seat while closing his eyes. "To do nothing but sit here and try to enjoy my coffee. Because it could very well be my last cup ever."

Antoni shoots a look of concern toward Kara, who answers with one of her own. Words hang on the edge of their lips, threatening to jump, but they both know there's nothing they can say or do right now that can help. So, they each take independent sips from their own mugs and sit in uncomfortable silence until the food arrives.

By the time Annie comes around with their breakfast banquet,

Kara and Antoni can hardly resist snatching the plates from her hands and digging in like a couple of safari-starved hyenas. In large part, it's because they're beyond famished but also because other than the golden oldies faintly spinning on the jukebox in the background, the awkward silence that Clayton started has finally bested their uncomfortable patience. Because at least when you're eating, silence is a welcomed departure from any awkward conversation.

It doesn't take long before the table brimming with loaded plates looks like nothing more than the inside of a dirty dishwasher. Antoni is the last one still eating, savoring every coiled bite of his warm, frosting-drenched cinnamon roll in between muffled, yet still noticeably audible, grunts of bliss.

Officially tapped out after her own valiant overindulgence, Kara reaches for the receipt Annie dropped off at the table along with the food.

"My treat, guys," she says, rummaging her oversized bag in search of her wallet.

"Ugh. I really hate being a girl sometimes," she murmurs aloud to no one in particular. "You know how hard it is to find your wallet, or anything for that matter, in the bottomless abyss of a bag?" Still aimlessly hunting. "I think we know so little about blackholes because we've been looking for them in the wrong place this whole time. They exist right here in women's handbags and purses, not the outer reaches of space."

By the time she finally locates her wallet from inside the canvas wormhole's void of space and time, she's managed to pull out her water bottle, eyeglasses case, a small bag of makeup, three random tubes of various lip balm, and the stolen prom picture. They're all spread out in front of her on the tabletop, strategically strewn between the landmines of empty dishes.

Annie approaches the table flaunting that friendly homegrown smile and hip-to-hip slip.

"Holy. Cow. Hungry was an understatement. Poor things, y'all were starvin'," she exclaims, surveying the amount of damage done to create the pile of happy plates before her. "I was gonna ask y'all if it was good, but I think actions speak louder than words at this point, amirite?"

She begins to clear the empty plates from the table when her eyes fall upon the personal items scattered about in front of Kara. They come to a full stop when they land on the old prom photo.

"Oh, my sweet baby Jesus, is that a picture of Shermer prom 1982? Egads! Now that's quite the trip down memory lane, y'all. A lonnnnng trip," she adds, looking up as if fondly rewinding the yesteryear night's nostalgia and then playing it back it in her mind. "That was such a fun night. So many memories. You know, I'd give anything to fit back into that dress again. Unfortunately, time and these gosh darn cinnamon rolls—" she guiltily jokes, taking Antoni's plate of frosting remnants away. "Well, they haven't exactly been kind to this ol' gal's figure."

An unexpected and renewed energy overtakes the table, as if let in by an open window. The lively gust infusing hope back into the trio, particularly Clayton. His mood shifts instantly like the flip of a backup battery switch in his brain.

"Uh, I'm sorry, ma'am," Clayton says, interrupting the recollection of her glory days. "Are you saying you were actually at this prom?"

"At it?" she scoffs, waving her hand in playful dismissal. "Sweetie, that's me in the hot pink sequin number in the middle front row." She points at the picture, cradling the stack of dirty dishes in her other arm. "Right there, looking all sorts of fine next to Chad Sommers and his date, Becky Gould, or Rebecca Klein as she went by after her marriage to the infamous Simon Klein. Guess you could say my claim to fame is that we were besties back before she ever became somebody. Still an absolute tragedy what happened to them."

A wave of adrenaline surges through Clayton's body. His fingers now tickling with anticipation, he tries his best to remain calm.

"I'm sorry, di—" He stammers a little and clears his throat. "—did you say . . . them?"

"Oh, yeah! Them," she reiterates, as if surprised by his utter lack of Shermer High history. "They were high school sweethearts, those two. A prized pair. Chad was the star quarterback for the football team and Becky was the most popular, and beautiful—I must reluctantly, but honorably, admit—girl in school."

Annie leans over to pick up an additional set of plates.

"The circumstances surrounding their cases are still eerie to this day." Looking down at their blind expressions, she can see they have no idea what she's talking about, yet they're hanging intently on her every word.

"But y'all don't know anything about that now, do you? And why would you?" Her voice grows louder and tone chattier. "I suppose things like what happened to them happen to people where y'all are from all the time, or should I say used to before The Hunt came along. But for Shermer, especially back then, heck, it was big-time news. A hit-and-run car accident and a missing person's case within just a couple days of each other. Two high school sweethearts who just so happened to be in town, attending the same Shermer High School fifteen-year reunion." She lets out a sigh. "I don't know. It still doesn't add up, if y'all ask me."

Clayton's former look of defeat has now been replaced by a wide-eyed lemur gaze as agape as his mouth, yearning for additional story time. He's so far forward on the edge of his seat that he's on the brink of sliding right out of the retro booth.

Annie adjusts the stack of plates in her arm and takes a quick look around the room. She leans in closer to the three, lowering her voice to a raspy whisper as if not to be overheard. Like it's townie gossip still fresh on the lips and in the minds of her fellow Shermerites.

"Just between me and y'all," she says softly, her breath faint with stale nodes of roasted nuttiness and a hint of menthol. "I think the whole thing screams something foul. Ya see, Chad and Becky had something special. Everyone who knew them back then knew it, too. And when she left Shermer for college life in the big city, Chad was devastated. They both were. But they were so young, puppy love and all that. They both had plenty of life yet to live on their own, and her parents, I think, pushed her to experience life outside of this place, being as they moved here from out west on account of her father's big oil deal early on in our junior year. And when I saw her and Chad at the fifteen-year reunion back in '97, it was like nothing had changed. They both still had that lost-love look in their eyes, and I think when they saw each other that night, they found it again." Her voice now just above a whisper. "Of course, what some people don't know is that they still wrote to each other after all those years. Emails. Love letters. Probably phone calls—you name it. Quite the secret scandal."

"What makes you so sure of that?" Kara asks, her chin firmly planted in her palms. Ears poised like satellites ready to receive more juicy transmission.

"Sweetheart, when you live in a small town, your gossip is everyone's gossip. And besides, Chad liked to make friends with the bottle, if you know what I mean, just like most men 'round here. One night he had a few too many over at The Giddy Up just across the street. See, I used to bartend nights there way back in the day. Back when I didn't need twice as much makeup to paint over all these wrinkles, and gravity hadn't betrayed the rest of me," she says with a turn and a laugh. Only the comedic relief isn't reciprocated by her audience who are all staring at her on edge with fixed eyes and loose jaws.

"Anyway . . ." she continues, "he kept going on reminiscing about the good ol' days—you know, high school football, Becky, this and that, and the like—and he let it slip that they had been talkin' again. Apparently, for quite some time," she adds, throwing in a slight "God is judging you" type of eye roll. "He said she was plannin' out her trip back for the fifteen-year Shermer High reunion and that they had 'other plans' after. Heck, he even showed me the wrinkled letter from her to prove she was serious about it. Pretty risqué since she was married to the up-and-comin', big-shot lawyer, Simon Klein, at the time. You know, before he became a household name with that whole

Hunt business. Not that I follow all that violent nonsense. Definitely a minority 'round here in that department," she adds, clarifying her stance while hiding her words with the back of her hand. "Anyway, he didn't make the trip out with her to Shermer for the reunion. No surprise there, though. I reckon a man with aspirations that big didn't have time for a small-town hoedown like the Shermer High reunion. But I just know the mystery surroundin' her death is what caused him to create The Hunt Initiative in the first place. Absolutely tragic, the whole thing. And now, all these years later, Becky's only daughter, Patricia, gets murdered by her own boyfriend. It's heartbreakin'. The Grim Reaper just seems to follow that family like they're the next wave of Kennedys or somethin'."

She fumbles the empty plates around again as their weight begins to wear on her arms. Clayton takes the small window of distraction to anchor down the brim of his Packers cap and angle more of his body toward the wall.

Finally, Annie gives up the losing battle of balancing their empty dishes and places them back on the table. Burden-free, she leans in and continues.

"You see, back when Becky died, there wasn't a lot of evidence with her case to go on, being a small town and all. And the cops 'round here"—she lowers her mild rasp to a hoarse whisper—"well, let's just say they're about as useless as a wool coat on an August afternoon. Which is why they chalked up the lack of leads 'round her death to a random hit-and-run. But if you ask me"—Annie leans in even closer after peeking over her shoulders—"Becky Gould wasn't accidentally killed in a hit-and-run that night. The night of the reunion she was murdered in cold blood. I just know it deep down. And the car that hit her wasn't Chad's, like some people 'round here like to speculate. As if he ran over the love of his life and just up and disappeared. He loved Becky more than anything, *anything*, I tell ya. And I say this lovingly 'cause I grew up with him, so I knew him well. Chad Sommers was a lot of things, but a murderin' criminal mastermind ain't one of 'em, darlin'. He wasn't exactly the type of guy who could outsmart the authorities on his whereabouts, if you catch my drift. No siree, Chad Sommers didn't kill Becky. And he certainly didn't just up and disappear, especially with his mom also being sick back then. He was murdered, too. They just never found the body or his truck. I know it. I truly do, deep down. I just can't prove it," she gasps, refilling her hoarse lungs with a much- needed extra breath. "And probably never will."

Practically sitting down now at the booth with them, Annie presses on. "I've never told anybody this, not even the authorities. Probably because they wouldn't've believed me, anyhow. And even if they had, they've always been more interested in getting to the bottom of Jack, Jim, and Johnnie than anything involving Becky. But the night of the reunion, I saw a strange man I'd never seen before outside in the school parking lot snooping around Becky's car when we were all leavin' the gymnasium. And I know he wasn't a husband of one of the women, because trust me, I know everyone and their significant others 'round here. It's a small town and an even smaller class, after all. But this guy . . . I bet I could still picture what he looked like if I closed my eyes."

Throwing inhibition to the wind, Clayton inches forward as much as the lack of remaining booth seat will allow him. "And what exactly did this guy look like?"

"Oh, hon, that was a long time ago, and god knows my memory ain't what it used to be. But I do remember he was an awful-looking man," she says, shaking her head. "The rough type, you know. The kind that made even the most hardened cowboys 'round these parts look like little Miss Priss. He was bald or at least baldin'. Stout with ugly tattoos on his arms and hands. Just a really intimidatin' presence. Oh, and he had some kind of red mark or somethin' on his face. Around his cheek, like a scar or a birthmark," she says, gesturing to her own rosy dimple. "Definitely didn't do him any favors in the looks department, I can tell ya that."

Clayton feels his entire being drop to the pit of his full stomach, followed by a vicious blow to the chest from a sudden bout of nausea. He comes touch-and-go close to bringing up the breakfast he just put down—one wrong swallow from spewing a half-digested number one all over the diner table. As he sinks back into the depths of the bench, there's only one face on his mind.

One name on his lips.

Marco.

Annie notices his sudden change in behavior and the wave of paleness that is now diluting the color on his face.

"Hon, are you okay?" she asks, studying Clayton with concerned motherly eyes. "You look like you just saw a ghost or somethin'."

She continues, glancing at the giant stack of dirty plates. "Did you eat too much?"

Stuck in this informational trance, Clayton pans his head until his eyes focus on the old tube television hanging over the bar. Right there for the entire diner to see is his face on full display. As he stares blankly at the boxed TV set, in a somewhat paralyzed spell, he notices the three men sitting at the bar turn in unison to face their table, suspicion painted all over their sun-hardened, pre-skin cancerous faces.

"Hon, you sure you're okay? Can I get you some more water?" He hears Annie ask him as he retakes the reins of his thoughts and corresponding motor skills.

"Uh, no. No, thank you, ma'am. I'm okay."

"We're not strangers here, sugar. You call me Annie," she orders.

"Annie . . . right," he mutters, as he kicks Antoni's leg underneath the table. His friend lets out a delayed groan of discomfort, partly from the kick but mostly from the overindulged gluttony of sodium and sugar-packed carbs currently testing the strength of his stomach wall. Emerging from his post-breakfast coma, he notices Clayton's concerned gaze and tracks it to the bar, turning to see the three men staring daggers at their table, talking among themselves. One of them even points at the TV set.

"Well, uh, thank you so much for the food and the story, Annie, but we better get going now. Still a long drive ahead of us," Antoni urges, as he hastily reaches over to grab the check and hand it to Annie with a pile of Kara's uncounted cash. "Keep the change. And thanks again. It's been, uh, enlightening, truly."

A big grin lights up Annie's face while she does a quick calculation, instantly noting that the money just given to her covers the tab and plenty more.

"Well, thank y'all," she beams. "It was my absolute pleasure. Y'all know who to come see if you ever come through these parts again, ya hear? Don't be strangers now."

"Of course, Annie. Will do," Antoni says, delivering his best pleasantries to conceal the forceful act of his shoving Kara out of the booth to leave.

"Geez. I can get out on my own, you know?" she gripes.

"Then do it, kid," he mutters in an aggressive tone while directing a clenched smile Annie's way. "We gotta go," he adds, nodding toward the men at the bar with two quick wags. "Right. Now."

Instantly, Kara notes the men, and the urgency of the situation becomes plain. She begins shoveling all of her shit back into her bag as fast as she can.

The three get up, and as quickly, yet calmly, as possible begin shuffling for the front door. Trying their best to ignore the mean-mugging from the gruff trio at the bar, they take the long route to the exit, weaving between narrow aisles of several seated two- and four-top tables along the way. They finally make it to the front door still in the clear, doing their best to remain calm. Once outside, however, the façade of coolness dissipates, and they make a mad dash for the truck that's just shy of an all-out sprint.

"Do you think they made us?" Antoni asks, hammering the unlock button on the key fob with the same thumbed vigor of a lost person desperately trying to locate where they parked.

"I don't know, but I don't plan on sticking around long enough to find out," Clayton responds, as they pile into the pickup.

Antoni wastes no time attempting to slide the key into the ignition, but before he can turn it over, there's a bang on the hood. They look up to see one of the three men from the bar standing in front of the pickup with his fists firmly planted on the truck's black lid. The other two spread out in a textbook flank formation.

"Where y'all going in such a hurry?" the man by the hood asks in a mocking tone. His bottom lip ballooning with an overzealous pinch of chew. Out of the three, he's the only one wearing a hat. A rusty fishhook is pinned on its faded and frayed bill.

The other two rednecks close in on the driver and passenger windows.

"Look, we don't want any trouble," Antoni speaks up, his hand still holding the keys in a half-twist position, hovering just outside of the ignition. "We were just leaving."

The man blocking their path forward sports a slight smirk; it registers more as a sinister sneer. A threatening expression to indicate he's not here to give them a friendly small-town sendoff.

"See, that's where you're wrong. Y'all ain't goin' nowhere," he snarls and shoots his camo cohorts a signal. "Not unless it's wit us. Get 'em, boys," he yells, as the man on the passenger side in a mossy oak camo hoodie cocks his elbow back and catapults it into the window like a battering ram. The glass shatters against the brute force as Clayton and Kara turn away to avoid the explosion of incoming shards.

Meanwhile, the man on the driver's side wearing a plaid, pearl snaps western shirt scales the back of the Silverado. His heavy cowboy boots clang against the metal tailgate as he hops into the truck bed. In front of the ride, fishhook hat finally makes his move and jumps on top of the hood. He begins mercilessly kicking at the windshield with his steel-toed boots. The glass spider webs from his successive blows but doesn't break.

"Toni, start the fucking truck," Clayton shouts, as he attempts with his one good arm to ward off the man in the hoodie from prying open the passenger door.

Antoni fumbles the keys in the ensuing panic, dropping them onto the floorboard.

"Toni!" Clayton gags, as a pair of calloused hands wrap around his throat in a diamond-shaped, vise grip. He can feel his breath shallowing with every cinch of the man's grasp, despite Kara's feeble attempts to help fend him off.

As Antoni hastily pokes around the floorboard for the keys, Kara feels a bicep slide around her own neck. The man in the truck bed has managed to open the rear slider window and snake his arm inside. She feels her legs leave contact with the seat as he attempts to pull her outside from the small opening. With just enough poise in between bouts of kicking and screaming, she turns her head toward the man's forearm and bites down—as hard as her jaws will clench until she tastes metal. Instantly, he releases her along with a yelp as she falls back into contact with the bench seat.

Antoni finally locates the keys and scoops them up. Stabbing them into the ignition with a shaky fist, he starts the truck and throws the shifter into Drive. His foot presses down on the pedal with all his force until it's met by resistance from the floorboard. Just like that, the truck peels out, leaving only the sound of screeching and the smell of burnt rubber in its place.

Immediately, the man atop the hood is flung from the jolt of acceleration. His fall is broken by the unforgiving concrete below. Still squealing and burning in a black cloud, the Silverado's wheels fight the pavement in a combative effort to straighten itself as the truck fishtails out of the parking lot and back onto the main drag.

With every slight millimeter increase on the speedometer's dial, the man's stranglehold on Clayton lessens until he can't hold on any longer or move his feet fast enough to keep pace with the accelerating truck. In desperation, he releases his chokehold for a more stable grip on the truck's window seal, but after a couple blocks up the barren two-way road, his legs give out from being dragged along the blacktop like a ragdoll.

Finally freed, Clayton undergoes a coughing fit as fresh air returns to his hungry lungs. Peeking into the trailing distance from his side mirror, he watches the assailant climb to his feet as a second red truck stops to pick him up.

"Fuck," he hacks in between another round of coughs, rubbing his throat to alleviate the spasm. "They're tailing us."

"No shit, tell me something I don't already know," Antoni barks back without taking his eyes from the road or his foot off the gas.

"Uh, guys . . . that's a future problem," Kara exclaims while pointing behind her. "What are we going to do about him?"

Everyone in the car turns around simultaneously to see the third man crouching in the bed of the truck, working his way back toward the rear windshield opening. But before they can address the dire issue behind them, Clayton whips back around and spots a white, wide-loaded Ford Dually accelerating toward them, head-on with its six overcompensating wheels in powerful tow. Just behind the Ford appears to be a silver truck with a tan SUV dragging up the caboose. It's officially a Hunting party with a growing procession of new recruits looking to play a good old-fashioned game of chicken.

"Uh . . . Toni, we've got more company."

Antoni flings his head back around in time to see the approaching Ford and its trailing parade gaining precious ground. They're less than a hundred yards away and closing fast.

"You gotta be shitting me," he sighs. "News really *does* travel fast in a small town."

"Oh god! What are we going to do?" Kara chimes in. Her once confident voice now quivering with panic. "We're trapped."

With little to no time left to think, Antoni has to make a decision.

Now. He looks back at the red pickup closing the gap behind them before refocusing his attention on the man in the truck bed who is once again doing his best to fight Kara and Clayton for control of the sliding rear window.

"Everyone, buckle up," he orders.

"Oh god, oh god, oh god," Kara squeals as she fastens her seatbelt and her eyes.

"What are you planning to do?" Clayton shouts, buckling his own belt.

"Just shut up and hold on tight!" Antoni roars.

At the last possible second, he cranks the steering wheel as hard left as the column can go. For an old truck, it handles well. The wheels responsively cut across the two-way road before flying over its shallow ditch and colliding with a makeshift barbed wire fence that spans a neighboring cornfield.

By the time Kara opens her eyes, her senses are met with the sight of ripe corn husks flinging wildly off the Silverado's cracked windshield and the not-so-distant sound of metal-on-metal aggressively slamming into itself at a high velocity behind her. She looks back to see the two main assailing trucks totaled from their head-on collision. The six-tire Dually is the clear winning loser in their grill-to-grill exchange, evidenced by the engulfing flames that stem from under what's left of the red pickup's accordioned hood.

"Holy shit!" she screams, as she turns back around. "Do you think they're dead?"

An even bigger boom echoes throughout the still countryside as the pickup's frenzied flames finally contact its ruptured gas tank.

"If they weren't then, they definitely are now," Antoni replies, doing his best to navigate through the dense barrage of harvest-ready starch. "But that's the first game of chicken I'm happy to say I lost."

Ahead, only slivers of blue sky are visible through the tall forest of maize.

"I can't see shit," Antoni continues, craning his head for any possible position that may offer better visibility.

Ears of corn continue to thwomp against the truck, assaulting their trek forward the deeper they drive into the abundant field. Behind them, the straggling silver truck and tan SUV, which Clayton can now see is an old Jeep Wrangler missing its iconic front grill, follow suit in their freshly plowed path.

"Seeing ahead is the least of our problems right now," he says while gesturing over his shoulder. "We've still got company behind us."

Antoni peers over to his driver-side mirror as a gunshot rings out. Where there was once a reflection, there now isn't.

"Fuckin' A, they've got guns now?" he yells, ducking down in his seat.

"God, guns, and glory," Clayton complements, taking his own cover while bringing Kara down with him.

Another series of shots ring out. Some harmlessly spatter the tailgate, while most whiz past, striking down innocent husks in the surrounding ocean of ears. The stray fire that does connect with the unsuspecting cobs causes tiny explosions of kernels like undercooked microwave popcorn.

After one too many times of being fired at, the realization that they also have guns infiltrates Clayton's mind. He fumbles under the seat for the duffle in their pursuit. But with no immediate luck, he rises back up.

"Toni, where's the duffle?" he shouts under duress. "Or the pistol you had on you?"

"I threw everything in the back of the bed when we got breakfast."

"You what?"

"I said I threw everything in the back of the—Oh, shit."

As if their heads were placed on synchronized swivels, they turn and face each other. With "Oh, shit" still firmly plastered all over their mirrored expressions, the disastrous panic hits.

Craning further back in perfect unison, they catch their truck bed assailant scrounging around through the bag in question. Within seconds, he's already found the pistol.

"Kara, get down!" Clayton shouts, as a lone gunshot shatters the rear-sliding window into tiny glass fragments. Their jagged edges adhere to her hair like burrs of crystal shrapnel as she cries out.

"Are you okay?" Clayton asks, bracing his arm around her.

"I'm okay," she whimpers. "I think."

Another unsteady shot burrows into the truck's center dashboard.

Kara shrieks again. "I lied! I'm not okay."

Fed up with the point-blank target practice, Antoni starts a game of tug-of-war with the steering wheel, snaking the truck violently back and forth in the hope of catching their relentless tailgater off guard. It appears to work as he loses balance and falls back into the steel bed, clanging his arm against the passenger-side wheel tub on the way down. The forced collision is enough to knock the gun out of his hand and across the bed in the process.

Clayton eyes the firearm rattling aimlessly along the truck bed floor, but it's still too far to reach. He knows if the man gets back to the gun, they may not be so lucky next time he takes aim.

Without saying a word, he unfastens his seat belt, slings it over his good shoulder, and dives over the bench seat out the shattered rear window.

"Clay, what the hell are you doing?" Antoni yells out mid-pursuit. "Get back here."

But it's too late. Before he can grab ahold of his friend to try to pull him back inside, Clayton is already steadying his sea legs on the bumpy bed—eyes locked with the man in the plaid pearl snaps, who has also worked his way back up to the sure side of his boots.

They stand facing one another in a swaying showdown while awkwardly trying their best to maintain enough balance. Clayton watches as the man's eyes fall to the gun that's clattering in between them on the bouncy bed. He makes the first move and lunges for it, but Clayton delivers an off-balance kick to his face before he can reach it.

Instantly, another round of gunfire from the trailing truck strikes the tailgate. The close clang sends Clayton ducking for cover.

In the swift move for safety, he feels a leathery hand grab his injured arm and drag him all the way down. An all-out scuffle erupts as the two men wrestle for the loose gun, tossing and turning wildly in a primal bout for survival as the truck continues its blind trek through the sprawling field. Clayton is the first to gain control of the fight and the gun after locking in a full mount, thanks to a well-aimed cross against the man's chew-packed jaw. But he quickly loses the upper hand when the man digs a thumb into the hole of his injured shoulder, deep enough to reopen the aggravated wound.

The familiar wave of pain causes Clayton to hunker over as the man wiggles free from under him. He follows up the dirty tactic with a succession of well-placed body blows that jostle the gun loose again. It lands back onto the truck bed, but neither fighter seems to make an immediate play for it.

Instead, they continue their wrestling match, wrapping one another up in a crouched grapple. Too injured to overpower his opponent or gain enough leverage, Clayton loses his ground and is thrust to the brink of the pickup's passenger-side edge. He just barely catches himself on the rim from tumbling overboard.

Before he can even fully regain his balance from the ledge, the man presses forward. He quickly advances, ramming his entire body along with its unsteady momentum against Clayton's top-heavy shoulders. He continues to shove with all his might, but in his lopsided attempt to cast Clayton overboard, the assailant compromises his own balance as the truck hits a deep, unexpected divot in the lush field. The fortuitous jolt affords Clayton just enough of an opening to trade positions and retake the middle of the truck's ring.

Now, back in control, he uses every ounce of his 180-pound frame to push the man's face over the side of the truck into the passing green blur of razor-sharp corn leaves. The green haze begins to turn a tannish brown as blood from the man's sliced-up face joins the crop's earthy color palette. Clayton continues to hold his head overboard until he feels the man's body finally give up the struggle.

With all the strength he has left in his one-and-a-half functioning arms, he pulls in the limp body from over the truck's side railing and shoves the lifeless figure. The wilted man staggers back on his wobbly legs until they catch the lip of the closed tailgate. Physics do the rest as the unstable momentum causes his upper body to topple head over feet out of the truck bed like a ragdoll. Mere moments after his barely conscious figure lands into the truck's plowed path, Clayton watches while the silver pickup hits an unexpected speed bump.

"Clay, are you okay?" Kara screams through the shattered rear window.

Her shrieks are followed by Antoni's series of shouts. "Clay? Clay? CLAY!"

As his spike in adrenaline finally starts to simmer, the muffled sound of their yelling gains clarity.

"Clay, answer us, goddammit!" Antoni continues.

But he doesn't. He just grabs the duffle bag and tosses it inside the truck through the broken rear window before following suit. Exhausted and battered, he melts into the bench seat, rubbing his numb, trickling shoulder—a subtle gesture to ensure it's still there.

"Clay, what in the actual fuck was that?" Antoni yells, as Clayton attempts to catch his breath. "The next time you think to pull some dumb shit like that, give me a heads-up first, so I can tell you not to do *dumb shit like that*."

With a short-lived hint of calmness returning to his nerves, Clayton looks back over his shoulder only to see the other two vehicles still trailing behind, gaining ground. The fresh wave of adrenaline floods any lingering trace of regained poise.

"Okay, all-wise one," he says without turning around. "What's your foolproof, non-dumb shit plan to lose them?"

Right on cue, a loud pop is heard as another bullet strikes the rear driver's side of the pickup. The trio slinks down into their seats in perfect unison. Seconds later, a couple more metallic bangs resonate as two additional slugs sink into the back of the truck bed just below the busted window.

Practically lying on the floor, Kara looks up to see a frayed hole in the back of the leather seat where her head was all but five seconds ago.

"Guys!" she shrieks, as another bullet pierces the metal frame, joining the previous seat hole. "Doc can't take much more of this. We got to lose them, like now."

Clayton looks out from his smashed passenger window. His view is still limited as countless stalks of corn streak by in a solid green blur, their leaves and tassels threatening to breach the truck with every passing second. Yet just above the wall of green distortion, he sees what appears to be a haze of dust hovering in a nearby sliver of sky.

Pointing into the horizon, he gets Antoni's attention.

"You see that cloud of dust in the distance?"

Antoni cranes his neck, practically lying in Kara's lap for a better view. After squinting his eyes until near closure, he finally spots a faint cloud of earthy debris about a hundred or so yards out—and it seems to be moving.

Kara peers out into the distance and spots it, too.

"Someone's harvesting," she says. "And as big as this field is, it's got to be a pretty decent-sized combine, probably a sixteen-row head, maybe even bigger."

"And you know that because?" Antoni counters.

"Because my grandparents' neighbors growing up had a huge corn field just like this one, and they had a twenty-four-header they used to let me ride."

Antoni and Clayton lock eyes as if a shared light bulb has just illuminated in their minds.

"Toni, are you thinking what—?"

"—Way ahead of you," Antoni cuts in, and slams on the gas.

He veers the truck right until the traveling cloud of dust in the distance is on a perpendicular path with the Chevy. Husks, ears, and stalks forcefully snap and flap under tow as the truck presses forward on its new diagonal route. Their assailants mirror the maneuver as Antoni gives the pedal a little more pressure. Again, the action is reciprocated along with a few added gunshots that whistle by, just missing their desired target.

Within a matter of seconds, the distance between the Chevy and the intersecting cloud of dust is cut in half. A moment later, it's halved again. And again, until they're so close to the soiled haze that they're actually in it.

"Hold on tight to something," Antoni laments, as he leans forward to brace himself with a death grip on the steering wheel. "We're about to go back for a second helping of chicken."

An instant later, the truck tears into a clearing in the field at top speed. On the other side of the breach, it's met by the roar of a massive diesel combine harvesting its seasonal crop. Each one of its growling twenty-four-row headers bulldozes a destructive path forward, devouring the entire crop in its hungry wake. Like a set of mechanical canines, its sharp pincers savagely strip the ears off the stalks while ferociously feeding the threshing cylinder bushels of the chopped crop through the spinning blades of its cutting bar.

It's a new game of chicken. Only this time, there's nowhere to go but straight ahead. Nowhere to turn and not enough time to stop. Six pairs of white knuckles grasp for anything they can find to brace themselves for impact.

"We're not gonna make it," Clayton roars, clenching every possible orifice on his body.

"Yes, we are," Antoni barks back.

"No, we're not."

"Yes. We. *Arghhhhhh*."

Antoni shuts his eyes and floors it as fast as the thirty-five-plus-year-old set of wheels will allow. The deadly wager turns out to be just enough, almost.

As the truck punches it past the combine's path of determined demolition, they're not quite lucky enough to make it out unscathed as the last header clips the pickup's back bumper. The small collision immediately causes the truck to fishtail. Belligerently swinging wide right, Antoni overcorrects the off-course maneuver by yanking the wheel in the opposite direction, a cutting gamble on the truck's center of gravity that should flip the vehicle under normal road conditions and laws of physics. But as the truck reaches the end of the clearing, a new barrier of unplowed corn provides just enough cushioning force to counteract its inevitable tumble.

Their pursuers, on the other hand, aren't afforded the same combination of fortunate timing and sheer dumb luck.

The silver truck that was trailing right behind them makes it halfway past the combine's plow path safely, but it's not near enough. Instantly, it's ensnarled in the center teeth of the ravenous row of headers, meeting its demise somewhere along the thirteenth or fifteenth incisor. The collision provides enough undertow lift to send the vehicle into a violent barrel roll. Metal, plastic, and glass unravel in heaping clusters of shrapnel, flinging 360 degrees with each and every flip until the truck finds itself capsized on the cleared field—barely even in one piece.

The Jeep doesn't fare any better. In an effort to avoid the same unforgiving flip of fate, the driver slams on the breaks, but it's too late and he's going too fast. There's not enough time or space, and the loose, nutrient-rich soil doesn't provide enough traction to allow for a safe stop. Instead, the Jeep barrels right into the side of the monstrous combine in a devastating T-bone collision that leaves little to the imagination.

Antoni stomps down on the brakes, and the truck's locked tires get to work, digging deep into the healthy soil. Clumps of earth and freshly cut vegetation fling everywhere as it comes to a skidding halt just inside the freshly plowed patch of cornfield. The three look back to survey the damage, but the dense fog of circulating dust is now combined with a thick overhang of black smoke permeating from the dual collisions. The entire scene is nearly indiscernible.

The creak of the combine's door can be heard as it flings open, quickly accompanied by inaudible wails from the innocent farmer who has heroically, yet hopelessly, hopped down to survey the wreckage and check for survivors.

For a moment, the three do nothing but sit as still as the idle truck, collecting themselves as they overlook the site of destruction. It's quiet enough in the cabin that their elevated heartbeats and heavy breathing can be heard pounding in rhythmic layers of synchronized harmony like orchestrated panic. Nobody says a word. Not a peep. Just fast, weighty breaths interspersed between the uncontrolled pounding of 150-plus beats per minute fill the space.

They all shoot one another concerned looks that say enough without saying anything. Clayton nods as Kara reciprocates the gesture. Antoni chimes in as well and takes the cue. He hits the gas, and the three drive off down the freshly plowed corn path back toward the road.

A road.

Any road.

Whatever it takes to get them away from danger and the hell out of Shermer.

A mile or so later, the beat-up truck comes to a clearing that leads to a narrow gravel lane. Antoni makes the bumpy turn back onto the unpaved street as silence and shock still loiter among the trio, making their party of three feel like a quintet. Lucky to be alive and, for the moment, fortunate to be alone, Kara is the first one to break the hush.

"Wow," she says, looking dead ahead still reaping the miracle of their grim escape from the scythe of Death. "You guys really know how to treat a lady to a weekend getaway."

Clayton and Antoni both blankly turn to face her before exchanging glances at each other. Seconds later the entire car is laughing in unified hysteria, replacing the silent stillness of shock with a much louder coping emotion. After the laughter subsides and the adrenaline with it, the reality of the situation slides back into the forefront of Clayton's mind. The gears and cogs begin to turn as the latest pieces to the puzzle fall into place even further, evolving a new plan.

"All this time. All these years. Simon Klein has been made out to be some kind of modern savior for his creation of The Hunt Initiative.

Blindly revered for revolutionizing a new justice system based on its oldest form—vengeance," Clayton says, reciting his inner monologue out loud. "But it wasn't formed out of sorrow. Or a flawed sense of justifiable revenge. That's just what he wanted everybody to believe. The reality is, he had his wife and her ex-lover murdered in cold blood to create it. To profit from it. To use as the foundation for building his entire bullshit legacy. And why? For what? Two of the most basic human instincts of them all—jealously and greed."

"Guess that's why they're called deadly sins," Antoni chimes in.

"The whole thing makes me want to throw up," Kara adds with a hard swallow.

Clayton tries to rewind some of his past engagements with Klein in his mind. Like a roll of film, they flutter by with the biggest highlights spliced together to form an unrehearsed replay reel. He recalls the time he went with Klein and Trish to visit Rebecca's grave on what would have been their thirtieth wedding anniversary. He vividly remembers how the son of a bitch held his weeping daughter. Not a drop of sorrow clouding his eyes. How he just stood there with his arm around her, telling her how much he had loved her mother. Missed her. Mourned her. Lying right through his murderous billionaire grin.

More memories try to play, force-feeding themselves through his memory reel, but Clayton's able to pull himself back to the present moment.

"I guess I always knew he was an asshole, but I had no idea he was such a monster."

"Clay, the man tried to have you killed," Antoni reminds him. The thought of which prompts a skim of the rearview for any sign of being followed, but there isn't a single car in sight. "Of course, the guy's a fucking monster."

"But, Toni, his own wife? The mother of his only child? And for what—Notoriety? Money? Control? All because she cheated on him? He may not have pulled the trigger, but he killed Trish, too. His own goddamn daughter."

"No, you're right, man," Antoni adds, apologetically. "He's evil incarnate with a résumé of the Antichrist. If I were you, I'd give anything to get back what he took away, too." He looks down at the finger on his left hand that holds a gold wedding band and the accompanying DB88 tattoo on the same hand's thumb. His thoughts drift to Sonya and Thad, praying they're all right. Aware that Desmond Baine and his own past sins nearly led to him losing the loves of his own life. "Bastard deserves a dose of practicing what he's preached. Let's take him down, once and for all."

Clayton nods in agreement but the rallying moment comes to an abrupt halt from a quiet voice between them.

"Umm, guys? Not to take over Antoni's role of Debbie Downer, but how exactly do you plan to do that?" Kara cuts in with an unwelcomed but much-needed reality check. "All we have is a plot hole-filled story from a way too caffeinated, gossip-oversharing waitress. Not to mention, zero evidence. Besides, your face is literally all over that city. I haven't checked your bounty lately, for obvious reasons—like almost dying back there and all—but I guarantee you it's even more now. I mean, it's not like we can just walk right into The Hunt for Justice and stroll up to Klein's office for a nice chat to sort everything out."

With cool eyes and a sly smile, Clayton turns to face Kara as she finishes her reality rant.

"Actually, it might just be exactly like that."

Clayton breaks eye contact with Kara to look at the sweeping countryside ahead. The sherbet layers of orange and yellow sunrays beaming through the vanilla-scooped clouds make him think of Trish, eating her favorite summer treat. Or, any season treat, really. With her sweet tooth, she never could turn down anything comprised almost entirely of sugar. If he didn't already know the danger that the road ahead had in store for him, he'd relish the beauty in this moment. But for now, there's nothing between them and Bannerton except for hundreds of miles of wide-open pastureland. And nothing on his mind except for what to do next.

"First things first," he says.

"Which is?" Kara asks.

"Ditch this truck," Antoni interjects.

"Exactly," Clayton responds. "If any word got out from the diner about what truck we're driving, there could be drone units scanning this road right now. Or worse yet, another backwoods Hunt party sniffing out our trail." He sticks his arm out the shattered window. A few bigger shards still remain snugged into the framed corners. "Not to mention, Doc's new makeover doesn't exactly scream discreet."

He looks apologetically back at Kara. "Sorry about that."

"And how exactly do we go about getting a new car?" she asks, grasping for a response that's actually grounded in some form of reality. "Unless one of you guys just happens to know how to hotwire a vehicle?"

The two friends shoot one another a wiry grin.

"Of course, you do." She shakes her head. "Why am I *not* surprised?"

Crossing her arms, she leans back against the center seat. She adjusts herself slightly to the left, avoiding the leather's frayed discomfort from its fresh cluster of bullet holes.

"Ugh, fine. But you guys owe me a new truck when this is all over."

"Get in line, kid," Antoni says like it's a known matter of fact. He shoots a scowl at Clayton, who avoids his peripheral scorn by shooting his own blank gaze out of the busted passenger window. "Don't think I've forgotten about Westport, Clay."

A few miles up the road, they spot the first semblance of civilization, a small farmhouse nestled a couple hundred yards past a sprawling wheatfield to the east. Antoni pulls the truck deep enough into the tall grain so it's not visible from the main drag. From about a football field away, they case the quaint homestead in the bed of the truck, watching for any hint of commotion. Any sign of life.

After ten minutes of nothing but the sound of country creatures orchestrating their Midwestern opus, they give it the all-clear and gather everything they need from the truck. Quietly, they slink their way in the home's direction. Halfway through the trek, the detail of the house starts to paint a clearer picture of the task at hand.

The rural dwelling is a traditional white farmhouse with natural wood accents and fresh Z-bar shutters. A decent-sized front porch, appropriately adorned with its very own complementary white porch swing, wraps around the exterior connecting the south and west quadrants, like a scene right out of *Little House on the Prairie* but on steroids. Behind the house to the north is a large, detached three-door garage, and stretching even further back than that, lies an old barn in the midst of being added onto and painted. It's freshly festooned with its own recently renovated, shutter-matching Z-bar barn door.

"All right," Clayton says, as the three lurch down behind a grove of trees somewhere in the generous acreage that is the farm's front lawn. "We break into the garage, pray they've got a set of wheels easy enough to boost, and then we—"

"Pinch a loaf and plant some corn," Antoni cuts in.

"OMG. Seriously?" Kara huffs. "Another poop-leaving joke? Right now, of all times? We almost *died* back there. You're unbelievable."

"Oh, c'mon. Even you've got to appreciate that one, what with our recent cornfield chase and all. In Journalism, they call that timeli—"

"Shhh, focus," Clayton hisses, attempting to swiftly nip any potential squabbling.

Once he's got all four eyes and ears trained back on him, he finishes relaying the plan.

"Okay. Kara, you're on lookout duty while Toni and I scope out the inside. Just stand outside the garage and make sure the coast is clear. Got that?"

"Outside? Really? That's so lame," she whines, her inflection indicative of her combined aggravation. "What am I supposed to do? Caw like a bird if I see someone?"

"I was going to say just bang on the garage door . . . but whatever floats your boat," Clayton responds with a shrug.

"Ugh. Whatever. Just hurry up," she boos, shooing them off in irritation.

The two friends approach the garage, staying below the windows as they hug the barn's perimeter and skulk around back. They try the side door despite having a pretty solid guess of already knowing the outcome.

Locked, as expected.

"Looks like we're going to have to improvise," Antoni says.

But Clayton's already a step ahead of him, removing his shirt and wrapping it around the hand on his good arm. He punches the smallest glass square closest to the deadbolt on the paneled door. It crumbles to shards from the stiff jab. Reaching his hand through the new hole, he flips the lock and the two are once again surrounded by near darkness in yet another unfamiliar room.

Antoni teases, "Well, this is beginning to feel a little too normal."

"Yeahhh. I'm really starting to hate the dark," Clayton replies. "All right. Let's split up and see what we can find."

The two part ways as Clayton goes right and Antoni veers left. Bumbling around in the dim obscurity, they come across the presence of a tarp-covered vehicle, but as Antoni pulls back the dust-laden drape it becomes clear upon closer inspection that it's just a large John Deere lawn tractor.

"Damn, that that won't cut it," Antoni whispers, gliding his hands across the shiny green veneer.

"Actually, that's exactly what it does," Clayton jokes. "But it's not going to help us get back to Bannerton anytime this week."

"Hey! I make the dad jokes around here, okay," Antoni reciprocates, as they share a short laugh.

For Clayton, it feels good to smile. To laugh. To make jokes again, even if there's still a long, unsure road ahead. It's just his life on the line. No big deal. But hearing Annie's story at the café instilled a new sense of hope within him. A sort of light at the end of the tunnel in his head. A dim one, far, far in the distance, but a light, nonetheless. The thought that all they've lost to get here hasn't been for nothing. That even though the odds are ridiculously stacked against them, they have a fighting chance to even the score. But first, they need a new set of wheels to get them off the starting line and away from this armpit of a town.

"I'm gonna check the other side of the garage," Clayton indicates with a point into the even darker abyss. "Why don't you scour the back to see if there's anything useful."

Antoni nods and walks toward the rear of the garage while Clayton makes his way past the tractor to the other side. Seconds later, two tiny illuminations of smartphone lights can be seen departing on separate paths adjacent to one another, dancing in the dust and darkness.

Within a few paces, Clayton spots a vehicle parked on the other side of the garage. He's pleased to discover it's an actual car this time. A beige Buick, that by first glance through the passenger window at its outdated dashboard, appears to be at least fifteen to twenty years old.

"Bingo," he mutters to himself, as he opens the unlocked driver's door.

The duffle bag thumps onto the concrete floor, and Clayton gets to work instantly removing the plastic cover on the steering column, one screw at a time. Within a matter of minutes, he's got the housed cluster of wires gutted and connected with their appropriate counterparts. A kiss of the starter wire to the connected battery wires and the engine purrs to life. Being careful not to be too loud, he gives the gas pedal a few gentle nudges, revving the engine so that the car doesn't stall out. The only thing left to do is break the steering lock, but with his bum shoulder he can't seem to get enough torque on the screwdriver using the trusted elbow grease method.

"Urggh, just a little more. C'mon . . . dammit," he grunts from the failed effort and twinge of tenderness. The dose of pain meds Sonya gave him before they left the shop have long worn off, and with the back-to-back lab and school break-ins, topped off with their chaotic corn chase, he hasn't had the chance or the thought to pop another.

That's when Antoni opens the passenger door from his own solo raid party with a handful of found goodies. Among the loot is a red, five-gallon tank of gasoline that he sloshes in front of Clayton's grimacing face.

"Check it. No rest stops for us on the way back," he cheers, placing the tank on the back floorboard.

As he slides into the passenger seat, he dangles another item in Clayton's view.

"Oh, I figured you might also need this," he says and hands Clayton a hammer.

"Good call," Clayton replies, grabbing the tool and pinning it in the wheel. Now with more than enough leverage, he gives it a solid crank until a hard crunch is heard and there's no more interior resistance.

Antoni reaches up to the sun visor for the garage opener, but Clayton grabs his hand before he can thumb the button.

"Wait. We should play this one smart," he says, slowly removing his grasp. "Let's keep it quiet. Go manual."

He nods in the direction of the garage door's red dangling pull handle.

"You wanna help a brother out?"

Antoni snickers and replies, "My pleasure. Besides, we both know you can't lift it right now anyhow, Rick Allen."

Confused. "Rick Allen? Who the hell is *Rick Allen*?" Clayton inflects.

"What do you mea—? It's Rick. Allen. Rick Allen?" Antoni questions, his palms to the sky. Equally annoyed that Clayton not only doesn't get the reference but that he also ruined a perfectly good punchline. "You know Rick Allen. The one and only Rick "Fucking" Allen!"

"Right. Because stupidly saying his name over and over again without context is going to magically help?"

"Oh, c'mon! I know it's been a hot minute, but my dad only used to play him, I mean them, all the time back in shop growing up, remember?" Antoni educates like it's a personal game of Wednesday night music trivia. "Rick . . . Allen . . . the goddamn Def Leppard drummer."

"Ohhh, that's right. I totally forgot. Damn, that man really did love his '80s heavy metal—AC/DC, Metallica, Iron Maiden—they were always on loop, too. But I still don't get the—*ohhh*," Clayton hmms, as the lightbulb finally flickers on. "Real clever. Rick Allen. Because the dude only has one arm," he replies, toting his injured shoulder along with a thick intonation of sarcasm. "You know what else I forgot?"

"What's that, Ricky?"

"That you always did think you were way funnier than you actually are."

"Haha—I mean, if the glove, and I do mean glove, *singular* in your case, fits," Antoni teases, barely able to complete the punchline between self-induced hilarity.

"Just go open the damn door, will ya, funny guy?"

"All right, all right . . . you don't have to get all *Hysteria* on me."

"Keep it up, and I'm going to *Pour Some Hurt on You* in a goddamn second."

Still giggling, Antoni swings open the Buick's passenger door and slowly slinks out of the once-upon-a-time, top-of-the-line luxury sedan. Clayton loses him on the other side of the garage as his figure vanishes into the darkness. All he can hear is the faint pitter-patter of his feet growing quieter in the distance. Then, a sustained period of silence is followed by the dulled sound of steel working against itself as Antoni does his best to muffle the screech of grinding metal. With each segmented sound of chain clanking along the rising track, another horizontal layer of outside light spills into the garage until there's just enough room for Clayton to pull the car out.

As soon as he's clear, Kara opens the boosted vehicle's back door and hops in.

"Took you guys long enough," she says, shutting the door as Clayton quietly drives off. "I was expecting Zebadiah and Billy Bob to run out of the house with shotguns blazing at any second."

Antoni deviously turns around from the passenger seat.

"Nah, they're probably waiting to do their killing until after church, like good Christians," he jokes. "Oh, and remember when we were leaving the lab and I told you, you'd be riding Backseat Bitch? Well, backseat, meet Kara's ass. Kara's ass, meet the backseat. I think you two are really going to hit it off."

"Tell me. When you fell out of the asshole tree, did you purposefully hit every branch on the way down?" she counters.

"Well, I have always said that anything worth doing is worth doing right," he quips and twists back around.

With a fresh set of wheels and a plan in the can, Clayton does something he hasn't been comfortable doing over the past couple days. He lets his guard down, chiming in rather than chastising their incessant banter.

"No, Kara. Falling out of the tree would imply that his becoming an asshole was by pure accident, when in fact, Toni's been practicing being an asshole since the day he found out he had one."

"Well played," Antoni says with a smile, holding Clayton's stare. "Not sure how I feel about this new two-on-one dynamic, though."

"Well, you've got about six hours to get used to it, so buckle up, buttercup," Clayton adds as they turn back on the road toward

Bannerton with the sun high in the sky and their fates hanging on the horizon.

The first uneventful hour on their homecoming passes by rather quickly, much to their surprise. No drones in the air. No sirens in the distance. No Hunt parties on the chase. The normalcy all feels a little too easy for Clayton. After all, it's creeping up on the better part of forty-eight hours since he's been on the run, and in that time, he can't recall what feels like more than just a handful of minutes spent outside of survival mode.

Looking over in the side view mirror at Kara, he catches a candid moment of her staring out the back window. He has absolutely no idea what she's thinking, but he owes his appreciation and his life to her. It's hard to believe that a woman who just hours earlier they held at gunpoint—a complete stranger—has risked not only her career, but her life to join his fight for survival.

She turns her contemplation from the backseat window, and they lock stares in the rearview's reflection.

"Kara, when we get back to Bannerton—" But she can already sense what he's about to say next before he can say it.

"I'm coming with you guys," she cuts him off. "We're already in this deep. The only thing left is to see it through, together."

But unbeknownst to her, the argument isn't up for negotiation.

"No. It's too dangerous. I don't need another innocent life on my conscience," he neutralizes. "I've already lost enough. Too much."

Not willing to drop it, Kara presses on, "Forget it, after everything we've been through, I'm in this all the way."

Realizing this back and forth isn't getting anyone, anywhere, anytime soon, he reluctantly tries another approach. To appeal to her reasoning, not his.

"All right then, why?"

"Huh?" she replies.

"Why are you so adamant to do this—to help us? To risk everything for me? We just met you yesterday. You don't even really know us—me."

Kara goes silent at the question. No longer pushing the issue or loading up another contrarian response. She just pauses a moment to gather her thoughts while looking back out the window into nothing, yet thinking everything.

"I don't know," she exhales, doing her best to filter her thoughts into words in real time. "Maybe because it's not just about you now. It's about so much more. It's about everyone and everything we thought we believed in. The absolute lie of justice we've all been force-fed into following for decades . . . that I've had to grow up my entire life with. It's about overcoming right and wrong. Not to mention, the fact that I've been obliviously helping him cover up his dirty work for the past six months, which just adds another checked box to the list. And regardless of the outcome, I don't want to look back and know I had a chance to help change things but did nothing except turn the other way. I don't think I could live with myself for that." Turning forward, she again meets Clayton's eyes in the rearview. "Could you, if you were in my shoes?"

He holds her gaze in the rumbling reflection for a beat before replying. The answer already written in the softness of his eyes before it ever leaves his lips.

"No. No, I don't think I could."

Silence befalls the car as they continue their trek back home. Antoni nudges Clayton with his elbow, getting his attention.

"I knew I liked that kid," he whispers.

She tries to hide it, but sincerity creeps across her lips, lighting up her bashful cheeks with an unabashed smile. She turns her head and goes back to window gazing. The open country road ahead paints the perfect blank slate of hope.

The opportunity for change.

After two more hours on the road, and one change in driver later, Antoni looks over from behind the wheel and catches Clayton incessantly rubbing his shoulder in between frequent texting sessions. A blurry red mass with a darker, deeper maroon blot in the center has engulfed his entire upper pec, courtesy of their cornfield scuffle, and it's seeped its way through the tightknit threads of his flannel shirt deeper than spilled cabernet on fibrous carpet.

"Shit, your wound opened back up," he says, tugging Clayton's shirt collar down to inspect the damage. "You should take another pain pill, and we should swap out your bandages. You haven't had a change since we left my shop."

"And swap them with what, exactly?" Clayton sputters between massaging groans. "It's fine. I may not be able to feel it, but I can still move it."

Antoni reaches across the Buick's matching beige seats to open the beige glove box—the sedan's whole interior just one continued monochromatic shade of light brown. Inside the compartment, wedged between an old, folded Road Atlas, a set of various crochet needles and skein of yarn, and the car's 2006 owner's manual, is a travel-sized sleeve of facial tissues.

He grabs the tiny Kleenex pack and tosses it on Clayton's lap.

"Take out a few of those," he orders while turning back to Kara. "Hey, check my bag, will you? There should be some duct tape in there."

"Classy," Clayton scoffs, still fiddling with his arm.

"I'll have you know that duct tape can fix anything," Antoni combats.

"Riiiiight," Clayton jeers, gingerly unbuttoning his shirt. "Except for all the things it *can't* actually fix."

"Pfft. Only if you're not using enough of it." Antoni grins, while Kara yanks out a large, used roll of the all-in-one silver fixer-upper.

She then unzips her own small bag, digging around for what's left of her water bottle supply. She hands it to Clayton who stops texting to lay the phone in his lap and douse his wound. Although still numb, he can feel the wetness. It's cold to the touch as it trickles down his chest and bicep, diluting the dried crimson streak in its path.

Kara unfurls a generous strand of silver tape, biting it off at the base. While Clayton does his best to hold a few tissues over the entrance of the wound, she applies her own wad over his exit maim and wraps him up from the back seat. It's not pretty. In fact, far from it. But it's good enough.

Clayton rolls his shoulder a few times to test its mobility. It's super stiff but it's mobile. Again, not pretty, but good enough.

"Not to press the subject, but we've got about three hours to figure out our next plan," Kara says while stuffing the duct tape back into the bag and tossing it on the adjacent seat's tan floor mat.

Clayton refastens his last shirt button and turns to face her. He waves Jayson's phone in her direction.

"Already on it," he says, lobbing her the device. She bumbles the pitch in her unexpecting hands a couple times before securing it.

"What *is* it, exactly?" Antoni asks, his eyes peeking back at her from the rearview mirror.

"Umm, looks like it's a group chat with some guys named Jayson and Hector?"

"Hmm, don't know 'em, but I was wondering who the hell you were so diligently sexting over there, Clay. Well, go on, Kara, read it," he urges, as she proceeds to read the text thread out loud.

***Clayton*** *(from Jayson's phone)*<br>
*Guys, it's me.*<br>
*I hate to ask this… but I need your help.*

***Hector***
*Clay? No estas muerto!*
*Gracias a Dios!*

***Jayson***
*Wow, you lucky son of a bitch!*
*I dunno if I'm happier you're still alive or that you've still got my phone in one piece. Carrying around my tablet everywhere is starting to be a real pain in the ass.*
*You OK?*

***Clayton***
*Nice to hear from you too, Jay.*
*I'm good guys but I need a favor. A couple favors actually.*
*But I'm not gonna lie, it's dangerous.*

***Jayson***
*Ohhh… so now you want my help. JK.*
*You know I got you.*

***Hector***
*Todo! Just name it, amigo.*
*What's up?*

***Clayton***
*I need you guys to help me break into The Hunt for Justice.*

***Hector***
*Are you loco, amigo???*
*What you need in there for?*

**Clayton**
*It's a long story but just trust me on this.*
*Are you guys in?*
*... Jay?*

**Jayson**
*Shit... I dunno man. Sounds like a death wish.*
*You know I wanna help and all but that's way beyond risky.*

**Clayton**
*I know. That's why I've got a plan.*
*But the only way it's gonna work is in that building...*
*In Klein's office to be exact.*

**Jayson**
*OK. Hex was right. You ARE crazy!*
*Are you fucking kidding me??*
*That's instant suicide!*

**Clayton**
*Maybe. Maybe not.*
*But I'm a dead man anyway, right?*
*Might as well go out on my own accord.*

**Hector**
*And you want us to help you dig your own grave, amigo?*

**Clayton**
*Of course not.*
*Look, I'm getting into the building with or without you guys.*
*But my chances are a hell of a lot better one way than the other.*
*So are you gonna help or not?*

***Jayson***
*Ugh. Yeah, I'm in.*
*But it's still fucking suicide if you ask me.*

***Clayton***
*Noted, Jay. Thanks.*
*Hex? What do you say, amigo?*

***Hector***
*Mi tambien, I guess.*
*What's the plan?*

***Clayton***
*Just stay tuned for now.*
*And set your walkies to channel 12 in about 3 hours. Around 4 p.m.*
*I'll call you guys when I'm close.*

***Jayson***
*You still have your walkie?*

***Clayton***
*No, I still have your walkie ;)*
*All right, talk soon.*
*And guys… thanks.*

***Jayson***
*Clay, wait! There's one more thing…*

***Clayton***
*What's that?*

***Jayson***
*There's something big going on here today.*
*Besides your Hunt, it's been all over the news.*

***Clayton***
*What do you mean?*

***Jayson***
*Don't know all the details but it looks like*
*the official public reveal for The Global Hunt.*
*They got a bunch of blockades set up and people are*
*starting to flock into downtown from everywhere.*

***Hex***
*Bunch of news vans out front too.*

***Clayton***
*FFS. Why can't something just go as planned for once?*

***Jayson***
*I don't know.*
*But I do know you're too damn stubborn to not come.*
*I just wanted to give you the heads up.*

***Clayton***
*Thanks, Jay.*
*Somehow this might actually play into my favor after all.*
*I'll see you guys soon.*

***Jayson***
*Unfortunately.*
*Just be careful will ya?*

***Hex***
*Si! What Jay just said.*

***Clayton***
*I'll keep trying my best.*

Kara finishes reading the exchange and tosses the phone back over Clayton's good shoulder. It lands unexpectedly in his lap.

"So, just to recap. You want to break into The Hunt for Justice? Into Klein's office, no less? In broad daylight? During The Global Hunt announcement parade?" she inquires, the tone in her ascending questions growing increasingly louder and more aggressive with each outlandish query. "I'm sorry, but that Jayson guy is right, 'Are you fucking kidding me?'"

"I've got to side with the kid on this one, Clay," Antoni piggybacks, shooting his eyes from the road to Clayton. "You *are* fucking crazy."

"Crazy? Desperate? Totally fucked? Pick one," Clayton urges. "But I do have a plan."

As he slides the phone back into his pocket, he catches the thin, red sliver of remaining battery life blinking in the upper corner. He can't help but notice the eerily similar parallels as his own fate clings to a sliver of life. The unsettling symbolism reaches full foreshadowing just a second later when the phone officially dies.

"Uh yeah . . . a plan that requires breaking into the very headquarters of the place that wants you legally dead," Kara snaps back.

"Which is exactly why it's going to work," he adds, tucking the lifeless device away. With an assured look of calm among the surrounding four eyes of panic, he continues. "Look, it's the last place they'd expect me to go. And as crazy as it sounds, the public address might make it even easier to get in."

He dives into more depth surrounding the details of his plan as Kara and Antoni apprehensively lend their ears. By the time he's finished, they admit that, in theory, it sounds slightly less crazy than expected. But the results of reality don't always equate to their on-paper hypothesis. Just having a plan doesn't mean everything will go according to it, especially when the steps to get there are as daunting as breaking the nation's most wanted man into the nation's most notorious building for killing wanted men. But time is running out, and if they're going to do this, they're going to have to up the ante. Even if that means going all in.

"For the record, I still think this plan royally sucks. It's nothing but a suicide mission for you," Antoni cautions. He can see the reckless abandon hovering just beneath the surface of Clayton's baby blues. "But knowing you, your stubborn ass is going to do it with or without us. At least with us, well, then maybe you stand somewhat of a chance."

Clayton nods his head in thanks at Antoni. Then, he cranes his neck to face Kara in the backseat.

"How about you? You ready to make that change?" he asks with a familiar twinkle of sincerity in his eyes—a look that matches the vulnerable softness from the first moment they met. "Something you can be proud to live with?"

Slowly, her constriction of crossed arms starts to slacken, loosening more and more as she unwillingly gives in to the idea.

"Yeah . . ." she sighs through a feeble smile. "I guess if we're going to go out, we might as well go out with a bang."

Clayton repays her support with a heartfelt smile of his own and turns back around. He catches the last green digit increase on the electronic clock just above the dash's obsolete 6-disc CD changer. It reads 12:57 p.m. By about four o'clock, they'll be back in Bannerton attempting to gain entry into a place they have no business trying to enter.

In the meantime, they've got some prep work to do and some prayers to offer up. God knows they're going to need a perfect storm of both to pull this miracle off.

Upon re-entering the outskirts of Bannerton, the real danger of their mission becomes overwhelmingly evident. What was quiet and desolate farmland just a few hours ago is now a maze of hustling and bustling city streets and sprawling suburbs full of Hunt-happy hordes of people. Droves of bumper-to-bumper traffic and waves of pedestrians populate every inch of the surrounding metropolis, making the treacherous concrete jungle even more of a hazardous hunting ground. And if that wasn't enough, it's the middle of the day where the luxury of night's veil isn't anywhere to be found, anytime soon.

Just outside the city, drones can be seen in the distance swarming the skies like scattered bands of robotic city pigeons. Each and every one programmed to be on the lookout for a facial match. So long as there's a face to be seen.

"Clay, how you doing back there?" Antoni asks.

A muffled voice from the backseat floor responds.

"Other than sweating under this heater of a blanket while trying to find a morsel of comfort with my bum shoulder? I'm fucking peachy."

"Hey, it's not my fault you jacked a car from an eighty-year-old crochet fanatic," Antoni says, glancing in the rearview. "Just count your blessings there happened to be a treasure trove of blankets tucked back in the trunk in the first place."

More ruffling and muffling. "Ungh, I don't get why I'm hiding under a blanket, anyway. Can't I just use the facial recognition scrambler to avoid any cameras around the city?"

"You could. But then you'd blow your load early," Antoni counters. "That scrambler works great on evading camera detection, but it's only good for about fifteen minutes tops. After each use, it needs to charge for thirty minutes or so. And forgive me, but I didn't exactly have the time or the foresight to pack an outdated 12-volt cigarette lighter adapter. Now, just shut up and lay low. We're only a few blocks away from The Hunt for Justice, and the last thing I need right now is a whiny voice coming from underneath an old lady's retirement hobby distracting me."

On the befitting corner of Hunt Avenue and Justice Street, the trio is greeted by an extravagant twenty-four-foot by forty-eight-foot digital billboard playing a short video on loop. It's an automated recording of Klein beseeching his fellow citizens on the importance of justice and the pillars The Hunt Initiative has provided for the foundation of their new republic. The end of his short address is followed by a photo of Clayton along with his wanted information, including last whereabouts. The reward has increased to just over a staggering two million dollars.

"Good god, two million?" Kara mutters aloud and looks at Antoni. "You know, that's a mill apiece, right?"

"I heard that" faintly resonates from the backseat.

"Hey, I thought I told you to be quiet back there?" Antoni snaps back. He turns toward Kara. "Go on, kid. I'm listening." A subtle bout of snickering emanates from the front seat—just enough to successfully shave off some needed tension from their current situation.

"Cool. I'm back here riding blind under this fugly, hot ass horse blanket while trying my best not to vomit thinking about my impending doom. And you two have jokes."

"Sorry, Clay, couldn't resist," Kara apologizes, trying to stifle her nervous giggle. "The good news is they don't have you pegged in Shermer for your last whereabouts. Then again, I'm not sure anyone we ran into back there is still alive or would be in any conscious state to report it, anyway. But . . ."

"You want to tell him?" Antoni cuts in. "Or should I?"

There's a brief pause of silence in the car, but for Clayton, the hushed seconds feel like an agonizing eternity.

"We've got some bad news," Kara hesitantly delivers.

"Bad news?" Clayton gasps, shooting up from the back as coverage from the floral crochet project cascades down his forehead, exposing his most critical asset. "What bad news?"

Unbeknownst to him, the streets surrounding The Hunt for Justice are far more littered than he imagined. Herds of people are parading around and celebrating, including a large gathering of Justice Hunters administering intimidation tactics on a smaller sect of their anti-Hunt protester counterparts. In a limited effort to keep the peace, masses of additional law enforcement and Hunt for Justice security personnel have been called in, along with a swarm of drones to survey and record the bustling scene.

The entire downtown is one massive hot spot of unsolicited activity. At the center of it all, erected atop the lengthy courthouse-inspired steps that lead to the building's main entrance, is a prepped podium flanked by stadium-sized projection panels. All the while, various press and news outlets are fighting for their front-row seats to what appears to be a forthcoming address from the likes of Klein himself.

A giant banner sprawls above the press conference setup. It reads:

THE HUNT INITIATIVE: GLOBAL PASS OPENING SOON.

"Well, the bad news is this place is an absolute zoo," Kara replies. "Worse yet, they've got every entrance to the building guarded and under watertight surveillance."

"So this is what Jay tried to warn us about. I mean, I was expecting bad. Bad I could do. Bad I could deal with. But this is a total nightmare," Clayton complains, throwing the blanket back over his head like a child seeking comfort from the scary unknown. "Just find a close place to park, and we'll take it from there."

Carefully navigating through the sea of pedestrians, Antoni does his best to distance the trio from the heart of the action, pulling into a tucked-away parking garage a couple blocks south. He finds a vacant spot at the end of the third floor and parks. Checking to see if the coast is clear, he gives the haphazard blanket sprawled across the backseat floor a subtle poke.

"All clear," he says.

Clayton surfaces from under the blanket like a whale coming up for air. After a tiny struggle with his uncooperative arm, he finally makes it up and onto the backseat, panting from his duel with the duvet.

"That was fun," he huffs, adjusting his shoulder and casting the wool sweat sack back onto the floor.

Opening the car's rear seat pass-through hatch, he grabs Antoni's duffel bag and Jayson's backpack. He takes the walkie out of the pack, and flips it on and over to channel 12, just like he instructed Jayson and Hector to do. He checks the time on the car's dashboard. It's ten past 4:00 p.m.—showtime.

The walkie goes from steady static to receptive silence when he clicks the page button.

"Guys? You there? Over."

Static again.

"Guys, it's me. I'm here. Do you copy?"

More static.

"I repeat, it's me. Is anyone there? Hello? Hellllooo?"

Negative thoughts of his grand plan blowing up before it ever began slip into Clayton's head and past his guard. The already paper-thin layers of hope that took him hours to fortify are shredded in just mere seconds of static silence as the foundation for his optimism continues to quickly erode. There's nothing now but the radio's unnerving flicker of feedback to keep him company.

Finally, before more of his quivering confidence can retreat, a familiar voice penetrates the idle hiss.

"¿Es tu amigo?"

"Holy sh—Hex!" Clayton yells in excitement. "Dammit, man you had me worried for a second."

"What? You didn't really think we'd leave you high and dry, did you?" Jayson's voice scrambles across the trembly transmission.

"Jay! Man, it's so good to hear you guys."

In a perfect world, Clayton would love nothing more than to play a game of twenty questions, filling them in on every grueling detail of the last two days.

The unwelcomed homecoming.

The DB88 shootout, and the whole getting shot thing.

The secret database.

"Kidnapping" Kara.

The school, the diner, the chase . . . all of the shitshow that was Shermer.

But right now is not the time nor the place.

"Look guys, there's a lot I have to tell you, but I want to keep this brief in case someone else is listening in on our line. Plus, we don't have a lot of time anyway."

Jayson responds, "Roger that. We've actually been trying to text you for a couple hours to warn you about what you've just strolled into. If you couldn't already tell, I was right. Klein is unveiling his plan for The Global Hunt today."

"I know," Clayton replies, looking ahead at Kara and Antoni who are sitting before him like a couple of dumbstruck tourists just doing their best to take everything in. "Your phone died on me shortly after I sent my last text. I figured there would be a crowd, but I had no idea this place was going to turn into a Thanksgiving parade of epic proportions."

"I'd ask you if this changes anything, but I think I already know and fear the answer to that question," Jayson adds. "So, let's just cut to it. What's the plan?"

Clayton takes a moment to recalibrate. "With all the entrances being heavily monitored, who's working the rear gate to the south entry door?"

"Yeah . . . you're not gonna like that answer."

Clayton mumbles under his breath, "Fuck, Rickers."

"Who's Rickers?" Kara butts in from the front seat.

"Dunno, but from the name alone, he already sounds like a real prick," Antoni adds.

"You have no idea. He's my"—Clayton catches himself—"*was*, my boss and just so happens to be head of security for the place."

Focusing his attention back to the walkie, Clayton asks, "Jay, you think you can distract him long enough to get us in?"

There's an extra-long silence on the radio.

"It's not gonna be easy, but I think I can buy you a little time. Getting you in the back entrance shouldn't be a problem, but it's all for nothing if you can't get past the gate—I don't have clearance to open it from the inside. And something tells me your employee credentials have been removed from the system. And, even if they haven't, you'd be one retinal scan away sealing your own fate."

"Umm," Kara juts in timidly. "I *might* be able to help with that."

Clayton turns to her, his eyes doing a better job of asking the question than the actual one that follows.

"Huh?"

"Well . . . I was . . . I mean—" she stutters, beating around every twig of the metaphorical bush. "Technically, I still am an employee of The Hunt for Justice with level three clearance . . . I just don't work at HQ, if you're picking up what I'm putting down."

Clayton steals a cautiously interested look at her from his peripheral. He knows it's a long shot, but what other choice do they have? If he gives it a go with his own credentials, he might as well just shout his name at the top of his lungs into the growing crowd outside. But no one knows that Kara is part of their party. He thinks for a moment, playing over every possible scenario.

Trying his best to choke down the same reality pill, Antoni speaks up. "You sure about this, kid? Because if we get to that gate and it doesn't work—"

"No, I'm not sure. I have absolutely no clue if it'll work," she interjects. "But we're wasting time just talking about it. Besides, we're here right now. Everything is already on the line. What do we have to lose at this point? So, I say let's liberate the brown trout and go do this shit already!"

Antoni cocks his head.

"I'm sorry, but—" he says, incessantly blinking his eyes as if his ears have suddenly deceived him. "Did—did you just make a shit-leaving joke?"

"Ugh, yes," she begrudgingly admits, hanging her head in instant shame as it bobs like her hair. "And I already feel gross and hate myself for—"

"*Yesss*, now that's what I'm talking about! Up top," he squeals, jutting his hand into the air while reveling in her reluctant elation. She plants a halfhearted high-five on his palm while fighting back the tiniest grin. "Have I mentioned I fucking love this kid?" he continues, shooting Clayton a gleeful gaze.

The same sense of joy, however, isn't reciprocated.

"Hmm. What do we have to lose?" he repeats Kara's question aloud tartly, watching as their smiles quickly fade into tight-lipped sobriety. "Other than putting the people I care about most in grave danger and risking my own life in the process? Absolutely nothing. It's all fucking sunshine and rainbows over here."

Racing the reckless thought back and forth in his mind, he ultimately crash-lands on the only conclusion his brain keeps feeding him.

"Fuck it," he caves, tapping the walkie-talkie against his head as if hoping to jog a better thought loose. "We've come this far. I guess it's now or never, right?"

"Jay?" he says into the radio.

"Here, buddy."

"How much time can you buy us?"

"I can tell Rickers there's been a disturbance reported at the main entrance. That ought to buy you guys some time, maybe five minutes or so, tops. But you'll need to get your asses in gear."

"Guess that'll have to do then. I'll let you know when we're in position. In the meantime, let's keep this line clean."

"Heard. Good luck, man," Jayson adds. It's the last thing uttered over the walkie before Clayton flips the dial and stuffs it in the bag. Looking back up, he pans his eyes from Antoni to Kara, pre-judging the likelihood of success by the level of nervousness reflected in their magnified pupils.

"All right. So, now all we've got to do is wade through a sea of insatiable Justice Hunters while avoiding detection from who knows how many surveillance cameras along the way, sneak past a flock of bird's-eye-view security drones, and break into one of the nation's most heavily secured buildings—on its most protected penthouse floor—all on the blind faith that Kara's security clearance will actually work," Clayton mocks, attempting to brighten an overwhelmingly dim outlook bleaker than the ocean floor. "What could possibly go wrong?"

He unzips and rummages through the duffle bag of tech tricks and pulls out the facial recognition scrambler.

"Toni, you said we've got a fifteen-minute window with this, right?" he asks, shooting his friend a questionable look that easily skews the inquisitive seesaw closer toward skepticism. "And it should bypass detection from the surveillance cameras and security drones?"

"Yeah, that's right."

"Well then, if we've got one shot, let's make it count."

Clayton opens the car door, but Antoni reaches back, grabbing his left arm before he can slide out.

"Clay?"

He turns to face his friend. "Yeah?" Hesitation inflected in the question back.

"The recognition scrambler will get you past the cameras . . . but the whole ball cap and sunglasses alter ego getup ain't gonna cut it in that hostile crowd. Your face is everywhere, literally. You're gonna need to double up your cover."

Antoni plunges his arm into the duffle. When his hand returns from the bag's abyss, it's holding the familiar, taser-like device. He tosses Clayton an apprehensive look—his eyebrows doing the heavy lifting. Timidly, he adds, "We're gonna have to mangle your face a bit."

Clayton slowly shuts his ajar door and cautiously accepts the device from Antoni's hand, like it's a baton bomb ready to detonate at the slightest fumble. Turning the expression compressor over in his hand, he studies the sleek device.

"If I use this, do I even need the recognition scrambler? Because we could save the scrambler for—"

But Antoni is already shaking his head.

"Nope. Those surveillance cameras and drones are like hawks, equipped with sophisticated lens technology that can pick up the most minute details from hundreds of yards up. That includes your eyes, ears, nose—all the features that make you, you."

Clayton's uneasy gaze consciously pans its way up the non-descript Mug Mangler before him. When it gets to the device's tapered summit, he releases the air chipmunked in the side of his cheek. The reluctant words escape in tandem with the anxious gust of carbon dioxide.

"Fuck it. Let's just do it." He surrenders, fidgeting with the device to camouflage the slight shake in his hands. "What do I do, exactly anyway? Ram it under my chin and press the little red button that just screams 'Don't push me'?"

"Uhhh yeah, actually. That's pretty much it," Antoni confirms. "You just gotta click that tiny switch on the side first to release the prongs."

"I'm sorry, did you say prongs?" Clayton whimpers.

"Yeah, prongs. Or barbs. Skewers? Whatever you wanna call the little spikes that pop out the top."

"Spikes? You never said anything about any goddamn spikes!"

"Sure I did. Didn't I?"

"Hell no."

"Really?"

"Nuh-uh."

"Hmm . . . are you positive?"

"Yeah. Pretty fucking positive I'd remember that tidbit."

"Sorry, guess I forgot to mention it," Antoni retorts, only his tone is far more apathetic than apologetic. "Though to be fair, I *did* tell you it would hurt like hell. So—"

"Oh, gee, thanks, buddy. That makes it all sooo much better."

Without further delay or complaint, Clayton clicks the side lever as a set of one-inch prongs switchblade out from the head of the device like a pair of mini cattle prods.

"Fuck me," he gulps, studying the combo of shiny copper spikes before him. "Here goes nothing. I guess . . ."

He lets out another long sigh before wedging the device firmly into the soft belly of flesh underneath his chin. Hovering his thumb over the red detonator, he clamps his eyelids shut as the rest of his facial pores and orifices follow suit, clenching in excruciatingly unanimous anticipation.

"Wait!" Antoni yells out, causing all the tension in Clayton's face to flee at once.

"You might want to bite down on this," he says, and hands his friend a handkerchief from his pocket. "Trust me."

Clayton takes the rag and lodges it between his teeth. The current of anticipated anguish begins to reconstruct in his fingers first, slowly moving up his arms then back to his face as he bears down with all the force his molars can muster.

"And remember, you have to keep it pressed under your chin for at least five seconds; otherwise, it won't take full effect," Antoni iterates.

"Sherioushly, yew tell me dat now?" Clayton mumbles through snarled teeth before spitting out the rag. "Is there *anything else* I should know? 'Cause if I'm going to wake up in five years with uncurable cancer or some shit, I should just save us all the trouble right now."

Antoni's eyes raise in their sockets as he ponders the question. "Uh, nope. I think that pretty much covers everything."

"Good, then can you do me a solid?

"Sure. Anything, man. Just shoot."

"Can you please for the love of all things holy just shut the hell up already?" Clayton mutters and stuffs the handkerchief back into his mouth.

On the internal count of three, he jets the dual prongs into the delicate underside of his chin as fast and hard as he can. They completely penetrate the flesh like a mechanical set of vampire fangs. The sting from their initial bite is nothing compared to what follows.

In a flash, inexplicable pain, unlike anything he's ever felt, shoots throughout his entire being like bolts of electricity pinging head to toe at lightspeed. Even if he wanted to let go of the button, his grip has seized so much from the ponging jolts radiating throughout his muscles that there isn't any control over what his fingers can do and what his mind wants them to do.

Clayton folds over in the seat as the shock courses down his chin past the fresh hole in his shoulder. After another second, he's nearly relegated to his back as his face begins to tighten and pull in a vicious tug-of-war from the outside in. It's only five short seconds, but it feels like painful perpetuity as he struggles against the concentrated charge of paralyzing kinetic energy—wreaking havoc throughout every centimeter of his connective facial tissue at blistering g-force speeds.

Finally, the device shuts off automatically after a series of quick beeps. It drops simultaneously to the floorboard along with Clayton as he fights to regain control over his liberated muscle groups.

Still visibly shaky, he slowly lifts himself from the Buick's spacious passenger floor. His insides feel fried, but at least the pain is gone—as fleeting as it was instant. He continues to gingerly work himself back into his seat with help from Antoni.

"Goddamn, my head is throbbing," are the first raspy words out of his hoarse mouth. They're immediately followed by a hand motioning toward his throat.

"Wait, why do I sound like that? Totally different. Like my balls just dropped for a second time, and I've been smoking two packs a day for the past twenty years."

"It's all part of the schtick, man," Antoni reassures. "Guess I forgot to mention that, too. Whoops . . . my bad." He cringes with a guise that yells "yikes." "You just rearranged and contorted almost every muscle and tissue in your face and your skin is currently fighting against gravity and everything it's ever known. You think it's bad now? Just wait until the post-headache hits later. Your forehead might as well be a stage because it's gonna feel like someone's heel-toeing *Lord of the Dance* on your face. But hey, at least you didn't shit yourself. That one's usually fifty-fifty."

Clayton shoots him a cold-blooded stare through taut eyelids and a distending brow.

"You tell me all this now? That info would've been really helpful twenty seconds ago, you dick."

"Just chalk it up to 'what you don't know can't hurt you?' Besides, I didn't wanna overwhelm you. Here, take a look at yourself," he adds, and flips the passenger seat visor mirror down.

The face Clayton's seen every day, for as long as he's been able to see it, is virtually unrecognizable. Forget puberty and those awkward freshmen year headshots, this is a whole other level of WTF metamorphosis. His cheeks have multiple folds and rolls like a giant manbaby, his forehead is jutting out far enough to be level with his nose, and his jaw is as bloated as a banged-up boxer that just went the distance in a landslide loss.

"Holy shit," he mutters through swollen lips. "I don't even recognize myself. Like, at all."

"Um, yeah. That's kinda the whole point, right?" Antoni jokes.

"Oh, is this funny to you?" Clayton snaps back.

"Me?" Antoni asks, openly choking back his laughter. "Erm. No, I . . . I—" But before he can dig out a response from the plot he's dug around him, they both turn to Kara who is trying her best, yet failing miserably, to conceal her own bout of amusement.

"*Really*? You, too?" Clayton demands in his new baritone voice. "What the hell, guys?"

"I'm sorry, Clay, but—" Her snickers blossoming into full-blown laughter. "—you look like you've got your own Benjamin Button thing going on. The Curious Case of Clay."

Not even a moment later, Antoni joins in her spell of hilarity. In between gasps for air, he adds, "You look like a sad, wilted penis with googly eyes, and I can't unsee it."

With as much irk as his mangled face can muster, Clayton glares at them through his droopy foreskin eyelids, looking back and forth between them and his wrinkled phallic reflection in the passenger mirror. But soon enough their laughter becomes contagious, and he can't help but join in on the merriment. Only his face is too tight to crack much of a smile and every chuckle is like a hammer to his already pounding skull.

"All right, all right. If we get out of this mess, you can roast me and my ball sack for a chin all you want, but we've got a job to do right now, and we're wasting precious time."

The laughter in the car dissipates as the three regain their composure, instantly reacquainting themselves with the gravity of the shit storm raging outside of the hard place they've put themselves in.

"Are we all clear on the plan?" Clayton gruffly poses, as two heads nod in unison.

"All right then, let's go," he says, slinging the backpack over his shoulder. "Try to maintain some distance out on the street. There's less chance of suspicion if we're alone. Once we make it to the gate, Kara, you're up. No pressure, but if your clearance doesn't work, well, then we're fucked."

"Geez, Ebenezer, when you put it that way, it really helps reinforce my already fragile nerves," she replies, her words full of anxious sarcasm. "Like other than impending doom, what else could go wrong?"

"I don't know," Clayton answers, ignoring the additional old man meets dickface jab. "But I'm not ready to meet my Ghost of Christmas Future just yet."

The stairwell door creaks open to a street-side exit, and the three slowly trickle out of the parking garage one at a time. Antoni makes his way out first with Clayton cautiously bringing up the rear. With all the excitement buzzing around The Hunt for Justice and the surrounding downtown area, a dull roar of voices can be heard from several blocks away.

A few hundred feet above the streets and alleyways, the steady hum of drone propellers adds to the reverberating mix. In some places, they're so dense in their swarm that only sparse blotches of blue sky can be made out in between the towering skyscrapers all around. The cacophony continues to crescendo the closer they get to the center of the commotion where a faint voice can barely be heard over the main speakers. It's hard to make out exactly what's being said, but it sounds like an old recording of Klein speaking about the genesis of The Hunt Initiative.

Closing in on the outskirts of the main block, more and more people can be seen pouring into downtown. A river of pedestrians quickly turns into a public sea when they round the corner of Hunt

Avenue and Justice Street. Wading now into the endless thick of it, like castaways without life preservers, the rally truly starts to take shape.

The spectacle resembles a demonstrative march with a record-breaking congregation of supporters toting quippy signs and hyping each other up with chants and exaggerated narratives of a better future through retribution. Even more drone clusters occupy the blue space just above the hub of humans like birds in migration surveying every inch of the sprawling scene beneath them. All the nearby billboards rotate between mirrored shots of the crowd and wanted photos for Clayton, including intel about his last whereabouts.

The bounty for his life is now an astounding $2.3 million. And growing. A man on a mission, wearing an olive-green puffer vest and red ballcap, aggressively pushes his way toward the larger main crowd. He blindly brushes right by Clayton as he storms past, shouting "Hunt Sparks. Preserve Peace."

His personal initiative triggers a small collective of similar-looking Hunt prospects to follow his plight and join in on the chant. Everything inside Clayton's being tells him to cut and run. That this plan is so far beyond a suicide mission that there's zero hope. But he knows there's nowhere to run to. Nowhere to go but forward. That he has to see this through to the end, even if it's his own. His choice is simple but far from easy: Die running or die fighting. And he's done running.

As the three continue their undetected journey toward the source of all the hustle and bustle, Kara notices a decent-sized flock of bystanders gathered around a single woman in vintage navy robes. Upon approach, she can hear her spewing an interwoven blend of Old and New Testament quotes along with Klein's own archived excerpts of equally biblical proportions.

"And the Apostle Peter says in First Peter Chapter Three, verse twelve, 'For the eyes of the Lord are upon the righteous, and his ears are open to their prayer. But the face of the Lord is against those that do evil,"' the woman preaches in her accosting homily.

"Don't you see it? Can you all see it? Simon Klein is our modern-day apostle. A descendant of Peter himself! It's even in the origin of his name, Simeon, before Jesus appointed him Peter. He is here to carry out God's will. To avenge thee. To repay thee. Just as Peter promised our Lord and Savior would. Rejoice in retribution, my brothers and sisters. Rejoice in the Hunt—for justice. For it is the Lord's will and our duty to see it through."

As if hypnotized zombies transfixed by a witch's hex, the entire congregation bows in unison and repeats after her, "Rejoice in retribution. Rejoice in the Hunt."

"Sheesh. And I'm the bad guy?" Clayton murmurs under his breath quiet enough for only himself to hear. "This brainwashed 'flock' doesn't know their beaks from their assholes."

That's when an eager, mustached Justice Hunter wearing an odd combination of a suit jacket with cargo pants while toting a shotgun, accidentally bumps into him.

The surprise encounter makes Clayton, who is still dwelling in the gospel according to crazy lady, lose his balance and drop Jayson's backpack. The contact causes his radio to fall out of the bag and clatter to the ground as it skids across the asphalt. The wardrobe-confused man bends down to pick it up with docile curiosity. He studies the device briefly, furrowing his brows in a scowl that eventually migrates to Clayton. The longer his concentrated gaze lingers, the more skeptical the look on his face grows.

Clayton reaches out to grab the radio, but the man yanks his hand back in a game of unwarranted keep-away.

Clayton's heart revs. The swelling suspicion that this stranger is bound to see through his mangled façade implants into his thoughts, triggering further palpitations. But more than anything, he's worried that either Jay or Hex could page him at any second and blow the whole plan before it ever really began. Just saying his name could be enough to reveal his true identity and put an end to any epic plan of proving his innocence—to prolonging the life he's barely clinging onto.

Clayton reaches for the walkie again, this time adding some peaceful commentary in hopes of breaking the staring stalemate.

"Thanks," he says, mid-reach.

But the man pulls the radio back again. His eyes squint harder as if sun-strained, and his lips start to twitch as if prepping for a response that got lost somewhere in his overgrown whiskers. Before he can locate the words in his unruly scruff, Kara bumps into him and snatches the radio from his unexpecting hand in the process.

"Oh, thank you, sir," she exclaims, stuffing the walkie back into Clayton's bag. "My brother is just so excited for today that he's a bit of a klutz. *Roy*—" she says with a balanced combination of calm condescension in her tone and stare. "Why don't you go radio the rest of the Hunting crew and let them know we're headed to the main congregation to grab a spot near the front."

Clayton hesitates momentarily before nodding his head and zipping up his bag. He resumes his trek toward The Hunt for Justice gate as Kara nods to the man, sealing their getaway with a cherry on top.

"Happy Hunting," she says, rejoining Clayton with Antoni a few deliberately spaced steps in tow. A look of impressed disbelief painted all over the latter's face.

As the trio approaches the rear entrance, the screens flanking the stage transition from their loop of Hunt propaganda and the latest news coverage to reveal a live feed of Klein sitting upon the throne in his office. There's a slight screech on the PA system before his initial audio hushes the crowd in a near instant.

"*My fellow citizens of Bannerton gathered here today, and to the millions watching at home, I commend you on your continued pursuit of righteousness. Shortly, I will join you all to reveal the official rollout for the next evolution of The Hunt Initiative. A collaborative initiative with a universal undertaking to—no. No, it is so much more than just that,"* he says sovereignly, prophesying his next batch of words off script. *"It is a worldwide revolution. A proven, moral way of thinking, working, and existing. It is the integrity that supports how we live and breathe as a collective society. Not just for America but for all humanity moving forward. To hold one another as human beings—all our brothers and sisters across the globe—accountable for our own actions. To become stewards of enforcing justice in every corner of the world.*

"*But—*" There's an uncharacteristic pause in his voice. "*—if I am being truly honest, I must admit that I am rather disappointed. This was meant to be a day of celebration. A fresh future for us all. But our flawless record of swift retribution has been broken—and with it, this day's laurels soiled—by the sustained evasion of the wanted murderer, Clayton Sparks. As you all know, this Hunt is extra special to me, personally. I lost my one and only daughter at the hands of this man. To this murderer. And the longer he walks free, the more I am reminded about what he not only took from me as a father, but what he has taken from all of you—from us, as a global community. He is a blemish. A tarnish on the reputation of our proud city and what we stand for—the shared belief of a united world.*

"*So, I am raising the ante yet again. If the cost for justice must include a higher price tag, then so be it. Four million to the man or woman who brings me Clayton Sparks. Dead or alive at this point. You have my word. I'm counting on you all to make me proud. To do the right thing. May justice be served. Happy Hunting.*"

The transmission ends and the new reward of $4 million is instantly reflected on the refreshed video feed. Within seconds, the pin drop silence of the crowd grows to a dull roar and then back to its previous free-for-all as they await Klein's upcoming address. The elevated energy and overwhelming thirst for more bloodshed disguised as justice continue to propagate with every salivating second.

Clayton, Antoni, and Kara finally reach the outskirts of the gate. The reinforced, story-tall, barred structure is all that separates them now from access to inside—to Klein. Well, that and several locked doors and 165 floors of high-security building clearance. But those are problems for Future Clayton when he reaches that step in the plan. Right now, it's getting past this fortress's barricade and the litany of security personnel currently shielding it, including none other than Rickers himself, who's standing guard square in the middle of the pack, looking particularly pissed off and on edge.

As much as Clayton would love to greet his former boss with a fist across his double chin right now, he does his best to hide his own face, even in its current unrecognizably mangled state. Rickers may be a dick, but he's not stupid. And if anyone could see past Clayton's rearranged potato head, it'd be him.

Saddling up to the gate, the three congregate at a safe viewing distance for a quick recon. All six eyes clustered on Rickers and the coveted entrance. Clayton motions Kara and Antoni closer, positioning them as a makeshift blockade from any potentially prying eyes. He slings the backpack off his good shoulder and digs out the radio.

Flipping it on, he hears the familiar drone of subtle static.

"Jay? You there? We're in position."

Silence.

Static.

Nothingness.

"C'mon, c'mon," he mutters under his breath, as Kara glances back to see what's happening. He tries again. "I repeat. Anyone there? We're here. We're at the gate."

More silence.

More static.

More nothingness.

"Pick up, pick up. Somebody *fucking* pick up."

Panic starts to burrow under his skin, disturbing the topsoil of his confidence like an invasive weed taking root. His mind drifts to the far end of the worst-case scenario spectrum:

*Maybe someone was listening in, and they got caught?*

*Did Jayson get reassigned?*

*Is the plan already fucked?*

As his doubt anchors deeper, he hears a familiar, unwelcomed voice call out behind him.

"Hey! You three!" the assertive voice barks.

Clayton's heart plummets faster than a stalled spaceship entering orbit. On the free fall down, he feels his heart leave the comfort of his lungs, pass his liver, and plunge into the gurgling depths of his stomach. It's enough to make him want to vomit on impact.

Standing just behind them on the other side of the security gate is Rickers, armed with his patented overcompensating authority and pent-up anger and no poor soul to currently use them on.

"You all need to step away from this entrance, now," he commands.

Clayton does his best to coyly drop the radio back into his bag as he slings the strap over his shoulder. The attempt isn't sly enough.

"What was that? What did you just put in your bag?" Rickers interrogates, stepping closer to the bars.

With his back still turned to an incoming and on-alert Rickers, Clayton looks at Antoni who is frozen in his own internal stalemate on what to do next.

"Hey jerk-off, I asked you a question," Rickers chides, his voice growing more hostile to match the hissing fuse attached to his explosive expression. His hand drops down to his hip, hovering over his sidearm. "You have three seconds to turn around before I make you turn around. You got that?"

The failed scenarios of how this plays out speed through Clayton's mind like the pages of a flipbook.

*Answer? And blow his cover. Get caught.*

*Run? And blow his cover. Definitely get caught.*

*Lie? And risk blowing his cover. Likely get caught.*

Out of options and time, Clayton slowly turns, hovering his hands in the air for added innocence. A scrutinizing 180 degrees later, he's face-to-face with his former boss. Rickers tilts his head to the side and squints his baggy eyes, studying the wrinkled man standing before him. Clayton can see the gears and cogs working behind the scenes while he inspects every newly formed crevice for any glimpse of familiarity in the strangely familiar face before him.

Before any more growing suspicion can take hold, Rickers's radio crackles. It's followed by Jayson's urgent voice.

"Rickers, I just got word on a disturbance at the main entrance. All available backup units are to report at once. Over."

Rickers diverts his attention to the source of the trebly voice transmitting from his breast. He bear claws the radio.

"Rickers here, roger that," he grumbles, refocusing his gaze on Clayton, Kara, and Antoni—a slight hesitation behind his response. "10–4, I'm on my way." He clips the radio back into place on his chest and turns toward the other guards stationed behind him. "Nastasio, Ward, Pinnell, and McAfee, you're all with me to the main entrance."

He starts to march away, leading the pack but pauses and turns around to face the gate one last time.

"You three," he says, aggressively jabbing a pointed finger at Clayton and Co. "I better not see you here when I get back. Understood?"

The three obediently nod in agreement as Rickers scuttles off in a tizzy back through the side entry toward the main entrance. His butt broomstick still firmly rammed up his ass like a witch brewing for a good time.

Clayton feels the g-force of his heart rocket back up through the layers of his internal atmosphere to its appropriate resting place. He drops his hands, leaking a sigh of relief.

"Goddammit, Jay . . . nothing like waiting until the last second," he exhales aloud. Kara and Antoni follow suit with their own reprieves. After a moment of group amnesty, Clayton breaks the celebratory exoneration.

"All right, gang, we've got a lot to do and not a lot of time to do it," he says, scurrying over to the gate terminal to check if the coast is clear. "Kara, be quick. Before they realize nothing is wrong and hightail it back on the double."

He steps aside as Antoni mirrors his movement, together flanking the sides of the ID kiosk. Kara struts up determined yet anxious and pulls out her badge. She looks at Clayton with evident hesitation. He repays the notion with his own stoic glance, followed by a forced but encouraging grin. He notices her hand trembling and imagines a forecast of doubt and anxiety thundering in her mind, clouding control of her extremities. He knows exactly what she's feeling because the same ominous storm is wreaking havoc in his mind, too.

"Kara, wait," he says softly among the clamor of the rowdy crowd while gently placing his hand on her shoulder. Her blurry eyes rise to meet his once again.

"Whatever happens," Clayton mutters. "Happens. No worries. Got it?"

She nods.

"Here goes nothing," he says.

She counters, "Here's to making a change."

She clenches her eyes shut and takes a deep, concentrated breath in. A sliver of courage begins to swell, freeing a determined gaze from its lidded stranglehold. Then, she exhales. Her fleeting bravery bests her anxiety as a wave of confidence steadies her hand, and in one fluid movement, she slides her stare in front of the retinal scanner and swipes her badge. Arrested by the anticipation, her body seizes from head to toe as the machine gets to work pinpointing her credentials. It's only nanoseconds but feels far from it. The click of the gate is what reaches her ears first, then she sees the terminal light flash green.

Clayton's grasp on her shoulder relaxes in unison with the savior light. He quickly wipes away the evidence of doubt perspiring on his overly wrinkled brow.

"Holy shit, it really worked!" Antoni exclaims in disbelief.

Kara spins around and gives him a mini-curtsey. "Bet you're glad you brought me along, now, huh?"

"I gotta say, kid, I'm impressed. Truly." Antoni continues with a rare, heartfelt smile that quickly turns smug. "Now, let's drop our beef with the butt burrito and—"

"Stop!" Kara interrupts mid-poophemism. "Let me have just this *one*, please? I think I've earned it."

Antoni pats her on the back, his smile big enough to bridge the gap between his ears. "You know what? You're right," he says, trudging forward through the gate behind Clayton.

"So, what's next?" he asks, still beaming.

"Jay should be coming around to sneak—" but Clayton's cut off as the backdoor flings open right on cue "—us in," he trails off.

"C'mon, move it, guys!" a frantic Jayson orders, waving the trio inside. "It's only a matter of time before Rickers and them discover they've been sent on a bullshit goose chase. He may be an asshole but he's not stupid." It's a sentiment that's shaping up to be the statement of the day.

Kara brings up the rear and Jayson shuts the door. The sound of its automatic lock clinks and clanks back into its resting place. They're in. There's no turning back now.

"Thanks, Jay . . . I owe you," Clayton says, nearly panting.

Jayson turns around to properly face Clayton and the two fresh faces for the first time.

"No prob—Jesus!" he shrieks in shock. "Clay?? Is that really you? What the hell happened to your face?" he flinches with a staggered step backward. "You look like literal dog shit. Worse, actually."

Clayton reaches up to touch the indistinguishable form of his own face. Even that familiarity feels foreign.

"Yeah, well, uh, that's a long story," he replies, letting out a deep, raspy sigh. "At least, you didn't say it looks like a ball sack."

Antoni juts in, "Ball sack. Dog shit. Benny Button. Is there really a difference?"

Jayson sniggers as he leans in to hug Clayton in a friendly embrace, something he thought he may never get the chance to do again.

"God damn, it's really good to see you, man," he adds, patting him on his good shoulder. "Even if you do look like an old man's soiled diaper."

"For fuck's sake," Clayton cries through swollen lips. "I'm gone for a couple days, and you become a comedian?" He pulls away, gesturing to his face. "I had to do all *this* to get through that crowd and security. And it actually worked, too, barely. Rickers almost ate our lunch, but he didn't recognize me."

"I'm just glad you're alive," Jayson says, giving all three of them another once-over. "I've been following the whole Hunt. Looks like you've been put through the wringer."

"You have no idea," Antoni chimes in.

"That bad, huh? What's all happened?" Jayson asks.

"Not now. It's a long story I'll have to fill you in on later," Clayton responds, grabbing his injured arm.

"Fair enough," Jayson ripostes, extending his hand toward Antoni. "I take it you're Antoni?"

"Guess my reputation proceeds me," he says, and juts his own arm out.

"I'm Jayson," he replies, as they shake. "Clay told me *all* about you guys."

"All? Oh, that's comforting."

"Yeah, well, I'm just glad to see you two worked it out and that you didn't shoot him on the spot."

"Wasn't for a lack of trying," Clayton cuts in.

"Ugh," Antoni shrugs. "Not this shit again."

Jayson laughs and pans his glance over to Kara who hasn't been this quiet since being held at gunpoint by Antoni when they first met. "And who's this?"

"That's Kara," Clayton continues. "It's . . . another long story."

"Right. Got it. Well, nice to meet you, whoever you are."

"You, too," she replies and shyly reaches out her hand. "Sorry to break up the bro fest, but thanks for helping us."

"Bottom line, I wouldn't be here without her. Without them," Clayton continues with soft eyes burdened by loads of gratitude. "They've saved my ass multiple times."

"Well, you're lucky to have made it this long, but it's far from over. So, what's the plan, man?" Jayson asks.

Clayton looks down the hall, scanning every visible nook and cranny to see if danger lurks out of sight. Deciding that it's safe enough to momentarily let his guard down, he turns back to Jayson.

"I need to see Hex."

The door to the surveillance room beeps, then flings open as the trio turned quartet file into the room. In typical pants-down response, Hex whips his head around from staring at his phone and not the monitors while his black ponytail plays catch-up from the surprise.

"Didn't you already learn your lesson about looking at porn on the job, amigo?"

"Cl-Clay?" Hex hesitates, as a smile grows underneath his sad soy sauce attempt at a mustache. "Amigo!"

"In the flesh and still breathing at the moment," Clayton responds.

Hex jets up from his control center chair ready to embrace his friend in their five-step signature handshake, but he pauses prior to the greeting process.

"Yo, why does your face look like my *abuelos's huevos*?"

"Wow, everyone's got jokes apparently," Clayton carps, staring at Jayson and Antoni who are snickering in the background like a pair of guilty school children.

"*Es* good to see you, homes," Hex adds, accidently patting Clayton on his injured shoulder. The friendly gesture causes him to release an agonizing grunt as he winces from the sudden sting.

"*Tu* all right, Clay?" Hex reacts, innocently panning over to the rest of the crew.

"Yeah, I'm fine," Clayton grits, gathering himself. "It's just been a helluva last couple days. Anyway, where's Rickers at now, Hex?" he asks, surveying the large bank of security monitors before him, his glassy eyes reflecting dozens of tiny lit cubes as his pupils dart back and forth.

Hex plops back down into his chair and slides another one over for Clayton. The rest of the gang circle up and close in. Antoni follows his loner M.O. and perches himself against a wall in the corner.

"He's on the move and he looks *muy enfadado*," Hex adds, pointing to one of the middle monitors where Rickers appears to be storming away from the main entrance in an unusually irate shamble. A dead giveaway that he's discovered the security backup was a false alarm.

Jayson pushes in, leaning over Kara's shoulder.

"Shit. Looks like he's on a mission to chew out someone's ass, might as well be mine," he concedes, reaching for his radio. "I'll try to buy you guys some more time but—" He pauses, and glances back at the monitor only to see Rickers hastening the pace in his feverish waddle as if his asshole has finally swallowed the metaphorically wedged broomstick whole. "—no promises."

As Jayson turns around to head for the exit, he's met by an unexpected force pulling him back. Spinning around to see the cause of the holdup, he finds Clayton's hand grasping his bicep.

"Jay, wait—" Clayton utters, stalling the words hiding behind his lips. His gaze dances around every part of his friend's face while avoiding eye contact at all costs. "—I need your badge . . . for the elevator clearance."

Jayson wobbles back at the initial shock of the request, wiggling loose from Clayton's grip. His eyes bounce around until they finally sync up with the rogue cha-cha-chá number that Clayton's are rehearsing.

But it's in that brief connection, that locked in two-step moment that he realizes there's no use trying to take control of this dance. He can see it in his friend's steely stare. Clayton has the lead and there's nothing he can do or say that will convince him to relinquish it. But like any good friend, he's not willing to entirely sit this one out. Not without at least an attempt to be the voice of reason.

"Clay, if you're planning on doing what I think you're doing, I might as well say my farewell now and just get it over with. That's your *big* plan? You're *aha* reveal? Confronting Klein face-to-face? *Seriously*? Going up there is suicide and you know it. Are you fucking crazy?"

"For the record that's now three votes for 'Are you fucking crazy?'" Antoni pipes up from the corner. "Just sayin' . . . please continue."

Clayton steps forward and corrals Jayson's shoulders into his hands.

"I'm tired of running, Jay. I've—*we've*—already lost too much," he says, glancing over at Antoni who shuffles his feet, repositioning his posture in the corner to an even more dramatic sulk. "If I'm going to go out, I'm going to make it on my own terms. Not running away. Not living in fear, constantly looking over my shoulder for what or who's coming after me. That's no way to live. That's not a life." He releases his tender embrace and steps back. "This is it. This is the only way."

Jayson shakes his head in rhythm with Clayton's back-pedaling.

"No," manages to be the first word uttered in between determined shakes. "No." And the second. "*No*." And apparently the third, with added emphasis. "I'm sorry but I'm not going to be the one responsible for your death. Not like this. Not after all you've been through," he continues between subtle shakes from left to right. "And if I give you my badge, you're already as good as dead. I just can't live with that guilt."

Clayton inhales, his head gracefully following the upward inflation of his chest. His next words closely adhere to a long, deep breath out.

"Yeah, I thought you might say something like that," he sighs and raises up his concealed right hand. Inside the clenched fist dangles Jayson's badge and unfastened clip. "That's why I didn't ask."

Jayson's eyes whiten as the involuntary reaction of surprise puppeteers his reflexes. He looks down at his belt in denial while frantically feeling around his waist for the suspended plastic rectangle that's no longer there.

"Pretty sly, Clay," he says, shooting a sarcastic grin at his friend, this time between nods. "That little fatherly gesture and speech was pretty slick. A real dickhead move, but slick. So, what now Evel Knievel? Into the fray without a helmet?"

"Two things, actually," Clayton says, revealing the retinal scanner that was hidden in his other hand. "First—" A click later and a brilliant red flash floods Jayson's vision blinding him.

"Argh! What the hell, man?" He flinches and immediately starts rubbing his eyes in a desperate attempt to help jog the sight back into them.

"Eeeesh. Sorry, Jay, I forgot how bright that actually is. But I figured if I'd asked, you'd have just said no again."

"Yeah, no shit. You just *Men in Black*-ed me."

"Sans the whole memory loss part though," Antoni chimes in again from the peanut gallery. "Just to be clear."

Jayson continues the rubbing and blinking fit as his dotted pupils start to slowly expand, readjusting to the room's dim lighting.

"Do I even want to ask what the second thing you need is? Or should I just curl up, close my eyes, and take cover?"

"Well, now that you mention it . . . I could really use that other distraction from Rickers," Clayton adds with a forced grin. "How's your ass feeling?"

Still trying to refine his vision, Jayson shoots a series of short and long pronounced blinks at Clayton, largely as aftermath from the scanner's disarray, but also to quietly and visually Morse code 'F-U-C-K_Y-O-U' in his general direction.

"Apparently, like it's ready to be chewed out," he finally responds.

With his sight returned, his blurry gaze lingers on his friend. He's not sure if the guise is a hopeless holdout for Clayton to change his mind, or if it's a subtle way to say his final goodbye should this be it. After a few prolonged seconds, he breaks eye contact and turns around to head for the exit. He grabs the handle but pivots back toward Clayton one last time.

"Hey Clay—" There's an uneasy urgency in his voice combined with a look of fear that Clayton hasn't seen other than during their narrow Hunt anniversary parking lot escape. "—don't do anything too stupid. Okay?"

Matching his sincerity, Clayton responds, "You know I can't make that promise, Jay."

"Yeah, I figured you'd say that," he sighs. "Just be careful. Besides—" A wave of light-hearted insecurity replaces his despair, forcing a small smirk. "—you still owe me a phone, and I can't collect from a dead guy."

Clayton digs into his pocket and pulls out Jayson's smartphone. "You mean this?" he says, waving the device. "How about I hold onto it then, for just a little longer?"

What was a forced grin full of nervous desperation is replaced by a genuine smile.

And just like that, the door shuts behind his exit.

Clayton wastes no time, diverting his attention back to the bank of monitors behind him. He watches intently, his eyes jumping from screen to screen as Jayson marches down the hall as tribute. He makes it around the long corridor's corner before finding himself on a collision course with a steamrolling Rickers. The head-on collision hasn't happened yet, but judging by the familiar hand motions and the violent head movement, Jayson is already one cheek deep in his foreseeable ass-chewing.

"All right, guys, we don't have a lot of time and—"

"Clay," Kara interrupts. "Your face . . . it's starting to go back to normal."

Clayton instinctually reaches up to touch is cheeks. He can instantly feel fewer wrinkles upon contact as his skin continues to give way to gravity by the second.

"Shit. Okay, we really gotta hurry," he urges, looking over at Antoni who's still brooding in the corner. "Toni, how much time we working with here?"

Checking his watch, Antoni holds up an open hand to indicate five minutes. "Tops. Give or take a minute or two. But your retinal scan should still be good for a little while after that."

"Good enough. This may be a stupid question, but can you program Jayson's retinal capture to match the remaining time I have left on my current scan?" he asks, tossing the scanner to Antoni. "I need it to go along with his badge to gain dual access to the executive floors."

"Sure can. Might take me a minute but shouldn't be a problem," he confirms.

"Hex?" Clayton says, swiveling his ex-coworker around in his chair while his hair plays pin-the-tail-on-the-caboose again. "I need you to be my lookout."

"I'm all eyes and ears here, amigo."

A smile spreads across Clayton's face as he plants one hand on Hex's shoulder and uses the other to grab the duffle bag. He plops it onto the control console in front of the bank of monitors.

"What do you say we *expand* those eyes and ears a little?" he adds through a cheeky grin. "Toni?"

"Uh-huh," grunts a preoccupied voice in the corner as Antoni looks up from initiating the scanner's retinal sync.

"You still got that duct tape handy?"

A couple minutes later, Clayton is back slinking along the winding bowels of The Hunt for Justice. Based on the surveillance footage he saw before leaving the others behind, Rickers and Jayson had moved their "discussion" (read: ass-chewing) into the breakroom at the far end of the hall, inconveniently right next to his destination—the elevators.

Despite the dire circumstances, skulking his way along the walls of these stark halls to avoid detection is something that actually feels quite familiar. Like it's just another day of being chronically tardy for work—albeit the current stakes substantially greater. Only now, he's got help. As he nears the corner to the first intersection, he pulls out his radio.

"Hex, I need those beautiful browns of yours."

"Coast is clear, amigo." Hex radios back. "Just be quick and careful, *comprende*?"

Clayton holsters the radio and keeps creeping along praying that every room he walks by has the door closed or is vacant. When he finally has eyes on the elevators, he can start to hear a heated dialogue in the distance. The exchange grows more audibly aggressive as he nears the breakroom. Now, nudged right outside the door, he can hear every word in vivid and violent clarity. By the sound of it, Jayson's firmly two cheeks deep with actual bite marks to show for it.

"Tell me again, Moore. How in the hell did you get a false security alert?" Rickers grills, inching closer to Jayson's face, further encroaching on the gap of already barely-there personal space. So close and just level enough he can see his jungle of untamed nose hairs fighting for daylight. "Are you that goddamn stupid? Is that it?"

"Sir, I swear," Jayson preps, teeter-tottering on self-admonishment. It's a perfected veil of professionalism and years of being subjected to similar ass-chewings, all working together in his favor to conceal his true emotions and provide just enough restraint while looking innocent by playing dumb. "I thought I heard a code 22 on the radio. I wanted to—" But Jayson loses his train of thought when he catches a glimpse of Clayton poking his head out from around the exposed doorway.

"What goddammit?" Rickers snaps back, staring at Jayson like he's mentally impaired. "You wanted to what? Do you even fucking know? Are you even capable of intelligent thought?"

Jayson tries to quickly collect himself, dropping his gaze to help shield the spit-spewing rain from Rickers's shouting as it pelts his eyelids.

"Sir, I just . . . I just wanted to be safe, not sorry, especially with all the activity outside. I just thought—"

"That's the thing, Moore, you don't think. Between you and your butt buddy, Sparks, you're lucky to have half a fucking brain cell between the two of you," he fires back between bouts of heavy wheezing thanks to years of cholesterol-loaded vending machine three-course meals. The crimson color pooling in his cheeks and forehead is now just a seamless continuation of his red security button up.

"Speaking of, how the hell is Sparks still alive? I swear, if I had the time, I'd hunt his ass down personally and claim that reward money myself. Then I'd quit this god forsaken job so I wouldn't have to deal with shit-for-brain rejects like you."

The timing is far from perfect, but at Rickers's infatuated mention of 'hunting his ass down,' Clayton's injured shoulder unexpectedly goes numb again and gives out. The sudden slack causes him to lose his braced grip against the doorframe and stumble into the wall. He does his best to stifle the accompanying grunt of pain with his other hand, but he fails in the unexpected attempt as a groan sneaks out through his loose fingers.

Rickers whips around at the commotion as Clayton swiftly ducks back behind the doorframe, clutching his mouth firmly with both hands this time.

"What was that?" Rickers inquires, his words still carrying an underlying hostility.

Playing dumb, which should come across as natural according to Rickers, Jayson naively responds, "What was what, sir?"

"That noise," Rickers clarifies, taking a step toward the doorway.

"Sounded like something out in the hallway. Is somebody out there?"

But before he can finish his left-right-left march to the door, Jayson takes two sweeping lunges forward to cut him off at the exit. Right before exposing Clayton, who is turning a violet shade from holding his breath, on the opposite side of the paper-thin drywall.

"I'm s-sorry, sir, you're right. It was my bad," Jayson confesses, reverting the subject back to ass-chewing ground zero. "I fucked up. It won't happen again. I promise. Do you want me to go back to my post to relieve Beck or . . . ?"

"Huh?" Rickers responds. His eyes still transfixed on the doorway and its phantom ruckus. "Oh, uh, yeah. Carry on," he mutters, slowly tracking his gaze back to Jayson. "Just make sure to remove your head from your ass; otherwise, our next conversation isn't going to end so well. Understood?"

"Understood, sir."

"Good. Now get the hell out of here," Rickers commands, shooing him away. As Jayson turns to leave, he catches Rickers charting a deliberate path to the corner of the breakroom—straight for the vending machines. Right on cue, if there ever was one.

With Rickers distracted by dozens of artery-clogging suitors, Jayson tentatively takes another step through the doorway, but by the time he reaches the hall, he's alone. There's no sign of Clayton anywhere. He breathes a sigh of relief.

"Good luck, buddy," he whispers. "You're gonna need all you can get."

# CHAPTER 41

Clayton flings himself into the elevator cab before the doors can fully part. Immediately, he pounds the Door Close arrow before even establishing that he's actually alone in the modern cube of pulleys and winches. Somewhere between the seventh and tenth poke, the doors finally reciprocate his urgency and shut.

He can't help but notice how fitting the whole scene feels, like the doors aren't the only thing being sealed. As if somehow his fate delicately hangs in the ensuing closure of their near-seamless gap.

"It's now or never," he whispers under the pull of a deep breath. "There's no turning back now."

He reaches down to his hip and extends the zip cord on Jayson's badge. Carefully, he touches the plastic rectangle to the magnetic pad while simultaneously bending over to prepare for the retinal scan. With a scrunched stare and his teeth gnashed in an agonizing duality of hope that all of Antoni's scanner tech actually works, he slowly eases the death grip on his eyelids as the red line submerges his line of sight.

"C'mon, c'mon, c'mon. Please work. Please work," he murmurs while doing his best not to blink.

Normally, the scan verifies authentication within one swift pass, but after its initial descent the light indicator still reads solid red. Dread starts to seep into his head causing beads of spontaneous perspiration to pepper his hairline. Each swelling droplet a further reminder of what's at stake.

"Shit, it never takes this long," he whispers anxiously, as the sweaty forehead globs begin to congregate, pooling into streams ready to gush.

The scanner beam rotates 180 degrees and begins its second ascending pass across his eyes. Still fighting the urge to blink or bail, Clayton maintains eye contact, praying that he hasn't run out of time with the recognition scrambler.

Halfway through its second scan, the red retina light stalls. He peers down without moving his face and sees the authorization indicator has flipped to his new favorite color—a flickering tint of green.

"Holy shit, it actually worked," he gasps, taking a step back to compose himself and wipe the streaking sweat from his brow. "All right, here goes nothing. And everything," he sighs and pokes the 165th-floor button to Klein's penthouse.

In the brief, idle moments while the lift soars above dozens of blurred stories, Clayton's mind goes blank as he catches his distorted features in the metallic doors. The warped reflection returning his gaze cues a flashback to the first time he ever rode this elevator.

He was on the way to ask Klein for a job. The whole thing being Trish's idea, of course. He didn't want to seem desperate, groveling for a handout as the boyfriend to the daughter of one of the nation's most powerful figures. But the truth is, he was desperate. He must have applied to fifty jobs when he was freshly paroled, but nobody thought twice to hire a recently released ex-con, nonetheless one with his rap sheet. Not unless he wanted to flip burgers at Chow Down with the local high schoolers and adult riffraff, dealing with the revolving carousel of asshole customers just to make the unlivable minimum wage of jack and shit.

He remembers being so nervous on that first elevator ride. Filled with all the anxiety of a teenage boy meeting his girlfriend's hard-ass father for the first time. But it wasn't that he feared Klein back then. Even now, on his way to the lion's den for what could surely be his actual end, he's not afraid. Just hesitant, like he was on that initial ride. Apprehensive about the lack of power and control he had going into a last resort situation. After all, it's never easy looking ultimate desperation square in the eye with a smile—accepting that no matter how hard he minded his *p*'s and *q*'s, how charming he was, or what he would swear to do to right his past wrongs, Klein would never approve of him being with his daughter. Knowing that he would hold this moment, and all that resentment, over his head for as long as he and Trish were together.

Looking back, it was always a relationship doomed from the start. He just never imagined it would lead him here. Like this. Back to the beginning and this feeling.

As the lift comes to an abrupt yet virtually unnoticeable stop, the doors chime and slowly part. The digital ding snaps Clayton out of his mental bout with paralleled nostalgia as he spots Alexa Holbech sitting at the reception desk at the far end of the swanky penthouse lobby.

She casually looks up from her computer screen only to follow the nuanced action with a quick, concentrated double take. Clayton notes the mini déjà vu moment and steps out from the elevator. She jets up from her chair, but she doesn't scream. She doesn't reach for the phone or go for a hidden gun secretly stashed in the top drawer of her meticulously organized yet adorably personalized desk. She doesn't do anything. She just stands there, gawking at the nation's most wanted man standing before her.

Clayton is the first to break the silent shock.

"Hi, Alexa . . . I—" but before he can finish his jumbled introduction, she finds her greeting. More specifically, the surprised salutation finds her.

"Clay . . . oh my god, you're alive! And here!" she exclaims, as she takes two steps forward and one baby step back. Not to seem too eager.

"Alive is one way to put it," he replies, repositioning his shoulder as a groan slips out. Playfully, he raises his hands. "You're not gonna pull out a gun and shoot me or anything, are you?"

A small, anxious laugh escapes as she snakes around her desk. She's wearing a short, barely below the thigh skirt with red heels that further accentuate the tone and contour of her olive legs. And her blouse's cleavage is dangerously stuck in an unbuttoned limbo—one clasp between the threshold of business professional and borderline stripper. It's a risqué ensemble he's pretty sure Klein is the mastermind behind.

"What? No. I would never," she defends at the playful slight. "I know you didn't kill . . . I mean, I know you didn't do it."

Clayton takes another step forward, this time with less caution in his gate.

"You do?" he lets out. "And how is that exactly?"

Alexa mirrors his approach, taking a small stride forward of her own.

"Because I . . . I saw the way you looked at her," she answers with her own steadfast gaze. Clayton tilts his head at the statement. "That night at the anniversary party—" She continues with a hard swallow, doing her best to prod gently around her next sentence. "—the night Trish *died*. In the gambling hall, I saw you look at her. Look at her like . . . like nothing else in the world even existed." Her gaze folds under the weight of his stare. "Like it was just her. And you. And no one else. Like true love."

Clayton parses his lips, thinking back to the last memory he has of Trish. Her trembling body slowly bleeding out while swaddled in his arms, helplessly watching the life escape her. He clears his throat, suppressing the all-too-familiar wave of grief.

"I-I think you're the first person outside of my friends who hasn't literally wanted to kill me," he responds while nervously running his hand through his hair. "Sorry for the bluntness. It's been a helluva last couple days."

He doesn't know why, but as his look lingers on her eyes, he's reminded again of Trish. Maybe it's the similar tenderness gleaming through her soft stare that's forcing the association, or maybe it's the fact that her hair is pulled back in a high and tight ponytail, just like Trish used to wear when she'd paint. He can't quite put his finger on it, but the random correlation completely derails him from his train of thought until he hears a page from Alexa's desk. They turn in unison toward the source of the trebly voice, and he notes an opened whiskey collector's set, featuring an ultra-rare bottle of expensive Irish cask next to the speaker phone. Nestled on the flanking doors of the collectible boxset is a fancy timepiece and an ornate Fabergé Celtic Egg.

"*Holbech, I'm due on stage in under ten minutes. Where is that bottle of Emerald Isle I asked for?*"

The vex of Klein's voice is enough to snap Clayton from his sidetrack of spoils back to the tension of the task at hand.

"Alexa, I need you to grab your things right now and leave," Clayton calmly orders while motioning for her jacket on the coat rack behind her desk. "It's not safe for you here, and I'm not about to put anyone else in danger, especially you."

Before she has much of a choice to respond, let alone react, he's already herding her toward the elevator in a frantic frenzy. He slams the call button, and the urgent action is instantly followed by a familiar ding as the stationary metallic slabs part. He gently pushes her inside, but as the doors close, she reaches out a hand to stop them.

"Clay, this is crazy," she says, continuing to hold the doors apart. "What are you planning to do? Please tell me you're not planning to—"

"You trust me, right?" he interjects.

She recoils with a blank stare back. Her initial look spells confusion, but it's grounded in more surprise from the question than actual misunderstanding.

"Y-yes," she squeaks. "I trust you."

A half smile teeter-totters on the corners of his lips.

"Then you've got nothing to worry about. I promise. Now, go down to the garage, get in your car, and don't speak to anyone until you get home," he cooly directs. A blank stare lingers on her face, as if not sure how to fully unload the command. "Okay?" he follows up.

"But I . . . I . . ."

"Do you understand?" he reaffirms.

"Yes," she sighs begrudgingly. "I understand, but this is crazy. What—?"

"Good." He cuts her off again, and places his hand on hers, easing her grip from the doors. Her skin as soft to the touch as it looks. "Thank you, Alexa."

"What for?" she poses, as the doors re-engage their shutting trajectory.

"For believing in me, when no one else would," he responds, as the last sliver of her face disappears behind the shiny steel sheets.

Clayton thumps his head against the closed doors' metallic finish in a futile hope that the crisp surface will somehow help him keep a cool head. Leaning into the prolonged pose, he does his best to refasten his frayed focus and fleeting courage, along with anything else he can find the strength to muster that will help him combat what ultimately looms next.

After scrounging up all the resolve he can, he drives his fist into the closed doors and spins away from the lift. Casually, he strolls by Alexa's desk and snatches the egg and bottle of the oldest and rarest triple-distilled single malt in existence from the lavish box-set. Tearing away the virgin seal, he pops out the cork and takes a big pull. The golden gulp ignites his insides with spicy notes of pepper and clove, refueling the fiery vengeance raging inside. He immediately downs one more sizable swig. Ready or not, it's time to tame the lion.

Pushing the historic cedar door aside, he spots his adversary sitting in his ridiculous throne of an office chair rehearsing a speech from a translucent screen atop his antique desk. The virtual text hovers in the air like words written in glass, free from the confines of a traditional monitor. Clayton can hear him reciting the address underneath his breath, perfecting that familiar *bow before me* tone that even God himself wouldn't dare question.

The arrogance more pungent than ever.

"*. . . That is why, my dear citizens, my countrymen—my brothers and sisters around the world—The Hunt: Global Pass will revolutionize the scale of universal justice as we know it. For I am just one man. But together. Together, we can revolutionize the world. And claim absolute righteousness for all.*"

"Were you always full of this much shit or did it all come with the job?" Clayton boldly interrupts, not an ounce of hesitation in his voice.

Without even bothering to look up, Klein stops rehearsing. The pause is quickly followed by the see-through screen receding into its sleek futuristic projector comically juxtaposed on his centuries-old desk. Scrupulously, he removes his bifocals with both hands, delicately tucks them into his breast pocket, and turns to face his surprise visitor. His gaze not so much slow as it is calculated to greet Clayton at the door.

"Ahh, Sparky," he retorts through a Grinch-like grin. "Bravo. Even I must admit. Although painstakingly irritated at your current existence, I am impressed. I never imagined you would last this long."

He reclines back into his throne, crossing his hands and legs in purposeful unison.

"Perhaps, I judged your character—your diligence—too quickly. After all, one cannot deny your spirit. Your irksome tenacity. You do have fight inside you, Sparky. I will give you that. But then again, that's exactly what got you into this mess in the first place now isn't it?"

Clayton takes a couple steps deeper into the jaws of the final boss's quarters. Again, surveying the taxidermied animal heads and ancient weaponry that bathe the walls in death, he can feel his primal instinct kick in as the feeling of fight or flight hits with each cautious stride.

There's nothing he'd enjoy more right now than to rip down one of the many broadswords from its hanger and take a swing across Klein's collar-tailored neck. To end it all in one vengeful blow—a dose of his own justice, just like that. But he doesn't act upon the impulse. He can't. And the fact that nothing is stopping him other than his own self-restraint feels almost ironic in a twisted way.

Instead, he takes another pull from the triple-distilled, single malt bottle and another step closer to Klein.

"You know, this stuff really is tasty. And to be honest, I'm not much for whiskey. More of a tequila guy, myself. Or mezcal. Trish and I *loved* mezcal. But this? Damn, it's good," he says, wiping the excess dribble of near-priceless liquor from his lips with his raggedy flannel sleeve. "It even came with this cute little egg thing. What's a posh set like this cost you anyway?"

"More than you'd know what to do with," Klein responds, aggravated as he watches Clayton toy with his perfectly good and stupidly expensive imported items.

"Oh, I'm sure," Clayton adds, studying the Fabergé egg's 18-karat yellow gold, hand-painted guilloché enamel, and diamond-encrusted Celtic knot clasp. "I mean, just look at this thing. It's absolutely gorgeous. Oh, damn, would you look at that. It even opens up. Whoa . . . is that *real* sapphire?"

"Yes," Klein resentfully answers.

"Hmm. That's a shame," Clayton remarks, before he violently chucks the bottle and egg against the trophy-laden wall behind Klein. Remnants of the rarest liquid gold in existence and shards of colorful glass and beautiful enamel splatter all over him and his desk as he fails to duck for cover fast enough. The immediate aftermath resembles the scene of a shattered, sacred stained-glass window. Slowly, Klein staggers back to posture. As he rises, he tugs on his suit jacket with one hand, wiping the whiskey residue from his cheek into his mouth with the other.

"Cute, Sparky. Very cute," he says, continuing to lick the accumulation from his fingers as he struts to the front of his desk. He attends to the remaining few glass shards clinging to his padded suit shoulder, brushing them off with thick insignificance. "I didn't figure you came here just to drink my expensive liquor," he adds, adjusting his diamond-cut Asscher cufflinks without missing a beat. "So, why *are* you here? You've either got bigger balls than I gave you credit for, or you're even dumber than I ever imagined."

"Well, you know what they say, Simon," Clayton juts in, taking another series of steps closer. "Keep your friends close and your enemies closer, right?"

"Hmm," Klein utters, delicately primping his liquor-dampened hair. "You have no idea how true that is."

"Oh, you see, but I do. I really do," Clayton pursues, going tit for tat with Klein's overconfidence. "Does the name Chad Sommers ring a bell to you?"

Klein's unwavering internal demeanor instantly shudders at the question. Clayton takes notice as his foe clenches his fist from the unsolicited sensation of his palms moistening. It appears swallowing has also suddenly become more of a chore for him. Subtly, he readjusts his seat against the front of the desk and does his best to bluff by playing coy.

"Chad? Chad, who?"

"You know what?" Clayton says as he digs his hand into his back pocket. "Maybe you're more of a visual guy. Yeah, you could definitely benefit from a visual aid. After all, you're a busy guy who knows a lot of people, right? A common name like Chad Sommers might not ring a bell. But maybe his picture will," he says as he tosses the old prom photo onto Klein's desk. "Go ahead, take a good, long look."

Klein does his best to ignore the picture. Clayton notices and pushes the envelope.

"Aww, what's the matter, Simon? Don't want to play show-and-tell?"

The slight opposition is all it takes. Reluctantly, a sparkling suit sleeve reaches across the desk for the photo.

"I'm sure you already know this, but just to help you out, Chad's the good ol' country boy with his arm around the cute girl in the purple prom dress. Her name's Becky Gould. Or perhaps you know her better as Rebecca Klein since you're not too great with names and all."

He reads behind Klein's eyes, finding the hairline crack where his bluff is weakening with every pointed question. "Yeah. That one rings a bell now, doesn't it?"

Klein continues to study the photo, but he's able to maintain a cool and collected gaze, even when his eyes stumble across his dead wife as a jubilant teen prom queen with her whole life still ahead of her.

"So, you have an old photo of my deceased wife when she was a teenager," Klein reiterates, crumbling the photo and tossing it to the floor. He adjusts the tautness of his double Windsor knot. "Who cares?"

Clayton smiles back. "You know, that's a great question, Simon. And I'm pretty sure I have an even better answer," he emphasizes, as he strolls behind Klein's desk, gesturing to the penthouse's view of the citywide commotion outside.

"Everyone will," Clayton continues. "Bannerton. America. The world. They're all going to care. And I know, somewhere deep down in that empty abyss where you should have a soul, you know *why* they're going to care."

He takes a page out of Klein's own playbook and gazes with a dramatic lingered look out the window before slowly turning back to face him.

"Sorry, what was I saying again? Oh yeah, of course, you do. Of course, you know why they're going to care. How could you not? After all, you're the one responsible for both their deaths. Or should I say one death and one disappearance? But let's be honest, you and I both know what really happened. You had Chad offed, too, didn't you?" Clayton accuses, as he takes a studied seat upon the throne, the symbolism not lost on Klein.

"But hold up a sec, because I'm getting ahead of myself now. So, let's just rewind a bit, shall we? You see, the day you blackmailed me, I saw you talking to a very questionable ogre of a man on the server floor. This big, bullish bowling ball-looking fuck that I now know as Marco. And I almost wrote it off. But then, I got a flash of his gun and I just had to investigate. So, I followed you guys and spied in on your conversation on the data floor. And that's when I heard him mention something revelatory. Something around the lines of 'yada, yada, yada . . . just like your wife.' And it occurred to me," Clayton continues, mimicking Klein by simultaneously crossing his legs while folding his hands. As if falling more comfortable into the plush of the chair and meat of his story. "How *did* Rebecca Klein actually die? You see, Trish never told me all the details because she never really knew them. Did she, Simon?"

He fires a rhetorical question in Klein's seething direction. "So, you know what I did next? I went to look up her file in the server room myself. Damn near got caught by you guys in the process, too. But when I finally found it, it was strange. Her report was practically blank. It was like her death had never happened. Like it didn't even exist." He pauses, reverting his attention to a power button pulsating from the cubed projector on the desk. He pushes the embedded icon on the device, instantly maximizing Klein's speech on the transparent throw screen, right where he left off rehearsing.

Clayton reads a few lines on the sheer screen and shakes his head. "Good god, where do you come up with all this messiah-wanna-be bullshit?" he asks, again rhetorically.

"Anyway, I keep getting sidetracked. where was I?" he says, again posing yet another rhetorical question with no use or time to await an answer. "Ah, yes, the server room and Rebecca's nonexistent file. But let's fast forward just a tad to the anniversary party because that's where things actually start to heat up. Remember? It was the night you tried to have Marco kill me after bribing me that very morning, and thus, starting this whole shit show I've found myself buried in—" He forces out the lump in his throat. "And not to mention, killing the woman I loved, and your daughter, in the process."

"I'd ask if you're following along, Simon, but the silent treatment combined with that murderous look on your face tells me you're keeping up just fine," Clayton adds, kicking up his dirty feet atop the one-of-a-kind desk. "So, can you guess what I did next? Just take a shot . . ." he trails off, surveying the surplus of floor-to-ceiling projectile weaponry behind the desk. "Yikes. Maybe a poor choice of words on my part."

Klein, who has slowly worked his way to the window overlooking the crowd stories below, protestingly responds with his back still turned.

"Why don't you enlighten me?"

"Ah, see. I knew you were still following along all right," Clayton teases before continuing. "Well, Simon, I *was* able to track her file down. It wasn't easy, I've got to admit. You did a pretty damn good job of hiding that shit. But I eventually found it. You know that secret data lab of yours in the West Bottoms truly is hard to find. Not impossible, but definitely not easy. And wow, super high-tech. But unfortunately, for me, even that wasn't enough info to go on. Again, I've got to hand it to you, you really did your best to cover all your bases. Or, so I thought," Clayton presses while simultaneously taking a moment to pet the plush, suede finish of the throne. "This really is nice, by the way. It's like a heavenly cloud cradling your ass. I can finally see the appeal of this ostentatious thing."

"That's a big word for a small mind," Klein says, finally turning from the window to size up Clayton.

"What can I say? I read on a high school level," he quickly counters. "Anyway, I didn't mean to leave you hanging, Simon, especially since this is where it starts to get really good," Clayton adds and drags his index finger across the desk through a small, shard-free puddle of the exorbitantly priced Irish whiskey. After one seamless swipe, he licks off the smoky remains.

"Mmm. Still good. So, can you guess where I'm going yet? Or would you like me to continue?" he pauses, letting Klein feel like he has a chance to speak before abruptly cutting him off.

"See, I got curious about where your wife *actually* died; after all, it's the one thing I did find in her report. So, I paid little Becky Gould's former residence a visit. You ever been to Shermer, Missouri, Simon? It's super quaint. Just this majestic little farm town in the middle of Nowhere, USA. If you ever do go, I highly recommend Louellen's Diner. The food was great, and Annie's service was impeccable. Five stars."

Clayton gives the lavish penthouse a once-over.

"Although, it's probably not up to your standards," he jests, again dragging his finger across the stark desk. "Too much dirt. Not enough class."

Klein's scorching scowl, much like his patience, appears to be flickering out from the abundance of theatrics, so Clayton gets back on track before he loses his hostile audience of one.

"Anyways, you'll never believe what I found out while I was down there. Any guesses?"

Klein doesn't say a word or bat an eye.

"No? Well, it turns out your henchman of the year, Marco, has also been there. In fact, he was there the night of Rebecca Klein's fifteen-year high school reunion. Coincidently, the very same night that she died, and Chad Sommers mysteriously disappeared. I mean, *really*, what are the odds?" Clayton asks, jutting up from the chair and walking back around the desk.

He makes it a point to stroll directly behind Klein who follows his movement carefully from his peripheral.

"Yeah, it turns out those two high school sweethearts had been secretly messaging each other for months before the reunion. Maybe even years. Emails and love letters all saying how Rebecca had told Chad she planned to take Trish and leave you to run off with him. Messages that outlined how you were never around, and abusive when you were, and that you didn't care about anyone or anything else aside from work and your next shot at notoriety. But why am I telling you all this?" Clayton eggs on. "This is all just old news to you, right? Her life just a stepping stone for your next great career move. The kind of story a young, hot shot lawyer on the rise like yourself needed to finally get to the next level. And you justified it all because you couldn't deal with the fact that you weren't enough for her. For them."

He takes another couple steps closer to Klein, the two now practically standing nose to nose.

"Oh, wait—" Clayton adds. His demeanor shifts to a more serious and deliberate tone. "There is just one more thing I think you should know. One big piece of news that you weren't privy to before Trish died. Tell me, Simon, did you know that your daughter was pregnant?"

At last, the hardened bluff of being dealt losing hand after losing hand by Clayton finally folds from Klein's fledgling poker face. It's replaced by a fragile sincerity in the form of glassy eyes. His onyx pupils reflect a rare, long-lost glimpse of humanity.

"That's right," Clayton reiterates, his own eyes swelling to a murky mess. "You didn't just kill your wife. And your daughter. You killed your grandchild, too."

Klein staggers back in retreat as the shockwave sends him on a heedless collision with his desk. He stumbles but composes himself just enough to grab a saving seat upon his throne. His glazed gaze wanders from focus, getting lost somewhere in the thick fog of his guilty conscience. Buried down deep in a grave of moral culpability.

Clayton steps forward and slams his fists upon the desk.

"How's that for a story, you son of a bitch?"

The impact triggers Klein's concentration to rise back to the surface. It's immediately overshadowed by the second logical phase in the five-step process of acceptance: anger.

"Why you . . . you little . . . fucking shit," he blurts out, suffering from a rare loss of preachy vocabulary while surrendering the moral high ground for once. "If you had just taken the goddamn deal and disappeared like I offered, my daughter and grandchild would still be alive. But just like your own life, you've gone and fucked it all up."

"Maybe," Clayton replies, removing his hands from the desk and easing back. "Maybe you're right, Simon. But even if you weren't the vile piece of shit that I know you are, and Trish and our baby were still alive, it wouldn't change the outcome for Becky Gould or Chad Sommers. Or anyone else you may have disposed of over the last two-plus decades that got in your way. At the end of the day, you're still the murderer. Not me."

"Hah! That slut and her redneck lover?" Klein scoffs at the accusation. His out-of-character, emotional burst devilish yet again. He reaches down and slides open one of the many ornate drawers in his old-fashioned desk. Clayton takes a reflexive step back in defense.

But when Klein's hands re-enter the safety of his line of sight, the only thing they're wielding are a cut crystal decanter and an empty rocks glass. He begins to pour himself a drink, acting as if this whole ordeal has been nothing more than a cordial catch-up among former acquaintances.

"As far as I'm concerned, those two got just what they deserved," he continues, topping off his stiff pour. "I gave my wife everything she ever wanted—a life of luxury, prestige, a family—and how does that whore repay me? By fucking around behind my back with some cornbread, backwoods, high school sweetheart townie."

He takes a long drink from the glass, making every single drop of the amber pour vanish. His mustache flinches as he bites to savor the sting from the aftertaste.

"Although, I guess I should really thank her for her unfaithfulness. Rebecca's heartbreaking death was just the thing I needed. The perfect sympathy crutch to get The Hunt Initiative up and running and capture the hearts of millions. And now, billions. It's truly amazing what a good sob story can do for business. I owe everything I have to taking her life. And now, I get the pleasure of taking yours for the whole world to see. To cement my legacy and all of which I've built. And there's not a goddamn thing you can do about it."

He pours one last glass from the accompanying decanter and throws it back in a single, seamless gulp.

"This is where your story ends, Sparky," he adds through liquored lips and his signature smirk.

Suddenly, Klein's office doors fling open, nearly escaping from their hinges as a patrol of security led by Rickers storms into the room with weapons drawn.

"Don't move, asshole," Rickers barks behind the overcompensating barrel of his elongated handgun.

"Remember earlier when I said you either had a bigger pair of balls than I thought or you're even dumber than I imagined?" Klein reinforces, as he gestures to a little red button underneath his desk. "I guess it turns out it's the latter, Sparky. A shame but I can't say I'm surprised."

He notions to Rickers and within a second, three of the security detail accost Clayton, throwing him without caution up against the vintage desk. The rocks glass, decanter, and lamp all crash to the floor from the violent impact.

"Careful with the desk, boys, goddammit," Klein beckons. "It's worth more than your salaries combined."

"You heard what Mr. Klein said, men. Take him to the ground. Now!" Rickers orders.

They continue to grapple as the scuffle moves to the floor. Clayton does little to resist as two of the men force his arms behind his back and slap handcuffs around his wrists. He holds in a cry of pain as the hand attached to his injured shoulder is involuntarily shoved into its metal restraint.

Rickers struts over to his captive. Towering above his shackled prey, he surveys the scene like a proud hunter who has just bagged his prize kill. He bends down, hovering just over Clayton's ear.

"Your ass is mine now, Sparks," he whispers.

Still stifling the anguish from his injured shoulder, Clayton manages a composed comeback befitting for the situation. After all, what else does he have left to lose?

"Flirting with the butt stuff again, huh Ricky?"

Clayton's cheeky punchline is immediately followed by Rickers's fat fist as it slams into his jaw in an attempt to rid the shit-eating grin from it. It doesn't have the desired effect as Clayton raises back up flashing a mouthful of peppermint-swirled Tic Tacs.

"That all you got? C'mon hit me again, Ricky, down there. Just for shits and giggles."

"Keep laughing you son of a bitch," Rickers mutters, and cocks his fist back ready to catapult another blow.

"That's enough," Klein commands, just in time to prevent the second pummeling.

Rickers lowers his fist and straightens back up, adjusting his distended utility belt and unintentional crop top security shirt in the process.

"What do you want us to do with him, sir?" he implores between heavy, out-of-shape-induced huffs.

Klein stoically gets up from his desk and turns to face the window wall yet again. He checks his watch as if curious to know the time but in no way bound to it. Meanwhile, the view of the masses below continues to increase in sprawl, pouring out into corresponding side streets for blocks on end as far as the eye can see. Their restlessness from awaiting his address growing more apparent by the uptick in volume, both in sound and size.

A smile fills the gap underneath the canopy of Klein's manicured mustache.

"Bring him down to the stage. I want to remind the world first-hand exactly what The Hunt Initiative stands for."

The massive, courthouse-like double doors to The Hunt for Justice open as the roar of the crowd soars beyond decibel recognition. Klein steps out into the daylight toward the glass podium that has been meticulously set up for him. There's an even richer air of confidence beneath his polished shoes as each step taken in his satin black wingtips is greeted by louder cheers and a growing barrage of camera flashes from the ground and sky alike. His every move graces the live broadcast on the massive, oversized monitors that flank the mobile stage—a viewable sprawl from miles away across Bannerton's entire downtown to the edge of its suburbs. Upon his arrival at the translucent podium, he looks out across the sea of people. His faithful followers. His flock. It's as close to being God as a man can get.

After a sufficient fill of basking in their adoration, he raises his hand to gesture for silence. It's granted almost instantly as a unified hush befalls the inspired congregation.

"*Justice,*" he begins with a single word. "*True justice is an enduring flame that lights our path. You can't extinguish it. You can't hide from it. It doesn't burn out with time. It is the beacon of truth, now and always.*"

He clutches the sides of the glass lectern and drifts into the familiar cadence of one of his grandiose sermons.

"*When I created The Hunt Initiative twenty-five years ago, I sparked that imperishable flame. Ignited that eternal truth. And look how many good people it has helped light the way forward,*" he orates, gesturing to the crowd in a simultaneous eruption of applause. "*And, today of all days, justice has burned bright yet again. Ladies and gentlemen of Bannerton and for those watching across the world, I have lived up to my word. For there is no better right in this life than righting a wrong. Today, I bring you the ultimate display of true justice.*"

The oversized front doors to The Hunt for Justice dramatically part again as Clayton Sparks is escorted by Rickers and a trio of security personnel up to the podium. The crowd explodes in a fiery frenzy as a large contingent of violent cheers and chants echo throughout the teeming city.

"CLAYTON THE KILLER!"

"MURDERER! MURDERER!"

"JUSTICE FOR PATRICIA!"

Clayton watches as a handful of overzealous Hunters—a little too eager to cash in on his fresh $4 million bounty—are flagged and quickly restrained by additional security along the stand-up gate at the landing of the tower's steps.

Rickers kicks the back of Clayton's knee, dropping him into a stance of begging—a genuflection fit for reciting last rites.

"Where are your jokes now, asshole?" he whispers into his ear while brandishing a satisfied smirk. "I'd start saying your prayers. You're gonna need 'em."

Within seconds, the hostile crowd's hurled vulgarities turn physical as trash and other random debris rain down on Clayton. Klein allows the scene of public pandemonium to partake for a few moments before he raises his hand once again, ceasing the unruly scene and calming the masses.

"*My fellow Hunters of justice, it is only befitting that on the very day we roll out the next iteration of The Hunt Initiative to the world, our Global Pass, that we also demonstrate the full power of what this righteous system and the principles behind it were conceived to do. That we make an example of this man and his sins against all that we've built. Against our very existence. Against me."*

Klein diverts his attention from the crowd to Clayton, who returns his fixation through a swollen, bloodshot left eye thanks to Rickers's right hand. He adds an extra layer of crude consideration by spitting a weighty wad of bloody saliva onto Klein's pristine Oxfords. He follows the repulsive manners with a courteous smirk.

Visibly agitated by Clayton's continued level of defiance, even now in the waning moments of his life, Klein subtly shakes his heel and continues with his address.

"*Because . . . as you all can fully see, you may run from the law, but you can't hide from justice.*"

A sudden, deafening squeal of feedback pierces Klein's audio feed. The alarming shriek triggers a cascade of hands to cover their ears in choreographed unison as it reverberates throughout the crowd. The flanking stage monitors flicker a few times, stuttering the live transmission, before ultimately fading to total black. When the feed returns a few seconds later, it's again broadcasting a video of Klein. He's wearing the same suit, only it's not the live feed of him at the podium they were all just watching. It's a new, shaky cam recording of him in his office. And the voice coming through the PA system isn't his. It belongs to Clayton.

"*Does the name Chad Sommers ring a bell to you?*

*Chad? Chad, who?*"

. . .

"*You know what? Maybe you're more of a visual guy . . . A common name like Chad Sommers might not ring a bell. But maybe his picture will. Go ahead, take a good, long look.*"

. . .

"*I'm sure you already know this, but . . . Chad's the good ol' country boy with his arm around the cute girl in the purple prom dress . . . Becky Gould. Or, perhaps you know her better as Rebecca Klein . . . Yeah. That one rings a bell now, doesn't it?"*

. . .

At first, total confusion stirs the massive congregation. Not sure whether this new feed is part of Klein's speech or some kind of random technical difficulty, a low murmur quickly blankets the assembly.

But as the recording continues to play, it arrests the entire crowd's attention. Each person intently tunes in and hangs onto every line while more and more of a loose story weaves itself into the truth. Even the drones above have halted their trajectories, and the city rumble of a million-plus has fallen deathly silent like a ghost town.

Klein himself can't help but just stand in awe, transfixed like a moth to a flame, entirely unaware of its own impending doom.

"*Turns out those two high school sweethearts had been secretly messaging each other for months before the reunion. Maybe even years. Emails and love letters all saying how Rebecca had told Chad she planned to take Trish and leave you . . . but this is all just old news to you, right? Her life just a stepping stone for your next great career move.*"

. . .

*"Oh, wait . . . There is just one more thing I think you should know . . . that you weren't privy to before Trish died. Tell me, Simon, did you know that your daughter was pregnant?"*

. . .

"*That's right. You didn't just kill your wife. And your daughter. You killed your grandchild, too.*"

. . .

"*How's that for a story, you son of a bitch?*"

. . .

Klein's resurgence of guilt knocks him out of his stupor like a KO'd fighter regaining consciousness from a whiff of smelling salts. But he's the only one out of a million that's lucid. Every single other person and twice as many eyes and ears are still glued to the screens and speakers.

The crowd in front of him.

The security behind him.

Even the drones above him.

All their senses tuned in like satellites absorbing the beacon of truth.

Panic quickly replaces his paralysis. He searches his frantic mind for the right words, but it's as hopeless as a foot fighting for traction uphill on loose soil. And the only foot his mind can fathom at the moment is the one firmly wedged in his two-faced mouth.

"C-cut the screens! Somebody stop this!" he bellows to the onstage crew but to no avail.

"*But even if you weren't the vile piece of shit that I know you are, and Trish and our baby were still alive, it wouldn't change the outcome for Becky Gould or Chad Sommers . . . At the end of the day, you're still the murderer. Not me.*"

. . .

"Turn it off now, goddammit! Right now!" he continues to shout at everyone—to anyone who might listen.

After finally succumbing to the notion that no one is responding, he storms away from the podium for a different approach. He begins waving hysterically for his security team's attention, but they do nothing. Not even a flinch in the general direction of his petitions.

"*As far as I'm concerned, those two got just what they deserved. I gave my wife everything she ever wanted—a life of luxury, prestige, a family—and how does that whore repay me? By fucking around behind my back with some cornbread, backwoods, high school sweetheart townie.*"

. . .

The come-to-Jesus moment of his fruitless cries for help to stop the video finally overtake his conscience, but his will isn't fully ready to concede defeat. Switching emotional tactics, he runs back to the podium and snatches the microphone in one last hopeless try to regain control of his downward spiral. Another sharp squeal of feedback consumes the speakers before his amplified orders echo throughout every major road and alleyway of downtown Bannerton.

"I demand this treachery stop this instant! Do you hear me? This *instant*! Or so help me I will . . . I will . . . I'll . . ."

He continues to bark incoherent imperatives into the mic, but his commanding tone wavers across the PA through noticeable stutters of unease and inflections of doubt—humanity's age-old recipe for fear. Something he hasn't felt in years.

"T-turn it off! Turn it off now! I c-command it . . . I-I, someone, please—"

Despite his boisterous directives, which have now morphed into nothing more than a ramble of pathetic pleas, there continues to be no response. No one to come to his aid. To even care. Just the stillness of a million focused faces hardwired to the video screens before them. Listening, learning—rehabilitating. Inadvertently deprogramming themselves from a *just* system founded on lies and the propagandized minds wielded to build it.

"*I should really thank her for her unfaithfulness. Rebecca's heartbreaking death was just the thing I needed. The perfect sympathy crutch to get The Hunt Initiative up and running.*"

. . .

Paralysis. Panic. Fear. And now, desperation digs in as Klein begins running aimlessly across the stage in search of a way to cut the power to the screens' audio and visual feed himself.

"*It's truly amazing what a good sob story can do for business. I owe everything I have to taking her life.*"

. . .

He continues to scramble on stage, trying to do anything but stand idly by as his reputation, his brand, and his life—everything he's built—comes violently crashing down on him.

"*And now, I get the pleasure of taking yours for the whole world to see. To cement my legacy . . . And there's not a goddamn thing you can do about it. This is where your story ends, Sparky."*

Right as Rickers and security break into the office to restrain Clayton, the video feed ends. The screens again briefly cut to solid black before flickering back once more to the live broadcast of Klein on stage. He's stooped over a set of large speakers, yanking handfuls of random wires and chords bundled together in color-coded electrical tape. The broadcast camera zooms into his current image, spotlighting a desperate and disheveled old man who hardly resembles the confident and powerful figure they all revere him to be. His pristine three-piece suit and pressed tie now wrinkled and sweated through. His perfectly manicured combover flapped mockingly in the wind much to his chagrin, revealing a glimpse of the freckled beige dome hiding underneath.

Klein freezes at the realization that two million eyes are now concentrated back on him once again. He stops ripping at the bundle of wires, and with the frayed threads of his remaining dignity, attempts to cinch his tie and readjust his hairpiece. Only the perspiration on his bald head has pooled so much that it's preventing any devotion to the assignment. His façade is finished.

And then, a single, distant voice carries from the center of the crowd.

"Liar!"

It's followed by another.

"Liar!"

And then another. And another. Until the dispersed chants of "LIAR" quickly turn into a more serious accusation as even more of the betrayed flock begin to incite their anger and betrayal in clustered unison.

"He's a MURDERER! A MURDERER!"

"MUR-DER-ER! MUR-DE-RER!" swells on the tip of their thirsty tongues, surfing throughout the sea of sheep-turned-lions.

Until finally, one chant swallows the entire congregation.

"HUNT! HUNT! HUNT! HUNT!"

The roar continues to build as more and more of the disgruntled masses chime in. The mantra of more than a million is deafening. Trash and debris from the hostile crowd again start raining down upon the stage, only this time honed at a new target.

Klein puts his arms up in a vain attempt to deflect the array of water bottles, half-eaten food, rocks, and other chunks of earth as they soar by, soiling his suit and reputation even further. In one last feat of utter desperation, he runs over to the podium and again grabs the microphone. With the poisonous combo of fear and despair more evident in his voice now than ever before, his shamble of words spill out.

"L-ladies and g-gentlemen, please . . . please," he beckons as a can of soda explodes upon impact with the platform, fizzing all over his jacket. "My f-fellow Hunters of justice, y-you don't understand. I can explain. I can . . . I can . . . I . . ."

But the thought doesn't reach completion. He just stands frozen, helplessly watching his flock continue to turn against him. A city full of justified Judases ready to hand him over for far less than thirty pieces of silver. And the spark that once lit the drive in his determined eyes, now extinguished—replaced by the dread of impending doom. There's nothing left but a vacant stare of hopelessness pleading for mercy. The very thing he built an entire empire preying on.

"Looks like you were right, Simon," Clayton leans over and says to him, still kneeling. "This is where *your* story ends."

Klein doesn't say a word. No hint of a condescending rebuttal. No attempt at a preachy homily. Just basic instinct as he lunges toward Clayton and throws his hands around his neck, shaking it in a fit of primal rage. Still shackled with a bum shoulder and his hands behind his back, Clayton can do nothing except writhe under the pressure of the choke as air quickly ceases to replenish his lungs. In between bouts of battling consciousness, a lone image of Trish floods his waning thoughts.

How her rose red lips perfectly framed her infectious smile. The way her jet-black hair used to look almost violet in just the right sunlight. How she seemed to make everything she touched better. How she made him better.

Before he can feel the life fully flee his body, three figures leap in and peel Klein away. Clayton rolls over alternating between bouts of dry heaving and violent coughing as his body naturally tries to jump-start the rush of oxygen back into his brain and body. He looks up through teary eyes to see a blurred view of Jayson and Hex standing over him, along with Rickers who is doing his best to detain a kicking and screaming Klein. Tucked in the background just outside of The Hunt for Justice's main entrance he spots Antoni and Kara.

Klein struggles to his feet spouting commands and threats to be released at his head security officer.

"Get your hands off me this instant," he shouts, squirming to regain control of the arms securely pinned behind his back. "I command you to release me. Do you hear me? That's an order, goddammit!"

But no such release is granted as he continues his futile fight for freedom. After enough of a tussle, the slow realization that nothing he can say or do will help, finally permeates his will and he stops resisting. Rickers follows suit and eases the tension on his grip, but the slightest slack gives Klein just enough opportunity to break free and draw the gun from his chief of security's holster.

Vulnerably restrained and still on the ground trying to catch his breath, Clayton has no chance at defending himself as Klein arcs the gun toward him. There's no pompous prophesying or famous last words. Just the guise of malice and rage as he aims the long-barreled revolver right between Clayton's eyes.

He can only clench them shut as the lone shot echoes throughout the downtown skyscrapers, silencing the crowd.

With his eyes still clamped, ready for death to come, Clayton waits. A second goes by, but there's no pain. Then another. No magical light at the end of the tunnel.

As he pries open his eyelids, slowly raising the fleshy curtains, Antoni blurs into focus. He's squirming on the ground next to him, holding the right side of his abdomen. His hands are covered in blood and a puddle has already formed around the perimeter of his prone outline.

Total shock paints Klein's already pale face an even ghostlier shade of white as he stands open-mouthed above the smoking barrel. Like any wild animal cornered against a wall and completely out of options, he has to make the instinctual decision between fight or flight.

He chooses the latter.

Scampering down the stairs of The Hunt for Justice, Klein fires a series of three warning shots into the air to clear a path in the crowd. The manipulated wave of bodies separates like a blood-red sea, affording him just enough of a trail to Moses his way through. Frantic and fearful with every fleeing step, he wields the gun in a mad frenzy, spinning around and waving the firearm at anyone he deems too close for comfort.

"Get back!" he yells, jutting the gun in all directions and capping off another sky-bound warning round. "Get back, I said. Or I'll shoot. I swear to God, I'll shoot. I'll shoot you all. Get back!"

He fires the gun again as a daring man wearing a black leather jacket tries to sneak up from behind him. The shot barely misses, but the effect is still successful as the pursuer retreats back into the crowd. Twisting around, he spots another man in a field jacket and Stetson hat make a move toward him. He takes aim and squeezes the trigger.

*Click.*

He tries again.

*Click.*

And again, in a feverish series.

*Click. Click. Click.*

The six-shooter is empty, but his cowering expression is anything but blank. With the realization he's out of bullets, the crowd snarls in on him like hunted prey. The resounding chants resume from all around.

"HUNT! HUNT! HUNT!"

"JUST-ICE! JUST-ICE!"

Within seconds, Klein is swallowed whole by the jaws of the hungry horde. Clayton watches but doesn't make out exactly how he meets his end. Being trampled to death seems like the most likely candidate. Or strangled. Maybe he was stabbed until he bled out. Perhaps his head was bashed in. The list of ways he met his demise goes on, but none of them matter. He doesn't need to know how. And he doesn't care. All that matters now is that the Hunt—his Hunt—is finally over.

He turns his attention to Antoni who is still lying on the ground, bleeding. Hex and Jayson flock to his side as Kara applies pressure to the gushing hole.

"Toni! Talk to me," Clayton orders, as he slithers closer.

"Mother fucker," Antoni grunts, and tugs on Kara for help sitting up. Struggling to lift and maintain pressure, she finally manages to wrangle his limp body upright with Jayson's help.

She lifts the back of his shirt to observe the fresh wound. There's an outer ring of runny red around a darker, deeper center pit in the side of his ribs.

"I'm no doctor but it looks like a clean exit," she says, studying the bullet hole. "As long as it didn't hit any major organs, and it doesn't look like it did, I think you'll be all right."

"Unngh, lucky me," Antoni groans, lowering his shirt back down. "Does my pride count as a major organ?" he jokes, only to grimace even more from the forced laugh that follows.

"You're a crazy asshole," Clayton adds. "What the hell were you thinking?"

Antoni continues to work himself up to his feet with the help of

Kara and Jayson. "I was thinking," he moans again from the sudden vertical adjustment. "I was thinking . . . we're even now."

The battered cohorts start to limp down the front steps when Clayton hears a familiar, hostile voice call out from behind.

"SPARKS!"

Slowly, he turns around to see Rickers speed-waddling up to him. Upon the usual unwelcomed encroachment of his personal space, Rickers stops and squares him up. There's a long, awkward stalemate before he aggressively spins Clayton back around.

"Rickers, what the hell?" he pleads.

A second later, Clayton feels the numbness flee his fingers as the flow of unhindered blood returns to his hands. It quickly works its way up his arm, delivering feeling back into his wounded shoulder. As he wiggles his way out of the open shackles, Rickers twirls him around again. There's a slight hesitation between the way he moves his mouth and the actual words that take shape.

"Ahem. I was, uh, I mean . . . they say it takes a big man to admit when he's wrong. And well, I guess I was, uh, wrong about you, Sparks," he admits in the most unapologetic yet genuine manner that couldn't be more Rickers.

Clayton rubs the pink abrasions on his wrists where the handcuffs were, trying to comprehend the surprise confession. A grin finds its shape across his mouth.

"You really are an outright prick, you know that, Rickers?"

"Yeah, well you know what they also say," he states through his own creeping smirk. "It takes an even bigger man to admit when he's an outright prick."

It's the first time Clayton's ever heard him make a joke, and out of all the opportunities it comes at his own expense, so he knows that even though it's subtle, it's heartfelt.

"No hard feelings?" Rickers requests, extending his pudgy right hand in a truce—the same one that acquainted itself with Clayton's face not more than half an hour ago.

Mirroring Rickers's now full-on smile with one of his own, Clayton offers his hand in return.

"Deal. As long as you leave my ass out of it."

Rickers chuckles mid-shake.

"Just get outta here already will ya, smart ass? Before I change my mind about liking you again."

Clayton nods and turns back around to rejoin the others as they continue their trek down the long series of steps—the literal foundation for The Hunt Initiative. The crowd pivots its full attention to the group, where they once again find themselves displayed on the massive stage monitors.

"Uhh, guys . . . is this gonna be a problem?" Antoni asks, doing his best to hinge his injured body and look over Kara's shoulder at the screen.

The answer comes quicker than expected.

What were raucous chants of "MURDERER" and "HUNT" just minutes prior fall to dead silence as the crowd goes still. The giant monitors continue to focus their video feed on Clayton, carefully tracking his every step. When the group reaches the bottom, a tall, clean-shaven man on the outskirts of his prime wearing a red "Justice Is Truth" ball cap steps into his path.

Again, the familiar feeling of panic detains Clayton's thoughts like the last forty-eight hours of déjà vu. After everything he's been through, maybe there is no way out. No escape. Maybe this is his fate. After all, no one has ever survived the Hunt. But the extended stalemate breaks as the determined man steps aside and removes his hat, lowering it to his chest. A shorter, stouter man standing next to him does the same. Then the five people behind him. And the ten after them. And the next twenty, then fifty—one hundred, until another Moses-like part trickles throughout the sea of justice supporters. The modern miracle is accompanied by an overwhelming roar of cheers.

Thirty minutes ago, every single one of these people wanted Clayton dead—even salivating at the chance to do it themselves—no questions asked. Now, they applaud him like some kind of hero. Like their new savior.

"So, where to now exactly?" Kara pipes up.

"Doesn't matter," Clayton responds. "It's finally over."

"True," Antoni moans, sandwiched between a series of groans. "But I'm thinking a hospital sounds pretty nice right about now."

It took twenty-five years for Simon Klein to build The Hunt Initiative to what it was—an accepted system of checks and balances based on controlling the masses through a veil of fear disguised as justice. With the circumstances surrounding his demise, it took less than twenty-four hours to tear it all down. Everyone around the world had just laid witness to the wild events that transpired outside The Hunt for Justice that day. It was everywhere, and there was no denying the truth now. No way to go back, only forward.

Klein's ultimate deception affected every Justice Hunter and sect of devoted Initiative supporters differently. But a system built on lies can't support an honest future. And a movement without a leader is nothing more than action without progress. The true loyalists sought another shepherd to lead them. But a chosen one never emerged.

Some fanatics rallied together in support as a few tame riots broke out that same evening and into the ensuing days. And like all causes, there were a few minimal protests that randomly popped up throughout the country over the next few weeks. But nothing big enough to stop the authorities from quickly stepping in and seizing control.

The apathetic majority of supporters carried on as if the Initiative never even existed in the first place. That indifference only grew thicker the more removed society got from the events of that fateful day. Other than a shortage in active law enforcement along with an overflow in misdemeanor incarceration numbers and some additional minor infractions, the Hunt's abrupt decline was nothing more than a blip in time. A soon-to-be-forgotten chapter in school history books about the de-evolution of society and the danger of blind belief. A mere teaching lesson that two wrongs can never make a right.

For Clayton, it meant a fresh start to a forgotten past.

"Oh my god, Toni, would you stop crying about it already?" Clayton urges, as he shifts the car into Park and kills the ignition. "I got shot, too, remember? But you don't hear me bitching about it every two seconds. Where's Kara to put you in your place when I need her?"

"Okay. First off, that kid never got the best of me."

"Yeah. Sure, bud," Clayton scoffs. "Whatever helps you sleep at night."

"And second, if you keep up this utter lack of sympathy for me saving your life, I may just finish what Klein started," Antoni continues, as he hobbles out of the car amid a series of dramatic grunts and groans. Careful not to tweak his recovering ribs.

"Real talk, babe, stop being such a baby. It's not a good look on you," Sonya adds, as she slides out from the middle seat with Thad in her lap. "Besides, I see worse wounds literally every day at the hospital."

"Yeah, Dad, stop bitching," Thad piggybacks Clayton's sentiment, heaping onto the hate parade. "Nobody likes a crybaby."

"Wow, et tu, little buddy?" Antoni gasps followed by a playful rub on Thad's head. "Okay, guess I'm shutting up now. Also, Clay, for the love of god, language, man. He's like a parrot to your pirate. Every time you cuss, he just regurgitates it back."

"Riiiight . . . because he hasn't heard any of those words from you before?" Sonya chimes in.

"Busted," Clayton adds with a smirk.

"Pshh, whatever. Just shut up and give me the keys already," Antoni orders. "You drive worse than my dead grandma."

"Hey, don't be mad at me that it hurt too much to shift. I'm not the one who shot you."

"Oh, you're right, I just took the bullet with your name on it."

The two friends meet eyes and match grins from across the shiny hood of Antoni's fixed-up 1955 cherry-red Chevy Task Force. Their attention gradually tracks across the street to a quaint house in a quiet neighborhood. A familiar, olive-green ranch-style home sits before them like a picture from a modern fairy tale. The grass, a perfect visual definition of the color green, and freshly trimmed, as always. The landscaping, flawlessly kempt as the lone weeping willow in the front yard wails in the cool dusk breeze.

Clayton takes a dramatic breath in and exhales.

Antoni takes notice.

"You sure you're ready for this?" he asks, shutting the passenger door.

"Nope. Not at all. I think I was less nervous facing Klein and a million people that wanted me dead than I am for this."

"Really?"

"Yeah. At least I had a somewhat of a half-ass plan for that one."

As Clayton's focus slowly drifts away with his gaze, he imagines that same perfect reunion scenario he's played in his head a thousand times. The one where he strolls up to the porch and rings the doorbell to his childhood home. Where his parents rush to answer it, embracing him and making amends for all their past sins and the countless fights they created, and relationships they ruined. That everything will be all right. More than anything, he wishes he could introduce them to Trish and tell them they're going to be grandparents. That they could all just start over as one big happy family cliché.

For a moment, he pretends that he can simply erase his past and do just that. After all, it worked for The Hunt Initiative, even if he did almost die several times to make it happen. But what about for something deeper? Something like family?

With enough nerve finally built up, Clayton takes his first step forward up the driveway. He doesn't complete a full stride before the screen door to the porch softly creaks open and a deep, yet sincere, voice calls out from the dim doorway.

"C-Clayton?"

He casts his attention up, toward the direction of the welcoming sound of his name to find two silhouettes residing behind the veil of the shrouded porch.

He takes another careful tread forward. The shadowy figures do the same.

Then, another step. And another, until his parents' faces are finally revealed in the receding daylight. His mother is covering her mouth in awe as tears roll over her wrinkled knuckles while his father stands content but cautious, his throat swallowing constantly, doing its best to hold back its own swell of emotion.

Both parties hasten their pace until they're standing teary-eye to teary-eye on the front lawn underneath the wails of the weeping willow. There's so much he wants to tell them. To share with them. Years and years of missed time and memories. But his words don't come out right. In fact, they don't come out at all.

"Welcome home . . . son," his father manages to whimper. It's only three words. Nothing, really. Just a simple greeting. But it's also everything. A first step. Another chance. And in one crashing wave of emotion, they all break down into a weeping embrace beneath that willow in a reunion that's only fitting for loved ones.

For family.

For a future.

# ACKNOWLEDGMENTS

In all my years of writing—from copywriting and poetry to blogs, even music, you name it—I don't think I've ever had such a love/hate relationship with words than that of tackling a novel. The good days are charged with an inexplicable verve of infectious creativity that seems to live effortlessly within the pages. These days possess you and make you feel almost invincible as the story unfolds before your eyes. You can't stop writing because you simply don't want to.

Then, there are the bad days. The days that leave you crippled with rampant fears of self-doubt, whispering in your ear to just give up already. That this is all just shit anyway. Even your closest friends and family can't save you on these days. In fact, sometimes, they're the paralyzing voice (or void of one) echoing upstairs. You can choose to either listen, and cave, or realize that motivation doesn't always come from entourage encouragement—or reinforced confidence. Sometimes, the opposite is just as potent. Sometimes, you just have to believe in yourself and tell the rest of the noise that it can politely fuck right off.

Now, with that author PSA off my chest, I have some very important people that deserve my utmost praise. I would love to give an irreplaceable thanks to my dad, Ken Wallace, for always believing in me. Your continuous support and interest in my creative ventures have been my North Star through more than you'll ever know. And to my mom, Karen Wallace, thank you for gifting me your way with words and never missing a moment to spin a solid pun. There are plenty in this book.

I would like to thank my wife, Taryn Wallace, for rekindling in me a love for reading that lay dormant for far too long as the hustle and bustle of life just kind of took over. Your insatiable hunger for consuming words on a page helped inspire me to not only pick up a book again, but to sit down and actually write my own.

I would also like to thank my creative counterpart, Ashley Dodson. Your boundless vision and drive are contagious, plus you're just a damn good human. The world needs more people like you.

A big shoutout goes to my buddy and talented cover artist, Dale Ley III. Thanks for wading through my conceptual vomit and atrocious sketches on more than one occasion to deliver something stunningly timeless and iconic. It's truly the cherry on top.

Thank you to my copyeditor, Stephanie Shiflett of White Rabbit Editing for bringing an eagle eye to my ramble of words. I've never claimed to be an editor and your thorough revisions definitely proved that correct.

I'm grateful to have stumbled across Bodie Dykstra of BD Book Design, and for his help formatting this chonky beast of a novel debut. His overall communication, speed, and professionalism (so, basically all the things) really helped create a canvas for my story so that my words could paint the page. Plus, his name is Bodie. It doesn't get much cooler than that.

Tons of gratitude goes out to Barry Brakeville for your mentorship, outside-the-box marketing strategies, and lunch rants over the finest Tex-Mex in town. Thanks for seeing something in me that I'm not entirely sure I even saw myself.

To Rebecca Coffindaffer, I appreciate you slogging through my very first rough (and I mean, rough) draft, and your welcome basket into the wild world of publishing. Be sure to check out her YA space opera duology, *Crown Chasers* & *Throne Breakers* for a fun, thrill ride of a read.

Thank you to my daughter, Rowan Wallace, for pushing me to be a better person every day. I hope when you're older you'll read this story and be proud of your dad, or embarrassed. Possibly horrified. Honestly, I'll consider any of the above a win.

And last, but certainly not least, thank *YOU* (yes, you, the one with this book in your hands right now) for supporting me by purchasing my ultimate passion project. I hope you enjoy reading this labor of love as much as I did writing it.

www.ingramcontent.com/pod-product-compliance
Lightning Source LLC
Chambersburg PA
CBHW030551310726
48979CB00011B/2106/J
*9798989781522*